Dead Magic
Book Four of the Ingenious Mechanical Devices

Kara Jorgensen
Fox Collie Publishing

Copyright © 2016 by Kara Jorgensen
Cover Design © 2016 Lou Harper

First Edition, 2016
ISBN 978-0-9905022-7-2
EBook ISBN 978-0-9905022-6-5

To pets,
Whose love makes life bearable.

ACT ONE

"I am all in a sea of wonders.
I doubt; I fear; I think
strange things which I dare
not confess to my own soul."
-Bram Stoker

Chapter One
Flesh and Bone

On balmy summer nights, Highgate Cemetery lay as still and silent as its residents, but as the witching hour approached, a shadow emerged. Footfalls echoed through the rows of vine-covered graves, their names impossible to read in the scant moonlight. Crickets fell silent and the grasses on either side of the well-worn path rustled with life just beneath the surface as Cecil Hale passed. Reaching for the shuttered lantern at his side, the young man stopped and listened for any sign of his compatriots. He had been instructed not to open the lantern until he reached the Egyptian Avenue, but the graveyard was harder to navigate in the dark than he had imagined. The dizzying rows of cockeyed graves seemed to go on forever, all nearly identical to the next.

Closing his eyes, Cecil drew in a long breath and released a wave of energy that began at his russet hair and passed through his feet. In the darkness beyond the curve of trees, he felt a flash of power pulse back. So they had ventured into the vault without him after all. As he rounded the bend, his heart quickened at the sight of the obelisk and lotus-columned entrance to the Egyptian Avenue. Leafy boughs and Jurassic ferns spilled over the top of the mausoleum's entrance, drowning out the tang of death with the scents of summer. He paused as the iron gate whined beneath his hand, waiting for the light of the night watchman he knew would not appear. A smirk crossed his lips. No one thought to worry about the dead.

Cecil's gaze swept over the faceless row of doors on either side of him until it came to rest on the wavering radiance of an oil lamp shining from beneath the threshold. Pulling open the door, he shut his eyes against the harsh light of the lanterns within.

"Did they not teach you how to tell time at boarding school, Lord Hale?"

Cecil Hale stiffened. If it had been anyone else, he would have cut them down to size for not only insulting a viscount but for daring to question the standing of the youngest practioner initiated into the Eidolon Club, but when his hazel eyes adjusted, he found Lady Rose glaring at him.

"Do forgive my tardiness, Lady Rose, but it wasn't easy to find my way here in the dark. Not all of us frequent graveyards," he replied before he could stop himself.

A low chuckle emanated from where she stood, but Cecil swore he hadn't seen her lips or chest move. Among the shadows of the mausoleum, her polished bronze hair and pale green eyes took on such an unnatural hue that he dared not question what he had heard. Of all the practitioners he knew, she was the only one he feared. If he stared too long, he could see the energy writhing and slithering around her, pulling at the flames positioned in a circle around the coffin at her feet. It was her power he felt when he cleared his mind's eye.

As Cecil pulled the crypt door shut, a lanky, white-haired figure emerged from the neighboring chamber. Cecil was accustomed to seeing Lord Sumner in the Eidolon Club's vast study, but seeing him standing in the mausoleum didn't sit well. It felt wrong, like seeing one's grandfather walk out of a Piccadilly brothel. He couldn't imagine him with his carefully trimmed beard and Savile Row suit anywhere near a charnel house. The man had a lineage as distinguished as any king on the continent, so what could be so important that he would risk being found prowling around a graveyard with the likes of Lady Rose? Perhaps Cecil wasn't the only one who didn't trust her.

"Will it be only us this evening?" Cecil asked, his voice reverberating against the vaulted stone as he stared into the darkened chamber.

Without looking up from the coffin edge, Lady Rose replied, "If you're worried about discovery, I hired a man to keep watch outside, but the ritual only needs one. His lordship is merely here to supervise."

"Let's hope the ritual won't be necessary," the elder noble murmured, averting his gaze from Lady Rose's makeshift evocation circle.

"Oh? Are you having second thoughts, Lord Sumner?"

"I think all of us would prefer to avoid such vulgarity. We can only hope his family thought it best to bury the damned book with him."

"So resurrectionists like us could find it? I doubt it," she said, running her bare fingers over the lid as if feeling for something.

"Did anyone check his estate and town home?" Cecil asked.

Lady Rose and Lord Sumner exchanged an incredulous look before turning their attention back to the casket. Her fingers slid over the decorative molding and around the brass bars affixed to either side, probing every cranny for hidden springs.

Resting back on her heels, she motioned for Cecil to come to her side with a curl of her finger. "Cecil, would you do the honors?"

For a moment, he wished they had left the door open to the crypt. The stale air pressed in as he drew in a breath and held it. Cecil steeled himself, ready to avert his gaze when the lid cracked open, but as he tried to yank it loose, a bolt of pain shot into his wrists and up his arms. Howling, he staggered back, nearly kicking over Sumner's lamp.

"The bloody thing's hexed!" he cried, rubbing his burning, twitching hands.

"The duke's underlings were smarter than I thought," Lord

Sumner said under his breath.

Grabbing a handful of dust from the floor, Lady Rose cast it across the casket top. A series of rings, lines, and scribbles appeared through the detritus. Cecil leaned in to get a closer look. He had never seen a sigil that actually worked. The Eidolon Club didn't endorse the use of such an out of fashion technique, so there had been no reason for him to bother learning about them. At the pulsing throb in his hand, he wished he had. Before he could finish tracing the twisting line with his gaze, Lady Rose pulled out a handkerchief from her Gladstone bag and scrubbed at the sigil. Cecil watched with wide eyes as she gritted her teeth and continued even as the arcane symbols crackled and arced with electricity beneath her palm.

She released a labored breath and wiped her forehead with the back of her hand. "Open it."

Cautiously, Cecil reached for the lid, expecting to feel the bite of electricity once more. The lid groaned under his hand, but as he raised it, the bile crawled up his throat at the overwhelming stench of putrefaction. The smell of rotting meat mixed with the bite of acid and the coppery sweetness of blood was so strong that he dared not look down. He had hoped that in the few months since his death, the Duke of Dover's body would have been reduced to nothing more than a skeleton in a suit. From the corner of his eye, he could make out an unnaturally blackened and melted face and a hint of bone peaking from the top of what he could only imagine had once been the duke's hand. As he returned to his station near the door, Cecil covered his mouth with his handkerchief, hoping Lady Rose and Lord Sumner wouldn't notice his sudden pallor, but she was already leaning into the coffin, her hands probing the body for the missing grimoire.

"Just as I suspected, it isn't here," she said, turning to Sumner.

"Then, what do you propose to do now?" he replied sharply, knowing the answer.

"The ritual. Unless you no longer want to acquire the book, but I highly doubt the Pinkertons or your investigators will be able to find it without hearing what the duke has to say."

Lord Sumner's lip curled in disgust as he locked eyes with the witch perched beside the coffin. She held his gaze, her green eyes at ease while the noblemen squinted at the pungency of the rotting corpse. With a final look at the duke's bloated form, Lord Sumner retrieved his cloak and hat from an empty niche.

"Do what you will, but I will *not* be a part of it. Leave a message for me at the club if you find anything, but don't taint me with your bone-conjuring."

Storming out of the crypt, Lord Sumner slammed the door, leaving Cecil and Lady Rose in silence. She stared ahead, her face betraying nothing even as she sat back on the dusty floor. Cecil dared not ask if she was all right.

After a moment, she licked her lips and swept a stray bronze curl from her forehead. "Cecil, if you ever want to succeed, never let theory trump practical knowledge. Despite your position, you're never too good to use what you have learned."

"I don't plan to rely on *theory*, Aunt Claudia."

Satisfied with his answer, she asked flatly, "Did you make the tincture I asked for?"

Cecil nodded, reaching into his breast pocket for the flask. It had taken him most of the day to prepare it from the notes she had given him, but it was perfect. It had to be. He had been so careful to check the thermometer and even test some of the precipitate to ensure he had created the intended compound. What it did, he had no idea. Plucking it from his hand, she sniffed and swirled it before setting it aside.

"Very good. Do you intend to stay for the ritual or would you prefer to wait outside, Lord Hale?"

"If you would permit it, I should like to stay."

"I see. Then, you must remain quiet and out of the way. You may be disturbed by what you see, but you must remain silent. Can you manage that?"

For a brief moment, Cecil considered slipping out the door of the crypt and getting into the first cab that would take him back to his flat, but he was an alchemist and to be taken seriously, he had to stay even when Lord Sumner would not. Sealing off his energy with a slow exhalation, Cecil stepped further into the shadows until his back rested against the damp stone. He watched as Lady Rose reached into the Gladstone bag at her side, pulling out a large, squat bowl, a bottle of what appeared to be water, a handful of narrow vials, and a rough obsidian blade. She emptied the bottle of water and three of the vials into the bowl. Placing it before her, she wafted the faint trail of smoke that rose from the liquid toward her. As she closed her eyes, her body rocked in time with the languid curve of her hand and a low chant resonated in her throat. Her free-hand skated through the dust at her side, scrawling tiny shapes he couldn't make out before darting for another vial to add to the bowl.

The air grew thick with the stench of sulphurous smoke until Cecil feared he would be ill. Lady Rose's lithe body writhed and snapped as her chant grew louder and more insistent. Sounds morphed into words he nearly recognized but were lost before his mind could retrieve their meaning. Drawing in a loud breath, the words ceased.

The obsidian knife flashed in the wavering candlelight. In one swift motion, Lady Rose ran it across the duke's hand. A few drops of a thick black liquid seeped from the wound and across her open palm where a bloated finger lay neatly severed from its mooring. Cecil silenced a gag with a tight swallow as the stench of offal overpowered his senses. Whispers raced across Lady Rose's lips as she raised the finger high before dropping it into the bowl. The smoke writhed and condensed, combining with the shadows lingering at the edge of the circle of candles. Monstrous faces flickered. They rose in open-mouthed grotesques only to be swallowed by another until finally the vague outline of a man solidified. His stern eyes and hollowed cheeks locked onto Cecil's hazel gaze before turning to Lady Rose.

"Duke Dover, we—the blind living—humbly ask for your assistance. Your divine sight sees all: past, present, and future. Tell us, sir. Tell us where the *Corpus Grimoire* lies at this moment," she pleaded, her voice level but tinged with yearning.

The duke's face dissolved, drifting and roiling until a new scene appeared in the smoke. A paper package sat among stacks of crates and bags of letters stamped *London, England*. The faint hum of a dirigible reverberated through the tomb. It was on a mail ship.

Lady Rose's eyes widened. "Duke Dover, who will receive the package? To whom is it going?"

Smoke twisted into a column before chipping away to reveal the soft curves of a woman. Her hair was fashionably curled into black coils that trailed down her neck and across the shoulders of her violet gown. Cecil leaned closer. Her rounded cheeks, the wide byzantine eyes, the tight set of her jaw in concentration. He knew her. During the season, he had sought her out at each dance, entranced by her wit and the warmth hidden behind her knowing looks and pointed remarks. Her figure fell in on itself before stretching higher into the form of a wiry young man. He would have been unremarkable, except for the long scar that cut through his left eye. How could they both have the grimoire?

A shadow stirred in the corner of the mausoleum. It climbed along the stone, straining and expanding until it nearly engulfed the entire wall. Cecil's heart raced as the shade solidified into the shape of a man. It lashed out with an arm and wiped the flames from the tops of the candles. The tomb plunged into darkness, the only sound the *swoosh* of the shadow and the clatter of the bowl as it tipped. Groping for the lantern at his feet, Cecil felt for its radiant warmth and quickly opened the shutter.

Even before he was able to see, he knew the spirits had left the crypt. Despite the godawful smell of the corpse, he no longer felt as if he would smother. Stepping closer, he could make out a spreading stain where the bowl had fallen over and spilled the brew. Lady Rose stood behind it. She glared down at her ruined ritual before turning her hardened gaze to Lord Hale. He swallowed against the flare of power emanating from her body. Questions hung on his lips as she snatched the empty vials from the floor and threw them into her Gladstone.

"You aren't going to try again?"

13

"There's no point. The duke didn't have much steam to begin with. He wouldn't have lasted through another question, let alone being resummoned. We have enough information. The book is in transit, and it will fall to one of them."

His mind trailed to the vision of the young woman with the dark hair and owl eyes. "How will you find them?"

"I have my ways," she replied, pausing to lock eyes with something in the darkness. "If it's in the city, one of us will feel it and find it."

"The girl, I think I know her," he said, not wanting to imagine what would happen if his aunt got to her first.

Lady Rose looked up from her bag, her eyes softening with interest. For the first time, her gaze was free of scorn as she searched his face. "Really? Can I trust you to keep an eye on her and report back to me? If she has the grimoire, it will be your responsibility to retrieve it."

"But what if she won't give it up?" Emmeline Jardine wasn't a stupid girl who could be easily swayed with his noble charms and a bit of flattery. "She's a true medium. I can sense her power at the Spiritualist Society. What if she wants to keep the book for herself?"

With a faint smile, Claudia ran her handkerchief down the length of the obsidian knife. "Then, we will simply change our tactic."

He swallowed hard. "And the other man?"

"Leave him to me."

Chapter Two
A New Regime

In Emmeline Jardine's eighteen years, she had learned two things for certain: people are nearly always dumber than they appear and nothing lasts forever. It was with this in mind that Emmeline told herself that Madame Nostra's reign at the London Spiritualist Society would be short. She loathed everything about the woman, from her over-sized hats and too orange hair to her rib-splittingly tiny waist and the wild patterns of her gowns. Standing with her back to the wainscoting and paisley wallpaper, Emmeline watched with an incredulous black brow as the other spiritualists swarmed the fake medium, listening eagerly to her recitation of her two month long European tour.

Madame Nostra let out a throaty chuckle and patted the massive ribbon affixed to her hat. "Oh yes, the King of Italy was a joy to read. I didn't want to say anything, but I did tell him about the death of a son he didn't know he had. His Majesty was deeply affected by the news."

Emmeline rolled her eyes as the others tittered for her to tell them more. One day back on English soil and they were already falling over themselves to be in Madame Nostra's good graces. Did they not realize she couldn't actually communicate with spirits? All it took was one reading with her for Emmeline to discover that Madame Nostra's spirits spoke in knocks that came from her left foot. It didn't seem right for *her* of all people to rise to the top, but with Lord Rose dead, Madame Nostra had the biggest name and the loudest mouth. If Emmeline had remained in Oxford, maybe things would have been different.

Someone bumped against Emmeline's arm, breaking her train of thought. She turned with a scowl at the ready only to find Cassandra Ashwood at her elbow, giving her a knowing smile. Against her will, Emmeline felt a grin cross her features. Ever since Cassandra arrived at the Spiritualist Society in March, they had been as inseparable as— and often mistaken for—sisters. Besides having the same brown eyes, round faces and short stature, they also shared the same opinion of the illustrious Madame Nostra.

"And I thought you would be thrilled to see the old girl back," Cassandra whispered, keeping her eyes on the middle-aged women hanging on Madam Nostra's every word.

Emmeline snorted. "Can't you tell I'm overjoyed at being ignored again?"

"I guess that's the end of our coregency," she replied, a faint smile crossing her lips. "It was fun while it lasted."

"Our holiday won't be long if I have any say in the matter."

Cassandra shook her head, a curl of mahogany hair dancing against her cheek. "It isn't worth staging a coup. The woman's harmless."

"Cass, you know stupid people are never harmless."

Locking eyes, Emmeline held Cassandra's gaze until finally her best friend relented with a shrug and a sigh. "Your aunt is rubbing off on you. Still though, aren't you happy that you don't have to manage everything now? You can be a medium again."

Words gathered on Emmeline's tongue, but she swallowed them

down in a bitter gulp. Even to Cassandra, she couldn't admit that she had enjoyed every moment she ran the Spiritualist Society. For most of her life, she had watched her mother manage the Oxford Spiritualist Society, so taking up the reins in London felt as natural as throwing a party. She had been fortunate that no one older or better known stepped up after Madam Nostra went on tour because she would have surely been usurped, but she might have allowed it, if it had been the right person. With Cassandra's help and calming words, they had managed the servants, tended to the account books, kept track of everyone's appointments to ensure there was always a parlor available for a séance, and had even organized a small dinner party for the benefactors of the society. It had all gone swimmingly, especially after the first week when the older members of the society finally realized she wasn't going to stop and acquiesced to her temporary rule.

"They may soon find that they miss my managerial style."

"I know I will."

Emmeline whipped around to find Lord Hale staring down at her with a cheeky grin. Her eyes ran appraisingly over his pomaded auburn hair and emerald waistcoat. He was the sort of man every woman imagined as her prince. She should have veiled her feelings for him as propriety dictated, but with a gentleman who was not only handsome but could dance and speak as well as Cecil Hale, it was nearly impossible.

"Lord Hale, what brings you here? Have you come to hear Madam Nostra's tall-tales?"

"No, much like you, I'm merely making a show of it." His gaze ran over her, lingering a moment too long before he caught himself and added with a cough, "Has the post come yet? I'm expecting a package. For the life of me, I can't remember if I addressed it for here or my flat."

"Why would you send it here?" Cassandra asked.

"At the time, I think I was between flats and wasn't sure if I would be settled yet. The parcel ended up being delayed, and well—" He shrugged. "Would you keep an eye out for it, Miss Jardine?"

Heat flooded her chest and cheeks as he flashed a vibrant smile. "Of course, I will let you know if I see it."

"Well, I guess I should pay Madam Nostra a visit. Good day, Miss Jardine, Miss Ashwood."

As Emmeline watched Lord Hale cut through the circle of women in the parlor, unabashedly tracing the curvature of his back and buttock with her eyes, she felt Cassandra's cold gaze upon her. "Don't give me that look, Cass."

"You're much too obvious, and he's a flirt." She waved a dismissive hand. "Anyway, I'm feeling peckish, would you like to come to the Dorothy with me? If we leave now, we can still get an eightpenny dinner."

Emmeline frowned. Even if she didn't love going to the women-only restaurant, it guaranteed that Madam Nostra and her entourage wouldn't be there. "Fine."

With a nod of satisfaction, Cassandra disappeared down the hall to retrieve their cloaks. Behind them in the hall, the mail hit the rug with a dull thump and a crinkle of paper. Emmeline sighed and scooped up the massive jumble of letters and parcels. If she didn't do it, she knew the others would let them sit there until they were trampled into the carpet. Emmeline flipped through the stack of letters with little interest. Most were advertisements for fake mediums with even worse acts than Madam Nostra or letters from clients hoping for a séance, but at the bottom of the pile was a package. The brown wrapping had been creased and torn at the edges in transit. Between smudges of dirt, Emmeline could make out the remnants of stamps and words written in half a dozen languages. The package had gone far in its time abroad, yet no return address appeared on the front or back.

Holding it in her palm, she judged its weight and smiled to herself. It had to be a book and a fancy, well-bound one at that. Her eyes flickered to Lord Hale, but as she took a step forward, she caught the words scrawled in tight script across the paper wrapping: *To the Head of the Spiritualist Society.* Lord Hale certainly was not it. It could have been Madam Nostra's as she technically had assumed the role as head of the society, but if it had been something she ordered, certainly she would have given the shopkeeper her name. If it wasn't hers, then… Emmeline's throat tightened at the thought of Lord Rose snarling down at her, his golden eyes alight like the end of his cigarette. He died by his own hand nearly six months earlier, but from the journey in faded stamps of ink, the book easily could have been ordered right before he died.

"What's that?" Cassandra asked as she handed Emmeline her cloak.

Emmeline opened her mouth to speak, the words tangling in her throat as she held the book tightly to her breast.

"It's nothing. I—" Dropping her voice, she said, "If you must know, I ordered a book that I don't want my aunt to see."

Cassandra's chestnut brows arched. "Another one? If that one is anything like the last, you had best hide it well."

"I'm lucky she hasn't found my cache yet."

Cassandra chuckled and slipped on her mackintosh. Releasing a silent breath, Emmeline slipped on her cloak and followed Cassandra out the door toward Mortimer Street. She bit her lip, glancing over her shoulder to see if anyone had seen her take it, but all eyes were on Madam Nostra. As Emmeline stepped outside, she kept the package under her arm and her hand tightly over the row of script written across its face.

⁂

The Dorothy Restaurant hummed with chatter only broken by the occasional sharp laugh. Emmeline resisted the urge to shift in her seat. She had been to the Dorothy several times with Cassandra Ashwood, but she never failed to feel out of place there. She had never been in a public place where men were not allowed. The room was overly bright even in the dreary weather with its red walls and gaudy array of colorful Japanese fans and parasols artfully tacked to the plaster. Around them all manner of women ate the same meal on identical white tablecloths

19

with vases of flowers. During previous visits, they had spotted Constance Wilde and the Countess of Dorset not far from a table of shop girls. In a space free of men, the women seemed to transform before her eyes into some strange perversion of the womanhood she knew. Cigarettes were lit and overheard table conversation often involved politics, women's rights, and even colonialism. Of course, there was gossip, but mixed in were stories of tête–à–têtes that bordered on elicit. At the Dorothy, they all seemed so free, yet surrounded by a complete lack of restriction, Emmeline felt stunted.

"You're very quiet today, Em," Cassandra said, looking up from her roast chicken and potatoes. "Anything the matter?"

Emmeline's eyes flickered over the window where rain pattered against the pane and through the drizzle, she inadvertently caught the gaze of a man peeking inside. What he expected them to be doing, she couldn't imagine, but gawkers, as she was quickly learning, were common at the Dorothy.

"Ignore him."

"Why are they always staring in? It's rude. It's a restaurant, not a sideshow."

"They don't like that we finally have some privacy. You know, you could have left your book in the coatroom. I'm pretty sure no one would steal it, especially when Miss Barker knows us."

"That's not what I was worried about." She paused. What was she worried about? "I didn't want anyone to see the title."

Cassandra shook her head. "Maybe I don't want to borrow it if you're that nervous about other people seeing it."

Emmeline gave her a weak smile. Her eyes traced the outline of the book beneath the crinkled paper. She had placed it on the table facedown with her reticule and gloves on top of it to keep Cassandra from turning it over. Her heart pulsed in her throat, ruining the taste of the meat in her mouth. She was itching to open it. Every time she looked away, she felt its gaze upon her, as if the book was watching her—beckoning to her—the moment she let her mind wander. For a moment, she wondered if she should just confess to Cassandra what she had done and open the bloody book.

Before she could act on her thought, Cassandra straightened with an excited squeak. She wiped her mouth and took a sip of tea before she asked, "Did I tell you about the gala?"

"What gala? The season is over."

"Well, it isn't a society party. It's a gala to celebrate a new ancient botanical collection at the Natural History Museum. I'm sure you heard."

When Emmeline raised a dark brow, Cassandra continued, "Your aunt's cousin, the Countess of Dorset, and her husband donated the main specimen, a silphium plant. Please tell me you know what I'm talking about. I'm sure your aunt mentioned it."

Thinking back to dinner conversations, she could vaguely recall some mention of a party at the museum. She hadn't paid much attention. "I don't think I was invited, but it doesn't matter. I don't want to go."

Cassandra's chestnut eyes widened and sagged.

"You actually want to go? But why? It will be so boring. All those old stuffy scholars and their pinch-faced wives."

"My friends will be there. I don't think you have met her, but Judith Elliott is my best friend—"

Emmeline stiffened.

"*One* of my best friends, and I'm certain you will love her as much as I do."

"Of course," Emmeline replied tartly as she stabbed a piece of boiled potato and brought it to her lips.

She could feel Cassandra's gaze upon her, eyes torn between annoyance and guilt. Somehow, Emmeline had never imagined that Cassandra could have friends besides her, that she had a life outside the Spiritualist Society. She only ever saw her at the Dorothy and the society, and she didn't appear to have a beau or that she was even looking for one. *Modern woman*, Emmeline scoffed. No wonder Aunt Eliza loved it when Miss Ashwood came for tea. Watching Cassandra go back to her meal, Emmeline's stomach knotted. How did she know so little about her even though they spent nearly every weekend and most evenings together at the Spiritualist Society? She knew Cassandra worked as a secretary somewhere, though Emmeline couldn't remember where, and that she lived in a flat not far from the society along with another woman.

From the edge of her vision, Emmeline studied Cassandra's features. She envied her prominent cheekbones and her expressive lips. When she smiled, it made Emmeline's face join in her joy, but it was her bearing that caught her attention when they first met. She had thought of quitting the Spiritualist Society for good until she spotted Cassandra waiting at the front door. She stood tall despite her short stature with her walking suit smartly cut to accentuate her curves and the color rich enough to bring out the flecks of gold and green in her eyes. There was a demure self-assuredness about her that didn't require words to enforce. Emmeline wondered if that was what five years of relative independence did to a woman. Still, it was troubling to know she had no suitors to fall back on or tear her attention away from the gloom and tedium of the Spiritualist Society.

"I shouldn't be telling you this since you have decided to be peevish, but Mr. Talbot's cousin just walked in," Cassandra whispered, her eyes darting toward the front door as a rush of swampy air washed in.

"How do you know it's her?"

"Because I just saw him drop her off."

Whipping around, Emmeline turned in time to see a dark-haired woman enter and a charcoal grey steamer pull away from the curb. "I can't believe I missed—"

The words died in her throat. Cassandra was holding the book, *her* book, regarding her with pursed lips. Emmeline reached to snatch it from her grasp, but Cassandra pulled it back. It wouldn't do to make a scene. Shaking her head, Cassandra handed the paper-wrapped book back to her.

"I knew something was wrong when you wouldn't give it up. You never wait to open a book. You can't steal her property, Emmeline," she replied in a harsh whisper. "Nostra is a fool, but this is hers."

Groaning, Emmeline placed the package in her lap and covered it with her napkin. "But she isn't even the head of the society, not yet anyway. Besides, it probably isn't even hers."

"If it isn't hers, then whose is it?"

Emmeline opened her mouth, but his name refused to leave her throat.

Sensing what she wouldn't say, Cassandra frowned. "But it's been over five months. Do you really suspect it was meant for him?"

"I don't know. I know taking it was wrong, but you didn't know him, Cass. He was evil."

"You think it's something malicious?"

She shrugged. "It could be. Would you want Nostra getting a book on soul-stealing or god knows what?"

Cassandra sighed, her gaze traveling to the book in Emmeline's lap before coming to rest on her concerned eyes and drawn mouth. "Maybe you should open it and see what it is. If it's just a book, we could rewrap it and bring it back tomorrow, and if it's something bad—"

"We can figure out what to do once we know what it is. Good idea."

Using her untouched bread knife, Emmeline carefully slipped it between the strings and paper. With a crack, the must of centuries old paper and ink rushed out. Emmeline locked eyes with Cassandra as she tipped the package and let the book slide into her hand. Lying across the front cover was a letter. Setting the book and torn wrapper on the table, she turned her attention to the missive. The sole page was stained with ink and flecks of brown, but the lines of the long, looped writing had been written with such force that it had been incised into the page. As Emmeline lifted it closer, minute beams of light broke through the parchment.

To the person the grimoire chooses,

I hope whoever reads this letter can forgive that I do not know your name. I don't have much time left. The duke is ailing and has entrusted the book to my care, but I fear my time will be as short as his. The grimoire is no longer safe. By the time you read this, the grimoire will have passed through many hands to keep it away from those who would pervert the knowledge within it. If you are reading this note, you may be the end of the line. It is my hope that the book has fallen into worthy hands.

Dark forces are in Berlin, and they are moving north to London. Those who would seek to keep the balance of death and life are being cut down by practioners wanting to tip the scale. They need what the grimoire possesses.

Protect it or send it to someone who can.

There was no signature. Flipping the paper over, she found the same note written in Latin. Emmeline's heart thundered in her throat. Dark forces were coming to London. What had she taken?

"What is it?" her friend asked, noticing her sudden pallor.

"I don't think the book was meant for Lord Rose, but I don't think it was meant for Nostra either. Here, read it for yourself."

Handing over the letter, Emmeline turned her attention to the heavy tome; she couldn't stand to watch Cassandra's reactions. Maybe she was right. She should have just left it alone. Running her fingers over the soft leather cover, Emmeline closed her eyes. Where there weren't deeply hewn arabesques or veins are fine as capillaries, it was as smooth as skin. She followed the lines as they hypnotically wove through one another to form not only a picture of a stylized garden but an intricate knot. Her fingertips hummed the moment the entire circuit had been traced, and in her mind's eye, she could make out the loops and whirls, seen and unseen, lying in her hands. *Open it.* Her freehand crept toward the latch.

"It has to be a joke of some kind. Something to scare off Madam Nostra. It has to be, doesn't it?"

Emmeline opened her eyes, her breath coming heavy as if she had just awoken. What could she say? She believed every word. In the past year, she had seen and experienced things no one would believe. Cassandra watched mediums like Emmeline tap into a different plane of vision to speak to the dead, but it was nothing compared to what she had dealt with. She had been resurrected and felt her own heart stop in turn to revive another.

She stroked the ridges of the book's spine. "I'm not so sure. What if it is true? I can't just put the book back now. What if it falls into the wrong hands?"

"You need to give it to someone else. The letter said to pass it on if you couldn't protect it," Cassandra replied, her eyes wide with fear. "I could probably find someone."

She eyed the women sitting around them suspiciously before turning her gaze back to Emmeline, who clutched the book close as if it was a cherished storybook.

Cassandra rolled her eyes. "I can't believe you. You're going to keep it, aren't you?" She dropped her voice. "Em, if you believe what it says, people will come after you. *Bad* people. They could hurt you. We need to figure out who to give this to. Did your mother know anyone that you can trust?"

"Perhaps. I could look into it, but for now…" *Keep it.* "For now, I can keep it in Uncle James's safe. No one would bother it there."

Emmeline's eyes traced the unending pattern carved into the supple leather. It felt warm in her hand, and if she let the world around her fade, she swore she could feel its steady pulse. It had a life within it, and it was hers to protect.

Chapter Three
The Junior Curator

Looking up from his research notes, Immanuel Winter bit down a grin. Everything was falling into place. After only eight days in London, he found that he suddenly had everything he always wanted. He had moved in with Adam Fenice, he had a job as a junior curator at the Natural History Museum, and he never had to set foot on Oxford University's grounds ever again. Immanuel leaned back in his chair, arching his back as he ran his hands through his hair and stretched. Wayward blonde curls sprang to life at his touch. The best part of this transition from student to professional was the privacy. No longer did he have to contend with constant rabblerousing from other students or having to find a secluded spot in order to work. Now, he had an office with a door he could close and like-minded employees who were, for the most part, peaceful.

His office was just how he had pictured it when Professor Martin told him that he had called in a favor with Sir William Henry Flower at the museum and secured a position for him in the zoology department.

Most of the room was taken up by his desk, which was already covered with stacks of paper after only four days of work. Behind him and in the space between the door and the windowed wall were shelves and drawers for taxidermy creatures, fossils, and jarred specimens. The office's previous occupant had been with the museum for years before it moved to South Kensington and had accumulated a veritable cabinet of curiosities and a small library of texts. At times, Immanuel felt as if he was merely borrowing the old curator's office, but he was glad he hadn't moved into an empty room, knowing he would have had very little to add besides a handful of textbooks from his time at Oxford. Even if the office didn't have any personal touches yet, it was bright and clean and his.

Something shifted in the damaged side of Immanuel's vision. He turned in time to watch a three foot swath of pale green wallpaper flop off the plaster. Immanuel sighed. That was the third time that had happened since he moved in. He opened the drawers of his desk one at a time, searching for anything he could use to secure it. *Pins.* He had seen dissection pins the other day, but where? As he yanked the bottom drawer, he heard the familiar tinkle of dozens of small things sliding together. Inside, surrounded by hand-written research notes and correspondence was a wooden box no bigger than a tea chest. Pulling off the lid, he snatched his hand away. Where he had expected to find a jumble of loose metal pins, he found a pile of bleached bones. Immanuel carefully lifted the box onto his desk, tipping it sideways to coax the bones to slide away from the skull. A blank-eyed face stared back at him with fangs bared. From the size and shape, he knew it had once belonged to a decently large housecat.

Immanuel stared down at the disarticulated creature. Its vertebrae lay scattered across the bottom of the box alongside ribs and leg bones, which had separated long ago. Why had the previous curator kept a cat skeleton in his desk? It wasn't as if they were rare or that the museum didn't already have a specimen on display. He chewed on his lip with his eyetooth, his eyes locked on the cat's empty sockets. The longer he stared, the more clearly he could imagine its pointy ears and the curve of its tail. Since he gained a hint of Emmeline Jardine's power, he had touched far too many corpses not to expect the cat's death to be gruesome. When he touched the dead, he witnessed their final moments, and most specimens' lives ended with the distant retort of a gun, the beast blissfully unaware while Immanuel screamed in his mind for them to run. Now that he was preparing his own lunch and helping with dinner, he often found his latent talents showed him the moment of squirming agitation before a chicken's head was lobbed off or a cow's throat was cut. It was enough to make him consider becoming a vegetarian.

He sighed. He had to know if the cat had met an unseemly end. If that was the case, at least he could bring it back to Baker Street and give it a proper burial. Adam wouldn't mind, and if he did, he would simply wait for him to go to work and bury it anyway. Drawing in a deep breath, he braced himself for whatever godawful fate the cat could have suffered. Immanuel reached into the box and gently stroked the smooth spot between the cat's ears. The bright office dimmed into a darkened bedroom. The moon peeked through the bed curtains and a fire crackled somewhere nearby, but the sound was drowned out by the rhythmic gurgle of purring. Ahead of him, he could make out a pair of fuzzy legs with the ink-dipped markings of a Siamese. A wizened hand lifted the sheets and pulled them up to the cat's chin.

Immanuel released a breath as his lips curled into a relieved smile, but it quickly faded as a wave of grief washed over him that he hadn't anticipated. The skeleton cat had been a beloved pet, one the previous curator had apparently kept until his own death. Maybe he should bury him after all. As he closed the box and carefully placed it back in the bottom drawer, he made a note to ask someone about the old curator. Opening the cabinet behind his desk, he found the jar of t-shaped pins he had been searching for. Immanuel dragged his chair over to the wall with the fallen paper. Taking a pin, he twisted it through the thick wallpaper and into the plaster, but when he tried to secure the other corner, the pin refused to sink in. With the heel of his hand, he hammered it home.

"Mr. Winter!"

Immanuel whipped around in time to meet the penetrating gaze of Sir William Henry Flower. The swivel chair spun beneath him as he tried to step down. Stumbling forward, the museum director caught his arm. Immanuel's face reddened, turning a deep shade of scarlet at the sound of pins tinkling behind him followed by the flop of paper. Sir William Henry Flower stared down his patrician nose at the young curator. He stood only an inch taller than Immanuel, yet his air of authority gave him a presence that made Immanuel wish he could disappear into the wallpaper.

"Is everything all right in here?"

Swallowing hard, Immanuel straightened and nodded quickly. "Yes, sir. I— I was just trying to secure the paper."

"We could hear you trying in the hall. Have Miss Nelson contact the maintenance staff to fix it." The museum director's light eyes roamed over the shelves before coming to rest on the jumble of books and papers across the desk. "How is the research coming? Have you found everything you needed?"

Immanuel pushed his chair back to the desk, suddenly aware of the chaos in which he had been working. Every inch of the six foot long tabletop was used to hold an open book or allow him to see multiple pages of notes. If he had another two feet of space, he knew he would have filled that, too. He hadn't even worked there a week, yet he was already making a mess. Drawing in a long, silent breath, he banished all thoughts of being fired. At least one of his colleagues had to be worse.

"Yes, sir. I'm still getting the lay of the land, but the librarians have been very helpful."

"Very good. It may be a good idea to check the specimen room in the storage cellars and take some measurements and notes yourself."

"I will, sir. I didn't know if I was allowed to do that. Touch the specimens, that is." He swallowed hard, hoping he could hold off visiting the basements until he could bring a pair of gloves from home.

"Museum staff can borrow whatever is needed to further their research. If you have any questions about protocol, Mr. Winter, just ask one of the other curators or librarians. As you may be aware, there is a staff meeting today at one in the Shaw Room. You haven't been with us long, but I think you should be present to see how things operate. Do you know where that is?"

"Yes, sir."

Giving Immanuel a firm nod, Sir William turned to leave but stopped on the threshold. A wave of nausea rippled through Immanuel's gut as he realized the older gentleman's gaze was resting on his brown-blotted eye.

"I have been meaning to ask, but have you had your eye examined by a physician?"

The urge to run his fingers over the bump of raised skin that bisected his right brow was nearly irresistible. Immanuel's hands twitched at his sides, but he quickly clasped them behind his back.

"Yes, sir. I was under a doctor's care after the—," he paused. What could he call it? Even after six months, he didn't know what to say when asked about how he received the scar that clouded one blue eye with a half-moon of blood-brown. Immanuel's jaw tightened and his eye burned. He wished he could pretend it never happened. "After the incident."

"Was it treated?"

"Sort of. At the time, there were more pressing injuries to treat. The doctor couldn't completely restore my sight in that eye, but it doesn't trouble me much. I have grown accustomed to it," he replied, his voice tightening.

"Very well. Remember the staff meeting is at one in the Shaw Room."

Holding his breath, Immanuel watched Sir William leave, shutting the door behind him. At the sound of the glass rattling in its frame, Immanuel darted to the window. He wrenched open the pane and leaned out on his elbows. Summer air flooded his lungs as he exhaled the vision of Lord Rose looming over him and breathed in London's unique perfume to keep his mind from conjuring the demon's smoky breath. The earthy fragrance of Hyde Park down the road brought him back to the reassuring pressure of his office's wooden floorboards beneath his feet and the paper on seal physiological evolution flapping against his desk behind him. Immanuel raked a rain-spattered hand through his hair. If Sir William had continued to question him, how long he could have lasted before the memories tore him from reality? *Lord Rose is gone*, he reminded himself as he did nearly every day. *Lord Rose is dead and gone.*

⋅◦҉◦⋅

Walking down the wood-lined hall, Immanuel's gaze traveled over the engraved brass signs beside each door. *The Shaw Room*, he repeated to himself as he made it to the end of the hall in less than a dozen long strides. It had to be there somewhere. He should have asked Sir William where it was. He thought he had known, but there were so many rooms named for founders, and after a while, they became as tangled as the streets he tried to memorize on his way to work. Rounding the corner, he resisted the urge to check the time. He didn't want to know how late he was. Immanuel's pulse fluttered at the thought of being dismissed in front of the senior and junior staff. It would take all his strength not to walk off London Bridge— if he could find it.

Why had they even hired him? It was something he had wondered since he received the news that the famed museum director had agreed to take him on as a junior curator sight-unseen. He had a hard time believing that Sir William had taken Professor Martin's word about his student's intellect and ability to articulate a skeleton as if by instinct. Perhaps it wasn't often that Elijah Martin called in favors, and it made him wonder what Martin had done for the director.

Upon meeting him on the day Sir William had agreed upon for him to start his duties, the only thing the director had asked was his position on evolution. Satisfied with his belief in Darwin's theories, he passed him off to the nearest curator, who happened to be Peregrine Nichols. At least it had been Nichols and not one of the museum gentry who were as white-haired and stoic as Sir William himself. Nichols was a junior curator, too, but had been hired a few years earlier in the botany department. He stood over a head shorter than Immanuel with boyish brown hair and long, dark eyelashes. Even if he was half a decade older, he had the fragile, delicate features of a child and the rapid-fire speech of a sideshow barker. As Mr. Nichols led him past cases of specimens, pointing out the ones he worked on along with those Immanuel would have to update soon, he caught him up on museum politics.

"You're lucky you weren't here for it. It was chaos, utter chaos for months when they left. Most were junior curators and assistants complaining that they couldn't pay for their wives. Pfft, a crock. You know how people are, they always want more money than they could hope to get. We get paid well for what we do. By the by, do you have a wife?"

"No," Immanuel answered a little too quickly as they skirted a mass of schoolchildren who stared up at the stuffed elephants in awe.

"Well, then I guess I don't have to worry about you running before you even get settled. It would be nice to have someone to talk to who didn't live with one of these," Peregrine said with a chuckle, hooking a thumb toward the mastodon skeleton. "Your predecessor, Mr. Masters, was nice enough, a bit eccentric. You will have to get accustomed to that. There isn't much that's normal in a museum. Anyway, just stay out of Sir William's way and do as he says. He's been eagerly awaiting your arrival."

When Immanuel's eyes lit up, Peregrine continued, "Albert Günther, the old Keeper of Zoology, retired early after a fight with Sir William over the theory of evolution being forced upon the new exhibits. If you can't tell, old Günther was more than a little agnostic when it came to evolution, and Sir William can't stand that. It's black or white with him. Anyway, he's been forced to manage zoology along with his duties as the director, but now, you're here to help bear most of the burden without the higher title."

"Do you have any advice? Is there anything I should know?"

Peregrine tilted his head in thought, his pink lips pursed. "You went to Oxford or Cambridge, right? Well, then you know it's all politics. It isn't just what you know but who you know. The good thing is you seem quiet, trainable, and you're replacing another German, so you should fit right in."

More than anything, Immanuel hoped he was right.

Immanuel froze at the brass plate marked, *The Shaw Room*. Taking a calming breath, he adjusted his notepad and smoothed a wayward curl over his scarred eye. As he scooted inside, a dozen grey heads turned toward him, murmuring half-hearted greetings before returning to their conversations. It was like being back at Oxford. The entire room was lined in richly polished woods from the far-reaches of the empire and smelled faintly of leather and brandy. An oil painting of the museum's founder, Sir Hans Sloane, hung over the hearth. The man's curly powdered wig hung down in long heavy locks like a spaniel, his eyes staring ahead impassively as his hand rested on a book of botanical prints.

Before Immanuel could locate a free seat around the long, mahogany table, Nichols caught his eye and pointed to the chair beside him. Immanuel didn't know how he missed Peregrine. His blue suit shone against a sea of somber blacks and greys, reminding him of Adam's penchant for flashy fabric. *Adam.* He suppressed a smile at the thought of what waited at home and shimmied behind the senior staff to the empty seat. The moment he sat and tried to steady his breath, Sir William called the meeting to order with a rap against the table.

"I'm certain you all know why I have called a meeting today. The gala is in less than a fortnight, and we have plenty of work to do. The invitations, food and other sundry have been taken care of, but *all* of the specimen tags in the museum must be up to date, especially in the great hall and the ancient botanicals exhibit."

A silent groan passed through the room while Immanuel and Peregrine stayed silent.

"Everything must be in top shape. You never know who will show up. We must present ourselves as if we know Her Majesty will be there.

Mr. Glenmont, are the preserved plant specimens ready?"

A middle-aged man with gold-rimmed spectacles lurched awake. "Huh? Uh, yes, sir. The live specimens from the horticultural society are also ready to be picked up."

"Very good." Sir William raised a white brow at the little man nearly bouncing beside Immanuel. "Mr. Nichols, do you have everything under control with the specimen cards?"

"Yes, sir, completely done. Well, except for the silphium, but I'm nearly done. The Earl of Dorset sent me his notes, but they are rather hard to read."

Immanuel's ears perked at the familiar name.

"Mr. Winter, do you have something you would like to add?"

At the sight of everyone staring at him expectantly, he opened his mouth, then closed it before uttering softly, "I— I would like to help if I could. I particularly liked botany and did well in it." He licked his lips. Should he say it? "The Earl of Dorset is my flat-mate's brother-in-law, so I could possibly speak to him and clarify any questions we have."

Immanuel paused as a murmur passed through the room.

"You know him?" Sir William said.

"The earl wrote his own notes?" one of the curators asked over him, his hoary beard in stark contrast to his lilting voice.

"I— I would assume so, sir," Immanuel replied, his eyes sweeping from face-to-face before returning to his lap. "From what my flat-mate has said, Eilian Sorrell is a well-respected mechano-archaeologist and researcher. He found the silphium at his estate in Dorset."

"Well, I'll be. Never thought you would know an earl," Mr. Nichols added with a shake of his head. "I would greatly appreciate Winter's help if you can spare him, Sir William."

Sir William thought for a long moment, his eyes flickering between the two young men. Immanuel resisted the urge to shrink beneath his hard gaze. Had he overstepped his bounds?

"It's a bit irregular, but I don't believe the zoological specimens are too out of sorts. Be sure to read and alter the cards for the pinnipeds. You are our resident seal expert, Mr. Winter."

Immanuel inwardly sighed at the title. That probably meant more nights coming home smelling like decomposing walrus. Poor Adam. Perhaps a trip to the arctic would be his punishment for not knowing his place or for ruining the gala with poorly written cards. As Sir William moved on to other topics of greater interest to the rest of the curators, Immanuel replayed the conversation over in his mind. His heart thundered in his ears, blocking the men's urbane, muted voices. It was like being before the dons and professors at Oxford. Every word had to be scrutinized to decode layers of forethought, alliances, lies, and useless politics. That wasn't his way. It was hard enough to remember to refer to Adam as his flat-mate after months of waiting to share a bed, but that was a matter of life and death.

"Meeting adjourned. Mr. Winter, please stay behind. I would like to speak to you for a moment."

Immanuel's eyes widened, but as he looked up, Peregrine caught his gaze.

As Peregrine pushed away from the table, he gave Immanuel a half smile. "I wouldn't be too worried," he whispered. "If he was going to sack you, he would do it in his office."

Swallowing hard, Immanuel clutched his notepad to his chest, waiting for Sir William to approach. When the last man filed out, the museum director turned to him, his face unreadable.

"You said your roommate is the Earl of Dorset's brother-in-law?"

"Yes, sir."

"Are they close?"

"Yes, but—" It dawned on Immanuel where this line of questioning was going. "Yes, sir, he is the only family the countess has left. Adam Fenice and I spent Christmas with the earl and countess in Greenwich last year, and I believe they have gone shooting together as well."

Sir William nodded, running a hand over his bearded chin thoughtfully. "I will have to extend an invitation to Mr. Fenice. If you and the countess are going, he may feel slighted if he is overlooked."

"His cousin and her husband are going as well," Immanuel added, staring at his feet.

"Who?"

"The Hawthornes, sir. Dr. Hawthorne is the Coroner to the Queen."

"Very well. The earl made a sizeable donation along with the silphium, and I won't lose their patronage over a slighted relative. Give my secretary his name, and I will make certain to personally invite him."

"Thank you, sir. I'm certain he will appreciate it."

When Sir William turned his attention to the snifter on the sideboard, Immanuel slipped out. A wry smile crossed his lips as he passed the men who had just been in the meeting. Their gazes fell upon him with a newfound respect. No longer was he some no-name German boy. He knew nobility and that would establish him better than age or experience ever could.

Chapter Four
A Blood Bond

Carefully pulling the door shut behind her, Emmeline listened in the stillness for any sign of her aunt or uncle, but the house remained quiet. Emmeline tucked the half-wrapped book under arm, keeping it away from her damp cloak as she tiptoed up the steps. The moment she hit the first landing, she darted up the next set of stairs and hurried into her room. As she reached the door, a familiar red head peeked out from a room down the hall.

"Emmeline, is everything all right?"

She quickly shut the door, biting down the urge to be snappish. *Go away!* she mouthed before replying sweetly, "Yes, Aunt Eliza. I'm just getting changed. Cassandra and I walked home, and I'm soaked."

"Be sure to dry your hair, so you don't catch a chill. Dinner should be ready in half an hour."

When she heard her aunt retreat, she exhaled, threw the lock, and turned on the gas lamps. Laying the book on the bed beside her reticule, she pulled off her soggy cloak and draped it across the hearth screen. By the time Emmeline had slipped off her muddy boots, the paper wrapper had fallen away to reveal the infinite series of floral swirls and symbols etched into the book's leather cover. The pink wallpaper and the sounds of Wimpole Street below died away as she drew closer until her gloved fingers brushed the tome's edge. A hum buzzed through her fingertips, and before she realized what she was doing, she had pulled off her gloves and pressed the flats of her palms to it. Warmth radiated beneath her clammy hands. She pursed her lips, debating if she should reread the letter again, but she knew what it would tell her. Pass the book on. Find someone else who can keep it safe. She should go down to her uncle's office, wrap it in clean paper, and send it off to someone in the Oxford Spiritualist Society. But who? Her mother had been the head of it until— Emmeline sighed. There was no one. Maybe if she read the book, then she would know who could help.

As if hearing her thoughts, the silver latch clicked open. Gently lifting the cover, Emmeline's eyes widened as they ran over a series of arcane rings drawn within. They looped and overlapped, catching and holding onto the next design's orbit like celestial bodies. She ran her finger across the ancient ink, energy rippling with each stroke.

"Ow!" Emmeline cried, dropping the book. A bead of blood formed at the end of her finger, but as she looked up, she caught a pulse of light. Emmeline blinked. *No, it had to have reflected off the latch*, she told herself as she sucked the blood from her finger and picked up the book with her other hand. Sitting on the edge of the bed, she cradled the unwieldy tome in her lap. Somehow it hadn't seemed so clunky when it was closed, but open, it covered the width of her thighs.

The title page was nearly blank apart from the words *Fiat experimentum in corpore vili origin* and an etching of a corpse and a man embracing. The man was dressed in the stockings and doublet of the Renaissance, his classical physique muscular and sinuous. He reached out, his hand caressing the corpse's skinless cheek. A dark robe hung loose from the corpse's form, revealing the bundles of muscle and the white of tendons beneath. If it was a medical book, why would anyone want it so badly?

Any thoughts of her uncle's copy of *Grey's Anatomy* died away when she turned the page. Both sides of the parchment contained saucer-sized circles filled with minute symbols that she swore she had seen before on old monuments or the altars her mother had built to Hecate and the Great Goddess. Others were alien, no more decipherable than scribbles, but there was something beautiful about the circles. Her eyes trailed along the curves of the lines before darting along the triangles and irregular shapes that connected the dissonant symbols. As she took them in, a wave reverberated through her mind like the silent *twang* of a tuning fork.

Amid the perfect hoops and lines was a red blotch. Raising the book nearly to her nose, she watched as the bubble of blood imploded into the crevice. It slid along the channel, forming a tiny river that flowed across the parchment. A little voice in the back of Emmeline's mind told her to drop the book, that it wasn't normal. She needed to wrap it up and pretend she never saw it, but her hands stayed locked on each cover until the blood hit the edge of the first sigil. The moment it entered the circle, it sluiced counter-clockwise around the ink, zipping across the straight tangents and shadowing the arcane letters in a halo of red. As the last line filled, a rumble passed through Emmeline's hands. The book shook until she could scarcely hold it and her bed's iron frame bounced against the wall. The red shadow of her blood burned black before flashing white-hot and finally fading to a burnished gold. Light gathered in the center of the sigil, casting a hot glow against her cheeks as it grew to the size of a grapefruit. The saliva evaporated from her mouth as the ball of light lifted from the page and hovered only inches before her nose.

The pop of shattering glass resounded from the sconce near the door. She wanted to scream as the lights on either side of the fireplace blew out in a hail of glass, but the ball of light held her wholly. The world slowed to nearly a halt as glass hurtled past her and scattered across the coverlet, the book and its ball of energy deflecting the blows. Gas hissed in the empty sconces but was overtaken by the sound of faint whispers. Words rose and fell from the orb, all incomprehensible, but in her mind, she knew it was speaking about her.

She stared into its depths. A maelstrom of faces and voices rose to the surface. A woman's face with familiar dark, strong brows and full lips held her gaze before dissolving into flames. Emmeline bit her lip against the sudden pain squeezing her heart, but before it could fully bloom, her mother's face fell away to reveal the kind, open features of a young man. He stared down at her with his mismatched eyes wide with fear. A ripple of energy shot through her hands as the sphere faltered. The images spun away as the whispers evolved into a droning chant. Its rhythm rang through her chest and the bones of her arms. It spoke to something deep within her, something she only rarely became aware of. She had felt it stir months ago when she had spoken to the Prince Consort's soul, but since then, it had remained dormant. With a final pulse, the wick lit and a glow filled her. Her head spun as the power infiltrated her form with a sickening heat. Her body tensed, jerking against invisible binds as the feeling ebbed. When Emmeline closed her eyes, a web slowly pulled away from her skin before flying toward the empty hearth.

Opening her eyes, she found the orb gone and the room slipping into darkness. She stared down at the book. Where her blood had once been, it now faded to a dull golden-brown. Behind her the globe-less gas lamps hissed. Closing the tome, she carefully stepped over the broken glass littering the rug and flipped off the lights. Glassy grit crunched beneath her feet as she walked to the window. As she forced it open, a balmy breeze caressed her cheek and blew away the lingering heat in her face and hands.

Below her on Wimpole Street, men and women pushed past in a crush of grey and black umbrellas and coats. Through the dull, beating rain, shadowed faces stared up at her. A man stood in the middle of the road his gold eyes locked on the upper window, heedless of the steamers and carriages rolling by. She averted her gaze as one barreled toward him, but when she looked again, he was still there. Two women darted across the road in front of him. When they reached him, she expected to see them separate and walk around him. Instead, they passed through him. The man's face rippled and condensed, yet his gaze never left her. Something about him was faintly familiar. He was too far for her to make out the details in his face, but there was a sheen of light hair and the power in his shoulders. Emmeline's heart pounded in her throat as she backed up and yanked the curtains shut. Even with them tightly closed, she swore she could feel his eyes boring into her through the veil of velvet.

She had to get rid of it. Grabbing the book, she spun, desperately searching for a place to hide it. If people were after it, it had to be bad, especially if it made her see things against her will again. From the force of the blast, perfume bottles and pots of lotion had blown across her dressing table along with her box of hair ribbons, which had spilled its contents in a jumbled rainbow across the floor. She ripped open the drawer and tried to stuff the book in, but it was too wide. Footsteps echoed up the hall from the stairs. Her eyes flickered over her dresser and trunk before coming to rest on her bed. Getting down on all fours, Emmeline slipped under the wooden frame. Bits of glass pressed into her back and knees as she stuffed the book between the slats that supported her mattress.

"Emmeline, what are you doing in there? I thought I heard glass break."

Emmeline slid out, grimacing at the sound of her dress tearing against a shard.

The doorknob rattled. "Emmeline, open the door."

What could she say to her aunt to explain the broken glass? A hairline crack had formed across the mirror as well as in the top of the window. Her aunt would surely think she had done it on purpose, a tantrum for something that had happened earlier. Looking down at her leg, she watched as a line of blood trickled a fresh scratch. She touched it to her cheek and applied a little under her chin. As she took a deep breath, Emmeline blinked until tears, half real from fear, formed at the edge of her eyes. Opening the door, she threw herself into her aunt's arms.

41

"Aunt Eliza, it was terrible! The lamps exploded! I don't know what happened, but they popped," she cried as she buried her face in her aunt's shoulder.

"Dear lord."

Closing her eyes, Emmeline felt Eliza's long hands running over her back and into her hair as she shushed her. She released a tight breath as her aunt pulled her back to inspect her reddened eyes and the blood smeared on her cheeks.

Eliza Hawthorne rubbed her niece's trembling shoulders and whispered, "Now, now, you're all right."

Her quick green eyes ran over the glass littering the fabric vines of the rug to the crack in the window. "How did this happen?"

"I don't know."

Eliza cocked a thin, red brow and sighed. "Let me fetch the dust bin."

As Eliza disappeared into the hall, Emmeline pulled back the curtain and shuddered. Standing on the street below, staring up at the window, was the same man as before, but now, he had company.

Chapter Five
Empty

Adam Fenice paused at the stove, listening as the grandfather clock in the hall struck six. A small grin crossed his lips. Immanuel would be home any minute, and Adam hoped to god he had a good day at work. They had only been living together eight days, but it was beginning to feel as if he had always been there. He had expected it to be harder to integrate their dissonant lives under one roof, especially when he had spent his life fighting to be seen as a separate person from George and Hadley and their businesses. With Hadley married and gone, Adam suddenly found himself alone, staring at gaps in shelves and empty rooms where she had once been. A quiet fell over the house that couldn't be silenced. Something was missing, something he couldn't fill alone.

When Immanuel appeared at the train station with only one trunk, Adam feared there would still be an emptiness, but soon science books appeared where ones on mechanics had once been and a sweet, soft voice singing in German chased away the morning silence. Suddenly it was as if he had always been there. No longer did his parents' marriage bed feel too large or the house too empty for a bachelor. Hadley's old room was stocked with Immanuel's somber wardrobe and soon her old workroom would smell like bleaching bones and varnish. What Adam loved most was seeing two dressing gowns hanging in their room and the shallow indent in the pillow where Immanuel's head had been.

With a groan, the front door opened. Glancing around the doorway, Adam could only catch a glimpse of Immanuel's blonde hair and the swing of his leather satchel as he pulled it over his head. Adam turned his attention back to the stew and waited. Quiet footsteps padded into the kitchen, and within seconds, Immanuel's hands were snaked around his stomach and his head was nestled against his shoulder. Adam drew in a long breath, inhaling the familiar soapy scent of Immanuel's skin. His lips brushed Adam's neck and cheek before returning to his shoulder.

"Have a good day at work?"

"Better than I expected," Immanuel purred, giving Adam a squeeze. "*I* got you invited to the museum's gala."

"Oh really? And how did you manage that?"

"I threw your sister and brother-in-law's names around. Once they realized we were all related and we shared a flat," he paused as Adam turned toward him with a questioning henna brow, "they wanted to extend an invitation to the Countess's brother, lest he feel slighted."

"I'm sure you were put out that you had to invite me. I'm but a lowly money-counter."

A grin spread across Immanuel's lips as Adam wrapped his arms around his. "Well, I see you every day, so why would I want to spend an entire night with you drinking champagne and waltzing?"

Adam turned, catching Immanuel's hands and pulling him closer until their hips were flush and their gazes met. Keeping their joined hands up, he tightened his grip around Immanuel's back and took the first step of a sweeping waltz. Immanuel stumbled after him, half a beat behind as he was twirled backwards.

"Waltzes aren't your strong suit anyway," Adam replied with a toothy grin, his pencil mustache curling in agreement.

"Thankfully, I would rather not be asked to join when I can't dance with my partner."

Slowing to a stop, Adam turned, his blue eyes softened with thought. Immanuel's grip tightened as he pulled him in for a kiss. Adam sighed, his eyes closing at the gentle push of Immanuel's tongue against his lips. Arching back, he wrapped his arms around the taller man's neck and his hand sliding into the curls of his hair. A chill washed over him at the skimming of fingertips over his spine. Immanuel's hand dipped under his jacket and made its way toward the top of his trousers.

"We should wait until after dinner," Adam whispered, licking his lips and resting his forehead against Immanuel's.

Adam wanted to say more. He wanted to bang his fist on the table and cry that it wasn't fair. That none of this was fair. At Hadley's wedding, he and Immanuel had sat at the same table for hours, watching other couples dance with arms and eyes locked. He caught their knowing smiles when bodies brushed while he and Immanuel had to pretend they barely knew each other. Staring into his glass, he had wished he could take Immanuel by the hand and dance alongside the other couples, but as he tightened his grip on the stem of his glass, a gentle hand squeezed his arm. When he lifted his eyes, he had expected to find Immanuel giving him a reproachful look. Instead, he found Hadley staring down at him, her eyes heavy with guilt. Did she regret inviting them both to the wedding when she saw the misery etched into her brother's features? That night when they returned to the house on Baker Street, anger had deteriorated into melancholy. Stripped of their finery, they had lain in each other's arms until daybreak, a tangle of limbs and lips making up for lost time. Would they always be making up for those impossible moments?

⁓⁓ ⁓⁓

Immanuel looked up from his empty bowl at Adam. He had been

abnormally quiet during dinner. Swallowing hard, he said, "I'm working with Peregrine Nichols this week, helping out with the exhibits."

"Who?" Adam asked, snapping back to reality as he grabbed his bowl and stacked it on top of Immanuel's.

"Peregrine Nichols. I'm certain I told you about him. He's the one who reminds me of an imp. He's always smiling and prattling. If he wasn't charming, it would be maddening. It might still be when we work together. You might like him, though. I'm sure you will meet him at the gala."

"Why are you working with him? I thought he worked with insects or something."

As Adam put the dishes in the sink, Immanuel took up the hissing tea kettle and poured them each a cup. "Plants, but he's behind on his work. With the gala coming up, it's all hands on deck, and having a hand in the preparations really isn't a bad thing for me. It will look like I have initiative."

"I guess so. Though, it might be better if you stayed out of it and kept to your work."

Immanuel frowned. "I know, but I can't stand to look at another seal or walrus. Somehow my reputation as the seal expert has followed me here. I don't want to smell like— like rotting blubber."

Adam froze at the way Immanuel spat the word *blubber*. When he looked up, Immanuel's face remained impassive as he doctored their tea and refilled the kettle, but he knew the old wounds were still raw. It was during a visit to Oxford that he heard of Immanuel's nickname for the first time. The name Blubber had originated from his preparation of pinniped skeleton's for the university's museum and the malice threading through it came from the nightmares that followed his captivity and abuse at Lord Rose's hands. Even now he wouldn't speak of it except in the vaguest terms, but his university roommates couldn't forgive him for crying out for mercy in his sleep.

"Immanuel, I can do that. Just sit down and enjoy your tea."

"I will in a minute," he replied with a weak smile.

Immanuel looked over his shoulder and spotted a vase sitting in the center of the kitchen table overflowing with fern fronds, forget-me-nots, and periwinkle traveler's joy. Adam had given them to him when he arrived, but now their edges were curled and turning brown while their heads dolefully flopped over the side. Immanuel set down his tea and took up the vase. As he made for the sink, he turned, expecting to find Adam behind him but found nothing. He went to take a step forward and was knocked off kilter by something hitting his chest. Heat seared through his veins, snaking through his core until it hit his heart and shot through his body one beat at a time. Swallowing hard, he leaned against the counter, busying himself with the flowers to keep Adam from seeing the fear in his eyes. This time it wasn't death gripping his heart. It was something that wanted in. He took a shuddering breath and closed his eyes, hoping the stutter in his heart would stop.

"Immanuel? Immanuel, are you all right?"

Immanuel jerked back as water overflowed from the crystal vase and ran over his sleeves. The creeping heat abated at the water's touch until it only lingered as a tight ball lodged near his heart. Releasing a pained breath, he swallowed hard and carried the flowers back to the table without a word. As he raised his gaze to the dying flowers, a gasp escaped his lips. Before his eyes, the flowers' heads uncurled and the bits of brown he had seen a moment earlier eating away at the edges of the petals disappeared. Across the table, Adam absently poked at a sugar cube bobbing in his cup, unaware of his partner's sudden urge to pitch the plants out the backdoor. Immanuel averted his gaze, but when he looked back, the blues and purples of the forget-me-nots were more vibrant than the day he arrived.

Something was wrong with him. Something was very wrong.

"I— I think I'm going to lie down for a little while."

Adam's arm wrapped around his shoulders, pressing Immanuel's back into his chest. "You look flushed. Are you feeling all right?"

"I'm fine," he snapped but caught himself. "I'm just tired."

"Well, I will come up with you."

Immanuel crossed his arms. "I can get up the stairs by myself. I'm not feeble anymore."

"I think you misunderstood me." Adam slowly raised his gaze to Immanuel's, locking eyes as he held his arms. "I *want* to come up with you."

Immanuel's mouth formed a soundless O, and before he could think about what Adam said, they were checking the locks on the doors and covering the windows. Darting up the stairs, Immanuel slipped off his jacket and tie and tossed them into his undisturbed bedroom as he passed. He waited at the threshold of Adam's door, watching his companion carefully close the curtains to ensure no one could see inside. It had become a nightly ritual that Adam had begun months before Immanuel moved in to avoid suspicion from their neighbors. When the room was dark, Adam took his hand and led him to the bed. His hand slid under Immanuel's shirt and ran along the flesh of his back. Even after a week together, Immanuel still hesitated, expecting someone to be just beyond the door. It seemed too good to be true to have such freedom.

"Mr. Winter," Adam whispered into Immanuel's skin as he planted a trail of hot, moist kisses down his neck, "I have been waiting for this all day."

But why? Immanuel suppressed the question that would only elicit a strange look from Adam and an equally awkward reply.

Before Immanuel could stop him, Adam's fingers were flying over the buttons of his waistcoat and shirt. He resisted the urge to stiffen and cover his deformed chest with his arms, and instead he followed Adam's lead. Beneath his bright dandy's clothes, Adam was as solid and strong as Immanuel felt frail. Adam pushed Immanuel against the bedpost, catching his mouth. His pencil mustache prickled Immanuel's lip as the redhead's tongue plunged and grazed against his. The breath caught in Immanuel's throat. Closing his eyes, he let his companion explore his mouth and his ever-changing body. Adam's hands worked along his sides before sliding over the firm flesh of his buttock, eliciting a soft groan from his companion. Heat crept up Immanuel's form, tensing every muscle in his abdomen and sending his heart out of rhythm. Immanuel blindingly unbuckled Adam's belt and felt his fine wool trousers slip down his legs. Reaching for his own, Immanuel kicked them off and pulled Adam toward the mattress.

The bed sighed under their weight as Adam climbed on top of him. His eyes drank in Immanuel's form while his hands rested on his ribs. Adam caressed the dents where his ribs hadn't properly knit together. Immanuel swallowed hard at the thought of being prone and unable to hide from Adam's mental dissection. He hoped it was too dark for Adam to see him, but his mind was silenced by a shiver rippling from his scalp to his curled toes. Immanuel raised his eyes to meet Adam's gaze. A wordless conversation passed between them, and Adam's lips curled into a knowing grin. Immanuel stiffened, his hips twitching, as Adam nipped at his collarbones and ran his tongue along his sternum and down the scant trail of hair leading to his flannel drawers. His fingers twisted into Adam's henna hair as a gasp escaped his lips at the rush of air and the goosebumps rising on the tops of his thighs as his drawers were pulled away.

"I want to make you feel better," Adam murmured, his voice husky and his breath hot against his stomach.

Immanuel closed his eyes, fisting the sheets as Adam drew him in. He needed him. He needed this. He needed to be reminded that even after all that happened, there was still love in the world. More than anything, he needed Adam to make him forget.

৹ৰৎ ৡৱ৹

Adam stirred. Something nagged at his sleep-drunk mind, but when he finally cracked open one eye, he found the bedroom dark and the street outside the window quiet. The bed shifted beneath him, followed by another quick jolt. Turning his head, he found Immanuel still beside him with the covers drawn up to his chin and his body curled into a ball. As he watched him, Immanuel's body trembled and a muffled squeak escaped his lips. Before he could stop himself, he released a series of soft sobs. A pale hand shot from beneath the blanket and pulled his pillow down. Hugging it close, he hid his face, reducing his cries to twitches and faint hiccups. Fear sucked the air from Adam's lungs as he watched Immanuel, keeping his eyes nearly closed in case he turned over.

The covers slid off Immanuel's back, revealing a cluster of shiny circular scars inscribed into his shoulder blade. Adam swallowed hard. He had never heard Immanuel's nocturnal cries. He knew about them from Immanuel's stories from Oxford, but as he listened to each pained sob and choked half-word, his stomach knotted. The idea that someone had used this against his partner sent rage climbing up his throat. But what could he say to make it better? Offering words of comfort wasn't his strong suit. He didn't even know why he was crying, so how could he help him? Maybe it would be best to close his eyes and pretend that he had never heard him.

Immanuel buried his face in the pillow as another hiccup escaped his lips. Adam resisted the urge to scratch at his wrist. Inching closer, Adam slipped his arm beneath Immanuel's side and rested his forehead against his neck. His partner stiffened in his grasp and drew in a crackling, drowning breath. He hesitated before slowly turning over to meet Adam's gaze. In the scant moonlight, Adam could make out Immanuel's glossy, red eyes. Immanuel blinked to squeeze away the burning ache behind his lids, but as he opened his mouth to apologize, Adam pressed his lips to his. Immanuel's body quavered beneath his grasp as he held him close. Heat radiated from his thin form, soaking the sheets and catching his hair in a sheen of cold sweat. As they parted, Adam caught his partner's bichrome gaze. Silent phrases passed between them, revealing months of pain and longing. There wasn't anything left to say.

Wrapping his arms around him, Adam pulled him closer until Immanuel's clammy forehead rested against his collarbone. Immanuel latched onto him, concealing his face and holding onto him as if he feared he would be set adrift. There was still nothing Adam could think of to comfort him, but hands and eyes could articulate what lips could not. As he rubbed Immanuel's back and gently hushed him, Adam watched him chew on his lip. There was something he wanted to say, something threatening to bubble out. What if he wanted to talk about Lord Rose or the terrible place where he was held captive? Adam wanted to move on. They were together now and life was good. That was what mattered.

Finally, Immanuel drew in a deep breath and met Adam's gaze. "I— I think something's wrong with me, Adam. I really do. Something *has* to be."

Adam wiped away the moisture clinging to the dark circles under his companion's eyes. "Why would you think that? You may have a bad eye, but like I told you months ago, spectacles might help."

Immanuel shook his head and shut his eyes, pressing them against Adam's chest. "No, that's not it."

"Are you in pain?" Adam asked, his voice tightening. "We could stop by James and Eliza's tomorrow. I'm sure he wouldn't mind taking a look at you."

"It isn't physical. Maybe it is, but sometimes—" The words hung in Immanuel's throat as he inhaled Adam's familiar lavender cologne in hopes it would steady him. "Sometimes I see things."

Immanuel hesitated. Should he talk about the cat skeleton hidden in his drawer? That he knew the cat had once been a beloved pet and because of that, he didn't know what to do with it. How could he explain to Adam that when he touched something dead, he saw what happened right before it died and that's why he couldn't handle raw meat? It was embarrassing. It was more than embarrassing; it made him question his sanity, which was already precarious at best. What would he think if Adam told him he watched a vase of plants revitalize before his very eyes? He would think he was losing his grip on reality, and perhaps he was.

"They're just nightmares, Immanuel," Adam whispered, pressing his lips to Immanuel's forehead, "and nothing more."

"Just—" A loose laugh escaped his lips. Immanuel shook his head. He had it all wrong. "They're not…"

"I know you still think you see Lord Rose, but it's just your mind playing tricks on you. You can't give into it. We know he's dead and can't hurt you now. If you keep telling yourself that, then all of this will stop."

It had all been said so sweetly, so innocently, and with such a gentle kiss on his brow that Immanuel didn't dare say a word.

His eyes burned with tears as he whispered, "Right. You're right. Good night, Adam."

Rolling onto his side, he felt Adam's arms wrap around his bare torso and the hot flesh of his stomach press against his back. As Adam settled into slow, steady breaths, Immanuel's eyes trailed to the narrow space between the curtains. Moonlight streamed into the room, illuminating the pile of clothes strewn across the floor. Biting back the urge to snatch them off the rug and fold them, Immanuel stared at the winking stars. *Adam didn't mean it that way*, he reminded himself. How could he know that putting his kidnapper and abuser out of his mind was hard on a good day and nearly impossible on a bad one? No amount of love or good fortune would dispel the damage Lord Rose had done. His ribs still ached on humid days from where they had been broken and the cigarette burns on his back seared anew the moment his mind lapsed into daydreams. But how could Adam know the pain the past still caused?

Immanuel drew in a wet breath and squeezed his eyes shut. Against his will, a tear bubbled out and slid down his cheek. Pressing his face into the pillow, he tried to push away the disappointment and fear pooling in his sockets. Adam had been there since the beginning. He had seen his body shattered, a hollow skeleton of its former incarnation, and he had watched him carve out a new form meant to resemble what he had lost, yet he still didn't understand.

For months Immanuel had counted down the days until he left Oxford and could finally be able to live without a mask, yet it wasn't to be. How could he tell Adam about the strange sensations and the visions if it meant losing the one anchor of stability he had? He sniffed and shifted until Adam's loose grip fell away.

Even with everything he could have wanted, there was no way to forget.

Chapter Six
The Reading

Emmeline wasn't certain what happened the night before with the book, but she didn't like its aftereffects. Dressing that morning, she pulled aside the curtain and was pleased to find the road below free of spirits. At breakfast, she quietly picked at her eggs, listening to the sound of her uncle's newspaper rustle while hoping her tea would begin working on her foggy mind after a restless night. She released a tense breath and tried to think about something other than how much she wanted to close her eyes. To sleep in meant she had to be ill and submit to her aunt's examination, and that wasn't something she could stand.

"What are your plans for the day, Emmeline?" Aunt Eliza asked casually, but Emmeline knew it was the beginning of an interrogation if she didn't approve of the answer.

Pursing her lips, Emmeline fought the urge to spit back an answer that would only cause her allowance to be cut until she was sufficiently miserable. "I'm going to the Spiritualist Society and maybe have lunch or tea with Cassandra if I feel like it. What do you think I'm going to do? She's the only one I'm allowed with."

Eliza Hawthorne's jaw dropped before snapping shut. As she began her usual diatribe on respecting elders, Emmeline's eyes traveled to the door behind her. The door to her uncle's laboratory had been constructed to blend into the wainscoting and the damask wallpaper with only the undersized doorknob to betray its camouflage. Normally, she scarcely noticed it, but now it was calling to her. Her aunt's words died away as she watched the knob, waiting for it to turn. The room grew heavy as if a storm would burst at any moment, and amidst the faint rumblings, it felt as if someone waited on the other side. Her heart pounded in her throat as a voice rose from the threshold. It came as a gravelly whisper, barely audible, but with each hissing syllable, it became clear that it came for her.

I am strong. I decide who I read. No one can harm or speak to me unless I allow it. I am in control, she repeated to herself, walling up her mind against the invader as her mother taught her over a decade ago. When she looked up, the air had cleared and the figure had gone.

Emmeline shook off the energy humming through her. That hadn't happened since she was a child. She had been so careful to keep her guard up in her uncle's house. With the basement being used for autopsies and the occasional procedure, it could be a place where spirits who died violently might linger. Rubbing her eyes with her knuckles, Emmeline released a tired sigh. If only her mother was still here, she would know what to do.

"Emmeline, did you hear what I said?"

Looking up, she expected to find her aunt angry, but instead, she found her green eyes softened with concern. "Yes, Aunt Eliza. I'm sorry for being cross with you. I didn't get much sleep."

"Why don't you stay home and rest?"

"No!" she cried a little quicker than she meant to. "No, I'm quite all right. I'm only going to listen to a lecture, nothing taxing."

Eliza nodded, probing her niece with her doctor's eye. "If you're certain, but I will walk you there. Just in case."

Shrugging off her aunt's arm, Emmeline slipped into the Spiritualist Society, her mind far away as she unpinned her hat and handed it to the maid along with her parasol. She released a huffed breath and smoothed her dark curls in the mirror, which had become frayed in the humidity and were expanding at an alarming rate. She should have brought the book with her. Since leaving the house, its absence nagged at her mind like a bad itch. She couldn't shake the image of masked bandits tearing her room apart and making off with the book before she could even properly look at it. Part of her wanted nothing more than to return home and make certain it was safe, but that was foolish. It would be fine as long as no one knew about it except her and Cassandra.

"Just the woman I was looking for," Cassandra called with a smile as she emerged from the hall. "You have a reading to do in ten minutes."

Emmeline bristled. "Are you joking? I didn't have anyone scheduled today. Did Nostra do this? I was supposed to be attending Sir Arthur Conan Doyle's lecture. She knew that, and if I miss it, I—"

Grabbing her arm, Cassandra dragged her into the empty front parlor. "Just be quiet and listen. I did it."

"But why? You knew I wanted to go."

"Yes, but I think you will like this much better than a lecture on faeries," she replied with a playful grin as her friend cocked a contrary brow. "It's your Mr. Talbot."

"Are you serious? Are you certain it's him?"

"As certain as I can be. The appointment was made for Nadir and Leona Talbot. That's his cousin, isn't it?"

"So she's taken her maiden name? Hmm. I guess the divorce is finalized."

"You really need to stop reading the gossip pages."

"Ugh! And today my hair decides to look dreadful," Emmeline cried as she broke from her friend, and pawed at her hair in the hearth mirror. "Is he as handsome as the drawings in the papers?"

"Even better. Well, go on. They're waiting for you upstairs in the Blue Room." She waited for her friend to move or at least look pleased. "What's wrong?"

Emmeline stared at her feet before meeting her friend's tawny eyes. "What if I make a fool of myself?"

"I highly doubt you will ever play the fool."

At the sound of Cecil Hale's smooth voice, Emmeline whipped around to find him standing in the doorway watching them with an amused glint in his eyes. Her face and breast flushed at the skim of his gaze over her dark red dress.

"I've seen your abilities, Miss Jardine, and you have nothing to worry about."

"That's very kind of you, Lord Hale. Will you be going to the lecture?" Emmeline asked, shifting to put her best features in view.

Tilting his head back to reveal his long, graceful neck, he studied the ceiling's tin tiles. "Actually, I was hoping to sit in on your reading if you don't mind an audience."

"I would like that," she replied, ignoring Cassandra as she rolled her eyes.

With a smile, Emmeline kicked herself for agreeing to do the reading. She hurried up the steps to the Blue Room with Lord Hale at her heels, her heart racing at the thought of having her favorite author and Lord Hale in the same room. It was a dream she didn't know she wanted to have until now, two men she admired, both watching her, maybe even wanting her. It was like a plot from one of her hidden books.

With a slow breath, she prayed to her mother to help her and opened the door. The room was as hideous as she remembered it with every surface, including the carpet and wallpaper covered in a blue paisley that had faded to periwinkle in the sun. Despite its hideous upholstery, it was her favorite room to work in. There were no tables or cabinets for a medium to hide behind in the Blue Room, and it was there that her powers shined.

Her breath caught in her throat at the sight of Nadir Talbot sitting on the sofa. She had seen etchings from the court case in the newspaper, but somehow, she had never pictured him as a living being. As the door creaked, Nadir rose and turned toward her, revealing a strong nose to match his expressive byzantine eyes and sensual lips. Waves of unfashionably long black hair dusted the shoulders of his fern-green suit, which had been expertly tailored to accentuate his gracile frame. He was as handsome as she had imagined, but as she approached her seat at the head of the circle, she tried to remember to breathe and not look too interested with Lord Hale hanging about. Sitting beside him was his cousin. While she shared his complexion and eyes, Leona Talbot's expression was somber, dour even, as she stared into her lap. Like a Renaissance Madonna, her features were in the constant war between softness and severity. Upon seeing Emmeline, Leona's reddened eyes ran appraisingly over her form before returning to her hands with a frown.

Curtsying to the Talbots, Emmeline bit back a smile at Mr. Talbot's smoldering gaze. She had never expected to be so close to one of her idols. She had followed him through the murder trial, and even if his character was still seen as dubious in many circles, she didn't take the lack of a conviction in the case to mean he was guilty. As Emmeline took her seat, she noticed how Cecil kept his distance, barely suppressing a sneer at her clients.

"Welcome to the London Spiritualist Society, Mr. Talbot, Ms. Talbot. This is Lord Hale, my associate. And my name is Emmeline Jardine. I'm a spiritualist medium." At the word *medium*, Nadir Talbot's lips twitched into a bemused grin. She knew that smile well; he was a skeptic. Locking eyes with him, she added flatly, "As you can see, my séances don't involve a table or spirit cabinet. They distract from the experience and are the hallmark of a fraud. So if you're expecting theatrics, I would suggest you find another medium. Now, who is the reading for or is it a shared relative?"

At her question, Mr. Talbot turned to his cousin. She released a tight sigh and reached into her reticule to retrieve a stack of letters tied in twine, their dark brown seals had cracked and their edges had been worn soft by many hands.

"He wrote these. Is that enough to—?"

"It will do," Emmeline replied with a smile, but when she reached for the letters, Ms. Talbot hesitated before placing them slowly in her palm. "What is it you want to know?"

Leona Talbot stared past Emmeline as she drew in a long, slow breath. "I'm not certain. I guess I want to know if he's all right... wherever he is."

Emmeline nodded. "Now, let's move closer and hold hands to keep our energy bound within the circle. Mr. Talbot, Lord Hale, please rest your hands on top of mine."

Emmeline didn't always tell her clients to join hands, but when it gave her the opportunity to be in contact with two handsome men, she would milk her gifts for all they were worth. Loosely holding the stack of letters she began to clear her mind until she felt the gentle pressure of a hand closing over hers. Nadir Talbot's fingers were warm against her hand, and if she focused her mind, she could feel the scrape of callouses where he held his pen. Another hand clasped hers. Emmeline shivered at the hum passing beneath Lord Hale's fingertips.

Closing her eyes, she fought to ignore the gazes of the men beside her and slowed her breathing. The sound of steamer cabs clattering a floor below disappeared and was replaced by the babble of water gurgling somewhere nearby. Emmeline's nose flooded with the damp of earth and the fragrance of greenery. Opening her mind's eye, she found massive palm trees rising all around her, turning the sun into panels of stained glass as it shown through their leafy boughs. For a moment, Emmeline thought she had been sent to a tropical forest or an uncivilized island, but as she pushed aside the branches before her, she found that she was encapsulated within a great steel and glass dome. Where had the letters taken her? A few feet ahead, the path curved out of sight into a patch of vines and low, scruffy plants. It was strange not to see the spirit standing before her. Usually, they were ready and waiting for her, but in this spirit's world, she had no choice but to follow the dirt-dusted bricks into the mist.

As she came around the bend, the foliage peeled back to reveal a square pool framed by soaring white columns and mosaics of nymphs. Sitting at the water's edge in a burgundy wingback chair was a man with a book. His aquiline nose and sharp grey eyes gave him the quiet ferocity of an eagle, which honed in on Emmeline the moment she stepped into view. Lowering her eyes to his chest, she could make out the faint outline of a ragged hole in his shirt and waistcoat, and as she locked onto his face, the image faltered. The stripes of grey in his hair overtook what was left of the brown, and for a moment, his face appeared wrinkled and pinched.

"What are you doing here?" he demanded, shutting the book and rising from his chair to loom over her.

His eyes sliced into her, lingering on her wild curls before running down her body in a languid line. Emmeline swallowed hard and steeled herself against his intrusive gaze.

"I was sent here to speak to you."

"Well, I don't want to talk to the likes of you, so get out."

Emmeline rolled her eyes. So he was going to be one of those. Most dead were very happy to have a human ear to gab in, but those who tended to be hostile in life continued to hold to old grievances and bad behavior even in the afterlife. People never changed.

"The joke is on you because I can't leave until you talk with me." Defiantly meeting her gaze, he turned and headed for his chair, so Emmeline added, "It was Leona Talbot who wanted me to speak to you."

He stopped mid-step, his eyes losing their edge for a brief moment. "Why?"

"She cares about you and wants to know you're all right. I don't know why she would care about a rude old man like you. If you don't want to talk, I guess I will be going, then. You seem fine to me."

Emmeline was about to leave the way she came when he called out, his voice less harsh than a moment before, "Leona asked you to check on me? Did she say anything?"

"No. I don't think she knows what she wants to say. You're Randall Nash, aren't you? Her life is quite unsettled right now because of you. Is there anything you want to say to her that would make things better?"

"Tread carefully, little girl, you aren't nearly as clever as you think you are. Leona was like you once." Turning his attention to the temple behind him, his eyes locked on a bald spot in the garden. "You can tell her that my plant is in jeopardy, and I want it to be safe again. It's the earl's fault. If he hadn't stuck his—"

Nash's voice trailed off as he and Emmeline froze at a reverberation traveling through the earth. The water in the pool rippled and danced with a roll of thunder in the distance. The air in the greenhouse grew still, thickening with the taste of rain tainted with the scorch of burnt wood. Emmeline's heart thundered up her throat as she met Nash's light grey eyes.

"If you're doing that, stop. You aren't going to scare me off."

Nash raised his gaze to the grey sky that had once been blocked by the greenhouse's metal beams. Cocking his head, he seemed to listen to something beyond Emmeline's senses. "They're coming for you."

Her pulse throbbed in her neck as another echo of energy passed through the garden and climbed her legs. It was like something out of a nightmare from her childhood. The giant's heavy footsteps chasing her in his garden. Closing her eyes, Emmeline tried to wrench her mind out of the vision, but every time she opened her eyes, she was still in the spirit world. *Oh, god. I'm trapped*, she thought.

Emmeline opened her mouth to speak and found herself alone. Nash had disappeared along with the artificial forest. All that remained was hulking and ancient. Before her stood a gravel lane lined with towering yews. They had grown unnaturally tall, twisting in on themselves like a bonsai and contorting into the vague suggestion of faces or beasts. Emmeline's breath came in icy puffs, roiling through the air before disappearing into the blackness pressing in around her. Something paced at the end of the path, and with each movement, the smell of water and fire grew stronger. The air suffocated her, burning her nose and throat. The thing was drawing closer. Emmeline willed her legs to move, but she stayed rooted in place. Where could she run to? When she had been in the greenhouse, everything had seemed so solid, so real, but now, the ground beneath her seemed only inches thick and would collapse under her at any moment, as tenuous as a puff of squid ink.

A face emerged from the shadows at the end of the lane. Emmeline's heart pounded in time with the pulse of energy emanating from the creature's body. It was barely more than the shades it hid within, but as it swept close, searching for her with wide, sightless eyes, she could make out the long face and branched horns of a stag. Where a body and limbs should have been, the darkness churned without forming anything that remotely resembled a body. A dozen skinny tentacles whipped toward Emmeline before sinking into its back, flicking out for a taste of her energy. *They're coming for you.*

"What are you?" she yelled, her voice cracking with fear and her body trembling. "Tell me. Tell me what you are!"

Raising her gaze to the hollow points where the creature's eyes should have been, the breath seeped from her body. There was no humanity in it. The cephalopodic monster had no life in it. Never had it been of her world, and as it fixed its gaze upon her, she could taste its hunger for flesh. Looming over her, it seemed limitless, the energy radiating from its wraith-like body overwhelming. Bile rose in Emmeline's throat as she turned her head and closed her eyes at the creature's tentacle skimming along the delicate aperture of her neck. It wanted her.

Emmeline felt the ground beneath her feet. She focused on the softness of it, the vision of it being no more than a shoe-sole thick. As the creature rose to swoop upon her, the ground gave way and she was falling.

Chapter Seven
Magic

Emmeline's body jerked forward, nearly falling off the couch if it hadn't been for Nadir Talbot's quick reflexes. She fell back against his chest, her head reeling as the room spun around her. Choking down the bile climbing up her throat, she stared at her shaking hands as she clasped Mr. Talbot's arm. Beyond them, the stack of letters had tumbled to the floor. After what she had seen, the familiar ugly paisley pattern beneath them was oddly comforting.

"I thought you said the reading was to be uneventful," Mr. Talbot said, his breath tickling the curve of her ear.

Her mind clung to the smell of coffee on his breath and the honk of a steamer outside as she dislodged from Mr. Talbot's grip and patted down her wild hair.

"My apologies. I don't know what came over me." Emmeline blinked and shook away the fading image of the beast in the forest. No matter what happened, she had to do this right. Her mother never would have allowed a client to leave without a proper reading. Clearing her throat and drawing in a slow breath, she said as steady as she could muster, "Ms. Talbot, I believe I saw Mr. Nash. He was an older gentleman with curly hair and very sharp eyes, like a hawk. Does that sound familiar to you?"

She nodded.

"He was in a garden with exotic plants and a square pool. He seemed very content… until I showed up. He wasn't very happy about that."

Leona Talbot released a stifled chuckle as Mr. Talbot gave her a knowing look.

"He was surprised that you wanted to speak to him. He wanted me to tell you something about his plant? He said his plant was in jeopardy and that it was the earl's fault. Does this make sense to you?"

"That bloody plant again!" Mr. Talbot cried. "Did you really expect anything different, Leona? He cared more about his stupid silphium than he did about you."

Leona's cheeks reddened as her eyes narrowed and her mouth pressed into a thin line.

"No," Emmeline interjected, "I do think he cared about you. He seemed genuinely surprised. He went soft for a moment. From what I saw, I can't imagine he was a man who did that very often. He also asked how you were. I wish I could have said more to him, but that's all I gathered before we were interrupted by a rather boisterous spirit."

A faint smile graced Leona's lips as she nodded. "Thank you, Miss Jardine. I appreciate the comfort, no matter how small."

"I do hope you will return. I would like to try to contact him again at another time."

Emmeline slowly rose as the Talbots gathered their things to leave. From the couch, she watched Leona's face lapse into melancholy while her cousin cast a curious glance back at Emmeline. Nadir met her gaze, probing her for something more. *Probably a catch or spring or something,* she thought, anything that would make her a fraud, yet there was no contempt or anger as he mouthed, *What are you?*

The moment the Talbots were out of the room, Emmeline put her head in her hands. She feared closing her eyes, but much to her relief, the monster or whatever it was, wasn't waiting for her behind her lids. Her chest felt hollow with spent fear while her head grew heavy with a pulsing ache. Without opening her eyes, she stretched her legs across the garish blue couch and was about to rest her head on the armrest when she brushed against something solid. Scrambling back, Emmeline found Cecil Hale watching her from his seat. In the chaos of awaking from the séance, she had forgotten he was even there.

"That certainly wasn't your usual reading. Were you trying to impress him?" He crossed the room and pulled open the window, chasing away the lingering reminders of the dark wood with a humid breeze. "I know that for someone like Nostra, that would have been part and parcel with her reading, but you aren't like that. You don't speak in tongues and thrash about."

Her owl-like eyes glistened as she tried to separate herself from the memory of the beast, but her body had no knowledge of what transpired while she was trapped. She cringed at what Lord Hale must have thought. "Is that what happened?"

"You don't remember?"

She shook her head. "I had no idea. It certainly wasn't on purpose."

"I can see that now. You're really shaken up, aren't you?"

Lord Hale sat beside her on the sofa and gently brushed the hair that clung to her forehead. The breath hung in her throat at his touch. His eyes softened as he stroked her cheek with the edge of his finger. Heat flooded her breast at the thought of him moving closer until their lips brushed. She had waited for it the entire social season.

"Tell me what happened," she whispered.

"At first, it seemed like a normal reading. You went into a trance as usual, moving your lips but not speaking aloud. Then, you started jerking, your limbs locked, and you opened your eyes. Do forgive me, but I thought you were possessed. You were staring ahead, your eyes wider than I've ever seen them, and you started speaking in— I don't know what to call it. It certainly wasn't English or anything I've heard.

You looked terrified." He locked eyes with Emmeline, his hazel gaze pulling her in as his hand came to rest over hers. "I know we aren't supposed to, but I was about to wake you when you came to."

"I must have made a terrible fool of myself. I complain about Nostra, and then, I do this," she replied, spilling frazzled curls as she shook her head.

"It isn't your fault. You said a spirit accosted you. Who was it?"

She opened her mouth to speak and was surprised to find her tongue had gone dry. There were no words to describe the thing she saw, and if she wanted to keep Lord Hale, there were things she couldn't say.

"Just tell me. I won't tell anyone, I promise."

"I don't know what it was. I'm most vulnerable when I'm doing a reading, but it was probably just a spirit trying to frighten me. Maybe something malevolent was attached to one of them or someone else here."

"Does that happen often?"

Emmeline shook her head. Honestly, she couldn't remember a time it ever had. Her mother had mentioned dealing with malevolent spirits before, but they came only when lured or invited by a medium. She had done neither. She swallowed hard. There was one explanation: *the book*, and the thought was as terrifying as the monster.

"Miss Jardine, you're shaking. Let me fetch you some tea."

Pulling the bell-rope near the door, he waited until one of the maids appeared. With a curt whisper, she disappeared down the hall and Lord Hale returned to the cushion beside her, taking her hands in his. Warming them between his palms, he gave her a weak but hopeful smile. Emmeline's stomach flitted at the closeness of his body to hers and the heat radiating into her hands in small bursts in time with his heart. Her skin prickled and the roots of her hair rose to attention as he ran his fingertips along her palms. As he closed his eyes, a wave of heat pulsed through her form, bringing a flush to her cheeks.

Lord Hale straightened at the reverberation of energy. Hers trailed somewhere far away. *A blood bond.* That was not what he had expected.

Cecil glanced toward the door before leaning close and whispering, "Have you ever thought of leaving the Spiritualist Society?"

"Of course not. My mother was head of the Oxford branch. It's been a part of my life for as long as I can remember. Why would I leave?"

Emmeline studied his features, which had softened with thought. Did he want her to leave because he wanted her hand? Plenty of married women attended the spiritualist gatherings and worked as mediums, but a man of his standing might prefer his wife to be at leisure. She suppressed a smile at the thought, but a voice that sounded vaguely like her mother's nagged at the back of her mind. *Would you really give it up for him?*

"I think your powers are wasted in spiritualism." He held her hands tighter as she stiffened. "Don't misunderstand me, you do great work. I have never seen anyone leave one of your readings without getting answers, but you could do so much more. Just look what you did when Nostra was gone. You practically ran the place, and yet they gave it all back to her. They would rather have a charlatan run the Spiritualist Society than give it to you. You should be somewhere your talents are appreciated."

She shook her head. Her eyes burned bitterly at the thought because it was true. No matter how much she did, they still saw her as a child. "And where would that be?"

"At the Eidolon Club. It's an exclusive establishment that caters to people with extranormal abilities. People like you and me."

"What extranormal abilities? You aren't a medium."

He chuckled. "Emmeline, there is more magic in this world than you could possibly know."

Closing the gap between them, Lord Hale held her gaze. The flecks of amber in his eyes glinted in the afternoon sun as his hand came to rest upon her cheek. He gently traced her cheekbones before sliding back into her loosed coiffure. Her heart pounded and she swallowed hard at the intimacy of the gesture. His eyes traveled to her lips. Leaning close, his breath skimmed her skin and suddenly his lips were pressed to hers. Warmth flooded her breast, traveling up her neck and cheeks until it tugged every hair on end. Emmeline slipped her hand into his hair, feeling the slick of pomade and the prickle of where it had been freshly cut. This was what she longed for all season. Even when the parties and balls lost their charms, he never did.

From the moment she spotted him, she wanted him. Tall, auburn-haired, with a decent fortune, and good-breeding, Lord Hale was all she could have asked for. What surprised her most was that he enjoyed the company of a girl like her. Dark hair, dark eyes, wide hips, and small breasts didn't make her the most attractive woman in the room, but at every dance, he appeared at her side with an outstretched hand, paying little heed to anyone else. After the social season ended, she had expected to not see him again under her aunt's strict rule, but one morning she arrived at the Spiritualist Society to find him standing in the parlor asking how to join. He had found a way to see her again.

When they finally drew back with hooded lids and quavering breaths, Emmeline lingered in his arms with her fingers tangled in his jacket and hair. As their gazes hesitantly met, matching smiles crossed their lips. In that moment, he seemed so young.

"And what do you call that, Lord Hale?" she asked breathlessly.

"Magic."

At the sound of a knock at the door, they scrambled apart. Lord Hale stood, waiting for Emmeline to finish straightening her hair and gown before letting the maid in. The dowdy woman eyed Emmeline and Lord Hale suspiciously as she placed the tray on a small table in front of the window. When she glared at Emmeline with a disapproving frown, Lord Hale drew to his full height and loudly cleared his throat. The maid quickly left but not without giving Emmeline one more strident look.

"Nosy servants. I will have a word with Nostra about that woman," he said as he poured Emmeline a cup of tea.

Handing her the cup and saucer, he let his hand linger on hers. They locked eyes, and Emmeline felt the stirring of heat and flutters in her core.

"I apologize, but I must go. I do hope you will consider my proposition, Miss Jardine. You have an extraordinary gift, and you should be with people who recognize it."

With that, Lord Hale let go of her hand and disappeared into the hall.

Emmeline's mind raced as she curled her toes in her slippers and bit down the smile that refused to leave her lips. She couldn't wait to tell Cassandra what happened, even if she would roll her eyes and chastise her for not resisting his charms. As Emmeline brought the cup to her lips, she stopped halfway to her mouth. Sitting where the cup had been was a black square. Emmeline set the cup on the cushion beside her and studied the strange card. On the front was an drawing of a grim tree with snarling roots that wove into symbols, some created several at once, while the leaves formed a star. Flipping the card over, it read, *You are cordially invited to the Eidolon Club.*

Chapter Eight
The Eidolon Club

Cecil Hale walked down Sloane Street, passing from the glow of each streetlamp without raising his gaze to determine how far he had wandered. He didn't have to. If he sent out a wave of energy, he could see the glow of the Eidolon Club from the outskirts of the city. Sweat trickled down his neck at the murky air seeping into his clothes. He should have paid attention to who was lurking in the alleys and shadows, especially in a heat that stirred violent blood, but he didn't care. Let someone try to rob him. It would be a satisfying way to channel the guilt and anger gnawing at him.

He had kissed Emmeline Jardine, and while he had wanted to for months, he felt as oily and disgusting as the gunk that seeped from Duke Dover's corpse. All through the season he had wanted to kiss her, but he hadn't been given a chance to with her aunt and uncle always nearby. He told himself he had ultimately done it because he fancied her. Deep down, he knew it had been a way to sway her to his cause. Emmeline was stubborn, but if he played on her need for love and reciprocated her feelings, she would listen. Jerking his hand into a fist, he cursed himself. He shouldn't have done it. He shouldn't have let Lady Rose get in his head. He should have just talked about Nostra and given her the card. Instead, he let his feelings get muddled with this mess with the book and—

Before Cecil could finish his thought, the streetlamp over his head blew out in a shower of broken glass. Darting out of the way, he let out a hiss as a tiny shard sliced across his cheek before dashing to the pavement in an explosion of dust. Muffling a string of profanities, he wiped the blood away with his handkerchief and kept walking. It had been a long time since that happened, since he lost control.

Ahead of him, just beyond the fog, he could make out the grey stone façade of the Eidolon Club. Like many secret things, it was hidden in plain sight among the rich who had so many of their own secrets that they didn't dare pry into theirs. With his free hand, Cecil rang the bell and tried to stifle his feelings lest anyone inside notice. He steeled himself. In front of them, he was Lord Hale, the youngest practioner to earn a place at the Eidolon Club.

Light streamed onto the steps even at that late hour as the butler stepped aside to let him in. Unlike the cheery atmosphere of the Spiritualist Society, the Eidolon Club's decor fit its purpose. Every room was trimmed in dark wood with crenelated arches and lined with hazy paintings of men or tempests. While there were plenty of cathedral-like windows punctuating the ceiling of the foyer, they did little to brighten the gloom. No matter how many electric lamps or fires were lit, the Eidolon Club never lost its chill, but that was a hazard of having so many practioners in one place. Passing through the front room, Cecil caught sight of Lord Sumner standing against the stone mantle, explaining something to another wizened gentleman in hushed tones. Cecil kept his eyes to the ground even as he felt their gazes upon him. On every story and in every room, extranormal people like him moved within, studying ancient texts, safely practicing magic within rooms that could withstand their power, or simply enjoying the company of those they didn't need to hide from. It was a place he had loved until he introduced his aunt. She brought something with her that he couldn't explain, something that made him feel as filthy as that stolen kiss.

Descending the stone steps to the catacombs, Cecil braced himself for what he would find at the bottom. Stale air tainted with dust and moldering water rose from below, carrying with it the reek of corpse flesh. It was a smell he wished he didn't recognize. A faint chant carried through the air, but as he grew closer, he realized it was the lilting melody of an ancient song. Slipping into the half-closed chamber, he found Lady Rose carefully arranging a series of mirrors and bowls around her in a loose circle. From a bag at her feet, she withdrew half a dozen tallow candles followed by a hunk of quartz crystal as long as her hand and a vial filled with a murky liquid.

"If you're going to stand there, you had better have something to say," Lady Rose murmured without looking up.

Lord Hale shifted uncomfortably at the glint of the wicked obsidian knife in her hand. "I have made progress with Emmeline Jardine. I invited her to join us here, and I think she will accept."

"That doesn't help us if she doesn't have the book. Mediums are useless anyway."

Gritting his teeth, he resisted the urge to kick the nearest bowl and ruin whatever ritual she was setting up. "If the book does what you say it does, then I *know* she has it."

He could still picture Emmeline's energy. Only a week before, it had been a short, compact flame with a trailing wisp, but today, he had seen a much different shape within her soul. It had been stretched until it fanned around her like a mandala. A catalyst was the only thing he knew of that could cause such a sudden change. What surprised him was how she could do it without the book on her person. Surely, it couldn't have fit in her reticule.

"Do you know how you will get the grimoire from her?"

"Not yet, but if I rush her, she will cut me off." He shook his head. "Then again, I haven't seen it. Maybe she doesn't have it."

Lady Rose stopped mid-turn as she traced a circle around her knees in chalk. "Then, why have you come if you have nothing useful to tell?"

"I want information." When the bronze-haired woman laughed and struck a match, he added, his voice edged in anger, "I have a right to know what I'm getting a dear friend into."

"*A dear friend.* You should have asked me when you agreed to help find the book."

"Well, I didn't think finding a book meant I would be crawling through graveyards and desecrating corpses. I'm not going to help you anymore unless you tell me what you want with the *Corpus Grimoire.*"

"Fine, you're dismissed. I will just have a talk with Miss Jardine tomorrow," she said sweetly with a smile that was anything but. Wiping the jagged knife on a rag, she locked eyes with Cecil. "How does that sound, Cecil? Shall I talk to her myself? I don't think you or she will like our conversation, but I'm sure I will get the book."

Cecil's hands shook at his side as the cords in his neck strained. He pictured himself seizing Lady Rose by the front of her silver gown and slamming her into the catacomb's wall. As much as he wanted to see her skull smashed, he couldn't imagine Lady Rose at the mercy of anyone, especially him. If he touched her, it would be the last thing he ever did.

"I will speak with her, but I'm not going to do anything that will bring her harm. She's innocent in all of this," he said.

"We will see about that." Looking up at Cecil, her eyes softened and her face lost its feral edge. "Keep your heart out of this, Cecil." She filled one of the bowls with a pale, murky liquid and put it only inches from her knees. As she closed her eyes and leaned back, she added, "If you must know, the grimoire may be the main part of the ritual, but there's more to find so we must act quickly. There are others in London who would love to find them before us and we're running out of time."

His eyes ran over the circle of mirrors and candles. It all made sense now.

"So you're scrying to find what remains."

A wry smile crossed her lips. "Clever boy."

Ignoring her comment, he asked, "And what else are we looking for?"

"An artifact, a compass of sorts, and a plant."

"What sort of plant?"

"Silphium. The oracles used it to get closer to the gods, and I fear if we don't have it and the artifact, the ritual will fail as it has in the past. No one had all of the pieces. Then again, no one had practioners like us. Have you heard of the Interceptors?"

"No."

"They are after the book and vivalabe but only because we want them. They want to stop us, Cecil, and we can't have that, can we?"

The candles sputtered around him, a wind fluttering the end of his coat. "But who are they?"

"Sometimes I forget that you are so young."

Heat rose in Cecil's cheeks, burning with anger to mask his embarrassment.

"If you had left England, you would be well acquainted with them. They live normal lives, pretending they have no abilities, and the moment any of us step out of line, they impose their morality upon us. They believe they have the right to tell us what is right or wrong."

Cecil watched her eyes steel again as she reached for the knife. His pulse quickened. *Someone wants to stop us.* He hadn't thought about the repercussions of what they were doing. Could it really be so grave that others outside the Eidolon Club cared enough to try to stop them? When he began studying magic as a boy, it had begun with a spark of talent, a bit of hedge witch blood from his mother's side, but what kept him at it was that magic had been limitless, taboo. It was uncharted territory where few dared to venture.

When he stumbled upon the Eidolon Club, a world of companions opened to him, and suddenly, the seclusion that had unnerved him at first only made it feel more exclusive. He was special and his diligent work and devotion to the subject quickly raised him in the ranks. Cecil swallowed hard, watching as Lady Rose chanted under her breath and stared deeply into the bowl at her knees. Suddenly the idea of rituals and magic books left a sour taste in his mouth.

The chanting grew faster as she brought the bowl closer until her nose and chin nearly dipped below the water. Just out of sight in the darkened corner of the catacomb, a shadow condensed until Cecil could discern a pair of broad shoulders and a towering frame. He had seen that shadow several times, lurking in dark corners or breathing down the back of his neck in ashy gusts when Lady Rose was around. As he turned to watch the mass of shadows, it seemed to glare back at him. Cecil knew who lurked beside her. He didn't like him when he was alive, and he most certainly didn't like him dead.

"Cecil, come here," Lady Rose whispered, beckoning for him to her side while holding the scrying bowl level in her other hand.

The nobleman knelt beside her, his eyes locked on the dark liquid churning in the shallow bowl. It pulsed, rocking with an unseen tide before settling into place. For a moment, the bowl was blank. Lady Rose's lips moved silently with the proper incantation, and as he cocked his head and drew closer, colors began to condense in droplets beneath the surface.

A room formed, grey and soaring with massive columns. Cecil drew in a tight breath at the thought of having to steal the necessary relic from a cathedral and hoped it wouldn't come to that. The building on the other end tilted, revealing rows of glass tanks housing an array of pinned butterflies over the fronds of a plant that had been set in resin. The image wavered, but through the murk, a man appeared. His face was thin and pale, and cutting through his eye was a long scar that tainted his iris with old blood.

"That man. He— he can't be. Can he?"

"He is," Lady Rose replied, lowering the bowl and blowing out the nearest candle. "We have been meaning to pay him a visit. Now that we know where he is, I will make certain we get what we need before the Interceptors have a chance to reach him." A thin smile graced her lips. "Cecil, please leave me. There are things I must attend to, and I doubt you will want to watch that ritual."

Giving his aunt a quick bow, Lord Hale retreated from the catacomb, happy to soon be free of the stink of rot and damp. Cecil lingered at the door. She had never shied away from scandalizing him before. He released a silent sigh. Somehow, he had never expected his aunt to be this way. After his parents and sister died, he had searched for Aunt Claudia, the only family he had left, and instead of finding a second mother, he got this.

The sound of clinking porcelain followed by the scrape of the obsidian knife against stone was too much to ignore. When he looked at her over his shoulder, his heart pounded in his throat. Lady Rose stood in the center of the circle, the flames of the candles on each point of the star glowing a pale green. She had her head thrown back as her throat worked in indecipherable words. As he stared, he watched her eyes grow dark until all that was left was an undulated darkness as terrifying as her shadowed companion. Her back contorted at an impossible angle before snapping forward. Lady Rose opened her mouth in a silent scream, but instead of sound, the smell of hot cemetery filled the tight room.

Cecil's legs trembled as he shook his head, trying to chase away the creature in her body, but when he looked back, the nightmare was real. His body lurched forward and suddenly he was running down the hall and up the steps, not stopping until he was out in the fog. He needed to go somewhere, anywhere he could pretend to be ordinary.

Chapter Nine
Impossible Devices

Immanuel followed Peregrine Nichols through the labyrinth of hallways leading to the bowels of the Natural History Museum. At first he had tried to trace the path they had taken in his mind, but after weaving through row upon row of specimens ranging from tiny beetles to elephant femurs, he was utterly lost. Shelves rose around them, boxing them into a forest of glass and wood so thick the air had stilled and tasted of decomposing paper and formaldehyde. Tucking in his elbows, Immanuel's eyes ran over the peeling labels affixed to the murky jars sitting at eye level. A cloudy sheep's eye lolled lazily in its container before meeting Immanuel's gaze.

"What did you say you needed my help with?" Immanuel asked, watching Nichol's disappear beneath one of the lower shelves.

Unseen glasses clanked together as the impish man's hand shot out with a flattened butterfly in a shadow box. Nichols waved the glass frame, and Immanuel dove forward to grab it before he let it drop. A thump echoed through the shelf above followed by a muffled curse.

Another hand shot out holding a long tube filled with coiled fern fronds.

"I needed a second set of hands, can't you tell?" Nichols replied from beneath the shelf. His striped wool legs flailed as he struggled to back out of the tight crevice. In his hand was a crowbar covered in dust with a trail of limp cobwebs hanging from its end. "I must thank Sir William for letting me borrow you. It's nice to have someone who won't throw out his back or keel over if he has to lift a crate."

"It still might happen," Immanuel murmured.

Nichols let out a loud cackle as he tossed the crowbar ahead of him and slid out. He dusted off his shoulders and knees before running his hands through his hair. A plume of motes clouded the air and recoated the shoulders of his jacket. With a Cheshire grin, he plucked the crowbar from the floor and motioned for Immanuel to follow him with a wave of his cudgel.

"You would be amazed how fast the curators' assistants disappear the moment you need help. Same with the dock men. You can't blame them. They think we're pampered scholars, so making us lift a few boxes is easy revenge. Then again, there are worse ways for them to get their jollies. Be prepared for them to torment you a little at first. It's happened to all of us. Well, the young ones anyway. They know who they can play with." His bright bronze eyes ran appraisingly over Immanuel's form. "And you're one of them. Don't worry, so was I. We get on all right now."

Immanuel gave him a nervous smile, which he kept plastered to his face as the claustrophobic rows of wooden shelves fell away to reveal a wide hall that opened with a welcome breeze. Men's voices rose at the end of the hallway, rough and raucous, the voices of men the scholars upstairs would pretend had no place in the running of a museum. The dock was as much of a storehouse as it was a port. Crates the size of men sat stacked on either side of the great doors, which stood open to the tree-lined divider that separated the museum from the street behind it. A hooked crane hovered overhead while four men wrestled a series of ropes around a long, squat box the size of a coffin.

The other five sat watching, passing a bottle between them. Upon seeing Immanuel and Peregrine Nichols enter, the bottle disappeared into the stacks.

"What can we do you for, Perry?" a man with pepper muttonchops said as he hopped off the box and met them out of range from the crane's swing. The man's shoulders sloped under years of heavy lifting and the muscles of his arms bulged beneath his rolled shirt-sleeves. His face had been sculpted with pleasing features surrounded by strong cheekbones and a fine chin. Quietly imposing was the best description Immanuel could manage.

"John, as you probably guessed, I need the gala goods. I've been sent to fetch all of the crates for the botany department and any left for zoology."

"So you want the whole lot then?" he replied, hooking a thumb toward the wall of boxes.

"If that's what's left, then I'm more behind than I thought."

"I can get them for you. You got the paperwork?"

"You care about paperwork now?" Peregrine patted his trouser pockets before fishing into his jacket. After a moment, he handed over a crinkled wad of telegraphs and letters.

John's ochre eyes narrowed as they scanned the names. With a wave of his hand for them to follow, he led them into the mess of crates. "Sir William does. Can't blame him with the break-ins."

"Break-ins?" The word escaped Immanuel's mouth before he could stop it. He fidgeted, adjusting the glass containers in his arms, which quavered with fatigue.

The dockhand looked at Immanuel as if for the first time. He cocked a grey brow, his eyes darting up his form like Peregrine had done. "And who are you?"

"John, this is Immanuel Winter, Mr. Master's replacement. Mr. Winter, this is John Daniels, our master dockhand."

"A pleasure," Immanuel said softly, jostling the specimens into the crook of his arm. As they shook hands, gnarls and rough callouses scratched against Immanuel's palm.

John pursed his lips, looking from Immanuel to Peregrine and the letters in his hands. He tapped them before saying, "We aren't supposed to let it get out. About the break-ins, that is. Sir William wouldn't want any reporters getting a hold of it before the big night."

"You know I won't tell," Peregrine replied with a vulpine smile. When John gave him an incredulous look, he added, "Well, he won't tell."

"That I might believe. None of your boxes were tampered with, but I came in last week and found a few cracked open and hay strewn about. It didn't look like they had taken anything. The bug men said everything was there that was supposed to be."

"What would they want with a box of insects?"

"I don't think it was bugs they were after. You would think a thief would take anything. They left a lot of valuable goods: butterflies, an Egyptian statue that should have gone to the British Museum, a handful of rare orchids. The odd thing is I don't know how they got in. Didn't break anything. Sir William thinks it's an inside job, so we need to check everyone's credentials before we can give them their packages."

Glancing over his shoulder for any sign of Sir William or the other senior curators, John leaned close and added, "Then, last night, one of the night guards caught someone down here. He heard them banging around and found a man climbing on the stacks. Tried to run after him, but he disappeared. The guard said he was strange too, didn't move like a man should. He was shambling around, like his limbs didn't work right."

Immanuel swallowed hard, the hair on his neck standing on end and the pendant around his neck burning cold against his chest. When he raised his gaze, he found John and Peregrine looking at him with matching conspiratorial grins.

"Was the ghost story part of the initiation you mentioned, Mr. Nichols?"

John chuckled as he led them to a stack of boxes ranging from a hat box to a hip-high crate. "Just a coincidence. Couldn't of made it up if I tried. The guards tell tall-tales. He was probably just an opium fiend or a drunk looking for a warm place to sleep. They've set up a night watchman here now, so your packages should be safe from night crawlers."

The dock man checked the papers one more time, his eyes running across the tacked packing slips and the less visible marks of names and addresses whitewashed across the rough wood. After a few moments and a lot of circling, he handed Peregrine the crinkled pages along with a small box. He reached to give the other to Immanuel but thought better of it upon seeing the fragile jars cradled against his chest.

"Where do you want the rest delivered?"

Immanuel watched as Nichols pursed his lips and squinted in thought. A grin crept across his features as he met John's gaze. There was a devilish glint in his eyes that Immanuel didn't like.

"Put half in mine and the rest in Mr. Winter's office."

⁖

When Immanuel returned from lunch ready to label and describe plant specimens, he was surprised to find his already cluttered office filled to the brim with rough wooden crates. From the look on Peregrine Nichols' face, he shouldn't have been. The boxes sat on the floor several high or across his desk with one massive, man-sized crate sitting directly behind his door that took up so much room he could barely slip inside. He couldn't imagine how the impressively stout dock men had been able to shimmy out, let alone with their trolley. With a sigh, Immanuel pressed his weight into the huge crate. It barely budged until he charged into it with his shoulder, and even then, it only inched forward with a scraping whine. He wished he could leave it and just shimmy inside, but he could imagine the look on Sir William Henry Flower's face if he tried the door and found a box barring his entrance. No matter how he played the scenario, it never ended well.

Testing his door, he opened it only to lock eyes with Peregrine Nichols across the hall. Nichols flashed a toothy grin before disappearing into his office, which appeared to be without a trolley-load of crates. *Half the lot, my foot*, Immanuel thought, choking down his anger until it oozed out at an acceptable level of frustration. *Don't take it personally. They do this to everyone*, he reminded himself. This wasn't Oxford and it wouldn't last the entirety of his career. He was the new junior curator, and the others would have a little fun at his expense to break him in. It was to be expected.

Quietly shutting his door, he spied a crowbar lying across his desk. Hefting it, he turned it over in his hands, unsure how to use it or what to use it on. The hip-high box seemed the easiest option, so he carefully aligned the metal teeth and wiggled the bar. With a sickening crack, the lid lifted to reveal dozens of nails hammered into the lid.

As he pressed and twisted, his shoulder blades stretched the fabric of his jacket, threatening to pop the seams. He cursed Adam for convincing him to wear something so tailored to work. Working at the museum should have been all books and dust, and instead beads of sweat were running down his back and dampening his collar. Since when did scholarship require physical prowess?

Immanuel jumped back as the lid toppled off to reveal a bed of straw. Pushing it aside, his hand brushed the waxy surface of a leaf. Inside were half a dozen pots filled with seemingly identical plants. Immanuel leaned into the crate, his heels lifting off the floor as he reached. He blindly placed the first one on top of the pile of crates, but when he went to place the second, the pot teetered. It hung precariously on the edge, but as Immanuel scrambled to grab it, it fell. Immanuel flinched as it shattered, sending bits of clay and dirt out in every direction. At his feet, the plant lay in a bedraggled heap, and apart from being without a pot or dirt to sit in, it looked all right. Picking it up by the stalk, he gingerly placed it on the windowsill. Maybe he could simply repot it and no one would notice. He hoped Peregrine might have a spare. He didn't look like the type to run to Sir William over a simple mistake.

After carefully removing the remaining plants, Immanuel stared down at the dirt strewn across his office. The soles of his shoes were coated in it and left a crumbling trail as he searched his desk and cabinets for a dust pail and broom. As he stooped beside his desk and rifled through the bottom drawer, a glint of metal under his shelf caught his eye. At first, he couldn't see it in the deadened portion of his vision, but when Immanuel lowered his face to the boards, he could make out a shiny ball halfway under the cabinet of curiosities. Immanuel reached under, ignoring the shock of cobwebs drifting across his hand. Along with a shard from the clay pot came an engraved brass ball. Flat metal rings encircled the ball, and surrounding them were tiny letters he could barely make out. Sitting back, Immanuel turned the ball over in his hands. It was surprisingly heavy yet fit perfectly in his palm. He ran his thumbs over the lattice of metal and chipped the dirt from the symbols. There was something beautiful about it. It was so utilitarian, so mechanical, but the intricacy of it was nearly anatomical. He stared down at the wider band running around its equator. There had to be some mechanical element to it. Running his fingers along the edge, he felt a slight lump. When he pushed it, a soft click resounded from within the device.

The top half fell back to reveal the inner workings of an astrolabe, or at least what looked like one. Immanuel had seen them in the science halls at Oxford, but the only one he had seen up close belonged to his uncle. As a child, he would snatch the gleaming disk from his uncle's mantle and spend hours spinning its dials, pretending to read the stars. The one sitting in his hand didn't quite look the same. While it still had the carved rete and plate, the readings were different. Instead of numbers, there were symbols etched into the rim, and lining the edge of the rete were minute beads carved from brightly colored stones. With the edge of his nail, Immanuel pushed the crystal miniature planet around its orbit. As it reached the midline, another click echoed through the metal. For a moment, nothing happened, but then his eyes caught the slow rotation of the inner most planet. The metal buzzed and tapped against his hand, and the series of disks that had formed the face of the plate eased into a raised orb. The center rose, bringing the matching orbits of the stone planets to soar around it. When

Immanuel held the device closer to his good eye, he noticed that the celestial bodies rotated in time with his movements. Holding it still, he watched the green planet travel in time with footsteps outside his door, stopping and turning in the opposite direction the person outside descended the stairs.

Holding the device to his ear, Immanuel could make out the faint, rhythmic ticks of gears working in harmony. He watched the colored stones dance, spinning on every axis before veering in a new direction as he turned his arm. It seemed impossible that it could have the ability to do such complex things in such a small form. Beneath his fingers, the machine pulsed with life.

But what was it? Immanuel's gaze flickered back to the door where he knew Peregrine Nichols and the other curators lurked. If someone knocked, should he toss it into the nearest drawer and pretend to be picking up shards or should he show it to them and risk having it taken away? He sighed. It wasn't his to keep. It was probably an antique tool that had rolled off some scientist's desk only to fall into the box of plants. Gently shutting the lid, he shoved it into his pocket and returned to the crate filled with straw. Immanuel tugged it forward, checking each side for a name or address, but the letters had distorted and faded during its journey. Holding his hand over the brass contraption jutting from his pocket, Immanuel slowly opened the door. From the threshold, he could make out Peregrine Nichols moving in his office through the door's wavering glass.

Drawing in a steadying breath, Immanuel knocked on Peregrine's door. When it opened, Immanuel's eyes widened at the sheer number of plants littering the tight space. Peregrine's quick gaze passed over Immanuel's features as he waited expectantly in the doorway.

"Do you need something, Winter? You can't possibly be done yet."

"No, but may I come in for a moment?"

Peregrine stepped out of the way, waving him in with a tin watering can. Immanuel stooped under the boughs of plants hanging from the ceiling and vines that seemed to grow over every surface.

They crawled up the walls and bookcases, leaving tiny purple flowers in their wake. He traced their path, but no matter what direction he went, he couldn't discern where each vine began. Every available surface was crowded with plants. Alien orchids, geometric succulents, and fairytale bushes covered with black berries lined the windowsill and shelves. A handful of small crates sat on the corner of the desk with a ledger propped beside it. Even without the massive crates, the walls seemed to close in on Immanuel as plants brushed his hair and tickled his neck.

"What do you need, Mr. Winter? I'm very busy right now."

"Well, I—," Immanuel paused, his hand pressing against the ticking orb in his pocket, "I broke a pot. Do you have a spare?"

With a nod, Peregrine reached into the cabinet beneath his bookcase and handed Immanuel an oversized porcelain flowerpot. "Adequate?"

"Yes, thank you." The botanist took a step toward his desk when Immanuel added, "I found something odd in the crate."

Peregrine arched a brown brow. "Oh? If it's an insect, get Bowker to take it."

"No, no, it was this." Immanuel pulled out the strange compass and held it out in his palm. "I found it when I dropped the plant. It must have ended up in the pot somehow because it rolled out with the dirt when it broke. I tried to figure out where it came from, but I couldn't find a name. I thought you might know since you have the papers it came with."

"Let me see."

Peregrine hefted the metal ball, rolling it between his palms. He pressed the invisible spring twice and the top opened to reveal the raised globe within. A small smile spread across his lips, his eyes running from the device to Immanuel's face. Immanuel resisted the urge to flinch beneath his penetrating gaze. What Peregrine was grinning at, he hadn't the slightest idea, but Immanuel knew it couldn't be good. Cocking his head, Peregrine carefully closed the lid and forced it into Immanuel's hand.

"It's yours."

"No, it isn't. It must have fallen in the pot by accident. Surely the owner must be looking for it."

The botanist stared at the device as he replied, "Sometimes things look for us. My advice is to keep it. You may need it."

"But I—"

"Trust me," Nichols whispered, trapping Immanuel's hand over the orb with his own. He straightened and laughed. "You had better get back to work, Mr. Winter, or you will be here all night."

Chapter Ten
Superstition and Fear

Immanuel quietly shut the door behind him. Guilt weighed heavily in his stomach as he caught the time on the grandfather clock in the hall. Even though he had sent a message home with an errand boy warning Adam he would be working through dinner, he hadn't expected to be this late. The house sat silent with the curtains drawn against any nighttime passersby. Fear welled in Immanuel's chest. His heart quickened, setting his body on edge as if waiting for the next thunderclap.

"Adam? Adam, are you home?" he called, hoping his voice didn't betray the panic tightening his throat.

"I'm right here."

Immanuel turned toward the voice. Taking a step into the parlor, he found Adam lying across the length of the sofa with a novel propped against the pillow. A silent sigh escaped his lips. What had he thought happened? Immanuel swallowed hard and perched on the edge of the cushion, his back pressed against Adam's hip. As Adam closed *The*

Tenant of Wildfell Hall and turned over, Immanuel slumped against his chest. Adam's arms wrapped around him, pulling him closer. For the first time all day, Immanuel let out a full breath.

"What kept you? I thought I was going to have to send Scotland Yard to find you."

"Gala work. I was helping Peregrine Nichols, and somehow, I ended up being saddled with most of the work."

"I told you to stay out of it," Adam murmured into the back of Immanuel's head.

Immanuel shivered against the brush of breath fluttering his hair. "If it wasn't this, then it would be something else. At least it's plants and not tarantulas."

Closing his eyes, Immanuel could feel the slow, steady drum of Adam's heart against his back, but could Adam feel his racing? That moment of panic when he thought Adam had disappeared refused to abate. All he wanted was to curl up in Adam's arms after a long day, but his muscles stood poised to move and his eyes snapped open with every creak or honk on the other side of the panes.

He licked his lips. He already knew the answer as he asked, "Adam, are you angry that I stayed late?"

The couch shifted behind him as Adam sat up. He furrowed his henna brows, his eyes coming to rest on Immanuel's pouted mouth and fitful gaze. "Of course not, I was just worried. I found your letter when I got home, and I hoped you would be home before dinner grew cold, but…" He shrugged. "Employers don't care who is waiting for you."

Immanuel nodded. He hadn't meant to stay so late. By the time he finished typing the last card at the secretary's desk, he found that the trolleys had finished running for the night. Passing an underground station, he stood with his hand on the rail and his eyes locked on its cavernous mouth. It would get him to Baker Street far faster than walking, but he couldn't do it. In the shadows shifting below, he could see Lord Rose in his devil mask glaring up at him. The fetid stink of the train station was too close. Walls rose around him, and for a moment, all hope of returning home fled. Metal claws sunk into his throat, tightening until he could scarcely breathe.

"Oh, I nearly forgot. A package came for you." When Immanuel merely stared up at him, Adam added, "It has German writing on it."

He blinked, the stupor leaving him as he rolled off the sofa and darted into the hallway. "Why didn't you say so?"

Adam smiled to himself as he followed his companion. By the time he reached his side, Immanuel had pulled off the twine and paper and was shaking the tight lid off the striped hatbox. Adam frowned thoughtfully as he watched Immanuel toss the lid aside and pull out a letter. Craning his neck, he could see that the box contained everything but a hat. Cradled in tissue paper were photographs, books, a new set of pastels, letters, and jars of what he could only imagine were jam. No wonder the box weighed so much when the postman hefted it into his arms. He looked up to find Immanuel chewing his lip with a nervous grin as he read the note.

"Who is it from?"

"My family," Immanuel replied, his smile widening. "Mutter, Vader, Johanna, even Onkel Theodor. They all wrote a little."

Adam couldn't imagine Immanuel with a family. He rarely spoke of them or what he left behind in Germany. The entire time he had known him, they had been a faraway entity, a hypothetical mother whose face Adam only saw as a pale, blonde blur. He couldn't imagine his father or sister. He couldn't even imagine a time when Immanuel only spoke German. He certainly couldn't picture the face of the boy who got Immanuel exiled from his homeland. When Adam thought of the moment that sent Immanuel to England, he could see only his own face at sixteen. For Immanuel, the lines of past and present never crossed. He was in constant motion, hurtling forward toward the future and pulling Adam along with him.

As his bichrome eyes swept over each line, Immanuel seemed happier than he had been since they met. A barb of envy stabbed at Adam's gut. Everyone in that letter knew Immanuel before Lord Rose had gotten him. Even if he hadn't known him then, Adam knew there were two Immanuels. The innocent was gone, but whether he had died in Germany the day the police came knocking or at Lord Rose's hand, he didn't know. Maybe if he knew him then, things would have turned out differently, or maybe Immanuel never would have needed him.

"What does it say?"

"Here," he said, thrusting the letter into Adam's chest as he reached for the photographs with his other hand.

"It's in German."

"Oh. My apologies. Sometimes I forget." Immanuel pulled it from Adam's hand and placed it on the hall table. "The usual letter. They miss me. They wrote about what's going on at home. They're very happy to hear that we are living together, and my mother wanted me to thank you for taking me in. I'm certain she would like you if you met."

"So she knows we're—"

Immanuel slowly flipped through the stack of cardboard-backed photographs. "I didn't say it outright, but she knows. I'm sure after seeing Johannes and Theordor, she knows what to look for. Do you want to see a picture of my family?"

Adam stepped closer and took the picture from Immanuel's hand. Staring up at him were three pale faces. His mother appeared to be the picture of maternal love. Her face and form were rounded and soft, and something in her eyes reminded him of Immanuel. He couldn't be certain if the shape was the same, but they shared a brightness that made him think they shared the same intelligence. When he turned his attention to Immanuel's father, the breath caught in his throat. They were nearly identical, twins separated by three decades. His figure had spread a little with age, yet their faces and necks and hands were all the same. Adam scratched his wrist. This would be the man he awoke with thirty years from now if the world didn't interfere. *If...*

"You look just like your father," Adam managed to say between tight swallows.

Flipping through the stack of pictures of the German countryside and Berlin, Immanuel turned away from his companion. "Do you really think so?"

Adam replied, but Immanuel couldn't hear him. At the bottom of the stack behind a picture of his sister was his face staring back at him. His eyes flickered toward the hall mirror behind him, but he quickly looked away from the crack running from his eyebrow to his cheek. He chewed on his lip as he slipped the photograph under the package out of sight. He couldn't let Adam see it.

"Here's a picture of Johanna," he said, feigning indifference as he passed the next picture to Adam. Averting his gaze, Immanuel picked through the box for something to take his mind off the young man wearing his face.

"Your sister is quite pretty."

"She's all right."

At the bottom of the crate, Immanuel found a small velvet pouch. Pulling the knot from the string, he dumped the contents into his palm to reveal two irregular balls of amber and a slip of paper. Written in purple ink were brief instructions in his mother's hand. *Put on either side of the doorway for good luck.* Holding the glistening stones close to his eye, Immanuel peered inside. Broken bits of fern leaves and the disarticulated wings of insects hung suspended in the saffron amber, but as he turned the stones, he could barely discern a scratchy manmade shape. Someone, probably his mother, had carved a rune into each precious stone. While the symbols marred their natural beauty, the inscribed amber felt at home in the space between his fingers and palms. He rolled them between his fingers, wishing he could keep them in his pockets. Leaving Adam with the rest of the photographs, he carefully tucked the first bit of amber against the doorframe, out of sight.

"What are those?"

Immanuel froze as he placed the second one on the other side. How could he explain it without making his mother sound odd? "They're— they're a housewarming gift from my mother. It's a tradition in our family to give stones like this when someone gets a new house. One is for protection and one is for luck."

"Oh. That was very thoughtful of her." Adam reached into the box and withdrew four volumes that had been lovingly wrapped in scarves and socks. "Well, that explains why it weighed so much."

Peeling away the colorful yarn, Adam laid the books across the hall table. The first three were bound in leather with vertebrae bedecked in gold and silver letters. While he couldn't understand the German titles, he could make out the names Charles Darwin, August Weismann, and Ernst Haeckel. He flipped through them, catching glimpses of sketched birds and creatures beside walls of text.

"Science books?"

Immanuel nodded as he reached his side. Lovingly running his fingers over the familiar edges, he said, "All on evolution. And look, none involve seals or walruses."

"What about this one?"

Adam turned to the last book. Unlike the others, it was slim with a soft vellum cover. There were no words written across the front to indicate who had written it or what it was about, but as he flipped through it, he found that the inside was handwritten. Text darkened the pages, stretching in crooked, irregular rows across the parchment only broken by the occasional drawing. Most were circles filled with shapes and minute scribbles of ink, discernable to only the writer himself. As Adam went to peruse the opening page, Immanuel clamped it shut.

"I don't know why my mother would send me one of Grandfather's diaries. It must have been a mistake. I will send it back to her tomorrow. Oh, look, Johanna packed some of her elderberry wine, and I think this is cheese. Would you take it into the kitchen and pour us a glass?" Immanuel said as he pulled the book from Adam's hand and replaced it with a bottle and tin.

"That sounds lovely. Just don't spoil your dinner."

When Adam winked and disappeared into the kitchen, Immanuel released a tense breath. He glanced toward the kitchen, making certain that Adam was occupied, before darting into the living room. Lifting the couch cushion, he tucked his photograph into the notebook and shoved it as far back as he could.

Adam could never see it. If he did, he would never think of his companion the same way, and Immanuel wasn't going to let that happen.

⚬⚬ ⚬⚬

Immanuel stared at the ceiling, listening to the gentle sigh of Adam's breath at his side. Carefully slipping out from under his companion's lax grip, he grabbed his dressing gown from the hook. At the door he paused, casting a glance at Adam's sleeping form. He wanted nothing more than to climb under the sheets and rest his head on Adam's henna-dusted chest. In his mind, he would close his eyes, lulled by the steady drum of his heart, and he would wake with the alarm's ring, feeling... He couldn't quite remember what a full night's sleep felt like. Perhaps he wouldn't worry so much and he certainly wouldn't be climbing down the steps at all hours, venturing into rooms meant to serve diurnal creatures.

As Immanuel passed, he checked that the front door and windows were still locked. Without flipping on the lights, he fished under the sofa's cushion until his fingers brushed against the frayed suede of the notebook. Pulling it out, he scooted into the kitchen out of sight from the street or the stairs. He lit the lamp in the middle of the table and settled in beside it. Shadows danced in the far corners of the kitchen, reflecting off the metal of the range and the wavered glass of the backdoor. Immanuel's pulse quickened, but he couldn't give into those thoughts. He couldn't go upstairs and hide yet.

Turning the leather journal over, the pages of tight, smudgy script fell open to reveal the cardboard-backed photograph. There was no point in ignoring it. Immanuel pulled it out and held it to the light. His eyes locked onto the boy's, which stared back at him from the paper with a smile-crinkled gaze, half a moment from a laugh. Immanuel's hand edged toward the glass globe of the lamp. It would be so easy to destroy him once and for all, to be rid of his mocking smile and clear

94

blue eyes. He raised the lid, inching the corner toward the dancing flame, but he kept trailing to the old Immanuel's face. His hand shook as he held it out. He couldn't do it. He was innocent. The boy posing for the picture had no idea what would happen to him. How could his younger self have known that a few stolen kisses would send his world crashing down around him? The boy thought the picture would mark his graduation and his transition to a university, a last boyhood portrait before he spent his days in deep study. The boy still had hope. He looked off past the camera to the world laid out before him. There was no hatred or fear in his world. The tragedy of Onkel Johannes's imprisonment was a twist of fate that would never happen to him. *He* would never worry that his love would bring out the worst in others, that it would send him into exile, that he would end up at the mercy of a madman. The boy had no idea that his bones would be broken and his body and face would be marred to where he no longer saw himself in the mirror. Why had no one warned him?

Immanuel shut his eyes against the tears threatening to escape. How could he be free for months yet still see his prison cell rising around him each time he entered an elevator? Why did he jump at every sound or feel reality slipping from his grip the moment a museum patron exhaled a puff of tobacco in his direction? It had been months, *months*, but it never stopped. It never got better. Shaking his head, Immanuel squeezed his lids and placed the card against the back cover of the journal. Adam would never see it; that he would make sure of. If he knew there had once been an undamaged Immanuel, he would surely want him instead, and there couldn't be two of them grieving for a lost boy.

Blinking the fog from his damaged eye, he turned his attention to the strange journal. What was his mother thinking to send it alongside his evolution books? He had told Adam it had been his grandfather's, but honestly, he had no idea who wrote it. While the pages had been bound within one cover, they varied in size, jutting from the edge of the notebook like crooked teeth. He flipped through the pages, watching the handwriting grow and shrink as he progressed. As rapidly as one hand appeared, another replaced it on different paper. Turning the book on its side, he could see where the pages changed where each new author spoke. The creator had disarticulated other books centuries ago and rebound them in a new spine, but why? What was so important that it had to be condensed to a portable volume?

He opened the cover expecting to find a title page only to meet a wall of tight text. Parts were in an archaic German while the rest was written in Latin. Immanuel scanned the first page, his light brows furrowing as the author dove into why certain mediums didn't work to create the desired reaction. For a moment, Immanuel thought it might have been a science book after all, but when he turned the page, he found a series of concentric circles littered with minute hooked figures. Immanuel knew what it was: *alchemy*. He resisted the urge to roll his eyes. It was ridiculous that his mother kept reminding him of their family's sordid past. Alchemists to scientists wasn't something to be proud of. No one bragged about having an alchemist in the family. It was embarrassing and— Immanuel's hand trailed to the chain and vial hanging around his neck. Giving the chain a gentle tug, he pulled it from his shirt. In the wavering flames of the lamp, the gold and silver leaves appeared to flutter. Engraved in the top of the stopper in Latin were the words *"Miscē cum Cruor."* Mix with blood. With a gentle twist, the lid came off and the sweet smell of the eternal forget-me-nots within wafted out. Whatever his ancestors had bottled all those years ago had worked. It had revitalized the pressed flowers and it had brought him and Emmeline Jardine back to life. After years of shaking off his mother's superstitions, her strangely colored rocks, her amulets, and her whispered chants, he wondered if she had been right. If his mother sent him the book, he had to believe there was a reason. He turned back to the first page and began to read.

Time passed slowly as he struggled to decipher the arcane words in his presumed ancestor's deplorable handwriting. At the third tolling of the grandfather clock, the idea finally clicked. The circles and lines drawn in the upper corner of the page were merely a way to convey meaning, to instruct the material how to bend to the person's will.

Immanuel's thoughts turned to hours spent next to bubbling chemistry sets, waiting for migraine-inducing solutions to drip into something worthy of turning in to his professor. It didn't take much to ruin a reaction. Perhaps alchemy had been nothing more than science mixed with superstition. His eyes trailed to the note below circle of symbols once more.

"*Protection. Best incised with a silver knife. Envision safety.*"

Immanuel looked down the hall at the pair of shoes sitting beside the front door. With his brain addled with fatigue and running high with latent fear, he couldn't stop himself from picking a knife from the kitchen drawer and carving the symbol into the sole. As he followed the path his ancestors left, he pictured Adam passing house after house and making it inside. The edges of the symbol were sharp and undulant, but if he couldn't be there at all times, he had to ensure that nothing bad would happen to Adam. If he had the opportunity, he would cut the sigil into Adam's flesh to make certain he would never be vulnerable. Adam was his one source of stability, and the thought of losing him…

Setting Adam's shoes back in their place, he released a choked yawn and quietly crept up the stairs.

Chapter Eleven
Dark Things

Emmeline stood outside the Eidolon Club. Her dark eyes ran over the brick Grecian columns and intricate ornaments above the windows. She never would have expected anything called the Eidolon Club to be in Chelsea. *Its members must have deep pockets*, she thought as she knocked on the door. After knocking twice with no answer, she checked the card Lord Hale had given her against the house numbers. She was in the right place. Maybe it didn't open until nightfall, but if that was true, she would need to find a better excuse to tell her aunt other than having tea with Cassandra Ashwood.

"So you found it!"

Turning, she found Lord Hale ambling up the pavement with a smile that flooded her core with a creeping heat. "It wasn't difficult, but it doesn't appear to be open. No one let me in."

As he reached her side, his gaze flitted over her form as he offered his arm. "That's because it doesn't know you yet. Only members can get in unescorted."

With a rapid knock, the door opened and Cecil gave her a knowing look. Emmeline's eyes widened as she stepped inside. The Eidolon Club was exactly how she had pictured the London Spiritualist Society before she arrived. While the Spiritualist Society reflected its middle class clientele with a multitude of photographs and paintings on every wall and furniture in garish patterns that matched the rugs and drapes, the Eidolon Club quietly spoke of wealth. The wood of the paneling and bannisters overhead had been polished to a lustrous sheen and the rooms had been laid out to heighten the open space. Everything was of the finest quality from the heavy curtains to the oil paintings by *known* artists hanging from the picture rail. Emmeline released a contented sigh. It reminded her of home. Closing her eyes to relish the familiarity, a buzz of electricity passed up her feet and through her body.

"Lord Hale, Miss Jardine, what a pleasure to see you," a woman's voice called from the next room.

Emmeline opened her eyes in time to see a bronze-haired woman emerge from the shadows. Lord Hale's arm stiffened in her grasp as the woman grew closer. She wore a gown out of a Parisian fashion plate. The dark red gown was overlaid with an intricate web of lace and had an Elizabethan collar that accentuated her long, sun-kissed neck and sensuous mouth, yet her eyes betrayed her youthful appearance. As Emmeline met her gaze, her body grew heavy and the weight of centuries pressed upon her. With a blink, the curious sensation dissipated.

Clearing his throat, Lord Hale began tightly, "Miss Jardine, this is Lady—"

"You may call me Claudia," she said as she grasped Emmeline's hand and gave it a gentle pat. "Why start with formalities when I'm certain we will be fast friends? I can already sense that you have far more to offer than one would expect. Do you mind if I call you Emmeline?"

Shaking off her stunned muteness, Emmeline replied, "No, I would like that very much. Your house is lovely."

"Oh, it isn't mine. It belongs to the society, which belongs to no one." Lady Rose gestured to the room she had come from. "Would you care for some tea? We have much to discuss."

Without waiting for a response, Claudia Rose led them into the parlor where tea and tidy sandwiches had been set on a table near the fireplace. As Lord Hale stiffly sat in the chair furthest from their host, Emmeline resisted the urge to study the tempest above the hearth. From the corner of her eye, the waves rolled in and the shattered ship sank, but when she finally turned, she found the painting remarkably still.

"You must know that a young woman with your gifts would be a great asset to our cause."

Emmeline settled into the armchair across from Claudia, turning slightly to avoid seeing the strange painting. "And that is?"

"To bring magic to the forefront, of course. To have the freedom afforded to those without extranormal gifts." Pouring the tea, a sharp smile crossed her lips. "You're so lucky to be a medium. You already have Her Majesty's blessing to perform in public. The rest of us... Well, we still have prejudices to overcome."

When Emmeline took the proffered teacup and stared at her with furrowed brows, Lady Rose continued, "Practioners, people with special abilities, were plentiful before Christianity reached the British Isles. They were oracles or served the gods as priests, but once Christianity became the norm, they were forced into hiding unless they wanted to face persecution. It seems ironic with Christ having extranormal abilities of his own, but that is human kind's nature, punish the outsider. You have certainly heard of witches being tortured or killed during the Inquisition and the Salem Witch Trials. It has been going on for centuries and continues to this very day, though not nearly as violently."

"How?"

"Well, between moral rigidity and the treatment of the fairer sex, it's surprising anyone discovers they have extranormal abilities at all. Society dictates you stay within the norm. The poor can't afford to be strange, and the middle class has no imagination. Only people like us have the imagination and civility to handle such a responsibility. Still, women are told it will have ill effects and men are led to believe it's unmanly. It's no wonder you don't see many practioners."

Emmeline stared into the blackness of her tea waiting for clarity. As the head of the Oxford Spiritualist Society, her mother had turned away dozens of frauds over the years and had warned her daughter against trusting those who claim to have powers, yet there had been strange things in Emmeline's life, namely a young man she shared a soul with.

"I don't mean to be rude, Claudia, but how do I know you aren't lying? I have never seen someone with abilities outside my own and my mother's."

A throaty chuckle escaped her lips as she put her tea on the table and shook her head. "My dear, no one could fault you for wanting proof. If you will allow me."

Claudia Rose drew in a deep breath and focused her eyes on a spot behind Emmeline's head. Emmeline stared ahead, refusing to move for fear of what she might see. The cups bounced in their saucers as the room rocked. The electric chandelier and the globes flanking the fireplace jangled in their sockets. Their filaments blinked, then glowed white hot until Emmeline had to shut her eyes against the burning in her retinas. Gripping the arms of the chair, Emmeline braced herself against the force of Lady Rose's energy. She turned her face and squirmed away from it, unable to pull herself from her seat. Just when she thought her throat would shut against the pressure, the energy burst like a bulb and trickled into the aether.

Emmeline panted as she opened her eyes, clutching her heart and running a hand over her clammy cheeks. Lady Rose watched her with her head cocked, her gaze probing her beneath the concern. When Emmeline finally faced Lord Hale, she had expected him to be as affected as she was, but he merely glared at Claudia from his chair, his fingers tightly wound around his teacup. Emmeline blinked until her mind could form coherent thoughts. This was no spirit thumping or table lifting. What Lady Rose had conjured was different. It had a palpable presence, a foreboding suck of energy like the silence before an explosion.

The only sounds left were her ragged breath and the teacup tinkling against its saucer. The words slipped from her lips in a breathless gasp. "I believe you."

"And I believe you can speak to the dead, among other things," Lady Rose replied with a smile that didn't quite reach her eyes. "Your mother was a medium as well, wasn't she?"

Emmeline nodded as she brought the cup to her lips, thankful for its reassuring warmth.

"What did she believe regarding your abilities?"

"She thought it was a gift," she said softly, her throat still tight. "That we had a special connection to the afterlife, and that it came from god."

A faint smirk crossed Lady Rose's lips. "Did she give you any rules?"

"Of course. If I don't keep my guard up, I can see spirits everywhere, so she would tell me to keep it up to avoid troublesome spirits. Mama said to always make sure I wanted to give a reading, and that I needed to give myself and the spirits permission before speaking to them." Emmeline released a nervous chuckle. "Avoid charlatans. Don't dabble in dark things."

Lady Rose leaned closer, her green eyes glinting with interest. "Dark things? What sort of *dark things?*"

Cecil clenched his jaw so hard that the veins of his neck rose against his skin but said nothing.

Looking from Lord Hale's tense features to Claudia's feline intensity, Emmeline felt as if she had stumbled into a past argument.

"The usual dark things, I suppose. Things humans ought not to be meddling with. Malicious spirits, faerie places, things that aren't human."

Lady Rose sat thoughtfully for a long moment. Adding another lump of sugar to her tea, she stirred it until it became a whirlpool. From her chair, Emmeline watched the rhythmic tide of particles rush by.

"Did you know Emmeline that the Eidolon Club has been studying how abilities like your own work?" Claudia asked, keeping her voice low and level and her eyes locked on the dark pool growing in her cup. "In remote places all over the world, there are people like you who can speak to the dead or what your mother may have considered *dark things*. These people are revered and feared for being able to see beyond the veil of what we call reality. That's what it is, you know, the ability to see past our limited field of vision. Like catching a spider's web in the light, you can only see the spiritual world from the right angle. Right now, you're choosing to only see things in a certain light, but what if you expand your abilities? Shamans, witchdoctors, the oracles of old, they all looked further and discovered more than they ever thought possible. Don't you want that? Don't you want to do all that you can to fully use what your mother passed on to you? Don't you want to be somewhere where you can grow instead of being used as a tool to please others?"

"I do." Emmeline's owl eyes widened at her unexpected response. The words slipped out before she even knew the answer.

A wide grin spread across Claudia's face. "See, I knew we would be fast friends. We can help you here. If you choose to stay with us, there will be a library at your disposal as well as experienced practioners who can guide you as you discover the full range of your Orphean powers. You will be safe here. No one will limit you." She drew in a breath, her eyes darkening, trailing off to an unseen time as she said, "No member of the Eidolon Club will ever threaten you with harm for pushing the boundaries. What do you think, Emmeline?"

Emmeline licked her lips and stared into the empty hearth. "I'm already part of the Spiritualist Society and have been my whole life. What you're suggesting would mean me leaving?"

"It would be difficult to balance both, yes, but we would let you ween off of it. Your leaving would raise suspicion, and we don't want them banging down our door, do we? We prefer to curate our members." Leaning forward, Lady Rose placed her hand over

Emmeline's and held her gaze. "My dear, since Cecil told me about your extraordinary abilities, I have wanted nothing more than to take you under my wing and nurture your gifts. You have so much potential and no one to guide you anymore. You remind me of myself at your age, and I wish I had someone to teach me about the world back then."

Pulling a chained watch from the pleat of her gown, Lady Rose checked the time and stood. "Emmeline, I must leave you as I need to attend to a man who is very unwell. I trust Cecil will escort you home. I do hope we will be seeing you against soon on a more official basis."

As Claudia flashed a final sharp smile and disappeared into the hall, Emmeline released a tense breath, her eyes trailing to the plate of untouched treats and her cold tea. Time had passed in a whirlwind, but when she struggled to read the mantle clock, she realized the hands weren't moving. Turning to Lord Hale, Emmeline put on a tight smile to counter his somber brows.

"That was interesting. Certainly not how I expected to spend my afternoon."

"No, but do you think you will join?" he asked, rising in time with Emmeline.

"It's tempting."

As Emmeline took a step forward, her drained legs gave out. Before she could hit the rug, Lord Hale's arms were around her, pulling her against his chest. She looked into his hazel eyes, watching them soften for the first time since they arrived, but something lurked behind them. Was it fear she glimpsed? As soon as it appeared, it was replaced by something warmer, richer. Something that aroused a part of her she secretly fed books she wouldn't dare let her aunt see. His eyes dipped to her mouth, and before she could pull away, his mouth was upon hers. Her body tensed as he tightened his arms around her, his lips working in time with hers. The tip of his tongue grazed her lip, but by the time she returned the advance, he was drawing back. For a moment, they lingered. Emmeline hung in his arms, half fallen, watching him wait for her reaction.

"We shouldn't," she whispered, the words rough against his

reddened lips.

"But why? I care very deeply about you, Miss Jardine. I don't think I should like this to end."

"Me neither." The smile dropped from her lips as he lifted her to her feet. Dropping her voice, she leaned close to his ear. "Do you trust Claudia?"

He stared ahead, his mouth pensively straight. After a moment, he said, "I trust her with my life."

⟨ᴓᴏ ᴓᴏ⟩

Lady Rose swept through the catacomb below the Eidolon Club, her heels echoing across the ancient cobbles as her skirts dragged through cobwebs and the remains of things long forgotten. At the end of the dank corridor stood a locked iron door, a remnant of the club's dark past. Wrapped around her waist a chain with a ring of keys clanked with each step. Some still hummed with energy left decades ago by other practioners and unlocked things far worse than what lay within the simple cell. As she found the key she sought, Claudia Rose paused, her eyes lingering on the dented metal door. She had to brace herself for what awaited her on the other side.

The last time she had seen Alastair alive, she had been dragged kicking and screaming into a waiting steamer by men from a hospital for the insane, and it had all been his doing. She hated him then with a venom that could have poison all of London, but the years had softened her. There were times she missed. Good times, while seldom, were all she dreamed of when she had pledged to spend her life with him. Shared glances, nights of passion, a mutual admiration that bordered on obsession. Now, seeing him degenerate into a vengeful spirit with no thoughts but one made her long for the man she once had. She put the key in the lock, drawing up her guard to drown out her emotions. Despite it all, she did what she could to make things better for him.

The door opened with a whine followed by the rattling clink of chains dragging across the floor. Sitting against the back wall, Alastair stared at her, the malice and charm still evident even on another's face. He rolled his shoulders and stood, towering over her. For a long moment, they merely regarded one another.

"Take them off," he replied hoarsely.

While the voice was not his own, the words were. No matter what body he inhabited, it was always *his*. He dominated it as he did all other aspects of his life.

"In due time. How do you like your new temporary home? Is it more to your liking than the last one? I tried to find someone closer to your physique."

"Of course not. You pick off some trash from Whitechapel and expect me to be pleased. Couldn't you have killed someone with at least a little class?"

A wave of power bubbled up Lady Rose's arm as she fought the urge to lash out at him. His body was senseless to physical blows, but one strike of her power would be enough to shove his spirit out. She had worked far too hard on the ritual to waste it.

"Sorry, darling, but you aren't worth hanging for." When he merely glared at her, she continued, "That is what I came to speak with you about. I would like to make a deal with you."

His dead eyes pierced through her. "I'm not in the habit of making deals with women."

"You do when it will get you what you want. I know what you offered to do for Her Majesty after my father died. You'll do anything to get what you desire if you want it badly enough."

"What do you want, Claudia? Is this revenge for what I did? You know you deserved it. You weren't fulfilling your wifely duties and you had to be punished."

Energy surged around her, jangling the keys at her hip. "Revenge would be leaving you to tear yourself apart as a spirit. That's what vengeful spirits do, you know. Instead, I give you a body and a mind where you can think straight for a change and you thank me with insolence."

"What's your deal?" he growled as he looked away.

"It's simple. Help me bring the god into this world, and I will get you a permanent body, a good one."

"And how do I do that?"

"You find the boy with the scar and bring me back the vivalabe."

Alastair's eyes brightened as she reached to free him from his fetters. "And what if I kill him?"

She held his gaze. If she stared long enough, she could see him through the mask of decaying flesh. "Then we'll both have what we want, won't we?"

Chapter Twelve
Sickening Clarity

Immanuel's head bobbed as his elbow slid across the papers at his side, sending them cascading to the floor. He rubbed his eyes and face, but the bags under his eyes and the heaviness in his limbs only grew worse. While sleep had seemed elusive at home as he paced the house and drew mysterious symbols on shoe soles, at work his eyes seemed to want nothing more than to close. He was fairly certain he had fallen asleep during the staff meeting. There were gaps in the day yet lines of untidy notes still appeared in his book. Scooping his papers into a loose pile, he tossed them on his desk and stared down at his notes for the new specimens. His handwriting sloped at bizarre angles and the words quickly trailed into a dragged line where he nodded off for a moment. How long would it be like this? He had hoped that after a week on the job, his body would grow accustomed to his new routine, but it only seemed to be getting worse.

A knock rattled Immanuel's door as he quickly shuffled his papers into some semblance of order. "Come in," he called, picking up his pen.

Peregrine strolled in, his mouth already running about disappearing curator's assistants, but as he reached the front of Immanuel's desk, he abruptly stopped. "Hell's teeth, man, you look dreadful."

"I know." He could picture how he looked: dark circles around eyes that had lost their luster, the hollows of his cheeks casting stark shadows while his hair stuck out at odd angles.

"You all right? If the hours are too much for you, you can go home. I was only joking about staying until all the work was done."

"I'm fine. I just haven't been sleeping well."

"If it's because of the gala, don't even worry. It doesn't—"

Immanuel shook his head. "It isn't that. I'm fine, really. What is it you need?"

"I was going to ask if you would do me a favor, but I don't think I should."

"No, it's fine. I can do it."

Peregrine Nichols frowned, studying Immanuel with a clinical eye. "I have a few things that need to go down to the storeroom. The dock men have gone home, and I would appreciate an extra hand while I finish something up."

Immanuel pushed away from his desk and made for the door when a hand landed heavy on his shoulder. Turning, he found Peregrine holding his satchel.

"Go home when you're done. Don't even come back up here. You're going to make yourself ill if you don't have a rest soon."

"What about Sir William?"

"I will take responsibility. I can tell him you're ill. Looking at you, I think he would believe it. Anyway, it's past closing. Any work you have can wait until tomorrow."

Licking his dry lips, Immanuel fingered the strap of the leather satchel hanging across his chest. *A favor for a favor*, he thought with a broken smile. "Thanks."

Kara Jorgensen

Immanuel descended the stone steps to the storeroom, holding the crate of specimen jars and old catalog ledgers in a white-knuckled grip. The murky jars clanked as he pushed open the door with his elbow, ready to hand off the box to the archivists, but found the desk empty. He deflated, his eyes traveling to the clock. Of course, it was after hours. Placing the crate on the table, he returned the ledgers to the shelf behind the desk and began checking the labels affixed to the tops of the specimens. Each had a row and shelf number carefully inscribed in wax pencil. His eyes trailed to the doorway. There were only five, after all; and he could easily replace them himself instead of leaving them for the archivists in the morning.

Checking to see if anyone was around, Immanuel stepped into the store room. A forest of shelves rose around him, all filled with strange creatures staring back through glass or bits and pieces of things made in clay or wood long since broken and unrecognizable. As he walked toward the far shelf where the first specimen belonged, he caught shadows moving in the corner of his eye. He turned ready to apologize to the head archivist but was relieved to see it was only his reflection staring back from a large jar housing a Portuguese man o' war. Immanuel released a nervous laugh and continued on with his head down.

As he replaced the first specimen, the door leading to the loading bay opened and clicked shut. Immanuel looked over his shoulder toward the door, but no one was there. Glancing at the next label, he quickened his pace, returning the jars and mounted specimens as fast as he could find their shelves. He wanted nothing more than to get out before they found him. After so many sleepless nights, explaining why he was running Peregrine Nichols' errands at night was the last thing he wanted to do. Bending to place the penultimate specimen on the bottom shelf, Immanuel's eyes widened at a pair of legs on the other side. His heart quickened at the sight of the man's grubby trousers, which were far too muddied to be a dockhand or curator. Immanuel slowly rose, locking eyes with the man staring him down from the other side. Something wasn't right about him. It was as if there was a hazy outline around him, collecting in his glassy eyes, which all at once seemed dead and wild. His stubble-lined face appeared grey and mottled with faint patches of purple. Despite his unkempt appearance, he stood with his shoulders squared and his brows furrowed in a predatory stare. Immanuel swallowed hard, unable to move.

"Remember me, *boy*?"

Immanuel dropped the box and ran. By the time he heard the shatter of glass, he was sprinting through the rows of shelves. The brass globe tucked into his satchel slapped against his thigh in time with the pounding of his footsteps. The voice, the body, everything was different, but it had to be him. There could be no mistaking the intonation or the roll of his shoulders the second before he chased after him. *Lord Rose.*

His eyes scanned the storage room as it blurred by. There was nowhere to hide and nowhere to run but out to the archivists' office and up the steps. No one would hear him down there. His lungs tightened against his poorly healed ribs, and before he could draw in a deep breath, the man's body collided with his. Immanuel fell hard into a wooden case, sending tiny jars of insects and stones crashing to the ground around them. The burn of formaldehyde filled his nose as he hit the floor and struggled out from under the man's weight. His massive hands pressed down on Immanuel's back, forcing the shards into his chest. Tears flooded his eyes as he futilely flailed beneath him. Glass glittered under the electric lamps only inches from him. The moment Immanuel's hand closed around a piece as big as his palm the man wrenched his body until they were eye to dead eye. Immanuel turned the point of glass over in his hand and struck. The ragged edge ripped across the man's skin, leaving a streak of congealed blood along the man's filthy neck. Immanuel's heart sank. The creature barely budged.

With a snarl, the man seized Immanuel by the arms and easily forced them over his head, the bloodied glass skidding under the shelf.

"Did you really think you would get away so easily? Did you really think I would forget what you and that girl did to me, you stupid boy?"

Immanuel stared into his face, his heart pounding in his ears. It couldn't be. It just couldn't. The smell of cigarette ash had been replaced with the sweet, pungent odor of rot, but the voice— the voice!

"But you're dead. You killed yourself. I saw it. I saw it," Immanuel whimpered.

Ignoring him, he pulled Immanuel's jacket aside and ran his hand up and down his ribs and along his hips. Immanuel froze at his probing touch. Satisfied he had nothing, Alastair reached over and patted Immanuel's satchel. A wicked smile cut his features as he found the orb.

"For this and your head, she promised me a new body. Not a bad bargain, really."

His mind scrambled for something that would save him. "But I— I can't die. Remember?"

"Oh, I don't want to kill you. I want you to suffer."

Immanuel squirmed and threw his meager weight as a switchblade appeared in the creature's free hand. He pushed up with his legs, hoping to throw him off, but the monster held him firm. His filthy nails bruised Immanuel's wrists, and the cold edge of the knife pressed into his side. A sob leapt in Immanuel's throat as he shut his eyes and turned away. It couldn't end like this.

Lord Rose paused at the whine of the store room door opening behind them. Locking eyes with Immanuel, he put the blade of the knife to his lips to silence him. Immanuel turned in time to see Peregrine's striped legs appear through the open-backed shelves. His heart writhed against his ribs as if it would stop at any moment as Peregrine Nichols' chipper voice rang through the empty room.

"Winter, you forgot the other box. I was going to leave it in your office, but I thought I would help you put them away."

As he came into the main aisle, Peregrine staggered back upon seeing Immanuel pinned beneath the intruder. "Hey! What do you think you're doing? Get off him or I'll—"

"Stay back!" the man yelled, angling the knife toward Peregrine. "Leave now or he dies."

Peregrine's eyes widened, running from the man's mottled face to Immanuel's pleading features. He took a step closer to the next shelf. "Just let him go."

"I said, leave or he dies," he said putting the knife to Immanuel's ribs.

"I can't do that."

Immanuel tensed, expecting to feel the thrust of the knife deep into his side or across his neck, but instead, pounding footsteps reverberated through his skull. The man jerked above him, his grip tightening on Immanuel's wrists before suddenly letting go. Keeping his eyes on the planks of wood ahead of him, Immanuel scrambled out from under him and ran on all fours. His legs wobbled and slipped out from under him. Immanuel turned in time to see the man raise the knife only to meet the end of Peregrine's crowbar.

"Help! We need a watchman! Come quickly!" Immanuel screamed, blindly searching for anything he could use to help.

The man turned toward Immanuel as Peregrine landed another senseless blow on the creature's head. "Winter, take cover. Now!"

His vision clouded. Where could he go? Through his good eye, Immanuel could make out a shadowed space, barely visible from the aisle. Pain radiated through his ribs and chest as he crawled over and squeezed his body into the narrow space between the shelf and wall. In the stacks, glass shattered and the thwack of skin and bone smashing echoed with sickening clarity. A voice rose through the wet gurgles and the rip of flesh. Shadows fell over the room as the lights blinked. His glass-coated hands trembled as he covered his ears against the crackling thuds and stammered chant.

Immanuel's head swam, the storeroom teetered around him, darkening into a dirt and brick catacomb. The acidic smell of alcohol fought against the sweet offal freed from the jars. His nose and throat burned as he swallowed against the lump in his throat. Blood frantically pulsed through his body, setting it aflame while turning his hands to ice. He rested his head against his knees. Time seemed to move in spirts. One moment he was crammed into the nook, nearly invisible as the night watchman burst past him, and the next Peregrine Nichols stood in front of him with a tissue-soaked crowbar hanging at his side. For a long moment, Peregrine merely stared at him, watching tears streak down Immanuel's now bloodied face while his eyes and body replayed a scene from months ago. It felt as if Immanuel stood at Peregrine's side, watching his own body twitch at unseen blows.

"He's dead now," Peregrine finally said when Immanuel quieted and stared blankly ahead. "Scotland Yard will be here soon. You need to pull yourself together, Winter, before they start asking you questions."

Grabbing Immanuel's trembling hand, Peregrine yanked him to his feet.

"*Fass mich nicht an*!" Immanuel cried, ripping his arm away only to stumble back into the cabinet clutching his ribs.

As Peregrine released him, he spotted a ragged, bloodied rip across Immanuel's side. "Hell's teeth, you're hurt. You need a doctor."

"No!" Immanuel cried. The thought of someone touching him sent bile up his throat. He wanted to go home. He wanted to lock all the doors and windows and scrub away the monster's fingerprints on his wrists. He wanted Adam. "No, I'm fine. It's— it's from the glass."

Peregrine's wide, round eyes skimmed over his form as he shook his head. "No, it's not. He cut you and you *need* a doctor."

Carefully lifting up his soaked shirt and vest, Immanuel revealed a two inch long cut that traced the edge of his old scar. His eyes watered with the searing ache of each movement. How could this happen again?

"Tell me who I can get for you. Surely you have someone who can help you home."

Immanuel blinked. No matter what it might look like, there was only one answer. "Adam Fenice."

ACT TWO

"There is a charm about the forbidden that makes it unspeakably desirable."
-Mark Twain

Chapter Thirteen
Home

Immanuel hung his head as he held his bloodied shirt up for the doctor. On the other side of the door, Sir William Henry Flower's stern voice rose and fell as he chased away unwanted reporters and interrogated anyone who had been on the premises during the incident.

"Of course something like this has to happen right before the gala! We *cannot* have a scandal, do you understand me? We will tell the reporters it was an attempted break-in and nothing more."

And nothing more. Immanuel couldn't get the image of the man's— the creature's—broken body. The skull had been smashed beyond recognition and dark matter leaked onto the floorboards, mingling with the preserved specimens and formaldehyde until it was impossible to tell them apart. He eyed Peregrine warily. Had it really taken that many blows to stop him or was there something savage hidden within his petite frame?

"Got any other wounds?" the doctor asked, clipping the end of the thread.

Immanuel stared down at the multitude of tiny cuts in his palms still crunchy with glass and the shallow slice where he had grabbed the shard. "No. Thank you, sir."

"You were lucky it wasn't too deep."

Hesitantly, Immanuel tried to tuck in his torn shirt, but when bits of glass dug into his palms, he let it be despite what others might say. Opening the office door, he met the director's steely gaze. Thus far, he had been saved from Sir William's probing questions and reproachful stare by the doctor's intervention, but with his wound tidied, he was at his mercy.

"Mr. Winter, I would like to hear your account of what happened in the store room."

"Is that really necessary, sir?" Peregrine said, putting himself between Immanuel and the director even though they could still see one another over his head. "Mr. Winter has been through a lot today, and I'm sure he would like to return home. He gave his statement to Scotland Yard already. Wouldn't it be easier to read that?"

"If I wanted to read it, I would have read it. Now, step aside, Nichols."

As the director edged Peregrine out of the way, the impish man caught Immanuel's eye. He silently commanded him to hold his tongue. What shouldn't Immanuel say? That Lord Rose, the man who had tortured him, was alive in a new body and had come back to kill him? Or was it merely that Peregrine didn't want him to mention that he had sent him down the storage room on a favor that rewarded him with an early night?

Sir William crossed his arms, probing Immanuel's bloodied but unscathed features for the truth. "Well? What do you have to say for yourself?"

Turning his face from him, Immanuel kept the director in the clouded side of his vision. His voice sounded alien as he spoke. It seemed too level—too normal—to be his own. "Like I said before, sir, when I was returning specimens, he snuck up on me and attacked me. Mr. Nichols walked in and fought him off with a crowbar. That's it."

"How did the man end up with his skull bashed in?" he asked, dropping his voice.

"Overzealousness on my part," Peregrine replied. "The man was dangerous. He stabbed Winter and threatened his life. I had to do something, or he could have killed us both."

"You didn't have to do *that*. Now we have murder allegations right before the gala. You're lucky we need you in the botany department because you might be looking for a new employer if it weren't for the gala."

"Sir." Immanuel swallowed hard and shook his head. "Sir, please don't take this out on Nichols. The man would have killed me if it hadn't been for his intervention. If he hadn't stepped in, there still would have been a murder."

Sir William released a huffed breath and turned his attention to the band of policemen milling in the doorway. The man in charge spoke to the retired bobby who served as the dock's watchman. "What I want to know is how he got past the night watchman. How in the world did he—"

A figure cut through the great hall, pushing past the police. "I was summoned by Detective Inspector Green's men. Now, let me through!"

Immanuel turned at the sound of the familiar voice and found Adam storming toward them. His red hair and bright blue eyes blazed against the museum's subdued granite. Adam's face was set in stony impassivity as he reached Immanuel's side. He tried not to look at him. Immanuel knew if he did, Adam's façade would crumble and that glint of horror in his eyes would spread, revealing all he couldn't say in front of others.

"Thank you for coming, Adam. I hope I didn't inconvenience you," Immanuel said as flatly as he could muster.

After all that had happened that night, pretending they were nothing to each other was the final twist of the knife. If they had been friends and nothing more, perhaps Adam would have put his arm around his shoulders to stop the trembling, perhaps he wouldn't have stood out of reach, perhaps he would have looked afraid upon seeing his flat-mate holding his ribs and appearing as if he had put his fist through a window. Perhaps in a different time or place, they would have feared what had transpired more than what others would think or do if they dared to show a hint of their true feelings.

"I'm glad to see you're all right." Turning his attention to Sir William and Peregrine, Adam added, "I'm sorry for intruding, but I was told to come here to escort Immanuel back to our flat. Has he seen a doctor?"

"Yes, but he can't leave yet. The police may want to speak to him again."

"How long is he supposed to stay here looking like this? If he's been seen to and has already spoken to Scotland Yard, then I'm going to bring him home. If anyone wants to speak to him, I'm sure you have his address on file. Come, Immanuel, the earl's cab is waiting for us."

Avoiding their gazes, Immanuel hung his head and followed Adam into the vestibule. A breeze whipped through his hair, bringing with it the unmistakable perfume of water and trees from Hyde Park. If he could, he would have dragged Adam into the hip-high grasses. Together they would sink into the earth until all they feared disappeared and all that remained were the stars and the familiar sighs of sleep. He wanted nothing more than to pretend the night never happened.

"Winter! Winter, wait a moment," Peregrine called behind them as they reached the throng of men near the front door. When Immanuel and Adam turned, Peregrine caught his breath and continued slowly, "I don't want you to leave thinking I sent you down there on purpose. If I had known, I never would have done it."

"I know. You couldn't have known he was there," Immanuel replied with a weak smile, forcing back the impending implosion. "I have to thank you. If it wasn't for you, things could have ended much differently."

"This goes without saying, but you probably shouldn't come in tomorrow. Take the weekend to recover. Don't worry, I will smooth things over with Sir William if need be, but it's unlikely anyone will argue that you should be here in your current state." He paused, the smile falling from his face as his eyes traveled to the bulge in Immanuel's satchel where the device sat swaddled in handkerchiefs. "I do hope you feel better, Winter. Anyway, let's hope that whatever he was after stays safe."

Immanuel's head swam as he watched Peregrine saunter into one of the galleries. He tugged at his collar and closed his eyes against the wave of nausea passing through his gut. Vomit gurgled up his throat, but Immanuel swallowed it down and gave Adam a reassuring nod. As they cut through the swarm of police and reporters, Adam stood behind him, fending off unwanted questions while pushing Immanuel forward with his body. The brief, forceful brushes reassured him. Adam was there. Adam was always there. At the edge of the pavement sat Eilian Sorrell's idling red steamer. In the window, Immanuel caught a glimpse of his disheveled and bloodied clothes and the feverish glint in his eye. He looked like something out of Bedlam. As he passed the reporters, he hoped none had gotten a good enough look to create an etching for the morning papers.

Adam nudged him into the cab and slid in beside him, fending off a pushy reporter who tried to force open the steamer's door. The moment the Sorrell's butler pulled away from the curb, Adam's features bloomed into horror and concern. His eyes traveled over Immanuel's face as if looking for the source of the blood streaking across it before lingering on the rips in his jacket and waistcoat. Finally they landed on his hands. Adam took Immanuel's hands in his, studying the cuts and bits of glass embedded in his palms. When he looked up, tears brimmed at the edge of his lids.

"Your poor hands. I thought a doctor looked at you at the museum. Why didn't he take care of you?"

Immanuel opened his mouth to speak but couldn't. His lip trembled and his throat thickened with moisture. "I didn't tell him," he croaked. "I just wanted to go home."

As he dissolved into sobs, Adam's arms wrapped around him. He rubbed his back, his fingers slipping into Immanuel's curls. "I know, darling. I know. When the police came, I feared the worst. I thought they would tell me I had lost you for good. You don't know how relieved I am to see you whole. There's no way I could have held together if you were any worse off."

Immanuel glanced toward the white-haired butler who drove with his eyes locked ahead. He heard their conversation and knew what they were but ignored it. Adam's sister and brother-in-law knew and, therefore, Patrick, the earl's manservant, must have known about them as well, but Immanuel trusted him as he trusted his masters. Releasing a wet, hitching breath, Immanuel closed his eyes against Adam's shoulder with his torn palms resting in his lap, thankful that he didn't need to hold it in anymore. The thought of giving into numbness on the walk back to Baker Street or pretending to not know each other in a hired cab made him sick. For over an hour he had tried to convince himself it didn't happen. No one had chased him in the storeroom. A knife had never sunk into his side. A detective from Scotland Yard hadn't questioned him like he was a criminal who had lured the man inside to be beaten to death. The man's body hadn't housed Alastair Rose's soul. Silent cries rocked his form, sending pains shooting through his ribs. He would have done anything to go home.

Immanuel lifted his head, straining to breathe. "Are— are Eilian and Hadley—?" He gasped for air. "Are they at our house?"

"Yes, I'm sorry. They came to surprise us with dinner. I'm sure you would—"

"No, I'm— I'm glad they're there. I should like to sit and talk with them, but look at me. This is all they'll see, Adam."

Before Adam could reply, the steamer slowed to a stop before their flat. The lights in the front windows were lit and the curtains had been pushed back to reveal the earl and countess's faces at the pane awaiting their return. Reaching for the door, Immanuel snatched his hand away at the sharp tear of glass in his palms. Pain rang through his body, filling every inch with renewed fear. In his mind's eye, he saw the man's lifeless eyes and the soupy black patch on the floor where bits of skull mingled with preserved tissue and broken glass. How had he ever thought stones and symbols could do any good?

Immanuel stood at the bathroom window, watching the Sorrell's red steamer pull away from the pavement and disappear into the evening fog. He didn't want them to go. The moment he arrived home, Eilian and Hadley had sprung into action. Adam retreated to the kitchen to reheat their dinner while the earl gathered clean clothes and sent Patrick out for fresh bandages. Upon seeing his hands, Hadley had taken him into the kitchen to soak them in Epsom salt and water. For nearly an hour she had patiently picked out every minute shard. In that moment, he loved them more than they could have known. He hadn't deserved their gentle smiles and tender ministrations. He had done nothing for them, yet his sister- and brother-in-law treated him like one of their own. If only they had stayed, then maybe he wouldn't have felt so exposed. Adam thought he would want solitude after the day's horrors, but he needed their cheerful voices filling the house to chase away the shadows of his mind. Despite the pain, they made him forget for a time. With four people in the house, surely no one would try to harm him.

Turning back to the tub, he sighed. Hadley's last kindness before she left was to fill the tub with piping-hot water. He had washed his face, but his body still smelled of formaldehyde and rot. Immanuel peeled off his waistcoat and shirt, trying to ignore the scratch of glass trapped within them. As he reached to remove his trousers, his stomach churned at the sight of fingerprints bruised into his forearm. *It's happening all over again*, he thought as he kicked off his remaining clothing and stepped into the tub. His flesh burned and the thoughts tumbled through his mind in the silence.

He was back. Lord Rose was back. The man who had destroyed his body and mind had died in the Hawthornes' basement by his own hand, but there he was in a new body—a *stranger's* body. Now, Lord Rose could be anyone. If he could invade a body once, he could do it again. Immanuel had to tell someone. He had to warn them.

Immanuel's thoughts were broken by the jiggle of the doorknob behind him. His heart quickened with fear, then beat faster at the sight of Adam standing in the threshold.

He reached to grab his companion's clothing off the floor when Immanuel murmured, "Don't bother, Adam. They're ruined."

"I figured as much." The rubbish bin teetered as he threw them in. "May I join you?"

"If you don't mind the smell."

Scooting closer to the far end, Immanuel folded his arms over the rim of the tub and rested his head against them. Water splashed across his back as Adam slipped in behind him. His legs appeared on either side of him, and his chest burned against his back. Soft hands tentatively caressed Immanuel's shoulders before slipping across his collarbones and down his sternum. Immanuel bit back a hiss as the water stung the field of tiny scrapes across his chest. Adam's hands stopped, his eyes tracing the stitches on his side. Certain he had taken in every new wound and bruise, Adam leaned back against the porcelain and closed his eyes with a relieved sigh. Immanuel grabbed the washcloth and soap, quietly scrubbing off Lord Rose's fingerprints and the blood beneath his nails. In the morning, he would do a more thorough job when Adam wasn't so close. His body stirred at the thought of his lover's soft, freckled flesh only inches behind him.

Immanuel leaned back until he rested in Adam's lap. Mustached lips brushed Immanuel's shoulder as Adam's hand snaked around his chest. "I'm so happy you're safe."

"Me too. I just wish someone was watching the door." The words escaped his lips before he could stop them.

Adam swallowed hard and removed his arm. The room fell silent, but he didn't move to leave.

"I'm sorry, Adam. I'm just afraid."

"And understandably so, but you're safe now. The culprit's dead, isn't he? It was simply horrible timing. At least, it couldn't possibly happen again. Three near-death experiences is plenty for one person."

Immanuel's eyes burned as he kept them locked on the bathroom window and his fingers tightly curled on the rim of the tub. "It wasn't a coincidence that he found me. He came looking for me."

"What do you mean he came looking for you?"

"He's back, Adam. He didn't die. He was never dead."

"Who?" Adam asked cautiously, his voice low.

Immanuel's breath crackled as he turned and locked eyes with his lover. "Who do you think? Lord Rose. He found me, Adam. He found me at the museum and came back to hurt me. He's still out there somewhere. What if he comes back again? What will I do if he comes here?"

Doubt lurked beneath Adam's somber exterior. He hid the tremor in his voice as he said, "Immanuel, we both know Lord Rose is dead. It couldn't possibly have been him. The man who broke into the museum was a thief."

"You didn't see him. You didn't look into his eyes when he threatened to stab me. I would know those eyes anywhere, Adam. I looked into them for months. It's him. He had a different body, but he moved the same, he sounded the same."

"Immanuel—"

"No! I know what you're going to say, but you *weren't* there! He said he wanted to make me and Emmeline pay for what we did to him. He wanted to make me suffer. A thief wouldn't know that." His voice rose with every word until finally he cried, "He wanted to torture me again, and you don't even care!"

Adam shook his head and scratched at his wrist. Opening his mouth, he tried to speak but couldn't when he met Immanuel's pleading features.

Tears welled in Immanuel's eyes. "You don't believe me."

"How can I? Lord Rose is dead. People don't come back to life."

"Emmeline did. *I* did."

"That's different. People can come around after nearly drowning, and maybe you weren't dead when Lord Rose electrocuted you. You could have simply fainted."

"I can't believe you."

Despite the ache in his ribs and back, Immanuel vaulted out of the tub, snatching up his towel and pajamas on the way out. Water sloshed behind him as Adam followed suit, but before the redhead could catch-up, Immanuel slammed and locked the bedroom door behind him.

"Immanuel, let me in. You're being ridiculous," he yelled through the door.

"No, I'm not!"

"Well, you certainly aren't being an adult about this." The doorknob rattled as he let his hand fall. His voice dropped, weariness overtaking anger, as he said, "At least let me in, so we can talk."

Immanuel slipped on his drawers and took a step toward the door. A pang of guilt crawled through his gut as he turned the lock. "All right, but you have to promise to listen to me."

Adam pushed inside, his eyes running over Immanuel for any sign of further injury or distress. Drawing in a long, tremulous breath, Immanuel averted his gaze and sat on the edge of the bed with his head in his hands. The mattress sank beside him as Adam joined him in only his towel, a gentle hand closing around Immanuel's knee.

"I believe you when you say that you saw Lord Rose's face in your attacker. I know you believe it with all your being. The man came with the intent to kill or injure anyone who got in his way, and so did Lord Rose. It would only make sense that you would draw parallels between the two, but they aren't the same man, Immanuel. Alastair Rose is dead, and he's never coming back."

He was right. Alastair Rose's body had died the day they tried to reanimate the Prince Consort, but Adam hadn't seen the swath of black flow out of the man's body. It had been his soul, and now, it was floating through the aether looking for a new host whose body he could manipulate and wear like a suit. Sweat dripped down his back at the helpless thought. *He could be anywhere and in anyone.* His head swam and his stomach gurgled to the point that he thought if he didn't lie down, he would vomit. Immanuel bit his lip as he lay across the bed facing the wall. Maybe if he closed his eyes, it would all be over, and the fear would lessen for a time.

Adam's hand ran along Immanuel's spine. "I'm worried about you, Immanuel. You don't seem yourself. You barely eat. You never sleep. I hear you pacing at all hours, and in the morning, you look as if you haven't slept in a week. You don't draw. You don't read. All you do is work. What can I do to help you?"

"Nothing," Immanuel said into the pillow, his eyes burning at the sound of the all too familiar word.

"Have you thought of seeing a doctor?"

"A doctor? You think I'm crazy, don't you? That I'm seeing things now?"

Images of being strapped down and electrocuted flashed through his mind. He couldn't end up there. They would murder his soul, and he would kill his body if they did.

"That's not what I said. Maybe they can give you something to help you sleep. If you were able to sleep, maybe you wouldn't have—," *delusions*, "so much anxiety."

Immanuel released a bitter laugh. "Sure, a little laudanum and I will be good as new."

Adam bristled. "I'm going to leave you be for now. I fear if I stay, I'm going to say something I will regret later. Just know that I want to help you, but you won't let me."

Listening with his eyes closed, Immanuel heard dresser drawers open and slam shut. Tears burned his lids at the sound of fabric slipping across Adam's back and up his legs. His footsteps trailed to the door when they suddenly stopped. Immanuel turned his head to find Adam staring down at him, his lips drawn straight and his arms tightly folded across his breast.

"I'm sorry, but you need to hear this. You need help. Ever since you went back to Oxford, it seems as if you're trying to slowly kill yourself, and I appear to be the only one who's worried. Do you want to die? I thought you would like living with me, that it would be better for you, but you seem miserable. We are taking a big risk living together, and if you aren't happy, then I don't know if it's worth continuing."

Immanuel bit his lip until the taste of copper welled in his mouth in hopes that it would silence the squeak crawling up his throat and the sob that followed it.

"Tell me, are you happy here or was this a mistake?"

His emotions bubbled out in a crackling heave that ended in a blubbered sob. His body rocked as he curled inward on himself and wept into his knees. He ruined everything.

"Oh, Immanuel," Adam whispered as he climbed into bed beside him. He wrapped his arms around the crying man and rubbed his uninjured side. "Tell me what I can do. Tell me what's wrong."

"I like living here," he cried. "It's not you. It's just… it's just that I don't know how to be happy anymore."

It seemed impossible. In the safety of Adam's arms, he released his pent up feelings in hot tears until his ribs and sinuses burned. All the love in the world couldn't cure the emptiness where something he could no longer remember had once been. He wanted to be happy. He wanted to love Adam and build a life without fear. He wanted to have fun again, but it all seemed impossible now.

Drawing in a thick breath, Immanuel's attention trailed to the icy spot on his chest where his pendant of perpetually blooming forget-me-nots hung. Whether anyone believed him or not, he knew Lord Rose was out there waiting. But who would believe an immortal boy and an impossible girl?

Chapter Fourteen
Shared Souls

It hadn't been easy to tell Adam to go to work. All through breakfast and getting dressed, Adam had asked him over and over, "Are you certain you will be all right by yourself?"

The answer had seemed so easy then. "Yes, I'll be fine. You go to work every day, don't you?"

But today was different. Today, there was no work for Immanuel to go to. There were no specimens to examine, no exhibit cards to write or edit. As Adam gave him a soft, lingering good-bye kiss, he sensed his lover's trepidation. There was an extra glance over his shoulder to give Immanuel ample time to change his mind, but Immanuel kept his lips resolutely shut. The front door closed behind him and all that remained was silence.

For a long moment, he merely stared at the coffered door, half expecting Adam to come bursting in declaring that he had changed his mind. When Immanuel finally headed into the parlor after locking and double checking the front door, he found that his mind was horribly clear. The night before, he had fallen asleep in Adam's arms, utterly exhausted from his breakdown and the ordeal at the museum that preceded it. Somehow he hadn't expected sleep to help so much. No longer did his thoughts come in dissonant bursts, but what happened the night hadn't changed. He knew what he saw, and his heart quickened at the thought that Emmeline was going about her day without knowing the truth. He would have to remedy that at a more reasonable hour.

Taking a half-empty sketchpad from the shelf, Immanuel retreated to the hatbox of gifts now sitting on the end table. Pawing through the box, he found the tin of brilliant pastels. The stitches on his side itched and stung with each step, but he needed to occupy his mind. At the back of the house, Hadley's old studio sat untouched. The last of the autonomous dioramas had been sold not long after her marriage to the earl, but hints of her past productivity remained in the loose bolts or stray porcelain body parts that littered the room.

Immanuel inhaled the fading scent of saw dust and oil. Beneath the surface, the workshop still hummed with her energy. Shutting his eyes, he drew in a deep breath, trying to level his mind with hers. His hand closed around a pastel, turning it over until the awkwardness dissipated and the chalk found its natural groove. After a moment's hesitation, his hand deftly swept across the blank page. From the random scratches, an eye appeared, followed by a familiar set of lips. For a moment, Immanuel was certain Adam's face would surface from the handsome lines, but the chin grew too wide, the eyes too narrow. Before the man's features could fully materialize, Immanuel tore out the page and ripped it to bits. His heart thundered in his ears as he sat staring at the new page. He needed something else to take his mind away from dark things.

His eyes roamed over the clockwork pieces in a box beside him and the pale disembodied limbs next to them until finally his gaze came to rest on a bee. Pressed against the glass of the alley window, the bee's fuzzy body lay on its side. Its legs curled inward while its wings jutted stiffly behind it. There was something sorrowful about the creature's pristine corpse. Bees were meant to be in motion. They were meant to work, to fly between flowers and produce something as beautiful as themselves, a self-portrait in sugar. They were never meant to die.

Immanuel reached for the gold pastel but let it drop. It felt wrong to draw it. With the edge of his hand, he carefully pushed its tiny body onto his sketchpad. He stared at the fluffy collar surrounding its neck, gently stroking its ruff with the tip of his pinky until the patch turned grey from a dusting of pastel residue. It deserved to at least be outside one more time. As he took a step toward the door to the flat's meager garden, the bee's legs twitched. Its limbs curled and flexed until it finally righted and drowsily staggered forward. Keeping the paper and bee ahead of him, Immanuel pushed open the window. It flew from the paper to the windowsill, its antennae twitching as it gazed back at him. With a shake of its body, it buzzed into the alley and disappeared.

Closing his eyes, Immanuel leaned into the sunlight. His lips curled into a hesitant grin at its reassuring warmth. Some things were worth living for.

⊙ ⊙

Emmeline reached under her bed, her hand creeping along the planks holding up her mattress. Beside her lay a sloping stack of books with titles and stories she would never want her aunt to discover, but they weren't what she was looking for. Squirming further under the bedframe, her hand brushed the soft, fleshy surface of the tome's cover. Carefully pulling it free, she laid it on the rug. It seemed larger than she remembered and more ordinary. Innocently latched, no one would have suspected that it could crack windows and shatter gas lamps. She quickly tucked her other books safely beneath the mattress and turned her attention to the *Corpus Grimoire*. Since it destroyed her room and sent her powers into overdrive, she hadn't dared to open it for fear that it would happen again. There was no way she could explain away a broken window to Aunt Eliza a second time, but she had to do something with it. After breakfast, she had reread the letter. Someone was after it who wanted to corrupt the knowledge within it, and she didn't want to run into whoever wanted it. But what knowledge was so important that it was worth chasing across the continent?

Running her fingers along the vision of Eden etched into the cover, Emmeline drew in a resolute breath. It had to be done. Just to be safe, she opened the windows and carefully removed the glass globes from her lamps, wrapping them securely in a shawl. Emmeline centered the book in front of her on the bed, holding her breath as the lock sprung open at her touch to reveal the bone and sinew man on the first page. Where her blood had been sucked in, all that remained was a sea of inky rings that rivaled a galaxy. Cautiously, she turned each page, her eyes running over handwritten rows of Latin with drawings of fantastical creatures and diagrams of circles containing queer shapes. The carefully lettered tome at times reminded her of a cookbook with lines of what she could only guess were ingredients, followed by instructions. One such page contained a woman lying prone with her arms crossed over her chest while another showed a man with his eyes alight like lamps, his lips parted as if in ecstasy. A thrill laced through her at the thought of what it could mean.

As the tome fell open to its middle, her eyes widened and her heart pounded up her throat. The creature she had seen during the reading stared up at her from the page. The shape of the horns and the intensity of the eyes were different, but there was no mistaking what she saw. It had stalked her nightmares since she fell into its lair, but what did it have to do with the book or the people who wanted it? Staring at the jumble of words, Emmeline picked out the few she could discern. Life, death, creature, sacrifice. Her years of French lessons were utterly useless against Latin. Flipping the page to escape the creature's intense gaze, she found a drawing of a man. His form had the hallmarks of Renaissance masters with an over-muscled torso and prominent Roman features. She would have believed he was created by Raphael or Michelangelo except for his eyes. They glared from the vellum at an unseen foe. At first glance, she thought the ink had merely run around his lids, but then she realized his eyes had been blacked out when a moment ago it had only been the irises. Emmeline lifted the next page to see if there was anything among the lines of Latin that could help her understand. When she returned to the man, his eyes merely stared without an ounce of venom.

She swallowed hard and shut the book. The moment she let go, the urge to snatch it up returned. Her hands faltered between attraction and repulsion. *Emmeline*, it whispered. She shouldn't be afraid of it. It was just a book. There had been so many books before it that had been infinitely more dangerous, but she wasn't supposed to have this one. Pushing it away, an idea sparked in her mind. Lord Hale had to know Latin, and his friends in the Eidolon Club would surely be better equipped to protect it from the dark forces the letter mentioned. She stared down at the cover, resisting the urge to stroke it. It had chosen to find her after all. Maybe… maybe she should keep it anyway.

Her body lurched at the sound of her aunt's light tread in the hall. Grabbing the book, she tucked it under her skirts and pretended to study her nails. The door creaked open to reveal Eliza Hawthorne's tightly bound red hair and subdued grey gown. Across her apron were minute spatters of something Emmeline would rather not identify. She looked disapprovingly from her niece's relaxed pose to the curtains flapping in the murky breeze.

"Miss Ashwood is downstairs waiting for you. She said you were supposed to go for a stroll in Hyde Park." When she noticed Emmeline cock a confused brow, she added, "Did you forget?"

"I—" Emmeline blinked. They hadn't made plans. "I lost track of time. Tell her I will be right down."

Eliza gave her nod, and as she backed out of the room, her gaze swept over every surface. Emmeline stared her down. She could look all she wanted, but she would never figure out what was going on if Emmeline didn't want her to know. The moment the door clicked shut behind her, Emmeline dug through her dresser to find her shopping bag. It was bulky and garishly tapestried with a bold Asian print, but it was the only one large enough to hold the grimoire. Quickly stuffing the book into the bottom of her bag, she covered it over with her neglected sewing sampler and a half-knit sock she had given up on months ago.

Pausing at the mirror to adjust her hair and check her reflection, Emmeline frowned. She swore she hadn't arranged to spend the day at Hyde Park with Cassandra. Part of her wanted to go downstairs and send Cassandra off with an excuse of ill health. Soon, she would be moving on from the Spiritualist Society, and she wouldn't need to feel inferior or slave away doing readings to please someone else. Cassandra wouldn't understand. For days, she had avoided her. Drawing in a deep breath, Emmeline steeled herself against the argument she was certain was to come. At least if they fought early enough, Cassandra would leave and she could get to the Eidolon Club before dark.

As Emmeline opened her door, she could hear her aunt and Cassandra talking animatedly in the foyer. She hated how they could discuss suffrage and careers while Emmeline stood awkwardly beside them once again feeling the sting of their judgment. Even with her best friend, she felt out of place. With Lord Hale, that was never an issue.

Upon seeing Emmeline appear on the steps, Cassandra's features brightened, but before she could invite her aunt to join them, Emmeline grabbed her wrist and pulled her away. "Cass, you're late. We must be off, mustn't we? Bye, Aunt Eliza. I won't be home for dinner. Cassandra and I will be going to the Dorothy instead. Sorry for not telling you sooner."

Stumbling outside, a cheeky grin spread across Cassandra's lips as Emmeline slammed the door shut and released a relieved breath at having a layer of brick between her and her guardians. For a few moments, they walked down the street in silence, but as they turned the corner from Wimpole Street, Cassandra slipped her arm into Emmeline's and pulled her closer.

"So we're going to the Dorothy, are we?"

"Certainly not. I'm cross with you," Emmeline muttered, eyeing the people around them for any sign of a thief who might try to steal her book.

"I'm sorry for springing this on you, but I'm awfully glad to see you."

"What was that about anyway? Couldn't you have just stopped by instead of luring me out? Now my hair is going to expand. I'll look like a poodle by the time we get home."

"You weren't at the Spiritualist Society, so I thought maybe you were ill. It seemed like a good reason to visit you. You're my best friend after all, and I was beginning to worry. I've never seen you away for more than a day." Her tawny eyes searched Emmeline's face, but she kept her head down. "Is everything all right?"

"I guess. I just wasn't in the mood to deal with Madam Nostra." The words hung in her throat, weighing as heavily as the purse on her arm. "I don't know how much longer I'm going to be part of the Spiritualist Society."

Cassandra stopped in the middle of the pavement, causing a man to bump into her and his companion to nearly run into Emmeline. "You're leaving?"

"I can't stand Madam Nostra, and I certainly will not stay in a place where I'm completely overlooked. I'm a *real* medium, yet people like Nostra get ahead by using cheap theatrics. It isn't fair."

"Then, let's change it. The Fox sisters were exposed and removed from their local chapter. We could do the same and get Nostra kicked out. Just don't leave," she said softly, gently squeezing Emmeline's hand.

"It might not work." Shaking her head, Emmeline looked in the direction of the park and hoped her resolve would hold out. She had to do this. "Besides, when the Fox sisters were exposed, it nearly killed spiritualism. It's already on shaky ground. Exposing Nostra as a fraud could ruin the London branch. No one would trust us if another major medium was a fraud."

Cassandra's round eyes took on a damp sheen. "Wouldn't you miss doing readings? Wouldn't you miss helping people get through their grief?"

"It isn't that I—"

The words died in Emmeline's throat as she spotted a familiar face cutting through the crowd. A long scar bisected his left eye, tinging it with a dark brown blotch where it should have been blue. What the devil was he doing there?

"Not him again."

The moment Immanuel Winter spotted her, he quickened his pace, grimacing as he politely pushed past a pack of older gentlemen filing into waiting cabs. "*Entschuldigung!* Emmeline! Emmeline, please wait!"

"Who is he?" Cassandra whispered, her eyes running appraisingly over his form. "Does Lord Hale have competition?"

Emmeline released a derisive snort. "Certainly not. He's merely an old acquaintance from Oxford."

"He looks like more than an acquaintance."

"Emmeline," he panted as he reached them. Grimacing, he stooped with his hand clutching his side and his eyes clenched tight against the pain. After a moment, he straightened, rubbing his ribs over his jacket. "I thought I had missed you. Dr. Hawthorne said you were going to Robin Row."

"*Rotten* Row," she corrected. "What is it you want, Immanuel?"

"Emmeline!" Cassandra hissed, elbowing her in the ribs.

As if seeing Cassandra for the first time, he gave her a quick bow and continued, "I need to speak to you. Something very strange has happened that you must know about."

"What is it?"

Stepping closer, Immanuel shot a glance toward Cassandra before dropping his voice. "I can't say here. Is there anywhere we can go to speak more privately?"

She sighed. "We're on our way to Hyde Park. If you insist, you can speak to me there."

Immanuel frowned, looking over his shoulder at the people streaming around them. Going toward the museum was not something he wanted to do so soon. "All right."

By the time they reached the lush lawns of Hyde Park, Immanuel's side was aching. He held his breath, biting down until the pain arced and passed through his ribs. The other girl cast him sidelong glances. Several times he caught her watching him with a sympathetic frown as if she could sense his discomfort or the fear quietly lurking beneath the surface. Emmeline merely charged on without a glance. If he hadn't been so accustomed to her demeanor, he might have been offended.

The park bustled with vendors selling cold drinks and snacks, calling out to men and women out for a stroll among the gardens. Immanuel tried to keep his head down as Emmeline led them through the clumps of people and into the more deserted paths, but he found his gaze sweeping over every half-shadowed face for Lord Rose. As Emmeline slowed her pace, the knot in Immanuel's gut loosened. The only person around was an older gentleman throwing bits of bread to a swan. Closing his eyes, Immanuel leaned against a tree to catch his breath. Before he could banish the stitches' sting, a hand closed around his arm.

"Are you all right?" the brown-haired girl asked.

"Yes, thank you, Miss—?"

"Ashwood, Cassandra Ashwood, and you are?"

He flashed a pained grin. "Immanuel Winter."

"Enough with the introductions," Emmeline snapped. "What is it you want to tell me?"

"Are you sure I should say it in front of—?"

"Out with it!"

"Lord Rose is back. He's alive."

Cassandra's eyes widened, her gaze running between Emmeline and Immanuel. "Lord Rose? I thought you said he was dead."

"He was." Against her will, Emmeline's throat tightened as she shook her head. "That isn't possible. We saw him die in the basement."

"I know. That's where it gets strange."

Beneath the shadow of the oak-lined path, Immanuel recounted the whole story: the chase in the museum's storeroom, the unmistakable look in the man's eyes, the way he mentioned both of them before sinking the tip of the knife into his flesh. The whole time he watched Emmeline's face. She listened with her arms folded across her chest and her lips pouted in annoyance, but her feigned attitude couldn't dispel the quaver of fear in her eyes.

"This is ridiculous. He couldn't just come back from the dead in a new body. When they did it with Prince Albert, it required all sorts of machines and chemicals. No one would revive him to stick him in some vagabond's body."

"I don't know how or why they did it, but I know what I saw. He's alive."

Emmeline shook her head, rolling her eyes with an exasperated huff. "I don't know what you *think* you saw, but—"

"Listen to me." Immanuel's voice sharpened as he leaned closer to Emmeline's face. "This is the clearest my head has been in weeks, and I *know* I saw Lord Rose last night. His face and body were different, but it was his filthy soul on the inside. I came because you need to know. I couldn't, in good conscience, let you walk around unaware— unprotected—while he's on the loose. If he could try to kill me, he could certainly go after you next."

"I'm fine, and I certainly don't need your help. Come on, Cass, let's go. We have wasted enough time."

"Em," Immanuel said softly, reaching for her arm but never touching it, "please don't discount what I saw. Last time you thought I was crazy for suggesting Lord Rose was Spring-heeled Jack, but in the end, I was right. Even dead, Lord Rose is dangerous. I wouldn't come to bother you unless I thought it was important."

"But what does he want from you?" Cassandra asked. "Revenge? Spirits are supposed to move on to peace."

"Lord Rose isn't the type to move on. We ruined his plans and he surely thinks we caused his death." His eyes trailed to Emmeline as he spoke, but it was easier to leave her in the blurry portion of his vision where he could ignore her derisive scowl. "Besides revenge, I think he's after something."

Emmeline's eyes widened, feeling Cassandra's gaze boring into the side of her face. *They need what the grimoire possesses.* "What could he possibly be looking for?"

"He came to get this." Reaching into his satchel, Immanuel withdrew a brass ball ringed and etched like an astrolabe. His thumb stroked the button that triggered the spring, but he thought better of it. "I don't know what it is. After he tackled me, he felt around for it in my bag. He definitely wanted it. Whether he was looking for me or the device, I don't know."

"May I see it?" Cassandra asked.

Immanuel eyed her for a moment, fighting the urge to hand the ball to her. There was something quietly reassuring about her, and her openness stood starkly against Emmeline's darkened countenance. He would have trusted Cassandra with anything without fear of retribution or ridicule. Meeting her gaze, a smile crossed her lips, and he handed over the device. Cassandra turned it over in her hands, tracing the intricate series of lay lines with her eyes. Without hesitation, she pressed the spring and the top popped open with a soft click. Pressing it again, the levels of orbits rose. The onyx piece spun on its axis, stopping beside a piece of sapphire. Cassandra's face lit up as she gestured for Emmeline to step closer. The black piece rotated in time with her movements, eliciting a cocked brow and deep frown from Emmeline.

"I haven't seen one of these in years. They're exceedingly rare, you know."

"You know what it is? I figured it was some sort of astrolabe or compass."

"In a way, it is. It's a vivalabe. If calibrated correctly, the person using it can supposedly align themselves with the spirit world." When Immanuel's brows furrowed in confusion, she continued, "See all the different colored balls? They each represent a type of energy, almost like elements. If you know what type of energy you're looking for, it can help you see the unseen."

But why would you need to? Immanuel wanted to ask, but instead said, "What about when it isn't calibrated with the spirit world?"

"You just need to know what you're looking for. It picks up energy of whoever is nearby. People who can see things like me and Emmeline, we can be tracked. See?" She held the vivalabe out and moved her hand in a slow circle causing the white, blue, and black stones to swing in their orbits. Her eyes flashed between the piece of quartz and Immanuel's form. "Well, it seems you have as much energy as we do. You're the white one. How fitting considering your surname."

"That's quite strange. I don't feel very energetic," he said, his cheeks burning at her bright eyes upon him.

Cassandra closed it and dropped it into his palm, her fingertips brushing the myriad of scratches and pinpricks. Squeezing the cold metal tight against his skin, he silenced the itching burn. At least now he knew what the device was and what it did.

"But why would anyone want it?"

Cassandra shook her head, a tendril of brown hair dancing against her cheek. "Nothing good. I would keep it somewhere safe and out of sight."

Immanuel nodded, his eyes trailing into the greenery beyond the line of trees, but he was far inside his mind. Gnawing on his lip, he felt the vivalabe grow heavy in his hand. Were they after him or the device or both? *Sometimes things look for us.* But why him? Why would it want him? For a brief moment, he saw himself following the familiar paths to the Serpentine he strolled at lunch. The carved ball hurtled through the air before disappearing beneath the water's surface with a satisfying splash. He could rid himself of the blasted thing and go home. If Peregrine asked, he would say he lost it or sold it, but he couldn't have it in the house. He couldn't put Adam at risk if someone should come knocking when he was at work.

"Are you all right, Mr. Winter?" Cassandra asked, noticing his sudden pallor.

"He's fine, Cass. He's always like this."

Immanuel ground his teeth, the vivalabe popping open at his tightening grip. Cassandra shot Emmeline an exasperated look, but she didn't notice as she picked at her cuticles.

"Miss Ashwood, would the vivalabe be safer with you or at the London Spiritualist Society with Emmeline?"

Shooting Emmeline a pointed glare, Cassandra replied, "No, we have had some thefts at the society lately, and I wouldn't want to chance it. Besides, I'm sure it will be perfectly safe in your care. You protected it once. Sometimes these things come to the right people."

He released a hoarse laugh that sent a shot of pain through his ribs. "You're the second person to say that. You would think the thing had a mind of its own."

Immanuel stared up at the sky as it greyed and the wind rustled through the trees. Their leaves rolled onto their bellies, awaiting the rain at the first hint of its sensuous perfume. As the sun disappeared behind the clouds, the shadows around them deepened, and he quickly stuffed the vivalabe into his bag. Breathing away the aches and pains, he looked up to find Emmeline staring at him, her eyes commanding him to take the path back home. Maybe he should, lest darkness and irrational fear sink in.

"Well, I guess I should let you go before the storm comes. My flat-mate should be home from work soon, and he will worry if I'm not there." Straightening to his full height, he stood before Emmeline. Her sharp, owl eyes bored into his sockets. "I know you don't believe me, Emmeline. I wouldn't either if I were you, but please, take care. I pray to god I'm wrong."

Before she could respond, Cassandra stepped forward to take his hand. "Be careful, Mr. Winter. Don't be a stranger."

A faint smile crossed his lips. "I won't."

As Immanuel Winter ambled down the path and disappeared the way they came, Cassandra turned to Emmeline with a reproachful frown. "You are incredibly rude."

"And?"

"You're going to end up an old maid with no friends if Lord Hale finds out how you really are."

"Well, he isn't going to, is he?" she spat, switching her heavy bag to her other shoulder.

Cassandra shrugged, slipping her arm into Emmeline's. "Tell me, where did you get that hideous— I mean, unique purse?"

"Now, who's the rude one? If you must know, I have errands to run."

"Oh. Would you like company?"

Gooseflesh rose along Emmeline's arm, traveling across her breast at the skimming stroke of Cassandra's nails against her forearm. She closed her eyes as drops of rain pattered down. They dotted her eyelids, leaving the taste of earth in her mouth. There was still time. She could still go home or to the Dorothy with Cassandra and forget all about the rich confines of the Eidolon Club, or the brown and green flecks within Lord Hale's eyes.

Tightening her grip on the bag, she pulled from Cassandra's grasp and veered down the nearest path. "No, I think I'll go alone."

Chapter Fifteen
Bewitching

Standing on the doorstep of the Eidolon Club, Emmeline released a tight breath. Was it fear that coiled in her breast and stole the air from her lungs? But what set her heart racing certainly wasn't. She was one threshold away from becoming something more than just a medium. If she couldn't succeed in the Spiritualist Society on her abilities alone, she would find a place where she could. Her mother hadn't taught her to be weak, to cower and sink into the hierarchy under the guise of respect. She was a woman imbibed with generations of power, and she would not go into obscurity quietly. Raising her hand to knock, the door swung open. Emmeline peeked through the crack but saw no one on the other side.

"Hello? Is anyone here?" she called as she slipped inside, shutting out the rain. "Lord Hale?"

Emmeline walked to the crackling hearth and rubbed her hands until the dampness's hold loosened. If there was a fire, someone had to be there. The book weighed heavily on her arm, and for a moment, she considered putting it down until a panicked voice in the back of her mind shot out a dozen what-ifs. What if it catches fire? Or what if someone takes it when you aren't looking? A silent laugh climbed up her throat. Maybe she wouldn't mind that.

"Emmeline, what a pleasure it is to see you on such an abysmal day."

She turned at the polished, familiar voice and found Claudia trailing along the grand staircase as forlorn as a specter. Her previously bright features and quick movements had been replaced by a dull pallor, and in her gossamer white gown, her bronze hair had tarnished. Her gaze flickered over the garish bag hanging on Emmeline's arm before returning to her face.

"Are you looking for Lord Hale? He isn't here yet. But if you would like to stay and wait for him, we can speak instead."

Emmeline glanced toward the window and the rain beating against the pane before returning to the green of Claudia's eyes and the sensuous curve of her lips. How many men had wished for that invitation? When Emmeline nodded, Claudia waved for her to follow her up the stairs.

"Where is everyone?" Emmeline asked, keeping her head down.

"Most have gone to their country estates for the summer by now. Only a small group of us is left in London."

As they made their way up the spiraling steps, Emmeline tried not to stare into the depths of the oil paintings lining the walls. All were darkened with smudged shadows and trapped or dying men. Bodies lay bleeding and ravaged on a battle field only inches from her eye as Claudia unlocked a room on the staircase landing. Emmeline feared that if she should hazard a look, she would find men being run through or see oil paint blood spurt from wounds while she stood helplessly, too real to do anything to stop it.

Beyond the door was only darkness. With a flick of the switch, the chandelier overhead buzzed to life, casting crystalline prisms across the carpet and curtains. The parlor was as big as Emmeline's bedroom yet appeared larger with its high ceilings and decorative wainscoting. On the far wall was a set of shut double doors that Emmeline imagined led into a sumptuous bedroom with silken pillows atop a tall four-poster bed. Claudia gestured for Emmeline to take the armchair across from the chaise where the lady stretched out. The undulating light from the window traced the curves of Claudia's form, pulling Emmeline's eyes away from her host's face.

"I have been hoping we could speak alone. I do love Cecil, he is my nephew after all, but it's so nice to speak with a woman. We're different. A man would never understand what we go through, and there's always a shortage of women here."

A smile crossed Lady Rose's lips, her eyes running over Emmeline's form and lingering on her strigine eyes. Emmeline should have seen the resemblance sooner. Though Cecil's hair was darker, he and Claudia shared the same ochre locks and mossy green eyes. Their faces retained little in common, but with a smile gracing her lips, Emmeline could see past the slyness of Claudia's features to see the full curve of Cecil's mouth that haunted her dreams. A knot tangled in Emmeline's stomach under the woman's stare. Claudia was the queen with Cecil as her heir apparent. There was no mistaking who pulled the strings, but how far did her reach extend? Had it been she who sought to bring her into their ranks?

"Do you know why there are so few women?" Claudia asked, scattering Emmeline's thoughts.

Emmeline's lips locked. She knew the answer—or at least part of the answer—but to say it was pointless. She shook her head, pulling her bag across her lap and covering it with her arms.

"Marriage. It's something we must contemplate very carefully when we are in a position of power. We aren't pulling ourselves up in the world, Emmeline. We're already there, but you must remember that a husband can be your closest ally or your greatest enemy."

Emmeline swallowed against the dry lump in her throat. Words escaped her as they trailed after the air in her lungs. She opened her mouth before closing it again. "Are you suggesting that Lord Hale—?"

"Yes. My nephew only has eyes for you. It's obvious to anyone with half a mind. Are you pleased?" she asked, leaning against her elbow and watching Emmeline from beneath her lashes.

A smile swept across her features as she stifled a laugh. "Very, though I should like to hear it from him before I get my hopes up."

"Clever girl."

Her lips lapsed into a fitful frown as she asked, "But do you think Lord Hale would stop me from using my gift?"

"I can't say. Lord Hale and I only recently reconnected, so I can't say much regarding his character." Claudia drew in a long breath, arching her back as she raised herself in the chaise to be eye-level with Emmeline. The edge that inhabited her gaze softened with her pouting lips. "I can only tell you my experiences in marriage, Emmeline, and they aren't happy ones. Seeing you with Cecil reminds me of myself at your age. So full of hope, so full of longing. I loved a young man then, more than I had ever loved anyone before, and I paid dearly for it.

"He had been beautiful then, which made his transgressions all the more forgivable. If he were ugly, I could have called him evil or bad and others would have believed me, yet they saw what I saw in my innocence: a beautiful, handsome young man so full of ambition and promise. What they couldn't see was the darkness inside him."

Emmeline sat transfixed as Claudia shut her eyes.

"I wish I had known then what I know now about darkness, but I wouldn't have believed it. I thought I could fix him. That with love, I could patch the hole and change him for the better. Make no mistake, Emmeline, having a touch of darkness is a very grave matter, but it can't be fixed. Not by you, and not by me. Darkness is a creature that consumes everything in its path, and by the time you realize it, it's eaten a hole through you."

"But Lord Hale doesn't have that problem."

"No, he doesn't, but we aren't born with it." Claudia leveled her gaze at Emmeline. "I'm telling you this because I don't want what happened to me to happen to you. Men are afraid of powerful women. We upset their image of the world when suddenly they have to share what they thought they were entitled to. My husband had extranormal abilities, or at least he did until his father beat them out of him. I tried so hard to bring his powers out, but in the end, all he had was strength and that all-consuming darkness, and he used them to keep me from using my abilities. If he couldn't have them, then neither could I. When they have nothing left, they take what's ours."

Her pale green eyes faded to a different time as she said, "First, he tried to beat it out of me, like his father. When that didn't work, he locked me up like a madwoman. The whole time, I foolishly thought I could still fix him. There's a reason women like us hide their powers, Emmeline, and that reason is men. My power exceeded his, and I had to be punished for it. He cut me from his life as if I had never existed to remove all reminders of his weakness. You're the only one who knows besides Cecil."

Emmeline licked her lips, her suddenly dry tongue sticking to her skin. "How did you escape?"

Claudia's features gleamed with a fleeting fire. A pulse of energy shuddered through Emmeline's body, traveling up the walls before shorting the chandelier above their heads in a hail of sparks. Emmeline yelped as the room fell dark. Above her pounding heart, all she could hear was the patter of rain against the panes and roof. Tightening her grip on her bag, Emmeline waited in the silence, fighting the urge to leap from her seat and head back to Wimpole Street as fast as her legs could carry her, but Claudia didn't move.

Summoning her voice, Emmeline rasped, "I'm so sorry that happened to you."

With a faint shake of her head, Claudia returned to the present and flashed a glinting Cheshire cat smile. Her gaze edged to the shadows beyond the door to the hall and narrowed at something unseen. "Well, it all worked out in the end. My husband is dead, and I'm still young enough to marry again if I so desired. For now, I think I will enjoy the freedoms of widowhood. After all, why would I want to expose someone to the darkness I inherited from my husband? At least, I can warn you in hopes that you will be spared."

Emmeline couldn't imagine it. Not a word of it. Cecil—Lord

Hale—wasn't cruel. She had seen darkness first hand. She had seen the damage ambition and anger could do to another's soul, and in Lord Hale, she saw none of that. If anything, he should have worried, for in the pit of her stomach she felt the tug of cruelty, that endless black vacuum as dark and cold as the depths of the sea. In seconds, it could well up, sweeping away all emotions and thoughts of mercy or kindness. She could ignore its cruel claws tearing through her, but at night, as she lay in bed recounting the day, she hated herself and the cruel words or sneers that issued from her lips before she could stop them. Perhaps it was he who should have been afraid of being swallowed up.

A soft knock sounded at the door before it squealed open. Emmeline's heart leapt into her throat at the sight of Lord Hale silhouetted in the hall's light. His brow creased with confusion as his eyes ran from the extinguished chandelier to the two women sitting in the gloom.

"Are we holding a séance?"

"No, just a little energy expulsion. The lights will come back on eventually. Why don't you take Emmeline down to the front parlor, Cecil? She came to speak to you, and I have kept her long enough."

A conspiratorial smile passed between the two women as Emmeline followed Cecil Hale from the room. She studied his frame as he walked beside her down the hall. He stood below six feet, but his gracile limbs and the pride in his bearing gave him the illusion of height. While he had lost the gawkiness of youth, his facial features had retained their sculpted smoothness. As they passed another hall of private rooms, his fingers brushed hers. They skimmed along the length of her fingers before caressing her palms. A shiver passed through her, and with one swift motion, she grabbed his wrist and pulled him into the shadows of the unlit passage. Her hand slipped behind his neck, pulling his lips within reach until she could kiss him. In a kiss, she tried to channel every feeling she had when she read her forbidden books or during dreams where he appeared in her bed, but her thoughts fled at the heat that spread between her thighs and crept through her core to tug every hair on end.

Lord Hale pressed back, pinning her against the wainscoting as he wrapped his arms around her waist. Hoisting her up, he raised her until their mouths were level and each kiss came as easily as breathing. Lips, hands, tongues all sliding and mingling to form a jumble of heat and chill, a wild thing threatening to escape. His fingers reached longingly for the buttons running down her spine but slid away. Emmeline tightened her grip, dragging him closer with renewed urgency despite the risk of someone finding them. If only they could move into one of the rooms. His arms faltered with her reaching for the unyielding knob behind her, and as he slid her down the wall until her feet met the polished floorboards, the breath returned to their lungs. Drawing back but keeping his bodyweight against her, a heavy smile crossed his lips. He stared down at her breathlessly. Her chest heaved as she rested her head against the wall, hoping the warmth in her cheeks and flesh wouldn't dissipate.

With the edge of his hand, he traced the soft lines of her jaw and the apples of her cheeks. Lord Hale raised her chin and kissed her. His lips burned against hers as the door behind her rattled on its hinges. Hands, firm and gentle, worked along her sides, one pulling her flush against him while the other explored the curves of her frame. Breaking from her lips, he slid to her neck. Quick, hot kisses pulled a stifled moan from her throat. Emmeline clutched at his coat. Her eyes slipped back in their sockets and her toes curled in her boots at the touch of his tongue. It was better than she had ever imagined. All she wanted was him, and she wanted more, more than they could offer each other at the Eidolon Club.

"I'm glad I showed up today," he whispered against her neck, each syllable sending a ripple of sensation that sent gooseflesh across her breast.

"Me too," was all she could manage as his tongue darted across her neck. "We— we shouldn't. Not here."

Lord Hale eased back to let her stand and straighten her mussed hair. Locking his heavy-lidded eyes with hers, he said, "You have witchcraft in your lips, Emmeline Jardine, and you have bewitched me."

"Good, then my charms are working. I'm certain I have it other places too, but you might not ever know about that."

He released a chuckle and scooped her bag off the floor where it had fallen during their moment of passion. "What did you want to see me for? Besides this."

Emmeline reached into her bag, feeling for the soft, pliable cover of the grimoire. Her heart pounded at the thought of it being out of her possession. Like their kiss, it felt somewhere between relief and panic, but she pulled it out anyway and dropped the bag behind her. Lord Hale's eyes widened at the sight of the leather tome. He reached out to stroke it but pulled his hand away before he could make contact.

"What is it?" he asked, his voice tight.

"I don't know exactly. It came in the mail at the Spiritualist Society addressed to the leader of it, but I took it because I didn't want Nostra to have it. I don't think it was ever meant for her, really. At times, I think it's an old book on science but then, it also seems magical." Her face darkened as she traced the vines and arabesques, picturing the strange circles within burning white when her blood touched it. "It's all in Latin, so I thought maybe you would be able to help me decipher it. You can hold onto it if you want. I don't want my aunt to stumble across it."

The air seeped from Cecil's lungs as he held the book. He closed his eyes and let the pulse of power wash over him. The book burned white hot in his hand while Emmeline's inner flame rose to match it. They had bonded. Lady Rose wouldn't be pleased.

"Are you certain you want me to have it? It would probably interest you," he replied slowly, leafing through the pages of strange drawings and arcane sigils.

"It doesn't help me much if I can't read it, now does it?"

"I could teach you."

"I would like that," she replied, a smile flashing across her lips before disappearing at her next thought. "There's another matter I wanted to ask you about if that's all right with you."

"Anything."

Emmeline drew in a deep breath, banishing Cassandra Ashwood's face from her mind. "I want to be a member of the Eidolon Club. I've realized the Spiritualist Society holds nothing for me anymore."

Hope welled sickeningly sweet in Cecil's chest. "Are you sure? Once you're here, you probably won't be able to go back. What about Cassandra? Does she know?"

"It doesn't matter what she or anyone else thinks. This life is mine and mine alone. I've made my choice."

Emmeline stared up at him with her owl eyes set firm, and he knew there was no other choice. There would be no way to spare her. "We will initiate you tomorrow. Come back at dusk."

Chapter Sixteen
Vive ut Vivas

Immanuel hummed to himself as he brushed the last of the butter and herb mixture onto the chicken he had bought at the market. While he had to brave the vision of the butcher with his cleaver, making Adam happy was worth it. He bit back a wide grin. Adam would be so surprised to arrive back from the earl's house in Greenwich to find a chicken roasting in the oven and a cake already cooling on the table. Immanuel's hands were gummed with flour and butter and his apron bore the tell-tale signs of cooking as he rushed around the kitchen balancing the timing of meat, side dishes, and dessert, but he didn't mind. It reminded him of happier days spent at the stove with his mother before their Sunday dinners with Johannes and Theodor. A spark of lightness he had missed for months glowed within him. And it was all for Adam.

Popping the chicken into the oven, he turned his attention to the icing he had assembled but abandoned to finish their dinner. He carefully tucked the bowl under his arm, whipping the sugar, berries, and butter as quickly as his tugging stitches would allow. As the balls of powder disappeared into the pink goo, the doorbell sounded in the hall. Immanuel froze, stopping mid-stroke as the song died in his throat. Adam couldn't be back already. He had to go over the books for the earl's estate and Hadley's toy company, and that would take a few hours at least. Dropping the bowl on the table and wiping his hands, he cautiously crept down the hall as the bell rang again. His throat tightened at the prospect of opening the door. He could dive into the parlor or Hadley's studio and hide until the shadows peeking through the front window disappeared. He could picture Lord Rose, his devil's gaze lurking just below the surface of whatever body he had stolen waiting on the porch to strike. Could he have found his home? Then again, what if it was Scotland Yard coming to ask him more questions about the break-in at the museum? Immanuel pulled off his apron and rushed to the door. He wouldn't let the police come barging into his life again. He would meet them on his terms.

Immanuel braced himself and opened the door expecting to see a plain-clothed detective in a cheap suit or a bobby in blue wool, but instead, he found Peregrine Nichols in his best violet and grey pinstripe suit. The botanist flashed a fanged grin as he doffed his hat. Looking over his head, Immanuel spotted two women. His eyes widened at the sight of Cassandra Ashwood waving at him with a reassuring smile beside a stern woman he vaguely recognized. He had only met her once, a few months earlier in Oxford when Adam had come to visit him. Back then, snow still fell at night to dust the lawns while memories surfaced against his will like a cry in his throat. Her arrival had been heralded with a swarm on dons flooding the university to stop her from opening a school for women with money from a dead heiress. She had lost the battle, but Immanuel had never forgotten the sensation when their palms met and invisible vines that prickled like lightning rushed up his arm and flared across his shoulder blades. Judith Elliott's military bearing and keen eyes weren't easily forgotten, but he couldn't imagine what she had in common with the others.

His eyes ran between them. "Mr. Nichols, Miss Elliott, Miss

Ashwood, what are you doing here?" His mind filed through possibilities, and a second later he added, "Have I been sacked?"

"No, no. Your job is quite safe, Winter, so long as Sir William is busy dealing with the gala and squashing rumors. May we come in? What we have to say is a bit more...," he trailed off, cocking a sharp brow and twirling his hand to speed the uncharacteristic silence.

"Pressing," Miss Ashwood finished. "It's nothing to be worried about, I promise."

"It's just—" Immanuel glanced over his shoulder at the bowl of icing waiting on the kitchen table. Adam would be home in an hour and the chicken wouldn't feed five. Swallowing hard, he said softly, "I don't mean to be rude, but I have company coming tonight."

"It won't take too long."

Stepping aside, Immanuel let the cabal file in. He rubbed his eyes, wondering if for a moment he had fallen asleep at the table and they had been a fabrication of his mind, but no, they were as real as he was. Making certain the front door was locked, he reached into the front of the satchel hanging on the coat rack and slipped the vivalabe into his trouser pocket. As Cassandra and Miss Elliott took their seats on the sofa, his eyes traveled to the space between the cushions where he had stuffed the journal of spells and photograph of his younger self. It was too late to hide it now. When he looked up, Miss Elliott had settled into her air of power with her brassy hair gleaming in the sunlight and her eyes set wholly on him.

"May I get you tea?" he asked, shifting uncomfortably under her penetrating gaze.

"No, thank you. Please, take a seat, Mr. Winter," Miss Elliott commanded, her American accent clipped in the quiet room. "There's no need to look so afraid. We only want to speak with you."

"It's rather hard to stay calm when people keep telling you there's no reason to be afraid. I don't understand why you're all here."

"Just sit and we'll tell you."

Immanuel tugged at his collar and chewed his lip as he sank into the nearest chair. His heart thundered in his throat in time with the clicking of the vivalabe against his thigh. The air hummed between them, raising the scant hairs on Immanuel's arms. At any moment, he feared one of them would move and the air would arc with sparks. Catching Peregrine's eyes flickering over the cuts littering his hands, Immanuel tucked them around his middle out of sight.

"As you probably guessed, we're here to talk about what occurred at the museum the other night," Peregrine began slowly. Upon seeing Immanuel's eyes widen, he put up his hands. "Not fired. You're not fired. It's about the man who attacked you. Was there anything strange about him?"

Immanuel's tongue turned to sand. He wanted to cry out that the man was dead, that the body he had wasn't his, that he belonged in hell after all he had done to him, but Immanuel kept his mouth shut. They were watching for his answer. They knew something.

Drawing in a deep breath, he pushed away the visions of that night. If he could be clinical, maybe he wouldn't lose his grip. "He wasn't right. His eyes were unfocused, but there was something behind them that scared me. It was as if he was wild, and he— he smelled like rot."

"Anything else?" Peregrine prodded.

"He didn't bleed. It was as if he was dead. He was, wasn't he?"

Peregrine and Cassandra nodded.

"But how? Was he reanimated? Is there another machine?"

"They don't use machines, no, but have you ever heard of a *neamh mairbh*? You might have heard it called a revenant," Cassandra said slowly, keeping her voice level.

"No."

"It's a reanimated corpse. Revenants are malicious spirits that take over fresh corpses, usually to take revenge on someone. It's rare to have a spirit be so evil or tortured that it doesn't move on. Between the level of malevolence and the power needed to create one, we don't see them very often. Thankfully."

"They're also bloody hard to kill," Peregrine added with a shake of his head. "Had to bust its skull like a coconut and still had to dispel it with a spell to finally kill it."

"A spell? What do you mean a spell?" Immanuel sputtered.

"It's— well, it's like the ward you have on the front door. Symbolic ingredients, a catalyst, focus, and intention, but on a much larger scale."

The ward. Immanuel's brows furrowed in confusion but loosened upon seeing the rune stones his mother had sent. "Those aren't spells. It's just superstition. They were a housewarming gift from my mother."

Cassandra and Peregrine locked eyes before turning to Judith, who had yet to take her gaze off Immanuel.

"He doesn't know," Judith said without a hint of surprise or emotion.

"What don't I know?"

"That you're a practioner."

"Of magic," Peregrine added.

"No, I'm not. That's not possible. I'm a scientist. Magic is just superstition."

A little voice inside of him whispered of flowers uncurling and dead creatures giving him a glimpse of their final moments, but he silenced it. He was normal.

"Magic is merely what science doesn't have an explanation for."

"I can't be a— a practioner. I don't do anything with magic."

"What's around your neck?" Judith asked, pointing to his collar.

Immanuel stared down at his chest. There was no way she could have seen the chain tucked beneath his shirt and waistcoat. Unbuttoning the top of his shirt, he pulled out the silver chain and the flower-filled vial swinging from it. How had she known?

"You became a practioner the moment you used that."

"But it wasn't mine! I didn't make it!" Immanuel cried, the pained words bringing back the filthy stone walls of the catacomb that had been his prison. "It's a family heirloom. I didn't know what it did."

Judith's brows furrowed. "I can see that your life line connects with another." Her eyes followed an invisible line running from his heart and through the window. "That's ancient magic. Alchemy?"

Drawing in a tremulous breath, Immanuel tried to silence his pounding heart. That's what his mother had said years ago. That they had come from a long line of alchemists turned chemists and scientists. Had he broken some rule when he rescued Emmeline Jardine?

"Am I in trouble?"

Judith's eyes softened. "No, not in that sense, but you are in danger. Peregrine told me what happened at the museum with the revenant, and we agreed that we had to speak to you. Did you recognize the creature?"

Fear-tinged relief washed over Immanuel. He wasn't crazy. He had been right when he told Adam it was Lord Rose's spirit he saw within the stranger's body.

"By face, no, but I know who he is. Can he come after me again? Is there a way I can protect us— I mean, protect myself?"

"Carry a gun or knife on your person, and be aware of your surroundings. While the revenant may have sparked a renewed urgency, it isn't the reason we have come to speak with you, Mr. Winter."

"Then, why? I have nothing to do with this supposed magic apart from the pendant."

"And the creature," Nichols piped up.

"We're here because Peregrine suspected you had higher levels of magic when the vivalabe chose you, but he wasn't sure if you knew of your extranormal abilities. Now, we know he was correct."

Immanuel released a tight laugh. "What *extranormal* abilities? I don't have anything like that."

Cassandra caught his gaze, and in meeting her taupe eyes, the tension sighed out of him. "Mr. Winter, *everyone* is born with magic inside of them. It gives us the ability to create and the spark of free will that sets humans apart. Magic is merely an affinity for something, a talent. A sculptor is thought to have earth magic because he can see inside the stone or clay and bend it to his will. Peregrine's abilities lie in horticulture. A green thumb blossomed into the ability to manipulate plants and change how they grow. The only difference between a normal person and a practioner is that practioners actively use their abilities and hone their skills intentionally. Do you now understand that abilities don't have to be grandiose or frightening? They're merely something we have a penchant for. Sometimes we lose our magic, after violence or we deny our natures until it goes away. We feared you might do that, and with the vivalabe in your possession, we can't let you take that risk."

"But I— I don't," he whispered, his eyes burning. All he wanted was to have a normal life.

"Mr. Winter, I can see it inside of you." Judith's eyes followed an unseen flame in Immanuel's core. It danced and whipped, growing immense before diminishing into the glowing embers of a pipe. Energy arced from the white-hot flame. "It's one of the strangest souls I have ever seen. It can't settle on a shape or size. Usually only infants have that happen, but you have been through things, terrible things, and that can lead to soul-uncertainty."

"How do you know that?" Immanuel's damaged eye clouded, blocking out Peregrine's form and half of Judith's. "Who told you?"

"I can see it within you. That's my ability, Mr. Winter, second sight. When I choose, I see the truth, the past, the soul. It's a very useful ability for a lawyer to have."

"Then what's mine? If I'm a practioner, then where do my abilities lie because I feel I have nothing of value," he cried, the words tearing from his throat before he could stop them.

Immanuel shrunk back at Peregrine's shifting, wide eyes and Cassandra's downcast gaze and pensive mouth. Was it pity he saw? Pity making them want to leave or avert their faces from him.

"I can tell you, but you must let me in. Relax and don't take your eyes off mine."

Regulating his breathing, Immanuel looked up only to find Judith staring back, unflinching. She locked onto his eyes, and as she drew in a deep breath, he felt his mind creak open. He had expected Judith's prying to hurt or feel as though he had stripped down to his most vulnerable parts, but it was as if she merely walked through a darkened hall, opening door after door to reveal what she needed to know. Her gaze focused in on something in the distance with her brows knit in concentration until finally she leaned back against the sofa shaking her head. Cassandra's gaze darted toward her, yet she didn't move. Had she seen him and Adam wrapped in an embrace? A bolt of panic laced through him, sealing his mind shut with a clap that radiated through his skull. A wave of nausea churned his gut, and for a fleeting second, he felt as if he were falling.

Judith shut her eyes. Her hand traveled to her lips as if to hold back the tide that threatened to overtake her. After a moment's pause, she met his gaze. Her brassy hair gleamed in the afternoon light as her eyes grew bright against a tinge of red. It seemed so unlike her. He hadn't expected to find something soft beneath the hard edge of her regal air, yet she suddenly seemed so human. Reaching forward, she wrapped her hands around his and gave them a firm squeeze. Warmth radiated through his icy pallor.

"You have no idea how special you are," she said softly, her voice crackling with a sorrowful laugh.

Special, his mind spat. That was his problem: he was too special to be left alone. He loved the wrong sex, he was never masculine enough to be like the other Oxford boys, he cried and couldn't stop.

She shook her head. "With all that you have been through, all you have seen— You have been put through the flames of hell only to be forged in iron."

"I don't understand." Drawing in a pained breath, he added, "You still haven't answered my question, Miss Elliott. What abilities do I have?"

"What is the one thing you wanted most?"

"What does that have to do with anything?"

"Just tell me."

Immanuel bit his lip and edged his gaze to the shelves behind their heads. He couldn't bear to see the questioning looks on Peregrine and Cassandra's faces. "To live a normal life and get back to how things were," he gestured to his scar, "before all of that happened."

"No," Judith replied solemnly, the word cutting any question of the truth. "What did you *really* want? What did you repeat every day in that cellar? What did you want?"

Tears burned his eyes. Gathering his strength, he forced out the words. "To live."

Cassandra looked between them in disbelief. "What did you say?"

"To live. I wanted to live. All I wanted was the possibility of a future outside of pain and darkness," he cried, wetness itching his cheek. "I didn't want anything else."

"That's your power, Mr. Winter, life."

Pawing at his cheeks, he rubbed his eyes. "No, I— I can't—"

"Think about it. You brought the girl and yourself back from the dead with that potion. I'm sure there's more. There always is. Strange things that you can't explain. Things so small that you do a double take and assume your eyes have played a trick on you. Once, long ago, maybe you were destined to be an alchemist or merely a talented scientist without ever knowing you were more than ordinary, but fate intervened. Fate has given you a gift you mustn't squander."

Immanuel wanted to pull his hand from her grasp but couldn't. He wanted to believe her. He wanted to believe that seeing the flowers come back to life in his hands had happened. He wanted to believe his life was worth something.

Turning to Peregrine, he asked, his voice thick in his throat, "How did you know? How did you know when I had no idea?"

A foxy grin spread across his features. "We know our own. It's a feeling, you understand? Like a vibration that lets us know we're close. Being around practiioners... it's like listening to a tuning fork. Sometimes if you're quiet enough, you can hear a faint reverberating hum that doesn't belong to the rest of creation, and you feel it echo inside you. Other times, you just hear the twang and know. We always find our own."

"What was it with me?"

"A bit of both. You aren't exactly hard to miss, but then, I tried to be quiet, very hard for me as you know, and I could feel the hum. Sometimes it's really loud. When you had the vivalabe and came into my office, I thought my bloody ears were going to fall off from the pitch. That's when I knew it belonged with you."

Immanuel's attention trailed to the cold metal bulging in his pocket. "That's why you're here, isn't it? The vivalabe?"

"Precisely. It was meant to come to me, you know. I heard of its departure from America to England through a friend's letter. I knew it was going to be in one of those boxes. That's what the break-ins were all about. I told you about them to scare you away from my boxes, and you *still* ended up with it." He chuckled to himself. "Hell's teeth, I brought it on myself giving you all those boxes to unpack and catalog."

"The point is," Cassandra began, shooting Peregrine an exasperated look, "there are people looking for the vivalabe, people who shouldn't have it."

"Why? What would they do with it? I thought you said it sees spirits or energy. That doesn't seem particularly useful."

"We don't know for certain what they're planning, but we think they're looking for a certain spirit. One whose power can disrupt the balance of nature."

Sweat rose on Immanuel's back at the thought. "A spirit?"

"Something not of this world, and to see it, they need a vivalabe and someone to walk in and find it. Nothing is certain yet. There's a book that they desperately need, and I happen to know where it is. It's safe for now. I trust its guardian, but we were worried that—"

Before Cassandra could finish, the front door clicked and open. Adam Fenice's face peered around the doorway, his mustached smile brightening with upon seeing company. Immanuel swallowed hard, fumbling for the right words.

"Adam, my colleagues decided to stop by and see how I was doing."

"That was very thoughtful. I'm sure it lifted your spirits."

He gave a weak smile. "It has. This is Miss Cassandra Ashwood. Miss Ashwood, this is my flat-mate, Adam Fenice."

"It's a pleasure to make your acquaintance, Miss Ashwood," Adam replied, bringing her hand to his lips with a graceful bow.

"The pleasure is all mine, Mr. Fenice," Cassandra said softly, her toffee eyes flitting between Adam and Immanuel.

"And it's good to see you again, Mr. Nichols. It was very kind of you to pay Immanuel a visit."

Peregrine looked at Immanuel from the corner of his eye before saying, "After all the chaos, I had to see for myself if he was fit for work on Monday. Couldn't let him come charging back if he was unwell."

"Good idea. I know my opinion holds little weight when it comes to Immanuel's work ethic." Adam proffered his hand and stared at Judith a moment before his eyes widened at the realization. "Miss Elliott, I didn't know you were in town. How goes the hunt for a women's college?"

"As well as one would expect. Well, Mr. Winter, Mr. Fenice, we should take our leave. We're glad to see you on the mend."

Rising with Cassandra and Peregrine, Judith locked eyes with Immanuel. The moment their hands touched, a buzz of electricity passed up his arm. When she pulled her hand away, he found a card pressed into his palm.

As Adam cheerfully ushered them out the front door, Immanuel turned the crisp filigreed paper over in his hand. Written in gleaming gold script was an address, and beneath it in pencil were the words *Sunday at seven.* When he looked up, he found Miss Elliott watching him over Adam's shoulder.

Her mouth never moved as her voice whispered in his mind, *We will speak again soon, Mr. Winter.*

Chapter Seventeen
Beauty and Tragedy

As soon as his guests were out the door, Immanuel darted into the kitchen, dumped the icing on top of the cake, and pulled the chicken from the oven in time to keep it from burning. Walking into the kitchen behind him, Adam's blue gaze brightened as it traveled over the assortment of vegetables and sweets.

"What's all this?"

"A token of my appreciation," Immanuel said with a grin. All thoughts of tears had vanished upon seeing Adam. "I wanted to do something to show you how I really feel about living with you. I'm sorry about the other night. I— I wasn't in my right mind."

Adam slipped his arms around Immanuel's waist, pulling him close until his forehead rested against his. In Adam's embrace, he felt invincible, as if the power imbued in his sigils ran through his lover's body. His lips reverently grazed Immanuel's cheek.

"Don't ever apologize for that. You've been through a lot." Drawing back, he stared into Immanuel's bichrome gaze, tracing the dendritic strains of copper that trailed into the remaining blue. "What happened has been bothering me, too. I got upset, but I didn't mean what I said. I want you here with me. I just want you to be happy."

"I know." Immanuel hugged Adam tightly before releasing him with a lingering kiss. "We both said things we shouldn't have. That's why I decided to make you a special dinner: to show you how much I appreciate all you have done to help me."

"Well, it looks fantastic. Have you been at it all day?" Adam lifted the pot's lid, inhaling the buttery warmth of potatoes. "Did we have these in the house?"

"No, I left right after you did." Immanuel pictured himself darting out the front door without looking back. "I bought it all at the market and cooked everything myself."

"Even the cake?"

Immanuel's face contorted in exaggerated outrage. "Of course."

"Hadley would be jealous. I think I made out better than she did. She received a title and a handsome husband, but I have a man who is brilliant and can cook. How many people can say that?"

Heat flooded Immanuel's cheeks.

"You seem lighter today. Are you feeling better?" Adam asked as he gathered plates and silverware.

"For now. It comes in waves. What happened the other night was the crest, and for now, the seas are calm. It never stays that way, but I'll enjoy it while it lasts."

Adam opened his mouth to say something but thought better of it. Finally, he said, "I hope it lasts for the gala. I'm looking forward to it."

A ripple of cold dread passed through Immanuel's form. *The gala.* There were so many opportunities to do something wrong. Sir William probably didn't want to look at him after what happened in the storeroom, and there were still a few days left for him to mislabel exhibits or fall further behind on his work. Then, there was the event itself. He could make a fool of himself or he could inadvertently expose Adam as his lover. It wouldn't take much. A lingering touch of the hand, an accidental kiss or embrace. He wouldn't be able to live with himself if he ruined it all.

"Are you all right?" Adam asked slowly, watching Immanuel's eyes fade into the distance.

"Yes, sorry, it's just pre-gala jitters. My waltz is rather awful."

"Well, at least you won't be going through it alone. I'll be there, as will Hadley and Eilian. You can show us the exhibits you worked on, introduce us to your coworkers, Then, I can finally put faces to all of the names you mention."

As Immanuel rearranged the plates and bowls to make room for the chicken, his eyes trailed to the vase of flowers sitting in the center. The petals had browned again and curled in on themselves. He made sure Adam was busy preparing their tea before blocking the flowers with his body. Gently stroking the edge of the once blue pedals, Immanuel pictured them alive, blossoming, smelling sweet like they did when Adam placed them in his hands. With each touch, the color invaded the dead tissue and the heads lifted toward the light filtering through the parted curtains.

Was that what kept the forget-me-nots alive inside his pendant? He had assumed it was due to residue from the potion his alchemist ancestors created, but what if it was him? The vial sat against his chest constantly. Was it that constant contact with his body that kept them alive or the desire to preserve one of Adam's gifts? *Adam*. Immanuel's mind rushed to his companion and what he wanted to do with him while his head was clear. Flesh on flesh, knotted together for hours each night. He wondered what his powers were doing to Adam. In his moments of frantic fear, he would do anything to keep Adam from harm, but the thought had to be banished. How would he explain to Adam that his latent magic might keep him young like Dorian Gray?

Immanuel snapped from his thoughts at the sound of Adam's voice.

"Eilian and Hadley were asking after you."

His cheeks burned anew as he quickly heaped a third spoonful of carrots onto his plate. "Really?"

"Oh, yes. They had hoped I would bring you along, but I understand why you were 'too tired' to come with this morning." He released a soft chuckle as he sat across from Immanuel. "Eilian was very concerned about your hands. He worried they would become infected from the glass and impede your work."

"You may report back that my hands are healing well. There are only a few slivers left to fester out, thanks to your sister. How are your sister and her husband? Are they planning to go back to Dorset any time soon?"

Adam playfully reached for the cake, but Immanuel swatted his hand away. "Actually, they're hoping to go in mid-July for a few weeks to avoid the worst of the heat. The earl has graciously invited us to stay in one of Brasshurst's guest rooms at any time. We could even go up by ourselves if we wanted. He just said to tell him when, so he can send a servant or two with us."

"I guess that means we will have to buy bathing costumes."

"Does it?" Adam shot him a smoldering look.

Immanuel swallowed a laugh and replied, "*Mein Gott*, you're scandalous. I, for one, won't be responsible for blinding old women and little children."

"I highly doubt either of us will blind anyone. Oh, Hadley also mentioned they might venture to Egypt in the near future, once the weather is cooler over there and the floods have passed or something of the sort."

"Why Egypt?"

Adam shrugged, popping a forkful of potatoes into his mouth. "The earl has always had wanderlust. I don't think he's going there to visit an archaeological site or to check on his company's investments. From what I gathered, he simply wants to introduce Hadley to one of his favorite places. I'm sure she will enjoy it. James and Eliza went there once and seemed to have a good time despite the heat and sand. They even came back with a mummified head in a jar." Releasing a laugh, he added, "That's sounds like something you might do."

"Probably. Maybe we will return from Dorset with a mermaid to display."

"So you want to take Eilian up on his offer? I was hoping you would but—"

"But?"

"I wasn't sure if you would be willing to step away from the museum long enough to go on holiday. Do you think you could get the time off?"

A few days where he could trade London's rumbling bustle for the rhythmic lapping of the sea might be just what he needed to calm his nerves. "I should. If I can't get it from Sir William legitimately, I could always cite my ill health. I doubt it will be a problem once the gala is over. It's not like seals are particularly interesting to the general public… or anyone for that matter."

"Good, then it's settled." Putting a forkful of chicken in his mouth, Adam looked from the plate to Immanuel. "Did you really cook this? You should make dinner more often." Adam stabbed a second helping and asked between mouthfuls, "So what were you up to besides cooking? Did your friends bring any news when they stopped by?"

Immanuel's mind raced. *Magic.* He wanted to cry that they told him of magic and spells. *They told me things that make sense. Adam, you must believe it. It all sounds so fantastical, but I think it's true.* His heart sank. *But you won't believe me.*

The words hung on his lips, but no matter how he played the conversation in his mind, Adam never understood. He valued logic, facts, and numbers. So how could he talk about magic when Adam thought he was losing his mind when he told him about Lord Rose in the vagrant's body?

"Nothing much, really." Biting his lip, he forced a tight grin. "Shall we crack into the cake?"

◦◦◦◦◦◦

Adam leaned back in his chair, his body heavy with Immanuel's surprise dinner. A gust of wind hot as breath swept along his temples. Even with the kitchen windows open, the evening was warm enough to make his collar stick to his neck. Behind the fluttering curtains, the sun stubbornly remained despite the late hour, a reminder of the imminent solstice. He released a contented sigh. A day that had begun with the tedium of figures had ended far better than he anticipated. Looking up from his tea, he found Immanuel's light eyes pressing upon him. His pulse quickened. There was an intensity he hadn't seen since they spent Christmas Eve together in one of the bedrooms in the earl's home. Beneath the blue fire, there was longing and focus where there was usually hesitance or sadness.

"Are you ready to retire to the parlor? I think I'll do the dishes later," Adam offered, gathering the remaining plates and filling the sink with steaming water.

"Let's go upstairs." Immanuel's hand curled around Adam's arm, his thumb stroking his wrist lightly enough to raise the hair on his arms. The corner of Immanuel's mouth twitched as he leaned close and whispered, "I want nothing more than to make love to you."

Adam's body tightened. "Did you say—?"

Immanuel opened his mouth, but no words came out. Staring at Adam, his brows furrowed as if he had to work up the nerve to repeat the words for a second time.

"Immanuel, are you all right?"

In response, Immanuel's long fingers skimmed across Adam's cheek before finding their way into his pomaded hair.

"Yes, it's— it's just that for the first time in weeks, months even, my mind isn't fogged, and all I keep thinking is how much I want to kiss you. I want all the things I dreamed about at Oxford." Wrapping his arm around Adam's waist, he pulled him closer until their hips were flush and their ribs met with each breath. "In the two weeks I've lived here, I feel like I've been watching my life happen, and I'm tired of it. I'm tired of fighting my mind to enjoy anything. I *want* to live." He dropped his voice, his breath skimming Adam's flushed lips as he said, "You have done so much for me. Please let me do this for you. That is, if you'll have me."

Closing the gap between them, Adam kissed him. It was slow and earnest and chaste, and it was only when he pulled back and placed another soft kiss on his lips that heat flushed his features. He could taste the sweet berries from the cake on Immanuel's breath mingling with the tang of tea as he exhaled.

"Of course I want you," Adam whispered. "I love you."

A fragile expression broke across Immanuel's features at the phrase. "You— you love me?"

"More than I could have known."

"Good." His lip twitched as if he might laugh or cry. "Because I love you too, Adam."

Immanuel wrapped his arms around his companion's back and bit back his joy. He shut his eyes and pressed his face into Adam's neck, his lips inching toward his collar and up to his ear where he nibbled and lapped at the lobe until Adam's hands tightened on his sides. Releasing him, he ran his fingers along Adam's jaw and gently lifted his head until their gazes met. He swallowed hard, taken aback by the look in Adam's eyes. Love was something he had nearly forgotten since he fled Germany, and in his companion's eyes, he saw the magnitude of its hold.

You don't deserve it. You don't deserve him, a little voice in the back of his mind hissed.

Pressing his lips to Adam's, he silenced any doubts. Adam's tongue slipped between his lips and his hands explored the parts of his body Immanuel wished he could ignore. A small smile inched across his features as his companion's thumb settled into the imperfection in his ribs where they never healed. Adam loved him, and he needed nothing more.

"*Mein Schätzchen*," Immanuel murmured as he pulled away, breathless. "Let's go upstairs."

Before his mind could clear, windows were quickly shut and their footsteps echoed up the stairs. At the junction between their rooms, they paused. As Adam took a step toward his bedroom, Immanuel caught his arm and pulled him close again. Drawing him in with a kiss, Immanuel worked his hands under Adam's jacket and slipped it from his shoulders. He carefully laid it on the dresser as Adam's fingers worked over the buttons of Immanuel's waistcoat. Beads of perspiration broke across their backs and necks in the muggy summer air, trapping socks and sleeves against damp flesh. Reaching to unbuckle his trousers, Immanuel caught Adam's lips in an urgent kiss.

Adam struggled for purchase as he stumbled back into the doorway, the molding pressing into his back. Immanuel leaned against him, using his added height to pin him in place. His long legs interlaced with his own, and as the hum of electricity crackled against his lips and arced across his tongue, Adam lost himself. For a moment, their bodies were one, still and frantic all at once.

His pulse raced at the thought of Immanuel's smooth skin beneath his palms and what lay beneath thin layers of wool and cotton. The belt uncoiled and fell at their feet with a clank only to be swept away by Immanuel's foot. Adam reached for the button of his lover's trousers, but Immanuel clasped his hand and brought it above his head. Adam's breath hitched at the pressure of Immanuel's length pressing against his thigh. He wanted nothing more than to break from his lips and tear his remaining clothing away, but he was trapped. Heat flooded his groin and abdomen at the thought.

When Immanuel finally drew back with bruised lips and hooded lids, he rested his forehead against Adam's to steady his heart. In the stillness, Adam's fingers flew across the buttons of their shirts until they hung open at their sides. Adam's eyes wandered over Immanuel's face and form. With his shirt covering his scarred side and a loose golden curl draped over his blotted eye, he appeared whole. His hand still held Adam's firmly above him, and in his grip, there was none of the trepidation or wavering he had known since they met six months before. Was this how Immanuel could have been? Without a marred eye, maybe he would have outgrown his shyness and been as confident in the world as he was in that moment. The image of when he first saw him flickered through Adam's mind, when Immanuel's face had been gaunt and flushed with fever. If Adam had met him before Lord Rose tore him apart, would they be together now?

Adam slipped his free hand beneath Immanuel's shirt and lightly traced the prickling stitches jutting from his side. No, if Immanuel couldn't have been taken away, Adam wouldn't have dared to love him. Twenty-three years of denying his true nature wouldn't have changed with a confident partner. He would have feared exposure and retreated, but he could trust a dying man who had so much more to lose.

Letting go of Adam's hand, Immanuel brushed against the soft flesh of Adam's stomach, sending a wave of gooseflesh across his thighs. With a quick motion, he pulled Adam's shirt away and swept the suspenders from his shoulders. Immanuel locked eyes with him, his hand resting on the button of his trousers. Sunlight glinted across his irises, setting their copper and turquoise aflame. Immanuel pressed him back toward the bed, and Adam obeyed. Standing at the edge, Immanuel let Adam's trousers drop in an inky pool. His drawers tented under Immanuel's hungry gaze. He wanted to do *something*, to reach out and touch him, yet his companion's hard expression stayed his hand. Adam eyed the wool trousers slouching on Immanuel's narrow hips and the blue of his drawers peeking out.

"What do you want me to do?" Adam asked, swallowing hard as he watched the vial of forget-me-nots dance in time with Immanuel's movements.

"Sit, and let me do the rest."

Adam sat on the bed and watched as his lover removed his shirt with a roll of his shoulders. The white fabric fluttered behind him, and when he looked back, Immanuel's hands were on his fly and a wicked smile graced his lips. Adam's body stirred at the sight of Immanuel's ivory flesh and the faint hairs that glittered like gold trailing to his waistband. He had never seen him in the daylight.

"Like what you see?"

"Very much so."

At the last word, Immanuel let his trousers fall. Adam's hands twitched, itching to touch him, to feel the downy flesh of his stomach or the smooth, otherworldly skin of his scars. His body tightened and his breath quickened at the thought. As if sensing his need, Immanuel slowly drew closer until he stood at Adam's knees. With his hands cupping his companion's neck, Immanuel straddled him. Adam closed his eyes and tried to ignore the soapy fragrance of his skin only inches away. His body shook with the urge to throw Immanuel to the mattress and do all he envisioned. It had never been like this with Immanuel silently commanding him to wait, all the while everything unbearably building. The German's long fingers worked through Adam's hair as his lips passed lightly over his eyelids and cheeks. With his mouth massaging the redhead's neck, he lowered himself over Adam's lap. Immanuel ground his hips against him, eliciting a low moan from his companion at each twitch and rock. Adam groped at his sides and back, his fingertips pushing in with renewed urgency, but he couldn't let the game end yet.

Sitting back on Adam's knees, they locked eyes. Their bodies breathed in sync as they waited for the charge between them to dissipate until they could speak. Immanuel hung his head, fighting to ignore the pulsing in his groin that urged him to go on. Fingers brushed against Immanuel's forehead, pushing the loose curls from around his eyes. Adam's hands closed around his cheeks and raised his head until they were eye-to-eye again. His companion studied his face, his quavering finger stroking the scar where it began above his eyebrow. He traced the ragged pink skin, following it until Immanuel had to close his eyes for him to continue. When Adam reached the tip of his scar where it disappeared into his cheek, he let his finger linger.

Adam stroked Immanuel's cheek, all the while staring into his damaged, half-blurred eye. "This one... This one is my favorite."

"How can you say that?" Immanuel asked, his voice hoarse and his eye blurring with the burn of moisture.

"Because it's different and beautiful, like you."

Immanuel bit his lip, averting his gaze. Snaking his fingers up Adam's neck and into his hair, he tried to regain the fire that had coursed through him a moment earlier, but all that was left was the growing emptiness of disbelief.

"Immanuel?"

"Why? Why do you love me? What do you see that I don't, Adam?" His lip trembled as he shifted, sending a bolt of pain up his side. "Because all I see is something broken."

Adam wrapped his arms around Immanuel's waist and urged him closer. Holding him tight, he kissed the crook of his neck and along the ridge of his clavicle until Immanuel's breath loosened.

"You aren't broken." Between hot, moist kisses, he continued, "You want to know what I love? I love how smart you are. I love how you sing to yourself while you're getting ready for work. I love how despite everything horrible that has happened, you keep going."

Immanuel's body tensed, his eyes shutting as Adam nipped at his neck and ran his tongue along the tender skin. The words swirled through his mind but scattered at Adam's deft touch.

"You're the only person I've ever loved." His hands ran up Immanuel's ribs and over the flat scars dotting his shoulder blades. "Your body bears tragedy as beauty, and every scar reminds me how close I came to losing you."

Shuddering, Immanuel pulled away. "But it *isn't* beautiful. It's—"

Adam put his finger to Immanuel's lips. "It is to me. I fell in love with you. *All* of you." He leaned back on the bed, stroking Immanuel's cheek while holding his bichrome gaze. "This is the only body I've known. This is the body I dreamed about while you were gone, and I love it, even if you don't."

The words died in Immanuel's throat as Adam drew him forward for a kiss. Adam lay back on the mattress, lowering Immanuel down with him. Their lips locked and slipped, parting to allow the reach of tongues and half-breathed phrases. Hands skimmed skin, memorizing the curves and planes of their forms until energy hummed between them. Insecurities died away beneath need and heat as the air grew thick with thunder. A chill passed over Immanuel at the brush of fingertips running down his stomach. He broke from their embrace to find Adam's hand resting on the edge of his drawers.

"Wait," Immanuel whispered, his voice barely audible above the tattoo of rain. Taking Adam's hand, he brought it to his lips. "I want to do something for you. That is, if you'll have me."

"Always."

Chapter Eighteen
Rites

Emmeline checked her reflection in the vanity mirror, licking her finger and running it along her eyebrows until every hair stayed in place. She had chosen to wear her favorite purple gown even though it was unseasonably warm, but if she was to be initiated into the Eidolon Club, she had to be at her best. Her gaze roamed over the pots and boxes littering her vanity until it came to rest on an oblong ebony box. An aria of tinny notes plinked out of hidden mechanisms as she opened it. Under the paste jewelry her aunt convinced her to buy were a shard of jet and an enamel brooch in the shape of forget-me-nots. Once upon a time it had been her mother's and she had coveted it until she let her borrow it. A thin smile crossed her lips as she held it in her palm and lightly stroked its periwinkle petals. If only she would have known it be all she had of her after that night.

Affixing it to her bodice, she looked in the mirror one last time. Behind her, dark clouds rolled over the city, gathering in grey clumps over Westminster. Emmeline drew in a long breath, relishing the sultry tang of approaching rain. Somehow it seemed fitting to have a storm on a day like this. Grabbing her purse and parasol, Emmeline eased open the door and listened for her aunt's mouse-like tread. When she was certain Eliza was occupied elsewhere, Emmeline broke from the threshold and bolted down the stairs, slowing her pace as she passed her uncle's study. James Hawthorne stooped over a microscope, obliviously turning dials and muttering under his breath. Emmeline kept her eyes on him as she slipped past. She could have stared at him for hours and he never would have noticed. If she had ever hoped for a loving, caring blood-relative, Uncle James was not it.

Carefully stepping over the creaking treads on the last staircase, Emmeline's pulse raced with the thrill of secreted freedom. She slipped on her mackintosh and reached for the doorknob when the boards whined behind her.

"Emmeline, where are you going?" came Eliza's voice from the parlor.

Gritting her teeth, Emmeline turned around with a tight grin. Eliza met her with an impassive look. While her mouth remained lax, her eyes sharpened with suspicion.

"I'm going out with Cassandra. She got tickets to an opera or a concert or something. I don't remember which."

"Like yesterday?"

Emmeline impatiently inched toward the door, her gloved palm growing sweaty around the metal knob. "Yes?"

"Strange," Eliza began as she approached with her arms tightly crossed. "A while after you left, Cassandra came looking for you. You must imagine my surprise when you weren't with her. I was about to call Scotland Yard when your uncle suggested you might be somewhere benign, like a shop. So where were you?"

Damn her, Emmeline seethed. "Why didn't you ask me yesterday?"

"Because I hoped it would be a onetime event. I didn't expect to find you sneaking out so soon."

"My apologies, I thought I told you," Emmeline replied tartly. "I was at the Spiritualist Society, yesterday, like always. I told Cass, but I guess she didn't hear me."

"Try again. I know for certain you weren't. Cassandra and I went there looking for you. She told me you haven't been there much lately. I thought we had a deal, Emmeline. You can come and go as you please—within reason—as long as you work at the Spiritualist Society. What could be so important that you completely ignore your responsibilities? They're counting on you. They're *paying* you to work."

Emmeline's grip tightened on the parasol's handle. She just wanted to leave. Was that so much to ask? Caustic words worked at her lips, but it was too late to stop them.

"What do you care? You're not my mother."

"Don't take that tone with me. I'm your aunt and guardian, and whether you like it or not, until you turn twenty-one, you're my responsibility."

"Your responsibility?" Emmeline spat. "What do you care where I go? You both barely care that I'm alive. You just feed me and order me around."

"That isn't true."

"Really? What have you said to me today before all of this? Hmm? Emmeline, take your books out of the parlor. Emmeline, do the dishes. Emmeline, see if your uncle wants anything."

Eliza's face fell but snapped back to its stern façade. "Emmeline, I don't—"

The cords in her neck hardened as she yelled, "Uncle James barely acknowledges that I'm even here. The only way I would have his full attention is if I was lying on a slab in the basement."

Her aunt reached for her arm, but Emmeline swatted her away with the handle of her umbrella.

"I hate living here. It's like I'm a bloody ghost! You never speak to me. You speak to Cass because you like her, but I'm not worth your time because I'm not perfect like her— like you. Mama and I actually spoke to each other. *She* cared about me."

"I do care about you. If you want to have conversations, then why don't you ever come downstairs and talk?"

Emmeline shook her head. Bitterness creeped up her throat, burning all in its path. "You don't understand anything. Why don't you just give me my inheritance and let me leave? You'll get your life back, and I'll be able to start mine."

"You know I can't do that, Emmeline."

"Why? Are you afraid I'll ruin myself and bring shame to the family? No one would care what happened to me. Do you think the corpses would care? Or are you worried about what the queen thinks since we made such a good impression last time?"

"That isn't it. There are rules," Eliza replied, keeping her voice cool.

Releasing a bitter laugh, Emmeline yanked open the front door. "Like you care about the rules. You lecture me about independence and autonomy, yet you won't give me control of *my* inheritance because of some rule. Am I the only woman who doesn't deserve to make her own choices or am I too stupid to handle free will?"

"You're still young. You don't have the knowledge to—"

"Then, I'll learn! I deserve the chance to try. You're a hypocrite! You think you can control me because you don't agree with what I want." When her aunt faltered, she spat, "I'm not nearly as stupid as you think."

Eliza Hawthorne fell silent. What little venom she had dried in her throat. "Emmeline, all I wanted to know is where you are going. We can discuss this later. I just want to know you're going to be safe."

"As if it matters," Emmeline muttered, opening her parasol as rain pattered from the roof in fat drops. Raising her gaze, she defiantly locked eyes with her aunt. "Maybe I'm going to elope or maybe I'm going to throw myself off Tower Bridge. I guess you'll find out when I come home."

Emmeline slammed the door behind her and started down the street, her heeled boots clicking on the pavement as she passed the unremarkable faces of Wimpole Street. She half-expected Eliza to chase her down the street and convince her to return home, but no one followed her into the storm.

Dead Magic

༄༅ ༄༅

Emmeline listened to the drops of rain pattering against the canopy of her umbrella. Its steady rhythm slowed her heart and lulled her body into a more peaceful pace. She should have still been angry, she should have fumed all the way to the Eidolon Club and back, but it had been a relief. She and Eliza had finally had it out. At least now she knew she was serious about how much she hated living there. As Emmeline rounded the bend, the Eidolon Club peeked through the steaming rain. A grin crossed her lips as she reminded her feet to slow down. She had to approach with dignity and confidence.

Stepping off the curb, a shadow skulked in front of her. Her heart tightened at the sight of the faceless man. Fear ran through her as she watched people pass behind him, their bodies visible through his shadowed form. Where eyes should have been, there was only piercing blackness. Emmeline grabbed her skirts and ducked across the street to avoid him, her pace quickening in time with her pulse, but as she reached the other side, a hand clamped on her shoulder. Swinging her parasol wildly, Emmeline whacked him. The umbrella's fabric released a dark winged flap as she blindly hit her attacker over and over, her voice rising in a high-pitched cry. Between thwacks, a familiar voice rang out.

"Emmeline, it's me!"

Emmeline stopped in time to see Cecil Hale grab the end of her umbrella before it made contact with his chin. She stiffened as he released it, lowering and then raising the mangled contraption over her head to block her hair from the downpour. He cocked an auburn brow, his eyes searching her face for any sign of logic.

"Who did you think I was? You nearly took my head off."

Her cheeks flushed with heat. "Lord Hale, my apologies. You startled me."

"Apparently."

"Did I hurt you?" she asked softly, laying her hand on his arm.

"I'm fine." He ran a hand through his hair, tidying the strands sent askew by her parasol. Regaining control of his faculties, his gaze softened, lingering on the purple fabric peeking through her raincoat. "I'm very glad to see you. I wasn't certain you would come."

She drew closer until she had to raise the parasol for her to see Lord Hale's face. "Of course I was coming. Why wouldn't I?"

"Because you're a spiritualist. I thought maybe you would have changed your mind. The idea of an initiation is enough to make anyone have second thoughts."

"What do you mean? What happens during the initiation?"

"Nothing, it's only that—"

Looking down the street to see if anyone was watching, Lord Hale took her hand and led her into an alley just wide enough to admit her umbrella. Emmeline's pulse raced as they stood chest-to-chest, his breath tickling her cheek with each exhalation.

He kept his voice low as he said, "Are you certain you want to go through with this? I need you to be very certain you want to be part of the Eidolon Club. If not, you still have time to leave without her seeing you. I can make an excuse for you."

"Lord Hale, you're scaring me. What's going on?" Emmeline asked, her voice tight as she watched him glance toward the Eidolon Club again. Lines appeared around his eyes and his mouth as he drew them into a frown. "Should I not join?"

"The choice isn't mine to make, but you will have to make an offering in order to be initiated. Here, this will be yours."

Reaching into his coat, Lord Hale pulled out the vellum grimoire. Emmeline resisted the urge to stroke its cover even as it beckoned to her. Why had she given it to him?

"I don't understand. What does the book have to do with anything?"

"Claudia doesn't know I have it. At the end of the ritual, she will ask you what you have to offer in order to join. Say the knowledge within the *Corpus Grimoire*, and I will give it to her, then."

Emmeline's heart pounded in her throat. "But the book is mine, and if it's my choice, then I—"

"No. I will not budge on this." His voice tightened with desperation. "If you join, this is your offering. You won't make the same mistake I did. Do you understand? This is for your own good."

"I'll do it if it's that important to you." She smiled nervously. "I have nothing else to give, anyway."

Lord Hale's face darkened. "Neither did I. That's why I needed to speak to you about it before you went in. I couldn't let them take advantage of you, like they did me."

She watched as his eyes grew distant and the rain pattered through his hair and trailed along the curves of his cheekbones and the edge of his jaw. For a brief moment, she considered putting her lips to his. Maybe it would chase away whatever troubled his mind, but something gave her pause. He seemed so grave, so afraid for her. Instead of a kiss, Emmeline slipped her hand across his palm, her fingers hesitantly sliding into the spaces between his. A small smile broke across his lips as he gave her hand a gentle squeeze.

Swallowing hard, she asked, "Lord Hale, what did you offer that was so important?"

"Only my life." Pain seeped into his features but disappeared as he turned his head toward the faint glow of the sun. "We should go. It's nearly dusk, and she is expecting you."

As they emerged from the alley, he proffered his arm. Emmeline gratefully took it, holding it a little tighter than she should have. Despite his obvious anxiety about the initiation, he seemed lighter now that they were in motion together. His eyes traveled over the purple fabric of her gown and the inky curls that had broken from her coiffure during the umbrella attack. Emmeline smiled to herself at his casually probing gaze.

The front door clicked open at his touch, and the moment they stepped inside, they met Claudia's gaze where she watched them from the parlor door. Lord Hale stiffened beneath Emmeline's grasp as he released her arm and stepped aside to take her damp parasol and mackintosh. Emmeline studied the plaits of Claudia's bronze hair, following the glossy braids where they seamlessly combined and parted to form an intricate net punctuated with pearls and bits of absinthe peridot. Her long, gracile neck and full cleavage were on full display in her flowing gown. The gossamer fabric had been carefully pinned and sculpted to accentuate her narrow waist and alabaster arms. With her elaborate coiffure and sheer gown, she was a goddess in their midst. As with their first meeting, Emmeline felt the press of power emanating from the woman's body. Claudia was charged and waiting for them.

"Emmeline, it is a pleasure to see you." Drawing close, she took Emmeline's face in her hands. Heat flooded Emmeline's cheeks before suddenly turning cold. The icy sensation seeped deep into her bones as the woman held her gaze. "You don't know how pleased I am that we will soon have such a talented young woman as one of our own."

With one last fond look, Claudia released her face and motioned for them to follow her. Emmeline's gaze edged to Cecil. As they trailed through the maze of rooms, his attention stayed fixed ahead of him, hard and impassive. While he didn't stop her, his body grew more erect and his jaw tighter the deeper they went into the building. At a set of stone steps, Claudia paused. The table at the threshold had been lined with fat tapers already lit and sweating beads of wax. Handing a candle to each of them, a wry smile crossed her lips.

"Watch your step. You never know what you may encounter in the dark," Claudia said, her green eyes glowing in the shadows.

Emmeline held her breath as she stepped off the landing. The murky air rippled away from her as if she had stepped into a pool. With each dip of her foot on the stairs, the cold creeped further up her body until it engulfed her, chilling her with its soul-sucking pressure, and for a second, she was falling. She was drowning, the air seeping from her lungs until her mouth opened against her will, and the flood of nothingness washed in. The moment Emmeline put her foot on the next step, she snapped back to the stone and mortar tunnel. Torches flickered on either side of the staircase, illuminating a hall that trailed into shadow. Emmeline swallowed hard, wishing she could grab Cecil's arm for reassurance, but they were clamped behind his back out of reach.

Following the glint of Claudia's headdress, she led them past empty rooms so dark their size and purpose was impossible to determine. Water dripped unseen in the distance and the sweet smell of rot lingered just strong enough to make Emmeline question if it was actually there or in her mind. Perhaps she didn't want to know what lay beyond her vision. At the end of the hall, light flooded Emmeline's eyes, blinding her as they entered the cavernous space.

The massive room had been painted with bright, flat figures in the style of Egyptian tombs. Winged women and animal-headed men lined the walls, glaring down at her with sharp, black-ringed eyes. At the center of the platform was a stone altar and behind it on the dais there was something Emmeline couldn't discern. It shifted, consolidating into a more solid mass before stretching to an impossible height. The shadows roiled, its attention concentrating on her. She wanted to cry out, demanding to know what or who was there, but the words died in her throat. As Claudia busied herself with mixing vials on the altar, Emmeline turned back to the shadow. A face appeared less than an inch from her nose. What little heat she had left leeched from her body at its intrusive, skimming touch. She stumbled back. It wanted her. It wanted to harm her. Emmeline tore her eyes away at the sound of Claudia's voice, but when she looked back, the shadow was gone.

"Kneel in the circle," Claudia repeated as she turned with a full chalice in her hand.

Holding her candle ahead, Lord Hale helped her step over the carved rings careful not to disturb the arcane symbols drawn haphazardly in chalk across the uneven stones. In the center, Emmeline sank to her knees. Her heart pounded in her throat as she faced the altar but let her eyes wander over the walls and ornaments.

Claudia lifted the cup over her head, a faint chant issuing from her lips in sharp whispers. The air stirred, brushing the curls against Emmeline's cheeks.

Smoke rose from the silver goblet and trailed over Claudia's hands as she chanted, "Gods of the unseen, hear my prayers. Accept

Emmeline Jardine into your disciples. Let her prove worthy of your greatness. Give her the strength to rise above all others. Let the god of death only greet her as a friend. If you deem her worthy, purify her with the sacred elements."

The stones beneath Emmeline's legs shook. For a moment, she thought it was merely her nerves, but then the stones before her rose and fell. The ancient cobbles clanked at the perimeter of the stone and between the grout came droplets of water. Moisture turned into rivulets that followed the narrow paths of Claudia's chalk symbols. The water danced, growing hotter until steam scolded Emmeline's hands and cheeks. Bursting like a geyser, the water transformed into thin flames. Emmeline bit down a scream, shrinking toward the center as the heat pressed in on her. She shut her eyes against the panic rising in her breast, pretending the all-consuming fire wasn't inches from her skin and that she wouldn't be burnt alive like her mother. The flames rose high above her head, fed by an unseen wind until the gale grew, snuffing out the pyre and the candles lining the room. Darkness fell heavily around them. Emmeline wrenched open her eyes, but all she could discern was the faint glint of the chalice near the altar. A match struck and a wisp of light appeared in Claudia's hand. As she raised it to the wick of the altar piece, Emmeline could see her lips curl into a satisfied smirk.

When the altar was alight, Claudia stepped forward until she stood at the edge of the circle. "Emmeline Jardine, by joining the coven known as the Eidolon Club, you have dedicated yourself to the study of life's mysteries and the strengthening of your extranormal abilities. As a member of this coven, you will bow to our gods and serve them as if their motives were your own, and in return, they will watch over you and protect you in all of your endeavors. If you break this sacred bond, you will face misfortune. Do you understand?"

Emmeline's throat tightened, the taste of ash and earth on her tongue. "I do."

"Emmeline, do you willingly enter this family?"

Her stomach knotted at the thought of her aunt's face when they fought. Would she have a home to go back to? "I do."

"What do you bring as a dowry? If you have nothing to offer, you may pledge your life to the service of the gods."

Her eyes trailed to where she imagined Lord Hale to be. "I offer the *Corpus Grimoire*."

Claudia's body locked. With a blink, the spell broke and her face returned to its somber stoicism. "Lord Hale, is this true?"

His voice echoed from the far corner of the room as he replied, "Yes, I have the book in my possession."

"Very well. Emmeline, the mysteries of the world beyond our senses are numerous. As a member of the Eidolon Club, you will learn our ways and abandon all thoughts of boundaries or impropriety. You will seek knowledge and the power it brings without restraint. May the Ancient Unseen Ones guide you." Holding the chalice before her, Claudia asked, "Will you uphold the values of the Eidolon Club and honor our gods?"

"I will."

"Are you prepared to be born anew? To begin a new life with a purpose higher than your own, to be an extension of the gods and their will?"

Emmeline swallowed hard. "I—"

"Then rise, and enter the collection of Eidolons, the children of shadows."

With a flick of Claudia Rose's hand, Emmeline's legs moved of their own accord. Something pushed her forward, bringing her toward the cup and the shades that hung from Claudia, like children at her skirts. Emmeline took the offered cup and drank deeply, the tang of the impenetrable brew within burning her throat as it slid down. Her head swam by the time it hit her stomach. She staggered forward, grasping Claudia's arm for purchase. Where was Cecil?

Claudia held her faltering gaze, and with a hand on each cheek, she kissed Emmeline's forehead. "It's time for you to prove yourself, Emmeline. In Eidolon, the god awaits you."

Her voice grew fainter as Emmeline's head grew too heavy for her neck and fell back. Her body was failing, and there was nothing she could do to stop it. The arcane reliefs faded to grey around her, the walls tunneling in until only a pinhole remained.

The world blinked, rippling in the darkness until it exploded out. It was different. It was all so different now. The room she had been in a moment ago fell into the background and over it lay a realm of trees and twisting buildings of a more complex design than humankind could ever hope to emulate. It lay over her world like a silk theatre curtain. She stared down at her own body. Inky curls fanned out around her head, her hands loosely folded over her stomach where she fell in the center of the stone circle. Its stone symbols glowed faintly in the space between worlds. Her gaze traveled to the white-hot flame housed in Claudia's body. It blinded her, a beacon in a grey world. As she stared through the woman's body, she locked eyes with a shade. Its hair gleamed gold as did its eyes. His features were familiar yet alien. Handsome and sharp but pinched to devilish points. Unnaturally black skin covered his body, gleaming like jet from an unseen light. Drawing closer, she could make out his incised skin and twisted features. It suddenly became horribly clear that only nightmares could live in the world of the unseen.

His lips curled into a Cheshire smile, sending a bolt of panic coursing through her breast. "Welcome to the Eidolon Club, Emmeline. We have been waiting for you."

Chapter Nineteen
A Family Affair

Cecil watched his aunt carefully lower Emmeline to the ground, her body limp. "This isn't how I remember my initiation. I applaud you on the theatrics. At least hers was less humiliating than mine, even if she did faint."

Lady Rose ignored him as she folded Emmeline's hands across her stomach. "She didn't faint."

"You poisoned her?" he cried, snatching the chalice from the edge of the altar.

"Don't be ridiculous. I gave her a silphium draught. I paid a dockhand at the museum to steal some. We will need more, but the Interceptors moved it after the first break-in. Since we don't have the vivalabe," she paused, her eyes darting toward the shadows, "I need her to go into Eidolon and tell me what she sees; otherwise we'll never know where he is."

"Shouldn't you have told her that before you knocked her out?"

"If she knew what she was looking for, the world would have bent to her will. No, her acting as a human compass is best. She can't complain. She was the one who wanted to join after all."

Lord Hale stared down at Emmeline's sleeping face. She lay still as death, her breast barely rising with breath. "Will she be all right? This isn't hurting her, is it?"

Lady Rose straightened, kicking away the clumsy sigil until all that remained was a trace of chalk. Turning to her nephew, she glared at him and held out her hand. "The grimoire."

"I said, will she be all right?"

"If you were so concerned about her well-being, then you should have taken the book and left her out of this." When his jaw hardened and his eyes narrowed, she added, "She's fine, as fine as anyone having a nightmare can be. Now, the book, if you please."

Reaching into his coat, he pulled the book from under his arm, where he had hid it during the ritual. Lady Rose's lime eyes brightened with glee. For a long moment, she merely stared at the cover, her fingers lovingly caressing the fine vellum and the alien flowers etched into it. Drawing in a steadying breath, she carefully opened the latch. She held her head high as if expecting something to occur, but when the cover merely flopped over her arm, her face fell and her eyes narrowed. Lowering it, she looked from the page of brown-inked sigils to Emmeline's supine form. The moment a wave of energy finished pulsing through the room, Lady Rose slammed the book shut.

"Damn it, Cecil. She's bonded with it! I told you to get it, and you let this happen."

"How was I supposed to stop her? She could have bonded with it the moment she found it. If you had intercepted it early, I wouldn't have had to earn her trust," he replied, keeping his voice low enough that Emmeline couldn't hear.

"Earn her trust? *Earn her trust.* You were supposed to infiltrate the Spiritualist Society, look for practioners who align with our beliefs, and then, find the bloody book. I told you to forget her when the season ended. Now, your dilly-dallying has jeopardized our plans."

"*Your* plans. I'm not sure if I want to be a part of this scheme anymore."

"Oh, don't start that with me. You're as deep in this as I am, perhaps even more."

"I did what you told me. I got the book, didn't I?"

"It's bonded to her!" she yelled, flinging the book at him. "It's practically useless."

Clutching the grimoire to his chest, he stormed after her as she descended into the crypt behind the altar. "It isn't useless. She can still do exactly what you wanted, and she will. If I ask, I know she'll do it. You're just cross because you didn't get the power you wanted. Now, you have to ask Emmeline."

"Cecil, I have been working to find that book since I left that godawful asylum, and someone else got to it before I could. She doesn't even know the power she holds!" Lady Rose gritted her teeth, her hand lingering on the old loop of metal that served as a latch for the catacomb. If her stupid husband hadn't gotten himself killed— Whipping around, she seized Lord Hale by the shoulders and pushed him against the damp stone wall. "Awakening the god is the only way for me to get my due. Do you understand what it feels like to have something ripped from you the moment you think you have it? Of course you don't, my sister made certain of that."

He sneered at her, resisting the urge to shove her back. His hand itched to move, but he would pay dearly for his transgression and so would Emmeline. "Emmeline is in love with me. With a little coaxing, she will do anything I say."

Leaning close, a wicked smile darkened her features. "I could kill her, you know. Slit her pretty little throat right now and be done with it. Then, the book would need a new master. Shall I? She wouldn't even know."

Lord Hale flung out his arm, throwing his aunt back against the narrow hall. A throaty chuckle escaped her lips. Before he could strike again, his body locked. Claudia stared into his eyes, her green gaze unrelenting. The air squeezed from his lungs as if they were being filled with concrete as she stared him down. His vision spotted and his heart stumbled out of rhythm. The world died away, the light faltering until his mind sputtered, *Was this the end?* With a wave of her hand, he stumbled back into the wall and slid to the floor. His head reeled as he drew in a lung-full of dank air. He coughed, reaching for his aching throat but found no fingerprints or bruises to tell of the ordeal. As he stood panting, Lady Rose shook her head, watching him with a triumphant smile.

"You need to learn to control your temper, Cecil, before you tamper with the wrong practioner. You wouldn't want Emmeline to have an accident on her way home."

"Don't you or your blasted revenant dare touch her. She's innocent in all of this," he hissed, pointing an accusatory finger at her. "You know she has nothing to do with this."

Swatting his hand away, Lady Rose drew so close he could taste the wine on her breath. "Not any more. You had better be right about her. If she isn't the compliant little maiden you claim her to be, I'll take matters into my own hands. I'm done with ineffectual men ruining my plans."

Cecil opened his mouth to speak but froze. Emmeline's voice echoed faintly through the chamber followed by the hesitant shuffle of feet. Lady Rose straightened, planting an unnervingly pleasant smile on her face.

"We're coming, Emmeline!" she called sweetly. "Smile, Cecil, your Sleeping Beauty is awake." When he didn't move to follow her up the steps, she turned and added, "If you would prefer to stay down here, you could always prep the body for Alastair's next outing. I had been meaning to ask you for another tincture. I'll need it by tonight."

"Already? Can his soul handle that sort of—"

"Leave him to me. Make the tincture or I'll be using your friend as his next host."

With a knowing look, Lady Rose disappeared into the ritual chamber. Cecil drew in a tight breath, his heart hammering in his throat. What had he gotten them into?

Chapter Twenty
Oil and Blood

Peeking at Adam from the edge of his pillow, Immanuel watched his chest rise and fall in a sleepy rhythm. He smiled, gently massaging Adam's arm as he laid his head on his shoulder. He didn't stir, but that was all right. It was late, and after the evening they had, Adam deserved the rest. Squinting at the clock ticking on the nightstand, Immanuel sighed. Despite being thoroughly satisfied with their time together and his limbs heavy with fatigue, sleep still eluded him. Thunder crashed throughout the night, rattling the windows in their frames and breaking the fragile veil of his dreams. Lying there would do nothing. With a silent sigh, he slowly slid from beneath the tangled covers, careful not to wake his companion. Words nagged at the back of his mind, words that no matter how hard he tried didn't dare come out between kisses or stifled moans.

Standing at the foot of the bed, he said softly, "My ancestors could do magic. They were alchemists, just like my mother said. The potion was real. Everything was real. Can you believe it?"

No, he wouldn't, and that's why he hadn't been able to say it aloud.

"I was right. Lord Rose is alive, and he wants to hurt me."

Immanuel's face fell at the realization of what he said.

"I'm scared, Adam. I feel so alone in all of this. I know you won't believe me, and that makes me feel like a freak… again. I don't know what to do."

Drawing close to Adam, he planted a kiss on his forehead before kissing his lax lips. He closed his eyes to relish the perfume of earl grey and the lingering sweetness of berries. When his companion still didn't stir, Immanuel slipped on his dressing gown. He paused with his hand on the threshold. A night bird cried beyond the rumble of cabs passing the house, alone in its mourning.

Watching Adam sleep, he whispered, "I wish you believed me."

Immanuel padded down the steps. His troubled mind tumbled over itself until it spiraled into hazy visions of Lord Rose in a devil mask. No, he was home. He was safe. As he confirmed that the front door was locked and chained, he flipped over Adam's upturned shoe, hiding the symbol incised into the sole. He lingered at the parlor door, his eyes fixed on the cushion where he had stashed his ancestor's journal. Only hours before Judith Elliot had sat there and pried into his mind. Had she known it was there? Plucking the journal from beneath the fabric, Immanuel disappeared into the workroom and flipped on the lamps. It all seemed so arcane, so strange, yet he couldn't push it from his mind. Science had been his whole life until now. He had grown away from his mother's superstitious runes and charms made of bound twigs and flowers, finally severing any remaining ties when he reached Oxford. The university was no place for fancy. His mind rejected the notion that it could be real. It had all been a coincidence. Maybe Adam was right and Emmeline Jardine had woken up after giving her the potion because she wasn't truly dead, but he had seen it with his own eyes. He hadn't made up the visions when he touched skeletons or dead bodies. He was anxious and fearful, but he wasn't crazy. That much he was sure of.

Sitting at Hadley's old workbench, he opened the journal. He read the lines of tight script, but little made sense. It had been written by someone who already knew why and how it worked. His gut gurgled with academic anxiety. Could he teach it to himself as he did science? But what if he never understood? The sinking feeling had consumed him during his first weeks at Oxford when English scarcely made sense and every stumbled syllable made him keenly aware of his tongue and teeth and lips. He grabbed his discarded sketchbook and flipped back to the page with the symbol for protection. In the predawn stillness, he struggled to copy the lines and make sense of how they related to one another. No matter how close he traced it, it didn't feel right. It looked the same as his ancestor's drawing, but it felt hollow.

What was it that Peregrine had said? *Symbolic ingredients, a catalyst, focus, and intention.* That's what was needed for a spell. He thumbed through the pages again. Ingredients were few and far between yet medium seemed important with circles and lines. The more permanent the medium, the stronger the spell. That was why he had carved the protection symbol into Adam's shoe. Immanuel stared down at the sigils scrawled on different colored patches of paper within the notebook. No matter their meaning, their structure seemed nearly identical with a series of concentric circles crisscrossed with symbols and lines. At first he had assumed the similarities were due to a repetition of words or meaning, but what if the spells used the same visual medium but varied with the practioner? Then, the symbolic ingredients were nothing more than characters with significance to the caster.

Ripping the page from his sketchpad, Immanuel inhaled and exhaled slowly, clearing his mind until all he heard was the distant tattoo of rain. He needed to focus, he needed intention, but most of all, he needed a symbol. With the pen loosely in his grasp, he closed his eyes and let his hand move. The pen lazily circled, following the cardinal directions. Walls rose in his mind, locking where the lines crossed. Tight arms closed around him. Doors shut with bolts slamming home. Adam whispered in his ear that everything would be all right.

When Immanuel opened his eyes, he found the workroom empty and a strange symbol in the center of the paper. What had begun as merely a spiral bloomed into something between a four-leaved flower bud and a haloed cross. He ran his finger along the edge of its cruciform arms where the nib had left behind a scratch in the paper. Energy hummed sleepily within. A small smile crossed his lips. It felt right. It felt his.

A thrill lanced through him as he stared at his pictograph of protection, keenly aware of how he longed to draw it everywhere. But where could he put it that Adam wouldn't notice and become cross with him? He had been lucky thus far that Adam hadn't discovered the graffiti on his favorite shoes, but carving a twisting rose and cross into the workroom door would have been much more obvious. And that was a conversation he wasn't ready to have yet. Tapping his pen against the nicked table, Immanuel's eyes trailed to the glass and metal pendent hanging around his neck. He turned it over, watching the sprig of forget-me-nots shift within. *Cruor.* Blood. Life-giving blood. If it had brought back Emmeline Jardine when mixed with his ancestor's potion and its remnants had been powerful enough to sustain rootless flowers, then maybe blood could be as powerful as a carving.

Picking through Hadley's tools and cabinets for leftover supplies, he found a bottle of mineral oil, a seemingly untouched letter-opener, and a painting palette. Immanuel sat on the stool and steeled himself as he dug the tip of the knife into his finger. Hesitant beads of blood bubbled out, dripping onto the palette with a squeeze of his hand. With the tip of his pinky, he carefully mixed the oil and blood together until the latter was nearly invisible. Standing at the backdoor, he pictured all he hoped to protect and everything that made him feel protected as his finger worked to trace the symbol from memory. When the last line connected, he stood back to admire its form. Something was missing...
A catalyst.

"Now," he said softly as he dotted the center of the pictograph.

Energy hummed faintly through the door like the vibration of a tuning fork. Carrying the palette into the kitchen, he set about marking every window and door. Like specimens on slides, the blood and oil symbols were only visible when seen by those who knew they were there. In the right light, they vanished completely; while at other times, they stood out as starkly as if they were engraved. With each new mark, Immanuel's body grew heavier and fatigue slowed the trajectory of his finger. By the time he reached the front door, he could scarcely keep his eyes open. His nicked finger lazily traced his mental image, dragging at the corners until the ends connected in a circuit. Immanuel dotted the figure and smiled.

In the faint, flickering glow of the streetlamps, the mark was nearly invisible. Maybe Adam wouldn't notice, but if he did, it was for a good cause. Even if Adam didn't believe, Immanuel did. How could he not when he could feel the house's hum in his veins? It pulsed in time with the beating of his heart, and with the final mark on the door, the circuit closed, knitting together the sigils in a ring around their Baker Street flat that would hopefully keep Lord Rose out. Laying his hand against the door, he closed his eyes. Visions of what life could be like with these new abilities flooded his mind. It all seemed so strange and new. Yawning, he wondered how different things would have been if he hadn't believed Judith, Cassandra, and Peregrine. They had feared he would ignore his abilities, but what would have happened? Was it really possible to beat the magic from someone?

Immanuel jolted awake as his face slid against the door's smooth grain. Rubbing his eyes with the heel of his hand, he padded up the stairs and into their bedroom. Adam mumbled under his breath as Immanuel slipped beneath the covers and laid his head on his chest. Adam's arms wrapped around him and drew him closer until their bodies were flush. Immanuel smiled, his finger tracing the protective symbol across Adam's skin as he lapsed into sleep.

Chapter Twenty-One
The Kingdom of Eidolon

Emmeline walked down Baker Street, her head pounding in her temples and forehead with each step. The brew Claudia had given her wore off long ago but the images remained burned in her mind. Nightmare landscapes of a madman's mind lurked just beyond the thin veil of London. As she passed familiar houses, she pictured the twisted spires of Eidolon. Half wood and half steel, they towered into the heavens with thorns and flowering vines choking them black with rot. What lay beyond their field of vision? Was it all deformed creatures with horns and stony skin or was that merely one layer? Under the potion's spell, she had walked through the city, following her strange daemon guide past Kensington Palace and its gardens until they reached a soaring castle preceded by a massive wasteland of arboreal stone outcroppings and a twisting lake of lava. The palace's walls gleamed like ragged obsidian, dwarfing her by proportions her mind couldn't fathom. Her guide's unnerving grin and pointed features sent her heart pounding with fear, but in the moment as they floated through the otherworldly palace, it had been impossible to think or speak. Ghouls of every size and form moved past her, paying her little heed. The occasional languid predator's eye fell upon her, sending a pulse of panic through her that threatened to spit her back into the inner sanctum of the Eidolon Club, but none of the creatures thought her a worthy meal.

"What did you see?" Claudia asked as she helped her off the chalk-dusted floor.

Her mind had been shredded, torn from what she ever believed to be true, yet she couldn't be sure if it was truly real or if what she had seen came from the strange herbs mixed into the wine she had been offered. She had seen a massive creature on a throne of cold fire. The image was blurred and in constant motion, but she knew it was the same creature she had encountered during her reading at the Spiritualist Society. Fear rang through her. The monster glared down at her with hollow sockets, its stag horns swishing in agitation as it eyed her at the base of its throne.

"Speak to it," her blackened guide commanded as he disappeared into the shadows.

Emmeline froze. The skeletal stag seemed to stretch above her until it stood as tall as a cathedral, ready to consume her the moment she erred. She opened her mouth to speak but found her soul or whatever vessel she traveled in had no jaw or tongue to articulate. Focusing her energy as she did during readings, she found the words she needed.

"What is it you want from us?" echoed through her mind, filling the vast hall.

Entry. A body. It paused, scrutinizing her in its hollow gaze. *A new world to conquer. But where is the other?*

Claudia smiled at her, patting her arm as she helped her walk back to the surface. "I knew it. I knew he would want to be part of our world. Emmeline, you have been such a help. Mediums have the easiest time traversing worlds, after all, so you were the obvious choice for the task."

"That wasn't part of the initiation?" she asked, her stomach churning as her head swam.

"Oh, it was. It was. Communing with the resident god is the polite thing to do when you join a society such as this, but you seem to have had a much clearer vision than Cecil or I would have had."

It felt as if her soul hadn't settled properly back into her body, and it made her sick. For several hours she had lain on a chaise in Claudia's private rooms, unable to convince her legs to move. Bile threatened to gurgle up from her gut at the thought of motion, yet it seemed even her stomach refused to act. Shutting her eyes against the harsh glow of the gas lamps, the next thing she remembered was Cecil asking her if he could take her home. Surely, she had agreed, but how did she get all the way to Baker Street?

He had driven her to Wimpole Street, stopping a few houses away from her aunt and uncle's flat. His russet brows furrowed with worry as he watched her rub her forehead and eyes. A gloved hand slid over hers, lingering until she finally met his hazel gaze.

"Would you like me to walk you to the door? You look ill. I could tell your relatives that you fainted at the club, and that's why you're late. We didn't want to let you leave until you recovered."

"I'll be fine."

Forcing a smile, she opened the door and staggered into the foggy night. Before she could step away, a hand lightly closed on her arm.

"Emmeline, I'm sorry I didn't warn you about the initiation," he said softly, reaching through the passenger door.

"Most rites are secret for a reason. Good night, Lord Hale."

With a pensive frown, he closed the door. As she watched the steamer pull away and disappear into the midnight gloom, she swallowed hard. The lights were still on in the parlor, which meant Aunt Eliza was waiting for her. Without looking back, she began to walk in the other direction. Through the heaviness of her vision and the pain jangling her brain, she knew she couldn't face her aunt. There would be a myriad of questions about where she went and it would spiral into an argument and her head would ache from whatever she drank. Aunt Eliza would assume she was drunk. If she could get to someone's house, she could hide out until morning when her head clear enough to string together a convincing lie.

Baker Street wasn't far, and Immanuel and Mr. Fenice were unlikely to turn her away in her such a state. Standing outside one twenty-six, a strange sensation passed over her. Through her hazy vision, she could make out a barely perceivable tether running from her body up to the window of the bedroom, but where the glittering rope hit the building's brick façade, it sparked. As Emmeline drew closer, the light grew brighter, violently popping until she took a step back. Vomit and tears rose to the surface, but she choked them down. Staying there would be impossible.

Fishing through her clutch, Emmeline found the note Cassandra had given her months ago. In the diffuse light of the streetlamps, her eyes clouded with moisture until she could barely read the address. She rested her head against the wet metal, holding its cold body for support as her knees threatened to buckle once more. Wrenching her attention from her thoughts, she hailed the first cab that came rolling lazily down the cobbles. The driver passed a cool eye over her wild hair and black-ringed eyes as she muttered the address of Cassandra's boarding house.

Collapsing in the backseat, Emmeline stared numbly out the window. It felt wrong. It all felt horribly wrong.

Chapter Twenty-Two
Misses Elliott and Ashwood

Emmeline's hand fell heavy against the doorknocker. The house in Bloomsbury was dark, but Cassandra had to be home. The driver had said it was the right place, but how could she afford it? She had expected a tidy but frayed boarding house. This building seemed far too nice for a girl with only a small job at the Spiritualist Society and maybe an allowance from a relative. Emmeline squinted at the building's white-washed façade through the steamy fog before returning to the card in her hand. It was the right address. Perhaps she shared the apartment with other girls. Letting the doorknocker fall a second, third, and fourth time, she rested her pounding forehead against the damp wood. Cass had to be home. There was nowhere else for her to go. She could have gone to Greenwich and imposed herself upon the earl and countess. They would have taken her in, but they surely would have reported her ringed eyes and inebriated state to her aunt.

Staggering forward, Emmeline's hand caught the edge of a brass plate. She raised her gaze and grinned at her fortune when she spotted a row of bells and names. Halfway down, she spotted *Misses Elliott and Ashwood* and held down the button until she could hear its distant buzz somewhere on the other side of the door. The vibration sent a wave of nausea through her as she waited, grasping the column of the portico for support. A light appeared on the third floor, and within a moment, footsteps rang down the stairs in a steady rhythm. The door opened a crack, revealing an almond shaped hazel eye and a pale cheek smudged with rouge. Her sharp gaze ran over Emmeline's face and rumpled gown, and for a moment, Emmeline feared she would shut the door on her.

"May I help you?" she asked, her American accent softened through a suppressed yawn but still jarring in the stillness.

"Is Cassandra Ashwood there?" Emmeline held out the calling card and forced her voice despite the pain in her head as she said, "My name is Emmeline Jardine. We're friends, and I was hoping she would let me stay the night. This is the right place, isn't it?"

The blonde woman eyed her suspiciously as she plucked the card from her hand and studied it under the hall light. There was something in her stare that reminded Emmeline of Lady Rose. This woman didn't strike the same fear and hesitance in her that the noblewoman did, but there was a silent power behind her, a radiant energy she didn't dare trifle with. As she handed the card back to Emmeline, a pale face appeared over her shoulder on the stairs.

"Judith, who is it?"

"Cass!" Emmeline cried, standing on tiptoe to peer over the blonde's shoulder. "Cass, it's Emmeline!"

Judith crossed her arms over her silken kimono as she opened the door wide to let her in. Taking a tremulous step forward, Emmeline's ankle rolled and the cramped foyer tilted on its side. Hands caught her arms, pulling her to her feet as they led her to the stairs. Cassandra leaned in close, her eyes wide to take in Emmeline's sallow features.

"What possessed you to come out so late? You could have been killed or attacked. I know you haven't lived in town long, but it isn't safe!" Cassandra cried in a harsh whisper, keeping her voice low enough that the other boarders couldn't hear.

Emmeline kept her head down. Swallowing down the dizziness, she closed her eyes and said slowly, "I was hoping I could stay the night with you. I had a falling out with my aunt, and I don't think I could go home and face her."

"What have you been drinking?" Judith asked.

Cassandra shot her a look. "Of course you can stay with us. Let's get you upstairs and into a nightgown."

"Thank you, but that really isn't necessary. I don't want to impose. I just want a place to sleep," Emmeline replied, eying Judith warily.

Cassandra nodded, sending waves of chestnut hair across her cheeks and the shoulders of her cotton nightgown. Looking up from Emmeline's shaking form, she silently pleaded with Judith. After a moment, the other woman nodded with a slight roll of her eyes and helped Emmeline to her feet. They led her up the stairs, past halls of brass numbered rooms, and into a spacious but spare parlor. The floors and walls were adorned with brightly colored Japanese woodblock prints portraying scenes of fishermen and women in robes with pale painted faces. Across the room over the fireplace hung a katana and a naginata. Emmeline wrinkled her nose at the masculine decorations. It reminded her too much of that dreadful restaurant Cassandra liked, the Dorothy.

Depositing her on the couch, Cassandra disappeared into the bedroom. Emmeline peered in after her but saw only a large bed, rumpled from sleep on both sides. As she turned her swimming head back to scrutinize the flat's furnishings, Emmeline met Judith's magnetic gaze. From the kitchen, she entrapped her. Their minds grew closer until they touched and Judith dipped below the surface, but Emmeline was powerless to stop her. Her mind had already been ripped raw, exposed to something she was never meant to see. With a snap, the other woman turned her face away. As Cassandra came out of the bedroom with a pile of clothes, Judith caught her arm and pulled her aside. They spoke in hushed tones so low Emmeline couldn't hear them even in the small apartment, but she watched her friend's eyes widen, her attention flickering between Emmeline and her roommate.

"Em, where were you tonight? What happened?" Cassandra asked as she perched on the arm of the sofa.

Something in the way she said it made Emmeline wonder how much she knew. Emmeline opened her mouth, her fogged mind racing to string together a sensible lie. Looking up, she found Judith staring at her from the ottoman. Her palpable intensity removed all doubt. She was trapped.

"I was at the Eidolon Club with Lord Hale."

Cassandra's lips twitched. "Why did you go there?"

After the day she had, she was in no mood. "Because he invited me to be initiated. Why? Why are you acting like I did something wrong?" Emmeline snapped.

"Because you did. You're part of the Spiritualist Society. I thought we would work there together, helping people."

"Not anymore. You know how I'm treated with Nostra running the society. At the Eidolon Club, they actually want me to use my powers. They think my gifts will be of use."

"Of course they think you're useful! You're a pawn to them."

"Don't you start with me. You don't know anything, Cass. You're just mad that I went without you. That I'm doing better than you."

Cassandra's mouth hung open as she shook her head. "How can you be so blind? And so stupid!"

"Cassie," Judith said softly, laying her hand on her arm to steady her.

"Do you know what you've done? They're using you!"

"And Madam Nostra isn't?"

"We could have spoken to her or exposed her as a fraud. You didn't need to join them. Why didn't you tell me they were courting you?"

"Because I knew you would tell me not to go. You never liked Lord Hale."

"At least you didn't throw back that I might want *him* for myself." Cassandra paused, her eyes distant as her mind raced. "You didn't give them the grimoire, did you? Please tell me you didn't do that," she pleaded.

Emmeline hung her head guiltily before defiantly glaring back at her. "It said to keep it safe or give it to someone who could. Lord Hale knows more about whatever that book is about than I do, so why wouldn't I give it to him? I don't understand why you're so upset with me. You never told me not to give it to someone else. You were the one who wanted to send it off in the first place!"

"Because I thought you were more sensible than to give it to them! I can't believe you. I can't believe that you ruined everything, that you threw everything away on that twat!"

Before Emmeline could say a word, Cassandra threw the extra nightgown onto the couch and stormed back into her room. Emmeline flinched as the door slammed and silence fell over the flat. Her head and eyes ached with a renewed vigor. She looked from her shaking hands to the flowered nightgown strewn across the couch. She ruined everything.

"You may not want to, but I would suggest you stay the night," Judith said. "Whatever they gave you was potent. You will have a headache in the morning, but a night's rest will recover your strength."

"But what about Cassandra? She hates me. She won't want me here."

"She will get over it." Judith rose from her place on the ottoman but stopped at the bedroom door. "Emmeline, do be careful with the Eidolon Club. Don't let Cassie's outburst overshadow what she said. She wasn't completely wrong about them."

Emmeline watched Judith slip inside. Their voices carried through the plaster, rising and falling with their argument, but no one emerged. Dropping the nightgown onto the end table, Emmeline slowly laid her head against the couch's arm. Her head pounded in time with her heart, drowning out the ragged sound of Cassandra's voice ringing only feet away. It had all seemed so right at the time, but what did she have now?

No family, no friends, no grimoire. Only the promise of a new life as tenuous as a spider's thread.

ACT THREE

"No man chooses evil because it is evil; he only mistakes it for happiness, the good he seeks."
-Mary Shelley

Chapter Twenty-Three
Her Majesty's Interceptors

Immanuel crossed the lawns of the Inner Temple Gardens, his feet crunching through the lush grass and uneven cobbles of the pavement. His gaze flickered between the card in his hand and the tall brick buildings surrounding the patch of greenery. Clicking open his pocket watch, he confirmed that he still had twenty minutes until his meeting with Judith Elliott. With a silent sigh, he sank onto the nearest bench, pulling his satchel across his lap. He closed his eyes and opened them again to take in the patches of tulips and sprays of wild flowers with a fresh gaze. In his blurry left eye, the view was as pretty as one of Monet's pictures. He had told Adam he was going to Scotland Yard to fill out another statement about the break-in, but now that he sat alone, he wondered if he should have taken Adam with him.

Leaning forward on his elbows, the brass bulge of the vivalabe and the corner of the notebook on top of it dug into his thigh. Immanuel drew in a deep breath, inhaling the sweet scent of flowers and the faint smell of the Thames behind it. With the imposing ornamental brick facades and wide lawns, he felt as if he were back in Oxford, but the moment his heart ticked with panic, he reminded himself of his new home and his new life. Oxford was far behind him. Turning his attention back to the gold-lettered card in his hand, Immanuel chewed on his lip. The front of the card had nothing more than Judith Elliott's name and the address of the spired red brick building behind him while the back was blank apart from *Sunday at seven* scrawled hastily in pencil. What did she want with him? He had already found out about magic and practioners and where he fit within their ranks, so what was left? A little voice inside of him repeated, *You're in trouble*. Maybe he had done something wrong after all. Maybe there was some unspoken law about practicing magic that he had broken in his ignorance. He bit down on his lip hard enough to draw a bead of blood. As he looked up from the glaringly white paper, his eyes locked onto a shadowed form in the distance.

A man stood across the lawn in the shade of an oak tree, watching him. His face was obscured in the gloom, but his eyes gleamed as he watched him. Realizing Immanuel had seen him, he refolded his arms and rested his back against the tree. Immanuel's heart quickened and his pulse raced through his temples in a steady tattoo. Without taking his eyes off the man, Immanuel stuffed the card into his pocket and walked backwards toward the line of buildings. Something about the man felt wrong. The shadows around him seemed too deep, his eyes too bright. Immanuel rang the bell and waited, keeping his bag tucked close under his arm. As he waited, his eyes darted between the door and the creature stalking him from the other side of the park. The man was coming closer, crossing the green in an uneven shuffle. Immanuel raised his fist, about to knock, when the door opened under his hand.

A grandmotherly woman stood on the other side of the threshold. Her questioning, pale eyes climbed Immanuel's face, beginning with the point of his scar. "May I help you, sir?"

"I'm here to meet with Miss Elliott. She asked me to visit her today. I— I have her card here somewhere," he blurted, resisting the urge to eye the man over his shoulder.

Dead Magic

A thoughtful frown creased her features until Immanuel fished through his pockets and found the card. She glossed over the front before flipping it to the back. With a nod, she opened the door wide and ushered him out of the tight vestibule and into the foyer. Light flooded his eyes as he stepped into the grand hall. In the ceiling, right above the winding spiral staircase stood an oculus and beneath it a crystal-encrusted chandelier that amplified the sun's rays and scattered them across every surface in a shower of rainbows. The floor was composed of marble laid out in black and white mosaics. As he walked further into the hall, dodging people on their way to the passageways running off the foyer, he realized that the mosaic tiles weren't random but formed the face of a massive sundial lined with Roman numerals. Leading him to the lower steps of the spiraling wood and iron staircase, the woman stopped. She looked him over once more, her gaze lingering on the pendant tucked under his shirt and the place in his bag where the vivalabe rested.

"Miss Elliott is on the third floor. It's the last door at the top of the second landing, dear, all the way at the end of the hall. Do you need me to escort you?" she asked, her eyes crinkling with good-natured affection.

"No, thank you, ma'am. I can find my way."

Immanuel gave the woman a tight smile before sprinting up the stairs a little faster than he intended, his satchel slapping against his leg with each step. At the landing, he slowed his pace. Even on a Sunday afternoon, the building bustled with life. Men and women passed down the tapestried hall, glancing in his direction before disappearing into the recesses of the building. A wooden door rattled in its hinges out of sight while voices rose and fell in all directions. Listening closely, Immanuel could hear the steady tick of typewriter keys and the dissonant whistle of a kettle.

Somehow, he had expected a dull school or a boarding house for wealthy widows or middle class women, but he had never imagined an office as busy as an anthill. Men *and* women. A small smile crossed his lips. If only the museum was more like this and less like the university.

Rounding the corner, Immanuel padded up a set of narrower iron steps that twisted up into the spire he had seen outside. At the landing, he stopped. The only sound was the squeal of the boards under his feet and the distant garble of women's voices. Had he gone the wrong way? He walked to the end of the hall, holding his satchel in place to silence its rhythmic swish. His eyes passed over the names painted in capitals on the glass of each door. At the end of the hall, he stopped before the one marked *Judith Elliott, Esq.* Immanuel glanced at the names on the other doors but none bore the accessory title. It didn't seem like a law firm.

He raised his fist to knock but stopped at the sound of two women's voices rising on the other side of the glass.

"I feel so foolish. I never thought she would do anything so stupid. I thought she was more sensible than that!"

"It happens. We'll figure it out," replied Judith, her American accent immediately recognizable. "She was enamored with him. It's to be expected."

"All over a man!" the softer voice huffed.

When they fell silent, Immanuel lightly knocked.

"Come in, Mr. Winter."

As he opened the door, he watched Cassandra Ashwood hop off the edge of the desk where she had been perched a moment before. Her normally open features had darkened with worry while a crease of annoyance appeared between her furrowed chocolate brows. Sitting behind the whitewashed wood desk, Judith caught Cassandra's hand, holding it tenderly until a hesitant smile graced the other woman's lips.

"Have I come at a bad time?" Immanuel asked softly, his gaze traveling between them.

"Not at all, Mr. Winter. I was about to leave, anyway. Mrs. Mills wanted to speak with me," Cassandra replied as she slipped past him, locking eyes with Judith one last time.

The door shut behind her, and he was left alone in the bright office with Judith Elliott. She stared up at him, her hazel eyes probing but not unwelcoming. It was as if her ability to see truths and lies seeped into every motion. Much like her starched and expertly coiffured figure, Judith's office was immaculate. Every wooden surface had been whitewashed to heighten the light drifting in from the tall window behind her. Glass-doored cabinets lined the walls, housing leather-bound volumes, bowls, jars of dried herbs and plants, glassware one expected to find at a chemist's, and an assortment of jagged crystals. Unlike Immanuel's desk at the museum, there wasn't a single paper out of order, only a bowl of succulents sitting on the far corner. As the sun emerged from behind the clouds, its rays hit a brass umbrella stand filled with long-stemmed parasols, momentarily blinding him.

"Please, take a seat, Mr. Winter."

Sitting stiffly in the sparse wooden chair at the end of her desk, Immanuel fidgeted. "Is everything all right? Miss Ashwood seemed upset."

"We had a visitor last night who came bearing some alarming news."

"I hope it wasn't anything too serious."

"Its gravity is yet to be seen. It does involve you, though, and what I wanted to speak with you about."

Immanuel chewed on the inside of his cheek. "Miss Elliott, I don't mean to be forward, but am I in trouble? If you've invited me to tell me I have broken some," he hesitated saying the word, "*magical* law, please tell me."

"No, Mr. Winter, you would have to do something very grave to end up on the wrong side of magical laws. You seem sensible enough and nervous enough to not trifle with dark magic. What I wanted to talk about has to do with our discussion yesterday. I sensed that you haven't told your Mr. Fenice about your abilities."

"Mr. Fenice is my friend, but—" The words caught in his throat at the sight of her cocked eyebrow and incredulous frown. His pulse quickened with silent panic. She knew. When she probed his mind to discover his abilities, she had found him and Adam interlaced, the sheets falling away as their bodies breathed as one. Had she invited him to discuss blackmail?

Upon seeing his wide eyes, she added, "Mr. Winter, you have nothing to fear here. Practioners have a different outlook on life than most. We have been a hunted group for hundreds—if not thousands—of years and only now are we beginning to gain acceptance again, at least in certain circles. We don't tend to persecute others who are feared and hated by those who would happily see us burn. You may get some backhanded nastiness or the occasional disapproving look but even that is rare here. You would be surprised how easily the queen is willing to overlook a few *eccentricities* when it serves her interests. She did with me and Cassandra."

Questions bubbled through his mind but the only one he could get out was "You and Cassandra are…?"

"Yes, just like you and Mr. Fenice. A Boston marriage, as they call it. Relationships like these are especially supported when the partner acts as an amplifier for a practioner. Much like your Adam, Cassandra isn't a practioner herself. Her talents lie in amplifying my ability to see the truth, and I'm willing to bet your Adam probably does the same for you, whether you know it or not. But that isn't what I wanted to speak to you about. I received a letter from Lord Sumner. Have you heard of him?"

Immanuel shook his head, his eyes wide. It was all so much to take in. "No."

"Lord Sumner is a member of the gentry and a theoretical practioner, meaning he's well-read on magical practices and abilities but does not perform any himself. Past incidents have cured his taste for actual magic, yet he enjoys the social aspect at a place called the Eidolon Club. You get it. Anyway, you must understand that covens are strictly forbidden in England to prevent a magical uprising. Over the last ten years, there has been a rise in magical groups that are reminiscent of a coven, such as the spiritualist societies, social clubs, secret orders, a few rather ambitious knitting circles, but they are disguised as religious or social organizations, which are perfectly legal. You would be amazed where they crop up. Her Majesty, in her absence, has allowed these societies to flourish, creating new issues for us to tackle."

Leaning close, Immanuel whispered, "Who is *us?*"

"You needn't whisper, Mr. Winter, you're already here. I'm a member of Her Majesty's Interceptors. We're a bit like the Home Office or Scotland Yard, but our domain is the extranormal. We investigate strange species, locations with magical phenomenon, and stop practioners from getting involved in dark magic."

"That— that sounds like a difficult job." How could he even say that? He shouldn't believe her. It couldn't possibly be true.

"But it is," Judith replied with a bright grin. "Even after all of your recent revelations, you still don't believe? Well, we can discuss my employment later, but we have much more pressing matters." Clearing her throat, she swept a blonde lock behind her eat and straightened. "Lord Sumner sent us a letter to warn us about a few members of his club getting into some… *darker* practices. Did you see the article in *The Daily Telegraph* a few weeks ago about the tomb that was broken into in Highgate?"

"I believe so. Scotland Yard said it was a grave robbery."

"That would be the one. Apparently, they did break into the Duke of Dover's tomb that night. The duke was known to us as a keeper of relics, and Lord Sumner suggests that the aforementioned members were the ones who broke in and desecrated the corpse in order to divine information."

Immanuel swallowed against the growing knot in his throat. His mind lapsed to dark rooms where corpses bloat until their features are distorted to the point of mutilation. The odor of rot overpowered his senses until his body was overtaken. He stared at the umbrella stand, hoping the bit of bile would settle before he spoke.

"Desecrating how?"

"Bone-conjuring. You asked about darker magic, well that's it. Bone-conjuring is a very old practice and one that is frowned upon. Anything that requires body parts isn't held in high regard."

"But why would he write to tell you about something like this? Wouldn't he fear being implicated as well?"

"He could, but as with Scotland Yard cases, we tend to reward those who help us. He didn't really turn to us to protect the world from dark witchcraft, it's because he doesn't like the grave-robbing riffraff that's now involved with his club. The Eidolon Club has been around since King George. It was where men of science and magic could speak freely, but even back then, it was mostly alchemists and theoretical practioners of nobility, so their approach to magic was respectfully hands-off until now. Lord Sumner would like us to deal with this problem for him while he sips bourbon and reads Pseudo-Geber on his country estate."

"What does this have to do with me?"

"I will get to that in a moment. Cassandra discovered that what they sought was a book—a very powerful spell book—that allows the possessor to interact with certain realms in the spirit world and manipulate the body and soul. Cassandra thought it was safe with our mutual acquaintance Miss Emmeline Jardine, but we found out yesterday that she turned it over to some very questionable members of the Eidolon Club, namely Lady Claudia Leopold Rose and her nephew, Lord Cecil Hale."

Immanuel's heart thundered in his ears. He knew that name. He had seen it scrawled on a sliver of burnt paper sitting in Adam's palm. They had found it months ago in the hell where he had been held captive, but he could never forget that day. His eyes trailed to the sun setting in the gardens behind Judith's head. Her brassy hair glowed red and her cheekbones stood in stark shadows in the waning light, yet what caught his attention was the man crossing the lawns. He stood close enough to watch the front door but out of sight of most passersby. Feeling Immanuel's gaze upon him, he looked up toward the upper windows, but Immanuel leaned back until he could no longer see him. What had Emmeline done?

"You know them?"

"Yes, I know Emmeline well, but no, not the others. The woman, I've heard her name before. I think she may have been married to the man who kidnapped and tortured me. Lord Rose is the man who—" Immanuel stopped, his voice trailing off as the man outside drew so close he disappeared out of view.

Watching his gaze, Judith turned. "What are you looking at?"

Immanuel reached into his bag and cradled the vivalabe in his palm. Pressing the button, the lid popped open to reveal a confused jumble of colored balls rushing in every direction while the white one sat perfectly still. A cracked grey ball steadily traveled along the brass curve before coming to rest a finger width from the white.

"That man, I think he's a… I can't remember what you called it."

"A revenant?"

"That's it. He can't steal a body himself, can he? She must have helped him." He swallowed hard, watching the grey ball pace around the perimeter. Gaols, filth, pain. It would never end. "He's waiting for me to leave or he's inside. I can't tell. I don't know what I'm going to do. He won't stop until I'm dead or he gets the vivalabe or both. How did he even find me?"

He turned to Judith, his mismatched eyes wide. "Is there a way I can sneak out?"

"Not really. Even if we did, he will only follow you home. I'm surprised he hasn't already broken in."

Immanuel stared guiltily at his lap, watching the orb move from the corner of his eye. "I— I put protection symbols on the entrances and windows."

"Really? What did you use?"

"This."

Dipping into his satchel, he pulled out his sketchpad and flipped to his pages of half-conceived symbols. She looked between Immanuel and the final symbol sketched in pencil, her brows furrowed in concentration. He fished around his bag for the slim leather journal and carefully turned to the page where he found the first sigil.

"My mother sent this to me. I decided to make my own. It's exhausting, but I think it worked better than the original."

"There's one way to tell." From the side drawer of her desk, she retrieved a silver lighter. With a quick flick, it sprung aflame. Carefully holding the page with the lone sigil, she applied the lighter. Flames danced and stretched across the page, but it remained unblemished. A satisfied grin spread across her face as she met his gaze. "Mr. Winter, you are just full of surprises. I have a proposition for you. I know how we can get rid of your revenant."

"How? I'll do anything."

"We must fight."

"Fight?" he coughed. "You didn't see him at the museum. That thing wouldn't die. If I kill him, won't he come back to life again?"

Miss Elliott pulled a naginata from behind her door. The long bamboo pole came to the top of her head while the gleaming blade stood two feet above her. Easily swinging it across her shoulder, she reached into the umbrella stand. From the bottom, she fished a black sheathed dagger, which she carefully tethered to her waist with a silk ribbon.

"You misunderstand me. We aren't going to merely kill him. We're going to sever his soul."

Chapter Twenty-Four
The Revenant

Immanuel's heart pounded as he followed Miss Elliott down an endless series of corridors and locked rooms. His ears popped at the bottom of the sprawling stone stairs. High above him, the stone opened into wide barreled catacombs that must have once belonged to a Roman cistern. For a moment, he feared the sights and smells of his prison would rush upon him and chase away reality, but the basement walls were strung with bright electric bulbs and lined with tapestries of unicorns to hide the cold mortar behind them. Immanuel stayed a step behind her, watching the sheath of Judith's dagger swing against her skirts and the blade of the naginata bob at her shoulder with each step. In his mind's eye, he saw a flash of Peregrine with the crowbar raised high above his head. Was fighting merely a part of the job?

"Is Peregrine Nichols an interceptor, too?" he asked softly, his voice reverberating off the high walls.

"Yes, though his powers are closer to yours than mine." As they neared a pair of metal doors carved with fantastical twisted and knotted beasts, she slowed her pace. "Here we are. The armory."

"Miss Elliott, I know I said this before, but I'm not a fighter. I don't know how to use a weapon other than a foil, and I haven't used one in years."

"Luckily, I can. You won't fight him, but you will finish him. Do you understand?"

Biting his lip, Immanuel nodded. There would be no stopping her, it seemed.

As she touched the iron knob, a barely perceivable ripple of energy passed through the hall, pulling the hair on Immanuel's arms on end. The castle-like tunnel fell away to reveal a vast steel and wood reinforced room complete with thick glass cabinets and locked drawers. A lanky man fit for a saloon sat on a stool behind the counter, carefully polishing a bulky crossbow inscribed with silver Chinese characters. His features reminded Immanuel of someone, yet they were wholly unremarkable. When he blinked, Immanuel swore that his irises had lightened from nearly black to a golden brown and his nose had narrowed. He shook off the strange sensation. It must have been a trick of the light.

"Caldwell, I need you to find the contraption they confiscated from Westminster a few months ago," she called as she rested her weapon against one of the glass cases.

The man stared at her a moment as if waiting for more.

"You know the one I mean. The one in the box."

He nodded before disappearing behind a swinging door without a word. Immanuel waited at her side, drawing in a slow breath to steady his heart. What had he gotten himself into?

The door swung open to reveal Caldwell hefting a wooden box. Placing it on the counter, he unlatched the lid and let it fall back with a clatter. Judith stood on tiptoe to peer into it. As she nodded that it was the correct item, the man pushed a ledger forward for her to sign.

"Take it but leave the box," she said to Immanuel as she filled out a page of forms.

Stepping up to the counter, Immanuel's throat tightened and his body reeled. Every nerve screamed for him to stay away, to bolt out of the room and get as far away from the box as possible. Inside sat a pair of familiar brass and glass lungs that were connected to an electric cord wired with sharp metal fangs. He looked from Judith to Caldwell only to find the latter watching with a curious eye. He had to take it out. He couldn't let them see the fear eating him hollow. Pulling the device from the crate, he tried not to look at it. If he wanted to stay strong, he would have to pretend the metal talons hadn't been thrust into his neck and the trigger pulled.

"Well, put it on."

"I can't."

"What do you mean? Of course you can. Just slip it on your back. The other part goes over your hand like so."

He drew in a trembling breath, his hands shaking as he laid the leather handguard beside the body of the device. "This was his. He murdered people with this. He tried to kill me with it? How can you expect me to use it?"

"There is a certain poetry in killing him with his own device, isn't there, Caldwell?"

The silent man nodded with a faint smile bristling beneath his mustache. Immanuel did a double-take, had that been there the whole time?

Turning to Immanuel, she rested her hands on his arms. He stiffened beneath her grasp, but she didn't let go. "Mr. Winter, we all must do things that scare us, and sometimes we must stoop to the level of our demons in order to destroy them."

Immanuel swallowed hard. What choice did he have? It was either fight Lord Rose or live in fear forever, and there was no way he would give up Adam and the promise of a good life for that wretch. Slipping his arms into the leather straps, he hefted the machine onto his back. He was surprised to find that it was much lighter than he expected. As he flexed his hand, Judith reached behind him and flipped the switch that sent the machine humming to life. It was him or Lord Rose, and he wasn't going to lose.

oe go

Holding the vivalabe ahead of him, Immanuel watched the grey orb grow closer until it came to rest only a sliver from his. His heart pounded in his ears as he clicked it shut and stuffed it deep into his pocket. Lord Rose was on the other side of the wall waiting for him.

Judith stepped closer, laying her hand on his shoulder. "Are you ready? Do you understand the plan?"

I'll never be ready. "I think so. I just hope you're better with a sword than Peregrine was with a crowbar."

A wry smile crossed her lips. "Don't worry about my swordsmanship; I was trained by the best. Now, go, before it gets too dark. Just remember, I'll be right behind you."

Keeping his hand on the doorknob, Immanuel closed his eyes and traced the protection symbol in his mind. If only he had told Adam where he was going before he left.

Immanuel inched open the door to the courtyard, the humid air hitting him like a wet blanket. Gas lamps burned through the thin fog, coating the brick façades in dark shadows while painting the cobbles with a bright sheen. His eyes roamed over the wide arches and sculpted topiaries but saw no one, yet something about the courtyard felt wrong. It was impossibly big. From the outside, there seemed to be barely enough space for a narrow garden, but here, in this bubble in space, a plaza had appeared.

His footsteps echoed as he crossed the stones and waited beneath the lamp. From his vantage point, he could make out the gleam of Judith's naginata where she waited in an arch. As he stepped forward, a boot scuffed in the darkness. Immanuel's breath quickened at the man emerging from the mist. A different beggar, a new body, but the same soul. He would recognize Lord Rose anywhere. Alastair raised his gaze, a crooked grin sluggishly crossing his features as he drew closer. *He's already dead,* he reminded himself.

"What are you doing here?" Immanuel called, surprised at his own boldness. "Why don't you go back to hell where you belong?"

A low chuckle erupted from Lord Rose's shambling form. "Because even the devil didn't want me."

He stopped at the edge of the light, but through the dim fog, Immanuel could make out mottled skin that had already begun to die and how the corner of his mouth hung ineffectively. A scratched machete glinted at his side.

"Did you think you could keep me out forever with your stupid little pictures, boy? Did you really think I wouldn't find—" Alastair's gaze swept over the cords and metal talons wrapped around Immanuel's arm. "You really are a fool."

Immanuel ducked to the left as the man lunged toward him with the knife raised. Before the machete could make contact, a figure burst from the shadows. Judith raised the naginata high above her head, bringing the butt down on Alastair's skull with a sharp crack. He stumbled back, a dark liquid oozing from his scalp that stunk of swamp water. Leveling his gaze to Judith, Lord Rose released a sharp laugh. Even with his eyes upon her, she stood firm, her knees bent and her grip firm on the naginata.

Without warning, he dove toward her. The clang of blades striking echoed through the courtyard. Using the length of the weapon, she kept him as far from her as possible, thwarting his blows with a twist of the pole. Immanuel watched Alastair's undead form in horror. It moved with a quick, unnatural gate, as if the skeleton and muscles no longer worked in harmony. Judith drove him back toward the trees with a series of short slashes of her blade. Alastair took an unsteady step back before making a desperate dive. Judith spun and slid to her knees. The machete embedded in the pole as he forced her down. A groaning cry ripped through the air as she sank, her boots scraping into the mortar of the cobbles. Immanuel's heart thundered in his throat. He ran toward them, swiping the back of Alastair's neck with the electrified metal claws.

The man whipped toward him, and in that brief opening, Judith swung her naginata and cracked him in the temple. The side of his face sunk in a fist-sized dent, but he didn't stop. He swung again, narrowly missing Judith by a breath. Sliding back, she sliced through his free arm. Vomit rose in Immanuel's throat as the limb hit the ground and skidded away. Alastair didn't seem to notice as his attention turned to Immanuel, his unnaturally cloudy eyes locking onto him. He raised his blade to hack into him, but a shriek broke through the night. Judith flew past. The curved metal of her naginata pierced through the revenant as she drove him back, the machete dropping from his hand. Alastair and the naginata's blade slammed into the trunk of a tree. The force of the blow nearly knocked loose her grip, but she held firm, pushing forward until the blade was fully embedded into the bark.

"Winter, do it now! It won't hold him long," Judith cried, locking eyes with Alastair.

A deranged grin accompanied the suck of tissue and muck as he slid his senseless body up the blade, grasping the shaft for leverage. "He wouldn't dare."

Grabbing the dagger at her hip, she drove the blade deep into his chest and pinned him again. He thrashed, his blood-slicked hands slipping up the hilt.

Judith locked eyes with Immanuel, her face red with effort. "Winter, finish him!"

Immanuel shook his head, his body locked in place.

"You're pathetic. Do you really think you can kill me?" Alastair said. The voice wasn't the one Immanuel heard in his nightmares but the tone, the cut, was the same. Those horrid eyes pierced him, burning through him with their unwavering hatred as he worked the dagger loose. "I'll come back again, and this time, I'll make sure you die in the filth like the waste you are. You don't have the gall to kill me, you little sod—"

Before he could get the word out, Immanuel lunged forward, sinking the triad of claws into Alastair's neck. Electricity surged across his back and down his arm, sending the creature's body dancing with convulsions. Bone slapped against metal as wet flesh tore. Alastair locked eyes with him, holding his gaze as what little light he had went out in his eyes. Judith stumbled back breathlessly as she watched Immanuel hold the trigger long after the life had left his body. Laying her hand on his arm, he released the gauntlet. Immanuel stepped back, staring at the corpse slumped against the tree as a sob escaped his lips. He covered his mouth, careful to keep the metal tines tipped with putrid flesh away from his face.

It was over. It was finally over.

Shrugging the machine from his shoulders, he laid it under the ring of lamp light. He twisted open the brass ribs and watched a shadow shimmer within the quartz jar. As he dislodged it from the needle, a face roared at the side before fizzling into motes of dust. Immanuel thrust it aside, the strength seeping from his limbs. The damp cobbles soaked through his trousers as he sank down and watched Judith yank the naginata from the tree and the putrid corpse before severing its head with a sharp slash. Bile rose in Immanuel's throat at the stench emanating from the body. Before he could stop himself, he vomited, grasping the lamppost for support. Wiping his mouth with his handkerchief, he hung his head and closed his eyes. A moment ago, the man had been alive and trying to kill him but now— It all seemed so unreal. If Judith hadn't been there, he would have thought it had all been a trick of his mind.

"It will take days to get the smell out," she muttered under her breath as she stepped over the disarticulated arm and came to Immanuel's side. She patted his shoulder before resting the naginata against the lamppost. "The others should be out soon to clean up our mess. How are you holding up?"

He rubbed his face and eyes. "I don't know. I— I keep thinking. Why couldn't I have figured out all of this before? If I had known I had this ability, that magic was real, maybe— maybe my life could have been different. Maybe I could have gotten out and not— and not—"

Immanuel swallowed down the cry in his throat, hot tears burning the backs of his eyes. Raising his head, Judith's stern form disappeared into the clouded portion of his vision. Maybe that wouldn't have happened if he had been able to save himself.

"This may be hard for you to hear, but sometimes the most horrible circumstances are what bring out our greatness."

"How can you say that?"

"Because it happened to me." Voices rose from the doorway. The thin beam of a torch cut through the evening murk as a pair of men emerged. "Come on, let's go back to my office. I'll have Cassandra make you a cup of coffee before you go home."

"No, I really should go. Adam doesn't know where I am."

"It will only be a moment. I just want to make sure you have your head on straight before you leave. Grab the machine and jar, would you?"

Giving into the numbness, Immanuel gathered the pieces of the machine, careful to avoid the dismembered body only feet away. He couldn't bear seeing the horrors of the man's final moments. Climbing the steps behind Judith, he watched in silence as she handed off her weapon to the silent Caldwell, who waited inside the door. With his other hand, he took the soul-stealing device, but when he reached for the quartz jar, Immanuel held it tight to his chest and turned away. He wanted to be as far from Lord Rose as possible, yet he couldn't turn him over, not yet. Judith whispered something to the strange man, and he strode down the hall without looking back. As they entered a set of well-lit corridors, men and women rushed past, heading down to the courtyard. They stared at Immanuel a little longer now, but he averted their gazes, not wanting to know what they saw when they looked at him. He wasn't one of them, he wasn't a member of their ranks. He was merely an outsider who possessed a power he couldn't even control. A man consumed by fear beneath the surface.

At the top of the tower, Cassandra stood waiting for them. Her face was ashen against her dark hair, but when she saw them emerge from the narrow staircase unscathed, her features brightened.

"Cassie, would you please find a cup of something hot for Mr. Winter? Something to steady his nerves."

She nodded and disappeared into one of the closed rooms. Sinking into the chair at the end of the desk, Immanuel finally relinquished his hold on the jar and sat it far from him. Lord Rose's black soul darted from edge to edge as if looking for a means of escape, lingering at the side where Immanuel sat. Miss Elliott perched on the corner of her desk, regarding Immanuel with narrowed eyes until her face broke into a smile upon seeing Cassandra return with a tray. She poured each of them a cup of thick, dark coffee before joining her partner on the desk. Immanuel took the offered cup, holding it far enough from his nose that his stomach didn't churn at the smell.

"What will they do with him? Will he be somewhere far from people so he can't escape?" Immanuel asked as he feigned taking a sip of scalding coffee.

"Have you heard of the legend of King Solomon and the djinn? No? Well, you use his method for troublesome creatures. Lord Rose's jar will be sealed with lead, sequestered in a locked box, and put in a vault where he will never see the light of day again. You needn't worry that he'll escape. Even if his jar breaks, the lead will hold him in."

"Are you feeling any better?" Cassandra asked, watching him take a sip with a wince.

"Much better, thank you."

"Now that you're a bit more steady, I must warn you that Lady Rose may come after you," Judith began cautiously. "She no longer has her revenant to do her bidding and she still needs the vivalabe. You need to be careful. Unlike Alastair Rose, she has no feelings attached to you, which will make you that much easier to dispose of."

Immanuel swallowed hard, the cup clinking against its saucer.

"You'll need to be especially careful this coming week."

"Why?"

"Oh, I never did get to the point before, did I? We aren't completely certain what, but Lady Rose and the Eidolon Club are planning a powerful ritual, an evocation. A ritual of this scale can only occur on a day when our world and the spirit world line up. The next time that happens is the summer solstice."

"The solstice is this Wednesday. *Mein Gott.*" Immanuel's eyes widened as the realization wrung the air from his lungs. "So is the museum gala."

Chapter Twenty-Five
Ruined Plans

Emmeline stared out the window, her head resting on the cool wood of the sill. Below, people passed along Wimpole Street unaware of ghosts or demons or the realm that lay just beyond their field of vision. Her head still pounded from the brew Claudia had given her, but that wasn't what bothered her. After her argument with Cassandra, she had begrudgingly slept the night on the sofa with the spare nightgown carefully folded on the end table. At the first sound of Cassandra and Judith stirring, Emmeline gathered her purse and disappeared out the front door. On the walk home, she braced herself for the tirade her aunt would deservedly unleash on her, but when she opened the front door, Aunt Eliza barely glanced up from the newspaper.

"Aren't you going to ask where I've been all night?" Emmeline asked from the doorway, her voice tighter than she had expected it to be.

"No, it's time I let go. You were right. I must trust that you can make the right decision. Is there a reason for me to be worried?"

"No." What had Eliza thought when she saw her come in with her hair a wild mess, her dress from the night before crinkled, and her eyes bloodshot? Anger and sadness welled in her throat as a knot of spite. She wouldn't let anyone think the worst of her. "If you must know, I fell ill and spent the night at Cassandra's. That's all."

Emmeline bolted up the stairs and slammed the door behind her as a cry worked from her throat. How could anyone care for her after what she had done? She lost her best friend and alienated her aunt, her only allies, within the same day. Up in her room, she lay staring at the ceiling, half dozing in hopes that the tears and anger would conjure a solution. Hours later, when, the sun had grown hot against her cheek and blazed through her closed lids, she blindly groped under her mattress for the grimoire. Remembering it was no longer there, she fell back onto the mattress. She wished she had understood what the *Corpus Grimoire* contained before her initiation. Maybe then she could have understood why what she did was supposedly wrong. Cassandra knew but hadn't given a reason. *Why?Why had she kept it from her?* her mind screamed. Had Cassandra thought she was protecting her? From what? She buried her head in the pillow and closed her eyes, pulled into an escapist sleep. When she awoke in the evening, her neck had grown so stiff that she could barely move. Rising, she crossed the room and pulled the stool from her vanity in to the window. Her stomach growled and her hands shook, but she refused to leave her room. She couldn't bear to face anyone, most of all her own reflection as she crossed the boards.

No one had visited her. No one had even questioned her or lectured her. No one cared enough to do so. Raising her eyes to the window, she watched a steamer roll down Wimpole Street, its passage only remarkable in its hesitation. A hired cab would barrel down the street and throw it in reverse if it missed its mark, but as the steamer neared the house, Emmeline could make out a vibrant coat of arms painted on the door. It seemed so familiar with its twisting dragon and crescent moon. Her heart thundered as cold sweat broke across her back. What was he doing here? Below, Lord Hale's driver opened the door and he swept out of his steamer. His auburn hair rustled in the warm breeze as he looked up but didn't see her. Emmeline forced open the window and stuck her head out as far as she could manage without falling.

"Lord Hale! Lord Hale, up here!" she cried, keeping her voice low but sharp.

He paused, looking up and down the street for the source of the voice before continuing toward the front door. Emmeline gritted her teeth. That man would ruin everything if he came to confess what had happened the night before to her aunt and uncle. She had salvaged whatever dignity she had left in Eliza Hawthorne's eyes, and he was not going to undo her lies with a noble conscience. Quickly slipping into a clean gown, she brushed out her hair, not caring as her ringlets turned into an unruly poof. She had to get down there and weave a tale that knit their versions of the previous night together. Racing down both flights of stairs, she rounded the corner to find the front parlor empty. Glancing out the front window, she found the steamer still idling across the street, but Lord Hale was nowhere to be seen.

"If it's Lord Hale you're looking for, he's up in the study with your uncle."

Emmeline turned to see her aunt watching her from the steps, her face set in a cultivated coolness.

"I didn't invite him," Emmeline replied quietly. "Did he say what he wants to discuss with Uncle James?"

"No. All he said was it was important and that he had to speak to him as soon as possible. Should I be worried, Emmeline?"

"No! Why do you keep saying that?"

Eliza ignored her, slipping past her to don her cloak and gloves at the door. "I'm going to the bank to open an account for you. If you would like your independence, then you shall have it. Though I doubt it will be for long."

Emmeline stared at her aunt with furrowed brows as Eliza stiffly excused herself and left. She stared at the door, unable to tell if she had destroyed what little remained of their relationship or if her aunt was learning to respect her, no matter how begrudgingly. Padding up the steps, Emmeline lingered outside the shut study door, but all she could make out were muffled voices and the occasional word. Her body ran cold as she retreated to the front parlor to wait for the verdict. Even if Cecil contradicted her, Uncle James probably wouldn't even look at her, let alone punish her. It wouldn't be until Aunt Eliza returned that she would learn of her fate. Emmeline's stomach churned, pulling and deepening as if fear had carved a void within her. Curling up in the corner of the sofa, Emmeline snatched her half-finished embroidery from the sewing basket beside it and applied herself to stabbing the minute stitches into the linen. No matter how much she tried to shut out the faint repartee of voices upstairs, the knots refused to leave her stomach.

If only her mother was alive. Her mother would have loved her no matter what she did, no matter how much of a disappointment she turned out to be. She wouldn't have treated her like unworkable clay. She would have sat her down the moment she saw a sign of distress and asked her what the matter was, and Emmeline would have told her everything. She would have told her mother about Cassandra and Lord Hale and the Eidolon Club and the book. Her mother would have known what to do and would have kept them both safe. But that was impossible now.

Emmeline snapped from her reverie, pawing at her moist cheeks as the study door squealed open. Boot-treads too slow and steady to be her uncle's clopped down the steps, pausing at the parlor doorway. Without looking, she knew who it was, and more than anything, she wanted to bolt from the room and escape Lord Hale's lingering gaze. She didn't want to see her uncle's reaction written on his face, and she certainly didn't want him to see what the initiation had done to her, how she had unraveled from the inside out. When she finally turned to face him, she was shocked to find Lord Hale grinning affectionately at her.

"Your uncle would like to speak with you."

Drawing close to him so only he could hear, Emmeline asked, "Cecil, did you tell him about last night? What did you say? We need to make sure our stories make sense."

"Last night? Why would I talk to him about that?" he replied with an ochre brow cocked in confusion. "No, I came to— I shouldn't say anything until you have spoken with your uncle."

Emmeline stared into the nobleman's eyes. Behind their somber, cultivated exterior was a gleam of joy, which only worsened the pit in her stomach. Her mind raced to concoct an explanation for not returning until the next morning. At the top of the steps, she paused, putting on her widest, wettest eyes, which, under the circumstances, wasn't hard to do. In his study, James Hawthorne sat at his desk, his ink-stained hands clicking across the keys of his typewriter. Emmeline crinkled her nose at the faint smell of formaldehyde and rot. She hated his office with its shelves of bloated specimens and bowler hat-wearing skeleton in the corner. If she looked closely any given day, she could spot gruesome postmortem photographs strewn between autopsy notes so detailed she could vividly picture every wound and body as if they were her own.

Without looking up from his notes, James said, "Come in, Emmeline, and close the door."

Doing as she was bid, Emmeline shut the door behind her and sat in the hard chair at the other side of his desk, locking eyes with the mummified head on the shelf behind her uncle. On the desk were two glasses. The one closest to her had been drained while her uncle's retained a thin layer of what looked like port.

"Your mother and grandmother would be proud of you for securing the affections of a noble as esteemed as Lord Hale."

"I beg your pardon?" she choked, her mind stumbling over her half-formed excuses.

"Lord Hale came to ask me for your hand in marriage."

Emmeline's eyes widened. Her corset suddenly felt unbearably tight as the heat rose in her cheeks and her fear dissolved into butterflies.

"I said I would give my blessing on the condition that I spoke to you first. This is a commitment that shouldn't be taken lightly. Marriage brings two lives together irrevocably, and I need to know you and Lord Hale are in accord with your feelings. No matter what anyone says, a marriage devoid of love is not something one can easily stomach." James paused to wipe his glasses with his handkerchief. When he replaced them, he locked gazes with Emmeline. His dark eyes darted over her features as if truly seeing them for the first time. "You look so much like your mother when she was your age. Madeline of all people would tell you how hard a loveless marriage can be. Archibald Jardine wasn't exactly her first choice, but he was the practical choice. Practical choices aren't always the right ones."

He sighed, leaning forward on his elbows. "What I'm getting at is, before you speak with him, I want to know how you honestly feel about Lord Hale. If you don't love him, I can send him away. You needn't feel pressured by an unwanted advance. Now, tell me, do you think you love him or is he merely the most pragmatic option?"

"Both," Emmeline replied without a moment's hesitation. "Against hope, I have wished for this, even if I thought him out of my reach."

"Very well. You may go and see your beau. Tell him, I have given my blessing."

With a wave of his hand, she was dismissed, and he returned to his typewriter and notes. A wide grin broke across her features as she resisted the urge to rush down the stairs and leap into Lord Hale's arms. Her legs shook with each measured step until she and Lord Hale stood face-to-face. She needn't say anything. The brightness in her features told him all he needed to know, and he dropped to one knee. Staring down at him as he pulled a box from his pocket and met her gaze with joyous hazel eyes, she found no trace of the darkness Claudia warned her of.

"Emmeline Jardine, would you do me the honor of being my wife?"

She nodded, words escaping her as she flung her arms around his neck and drew him in for a kiss. He stumbled back, catching her mouth and waist in the same motion. Heat rose through his form at the brush of her lips on his and her fingers creeping along his neck and cheek. Drawing back, he found her sitting on his outstretched knee with her arms around his neck and her forehead resting against his. With unsteady hands, he pulled the ruby ring from its box and slid it up her finger. The gem glinted in the light as she inspected her hand.

Drawing in a tense breath, he stifled an anxious laugh. He leaned in close as he said barely above a whisper, "You have made me the happiest man, Emmeline. We will be unstoppable together, and with our combined lineages, we could create a dynasty of practioners the likes London has never seen."

"My mother would have liked you. Cunning, handsome, and with a title. Best of all, you're obviously very brilliant."

He looked at her strangely, but then a wan smile crossed his lips. "And why am I suddenly so brilliant?"

"Because you picked me, of course."

Chuckling, he helped her to her feet and placed a kiss above her brows. "I hate to leave so soon, but Aunt Claudia is waiting for me to return. She has something she wants me to do before nightfall."

"I understand. I do hope we will see each other soon."

"Actually, I was going to ask if you would like to accompany me to the Natural History Museum's gala. Now that we're engaged, no one should complain when I hog your attention."

"I would like that very much."

"Wednesday, then. I'll meet you there."

He bent down, placing a soft reverent kiss on her lips. When he pulled away, Emmeline could make out the unmistakable coil of fear within his eyes, but his face softened before lapsing into stony sobriety as he slipped out.

Emmeline closed her eyes and bit her lip with glee. Lord Hale wanted her. He *loved* her, and soon, she would be Lady Hale. A lady with a handsome husband, multiple houses, and staff to keep her company until they had children. She would never be lonely again.

The boards creaked behind her as she gathered her wits and smothered her mirth to an acceptable level. James regarded her blandly as he turned down the hall to descend into his basement laboratory. At the threshold he stopped and looked back at his niece.

"It's strange that it should be Lord Hale. I thought we were done with Lord Rose and his ilk, but at least Lord Hales seems to be of different stock."

"Lord— Lord Rose's ilk, what do you mean?"

"Charles Leopold, the one who passed the London Spiritualist Society to Lord Rose, had a daughter who married a Lord Hale. He must have been your fiancé's father."

With a shrug James disappeared into the shadows. Emmeline's lungs tightened as she stared at the blood-red stone on her finger. *Lord Rose's ilk.*

Chapter Twenty-Six
By Invitation

Immanuel kept his head down, his eyes scanning the words typed in rickety letters without reading them. His gaze flickered to the open door across the hall where vines trailed over nearly every surface and poked out the door as if looking for their owner. Peregrine had been gone nearly all day. Immanuel had seen him in the morning when he first arrived, talking heatedly to Sir William but hadn't seen him since. His gut gnarled when he added the hours and realized how long Peregrine had been gone. Immanuel's mind raced to half a dozen horrible possibilities. What if he was down in the storeroom dead or maimed while Immanuel sat at his desk pretending to work? It was foolish to think. After all, Lord Rose was gone for good, and it was obvious that Peregrine could hold his own despite his short stature. Immanuel tried to ignore his foolish thoughts, but he knew he had to prove he was alive and well if he wanted to get any work done.

He chewed his lip. If he walked around the museum asking after him, someone would notice. There was only one way to find him quickly. Slipping from his chair, Immanuel closed his door and pulled the vivalabe from his bag. With a click, it sprung open and the marble and stone balls rolled away. Most stayed locked in their places, but the green ball sprang to life and set off across the etched grid. Immanuel stared down at the vivalabe, trying to match it to his hazy mental map of the museum's many halls and alcoves. When the ball stopped not far from his own, he knew he had to be below him in the hall reserved for the *New Ancient Flora and Fauna Exhibit*. Stuffing the vivalabe into his pocket, he snuck out of his office and darted down the stairs.

Pushing past clusters of patrons milling around stuffed specimens of lions and bears, Immanuel spotted the wooden doors leading to the new exhibit with their polished wood and red-lettered sign that read *Museum Employees Only*. Despite being inside the secret ancient flora and fauna exhibit nearly every day, seeing the sign and knowing he could go inside unimpeded still set Immanuel's heart aflutter with the fear he would be caught. He was an imposter, an invader, and part of him still worried he would be discovered.

In the exhibit's main hall, Immanuel slowed his pace. Hugging the wall, he kept his face downcast as he passed Sir William Henry Flower barking orders at curators' assistants and a few men he recognized from the loading dock. If he caught Sir William's eye, there was no telling what task he would be given and he needed to find Peregrine. Immanuel wandered away from the main hall only to find walls of specimens carefully hung and mounted, their cards tacked beside them. Stopping before a cabinet of dried seeds of ranging from minute sprigs to heart-shaped pods, a smile spread across his lips. He had written the information for them. It was strange to see his work amount to something. In the days he had been absent from the museum, the exhibit had gone from crates and stacks of research notes to an exhibit worthy of an educated audience. Part of him wished he could have been there to help.

He followed the trail of specimens until he reached a dead-end hall lined with shadow boxes of leaves from all corners of the globe. At the end, Peregrine Nichols stood in front of an upturned tree stump the size of a steamer. The petite curator stared up at it, his mouth agape and his head shaking. Muttering under his breath, he dipped a rag in wood polish and stood on tiptoe to apply it to the edge of the massive stump.

"Peregrine, I—"

"Look what they sent me! Look at this thing. What am I supposed to do with this? Bloody Americans decided to make an endowment only days before the gala. Now I'm supposed to count tree rings until I turn blue. Do you know how long that'll take? All bloody day, that's how long!"

Immanuel swallowed hard, watching the shorter man muttered again as he wiped the oily spot where he had attempted to polish the wood. "Do you need any help? I can't reach the top, but I can do something."

"You aren't busy?" When Immanuel shook his head, Peregrine hooked his thumb toward a bucket of polish and the pile of rags behind him. "What are you doing down here? Didn't Sir William leave you with a stack of cards to quadruple check?"

"He did, but I've read them so much I can't bear to look at them again. They're fine. I actually came down to speak with you."

"Oh?" Peregrine raised an eyebrow, casting Immanuel a glance as he easily reached far above his head but recoiled with a grimace. "Side still hurting?"

"It's healing," Immanuel winced. Dropping his voice, he stepped closer until their arms nearly touched. "Have you spoken to Miss Elliott since we met?"

"Not really. Why?"

"Yesterday, I stopped by her office, and we got to talking. She thinks the Eidolon Club might be planning something for the night of the gala."

Keeping one eye on Sir William, he told Peregrine the story of the battle with the revenant, the spell book and the powerful ritual the Eidolon Club might attempt. Peregrine released a low whistle and shook his head.

"Fantastic. Just what we need: a bunch of radical practioners trying to summon god knows what *and* the director breathing down our necks. Elliott better be on top of this because I'm not. I can't not attend the gala."

"Do— do you think anything will happen at the gala?"

"Do I think they'll hold a ritual in the middle of the great hall? No."

"But they supposedly need the vivalabe, and they only have two days to get it. Unless they catch me between now and then, the gala would be the best place to steal it." Immanuel swallowed hard but snapped to attention when he realized he was drawing a sigil across the wood's grain.

"Did you ask Elliott if Lady Rose will be there?"

"No, but I have this sinking feeling that something is going to happen."

"Of course you do. You were knifed in the storeroom. I would be punchy too. Look, if you're so worried, why don't you look at the guest list and see if Lady Rose is on it?"

"Where is it?"

"In Sir William's office."

⁕

Immanuel held his breath as he stood next to Sir William Henry Flower's office door. His heart pounded in his ears, but it couldn't drown out his own reservations. He could get caught. He could get fired, but he could get killed if he didn't know who would be at the gala. Watching a flock of white-haired curators and benefactors pass, Immanuel smiled and nodded a greeting as he pretended to give his exhibit notes one last look. The moment they were out of sight, Immanuel ducked inside Sir William's office. Standing with his back resting against the molding, he exhaled a slow, silent breath. The room was as imposing as its owner with hulking dark wood on every surface and windows with their curtains drawn to cast the room in a somber grey gloom. Sir William's heavy desk was flanked with stacks of papers in neat piles precisely squared and set an equal distance apart. Immanuel quickly rifled through the piles, feeling exposed in front of the door's blurred glass. If someone saw him— He banished the thought as he tidied the papers and turned his attention to the drawers on either side of Sir William's great leather chair.

Rooting through the first one, Immanuel found financial reports, copies of employee files, and a large tin of Palmer biscuits. He shoved it shut with a huff, but as he opened the next, his eyes lit up. A copy of the gala invitation stared up at him, covered in etchings of a primordial forest framing bold letters that announced the grand event. Beneath it, he found the menu along with a series of names and addresses. His eyes trailed down the names, flipping the pages until he found Miss Judith Elliott, Miss Cassandra Ashwood, the Earl and Countess of Dorset, and on the final page, Lady Claudia Leopold Rose. Immanuel sat back, his mouth dry and his pulse rattling the vessels on his neck with each beat. All those names... None of them had any idea of what was to transpire. Worst of all, Adam and the people he loved would be there. If they couldn't get the vivalabe from him, would they hurt Adam instead?

As he carefully replaced the papers and stood to leave, a shadow fell across the door's frosted glass. Immanuel looked at the desk and the narrow space behind the chair but knew he would be found the moment the director went to sit. His heart thundered with panic. There was nowhere else to hide. The doorknob whined, but by the time the door fell open, Immanuel stood behind it with his back and cheek flat against the wall.

"Indubitably. The reporters have backed down. They have more scandalous things to talk about. With beheadings and grave robbery, a little murder is mundane."

At the sound of Sir William's voice, Immanuel's body locked and his eyes clenched tighter. He flattened against the wall paper, hoping he could disappear into it as the director pushed the door toward his chest.

"Yes, sir. Right, sir."

Peregrine! Immanuel's mind cried.

"Do you have a moment? I really need to show you something in my office."

"Not now, Nichols. I have a meeting to attend."

The door jerked forward as Immanuel slid out and braced himself for a solid hit and subsequent discovery, but the door hovered an inch from his face.

"Wait! Sir William, I heard Dr. Quinn calling for you."

"Quinn? What does he want now?"

The director released the knob and pulled the door shut behind him. Immanuel released a tremulous exhalation as his energy drained from his limbs, leaving his legs weak and his hands clammy. The moment Sir William disappeared around the bend, Peregrine poked his head in and waved for him to come out. Casting a glance in either direction, Immanuel darted out to stand at Peregrine's side. He drew in a tremulous breath, hoping the flush would leave his cheeks. The moment his heart calmed, he looked up in time to see Sir William return, his brows arched in confusion at the two men lingering outside his door.

"Quinn must have gone out." Seeing it was Immanuel, the director released a huff and reached for the door. "You too, Winter? What is it you want? Get on with it. I still have the press to deal with because of you two."

Immanuel reached into his jacket and handed over a pile of typed notecards. "I finished the exhibit cards you asked for, sir. I figured you would want to give them your final approval. Nichols, would you come to my office? I have a question about a certain botanical specimen."

The director watched them as Immanuel and Peregrine turned on heel. Out of Sir William's sight, Immanuel released a tense breath the second he could. He had gotten away with it. He couldn't believe he had done it.

As they reached the wide hall of offices, Peregrine cast a glance over his shoulder and asked softly, "So, what's the verdict?"

"I think we're in grave trouble."

Chapter Twenty-Seven
The Memory of Bones

Peregrine's reassurances of his safety did little to put Immanuel's mind at ease. Though he had seen the amount of strength hidden within the botany curator's small frame, Immanuel couldn't help but think it would prove useless against someone like Lady Rose. Staring at his stack of notes, his left eye blurred. Immanuel futilely wiped at it, but the smudge in his vision stubbornly remained. He released a frustrated sigh and closed his eyes. Lord Rose had been a cruel, ruthless man, and she had married him. *A wife.* It was hard to picture the man in the devil mask standing at the altar promising to love and cherish anything. He couldn't help but wonder if she, too, suffered from his cruelty. If she was anything like him, he didn't stand a chance.

A light knock rattled the glass of his door, and when Immanuel looked up, he found Peregrine Nichols slipping inside. The little man's eyes ran over him, lingering on his face before sliding along the contents of his desk. Immanuel mustered up a neutral expression, but even he knew it was a wasted effort.

"Still fretting about the gala?"

Staring down at his ink-stained hands, Immanuel nodded.

"I can't say I blame you. I don't know much about Lady Rose, but you seem to. Look, you need to just keep your wits about you. I'm going to stop by Interceptor headquarters and catch Elliott before she leaves. I'll tell her what you found about the gala invitations."

"Thanks. Let me know if she has any advice or if there is a plan of some sort. I can only imagine the Interceptors would do something to stop her."

Peregrine shrugged, picking up a jar of seashells from the nearest bookshelf. "It's hard when you don't know what they're planning. I mean, if there were more people involved, it would be easier. Someone always talks, but with a cabal this small, who knows. They were lucky Sumner said anything. It must be unsavory if a man like him is willing to tarnish his reputation by admitting he even knew of it."

"But what do *we* do about it? If they're coming to the gala to— to do something, shouldn't we be prepared?"

"*We* will figure out a plan. *You* will stay out of it," Peregrine said, his voice sharper than Immanuel had ever heard it.

Immanuel rose from his chair, dwarfing Peregrine as he cried in a harsh whisper, "How can I stay out of it when they're after me? *Mein Gott!* They have tried to kill me twice, and you tell me to stay out of it. Do you expect me to sit here waiting for them to come after me and the vivalabe?"

"Look, Mr. Winter, I get it, but you are a fledgling practioner and nothing more. You have never dealt with something like this. The best thing to do would be to lay low and let us sort it out. The Interceptors will deal with Lady Rose, trust me."

"If you wanted me out of it, then you need to let me know what danger I'm in. Miss Elliott was kind enough not to spare me or give me the brush off."

Or was that why Peregrine wanted him to keep out? Because Miss Elliott had confided in Immanuel before discussing the Eidolon Club's plans with him. Immanuel locked eyes with Peregrine. His annoyance was obvious in his straight brows and deadpan stare, but Immanuel refused to sit. Finally, Peregrine released a rough breath and shook his head.

"I don't know why you're so insistent about this. You have made it through relatively unscathed thus far."

"I can't expect to be saved by someone else every time."

"Fine, you can borrow this." Reaching into the inner pocket of his purple plaid jacket, Peregrine pulled out a sheathed knife and dropped it on the desk. It was as long as a letter opener but as thin as an icicle. "Give it back after the gala."

Before Immanuel could reply, Peregrine was out the door and gone. Sinking back into his chair, Immanuel sighed. He pushed the stiletto around his piles of paper with the tip of his finger. That wasn't the answer he had expected. He wanted information, not a weapon he could barely wield. Picking it up like it was poisoned, Immanuel dropped the knife into the inner pocket of his coat and pulled the vivalabe from his trousers. He rolled it between his palms. Why did they want it so badly? What did they need to see in the spirit world?

Immanuel scoffed. Magic, the spirit world, practioners, and all under the roof of the Natural History Museum. And what useless ability did he have? Life. He chewed his lip, remembering the feeling of his mind cracking open like a stuck door when Judith probed his mind. That at least was useful. Maybe if he had an ability like that, Peregrine would respect him and appreciate his help, but life... life was useless.

Picking up his pen, Immanuel tried to push all thoughts of magic and nonsense aside. After all, the gala was in two days and he should turn his attention back to his research on the evolution of pinniped anatomy, but his mind had other ideas. His pen flew across the blank page, his mind flickering to bees and flowers, children laughing, his lips on Adam's, the shiver of life, the beating of a heart. He blinked, the trance rapidly lifting. The page had been covered in overlapping spirals infinitely more complex than the protection symbol he had scrawled all over the house. Helices twisted, dividing into forked curves before dissolving into vines of forget-me-nots flowering into a chain. Within the myriad of inky lines were the vague forms of animals and people. A face. An eye. A sacred pattern. This was what life looked like.

Immanuel traced his handiwork with the tip of his finger, feeling the hum of energy growing beneath it. New details emerged with each pass, but as he grinned and raised his gaze to the clock ticking on the opposite wall, he found Sir William's tall, stately figure heading toward his office. Without taking his eyes off the door, he opened his drawer and shoved the paper deep into the tea box of cat bones. Immanuel grabbed his pen and turned his attention back to his book on extinct pinniped species. When a knock sounded and the museum director entered, Immanuel rose to his feet, but Sir William gestured for him to sit back down.

"Are you busy, Winter?"

"Just doing a little research for a paper, sir, on seal evolution," Immanuel replied, hoping the director wouldn't press him for further information.

"Ah, very good." Sir William's hawk eyes sharpened. "Have you, by chance, heard anymore from Scotland Yard about the *incident*?"

"I—" Immanuel paused at the faint sound of scratching near his feet. "I haven't, sir. I assumed the case was closed."

The director nodded, seemingly unaware of the scraping and rapping at their feet, as if a hoard of mice had decided to descend upon his office's floorboards. "Mr. Winter, since you have returned to your usual duties, I would like you to perform a preliminary inspection of all of the gala exhibits tomorrow. I trust you can evaluate each exhibit and specimen for completeness and make a list of any mistakes you find."

Something thumped, but this time, there was no mistaking that it came from his desk. Keeping his eyes locked on the director's, Immanuel replied, "Yes, sir. I'll be sure to do it as soon as I get in tomorrow."

"Very good." Sir William Henry Flower rose to his full height, dwarfing Immanuel as he followed him to the door. At the threshold, he paused at the sound of something thumping and scraping behind them. "Are the pipes always this loud?""

"The pipes? Oh, the pipes." Immanuel released a nervous laugh. "I hardly notice them anymore. I will make sure to inspect the exhibit thoroughly, sir, and report back any issues I find."

With a final disapproving look, Sir William swept out. The moment the director was out of earshot, Immanuel locked the door and cautiously approached the desk. He steeled himself, expecting to find a large rat lurking beneath his shelf or desk, but as he bent down and found nothing, the scratching began anew. Swallowing hard, he grasped the pull and threw open the bottom drawer. Papers slid beneath the tea box, which crashed into the front of the drawer at the sudden motion. Immanuel jumped back as the box rocked on its corners. Something skittered and clunked within it, knocking at its lid. A rat. It had to be a rat, and it was probably nibbling at the sigil he barely had the chance to look at. He hadn't seen the creature when he tossed the paper in, but that didn't mean it wasn't there. Just what he needed after a long, stressful day: a rat eating his notes. Grabbing a heavy tome off his desk, Immanuel squatted beside the drawer, ready to strike if the rodent lunged at him. He drew in a steadying breath and threw open the lid.

The hollow sockets of a bleached cat skull stared back at him within. He leaned closer, looking for the source of the noise when his gaze fell upon a series of jagged claw marks on the lid's underside. As he reached for his paper, which had slipped under the articulated cat skeleton, he froze at the sound of nails clicking. Sitting back on his heels, the breath caught in Immanuel's throat as the cat opened its jaw in a silent hiss. Its vertebrae-spiked back arched and its feet flexed on the edge of the box. Immanuel opened his mouth in a scream but all that came out was a ragged breath. With a shake of its hips, the cat leapt from the box. Immanuel dropped the book and fell back into the shelf. His back ached as he scrambled away from the creature on his hands and knees.

The skeleton cat paced the floor, its sightless sockets sweeping over its surroundings before landing on Immanuel. With each step it took toward him, Immanuel backed up until the only place he could go was on his chair. His heart thundered in his ears as the cat placed its bony feet on the seat and sniffed the air at his loafers. It couldn't be alive. It just couldn't. Immanuel slapped his cheeks. He had to be sleeping at his desk or hallucinating. Maybe his insomnia had finally caught up with him. He had touched the cat's skull and seen its final moments of life, nestled in the previous curator's bed, so maybe it was all a dream.

He watched the cat skulk behind his desk before jumping on top of it. It sniffed his papers and inkwell until finally it stood squarely on his book and flopped onto its side. Cautiously climbing off the chair, Immanuel drew closer. At the bottom of the tea box was the crumpled life sigil. His mismatched eyes ran between the inky figures inscribed on parchment and the skeleton cat who lay on his desk languidly licking its foot with an invisible tongue. Immanuel swallowed hard. This is what life looked like.

"*Mein Gott. Was habe ich getan?*" What had he done?

Slowly approaching the desk, Immanuel bit back his fear. The cat stopped, watching him as its body tensed and its bony tail flipped in warning. He stuck his hand out, letting the cat inspect it. Cold bone bumped against his fingers as it sniffed. Immanuel's eyes locked on the spaces between the bones, searching for strings or mechanisms, anything that could have proved it to be an elaborate hoax, but there was nothing. It was as if the bones knew what they once were. As if within their salts and strands of tissue, they remembered how to strut and stretch as they did in life. With a final nudge of its head, the cat rubbed its naked fangs against the side of his hand before rubbing the length of its body against him like a real cat would. Immanuel bit his lip, his hand hovering over its back as it watched him. *It's just a cat and nothing more*, he reminded himself, running his hand along the cat's spine. At the touch of his hand, the cat looped back for more affection. A small smile crossed Immanuel's lips at a gentle buzzing in the cat's bones. It was purring.

Glancing at the clock near the door, Immanuel watched shadows pass. Everyone was heading home for the day. The skeletal cat nudged his lamp before swatting his pen until it flew off the side of his desk. Immanuel chewed on his lip. There was no way to leave it there. If a maid came in at night to clean, she would surely see it, and if it got out— He would have to take it with him.

It was time. Adam had to know.

Gingerly shutting the door behind him, Immanuel kept his scratched hand tightly on the lid of the tea chest even as the cat thrashed and scratched inside. "Just a few minutes more. I'm sorry," he whispered into the wood.

The front parlor stood empty, but as Immanuel slipped off his shoes and hung his satchel on the coatrack, he listened in the stillness for Adam's tread. In the kitchen, a kettle whistled and the faint melody of a hummed tune broke the stillness. Immanuel lurched forward, keeping his hand clamped on the box. The cat threw its weight into the box's side and nearly jettisoned it from his grasp. He looked from the tea chest to the handsome redhead standing at the stove. How could he ever begin to explain this?

"Adam! Adam, I need you to come here for a moment," he called, his voice dry and tight in his throat.

His companion's concerned gaze ran over Immanuel's form at his tone. "Is everything all right?"

"We have a… a situation."

Placing the box on the floor, he released the lid and the cat sprang out with a graceful pounce. Adam stared at it for a long moment as the skeletal creature pranced across the rug, flexing its claws into the fabric.

"That's rather clever, if not morbid. Is this what you have been working on when you were staying late at work?" Adam craned his neck. "It's fantastic work. You can't even see the gears. Did Hadley help you?"

"Adam, it isn't mechanical."

He looked from Immanuel's tense features to the creature curled up on the floor. "What do you mean?"

"Look." Immanuel carefully picked up the cat. Wrapping his hands around its ribs, he held it close enough that Adam could see the spaces between the cat's ribs and the organ-less hollow beneath it. Immanuel stuck his fingers into them, ignoring the cat as it struggled to kick him away with its hind legs. "No gears. No mechanisms. It's real."

Adam stared at him blankly.

"Adam! It's a *real* skeleton, and it's alive."

He locked eyes with the creature as it opened its mouth in a silent meow. Adam's breath quickened at the void in its throat and sockets when it stared at him. He could practically see its eyes, yet all there was were empty holes of bleached bone. The more he stared, the more horrifying it became. Every crack and fissure stood starkly against the rug, and as it languidly stretched, Adam could see the spaces between its vertebrae expand. He could see right through them.

"What is that thing? What's wrong with it?" he cried, stumbling back into the sofa as the cat padded toward him. It went to rub against his legs, but Adam jumped onto the chair, leaping across the room to the armchair as it scrambled up to follow him. "Is it diseased or something?"

"Adam, it's dead!" Scooping up the cat, Immanuel cradled it against his chest and stroked its smooth skull until it stilled. "See? It isn't bad or evil. It's just dead."

"Why is it moving? Why is it doing that if it's dead?" Adam asked, his eyes wide with fear.

"Because I used magic." Reaching into his pocket, Immanuel held up the folded sigil for life. "I drew a symbol imbued with life, and I put it in the box of bones. The next thing I knew it was alive."

"That isn't possible. Magic— magic isn't real, Immanuel. Things don't come back to life." When the cat began to lick its paw, Adam cried, "This isn't funny. Shut it off."

"Adam, get down and listen to me!" Immanuel snapped. Grabbing

Adam's hand, he put it against the cat's ribs before placing it over his own heart. "He's real. I'm real. And you still won't listen to me. You think I'm going insane, but look at what's right before your eyes. I did this. I brought it to life."

When Adam stared at him shaking his head, Immanuel darted into the kitchen and returned with the vase of wilted flowers wrapped in a towel. Ripping away the tea towel, he grabbed the vase and pictured the flowers as they were when Adam gave them to him. His lover gasped as the heads sprung up and the brown pedals suddenly brightened with color.

"How— how did you do that?" Adam stammered.

Immanuel sighed, setting the vase down on the mantle. "I told you. It's magic."

"Have I gone mad?"

"If you have, then so have I and a lot of other people." Immanuel gently laid his arms on Adam's and coaxed him to come down off the armchair. "I have a lot to explain, but you must believe me. Will you listen and not say a word?"

Adam's eyes flickered between the cat's bare skeleton slinking around the sofa's wooden feet and Immanuel's pained, earnest gaze. Could Immanuel have been right all along? His head hurt. Nothing made sense. Immanuel's long fingers trailed across Adam's cheeks and gently raised his chin until their gazes met. In wordless phrases, a wave of calm passed over him, silencing Adam's screaming brain until the fear came only as a whisper.

"Please, just listen to me. If you love me, you will listen."

After a moment, Adam nodded and let Immanuel lead him to the sofa. Sitting at his side, Immanuel told him everything he should have said long ago. How he saved Emmeline Jardine's life in Oxford with the potion his ancestors made, how he felt his heart stop the moment before she awoke, how he could see the final moments of any creature or person with just a touch of their corpse, how he had seen Lord Rose in the man who attacked him in the museum, how Miss Elliott and the other Interceptors had told him of his magical gifts, and how they feared what ritual Lady Rose and the Eidolon Club might try to perform.

Adam released a tense breath as he scratched his wrist with a wince. The skin had been rubbed raw with each added fact. He swallowed hard, watching as Immanuel pulled the pendant from his shirt and studied the vial filled with forget-me-nots nearly half a year old. How had he not realized it sooner?

"Does it make more sense to you now?" Immanuel asked when he caught Adam watching him.

"Yes. I believe you. I do. At this point, I don't think I have any choice, but you must admit, it's just a lot to swallow."

"I know. Trust me, I had a hard time with it myself. When Miss Elliott forced me to look into myself, I didn't want to believe what I saw. How could my gift be life when my whole life feels like I have been one step from death?"

A hesitant smile, curved Adam's mustache. "Because you have made it through. That I believe. Is that why you seemed so much brighter after they came to visit?"

Immanuel nodded. "It was the strangest thing I had ever heard, but it made me feel less alone, less different." His eyes moistened against his will, but he fought it with a smile. "I have spent a lot of my life feeling like an outsider, and I found more people like me."

"Why didn't you tell me earlier? Why didn't you tell me why they were really there?"

"Because I didn't think you would believe me. If I barely believed them, how could I expect you to? You didn't believe me when I told you about Lord Rose attacking me. I had no proof, and I was afraid you would think I was losing my mind."

Adam sighed, his features falling as he took Immanuel's cut-up hands in his. "I didn't mean to make you feel that way."

"I know, but I was afraid. I love you, Adam, and I thought I would lose you if I told you all of the strange things that were happening. I thought I was going mad, so why wouldn't you? Any reasonable person would. I didn't want you to know about my family's involvement in witchcraft or that when I touch something, I can see its last moments. It's morbid. It isn't normal. And I couldn't bear to lose you if you couldn't handle the truth."

As a wet breath escaped Immanuel's lips, Adam crushed him to his chest. He clung to him, rubbing Immanuel's back with one hand and keeping his head against his cheek with the other. Immanuel shut his eyes, tears of relief trickling from their corners as he drew in Adam's lavender cologne.

"It would take more than a bit of strangeness to chase me away. I love you more than anything." After a long moment, he let him go. "Now that it's out in the open, you must tell me about this magic of yours."

"I will," Immanuel replied softly, wiping his eyes. "I have been playing with symbols and how they can be charged with energy. There are only two I have tried: protection and life. You see what the latter has done."

The cat leapt onto the back of the armchair and stretched across it.

"What about protection?"

He chewed on his lip. "Look at the bottom of your shoe."

Adam's brows furrowed as he crossed his legs. Beneath the dried dirt, he could make out a wavering figure carved into the sole. He released a tense breath, caught between annoyance and flattery.

"I put them all over the doors and windows, too. Seeing Lord Rose made me paranoid. I figured we would be safe if I warded the whole house."

"A sound thought. So, what are we going to do about your little friend? Do you think it will wear off?"

"I have no idea. I could ask Miss Elliott or Peregrine tomorrow, but for now, I think our deceased Siamese needs a name. I wish I knew his real one, but his previous owner never said it."

"What about Oscar?"

Immanuel cocked a blonde brow. "No. I hear enough about him already."

"Fair enough. What about Percy? Percival. Formal but sensible for a cat."

"We can't exactly call him Fluffy, can we?" Immanuel said with a laugh. "Percy it is."

Adam snapped his fingers and clicked his tongue until the cat languidly strolled over. His hand hovered above Percy's meatless back. For a moment, the image of Immanuel months ago flashed through his mind. Skin and bones with nothing but a faint glow of life. He had loved him then, and really Percy wasn't so different. Putting his hand out, he let the cat rub his bare head against the back of his palm. If he looked at him from the edge of his vision, he could almost make out the phantom outline of ears.

"Do you think they remember?"

"They?" Adam asked.

"Bones. Do you think there's something deep in our bones that remembers everything? Our memories, hardships, trauma. Do you think they become a part of us? That one day someone could study our bones and learn all the secrets we strove to hide, or maybe we could rise like Percy, fleshless but in full knowledge of what we were."

Adam looked up to find Immanuel regarding him, his eyes far away.

"Do you think they ever forget?"

Chapter Twenty-Eight
Unseen Complications

"Something is wrong, Cecil. Something has gone horribly wrong," Lady Rose cried as she grabbed a bottle of wine from the service near the window.

Standing in the doorway of her suite at the Eidolon Club, Cecil released an irritable huff and pulled the door shut behind him. What now? All he had wanted was a night with Emmeline away from the Eidolon Club and especially away from his aunt, but a messenger had come knocking at his lodgings before he could even finish his note to Emmeline's uncle. If they were to marry, the Hawthornes should get to know him better, but as he drove to the club, he wondered if he and Emmeline would still be together after the gala. If he was her, he would run upon learning of Lady Rose's plans. He wished he still could.

"What now?"

"Alastair never came back. I don't know where he is."

Her bronze hair sprang from its pins in wild waves while her flushed face glistened with moisture. If he hadn't heard her voice, he wouldn't have recognized her. Even when he rescued her from the asylum, he had never seen her unhinged. Reaching into the trunk at the foot of her bed, Lady Rose retrieved a shallow black bowl and a set of vials. She rushed into the sitting room, spreading her equipment around the bottle of wine. Cecil did a double take at her trembling hands as she poured the wine into the bowl. Drips dotted the lace tablecloth with each slosh of liquid.

"I thought you hated him."

Lady Rose wiped her flushed cheeks and swept the matted hair from her face. "I don't hate him. I need him."

"Are you joking? You don't *need* him. That repulsive man sent you to the madhouse, so he could have dalliances."

"It's complicated, Cecil. You wouldn't understand," she snapped, tipping a bit of each vial into the bowl.

"I don't understand? I understand that he locked up my only living relative and that it took me months to find you after Mother and Father died in the dirigible crash. He made certain no one would find you. What he did… what he did made you like *this*."

"Like what, Cecil?"

His throat tightened as the words he longed to say for months burst out. "You sold me, so you could gain power from some… some creature you can't even see. Do you know how pacts with the devil end? Everyone ends up screwed."

"You know nothing about any of this," she growled, the lights overhead dimming.

"I know you used to be kind to me. I went looking for you because you were like my mother, but not anymore. Did you even think about how tying me to that thing would affect me?"

"I don't recall you fighting when you pledged your life to the Eidolon Club's benefactor. You seemed quite pleased until you realized you might have to make good on your offer."

Cecil clenched his fists so hard his nails bit into his palms. "What do you want with me? I have plans tonight."

Staring deep into the murky water of the bowl, she held her hand up for silence. From her lips came a low chant. The words grew louder and louder, their meaning unintelligible, but he knew she had to be scrying for Alastair Rose. Cecil relaxed his body and mind until the pulse of energy washed over him and through his feet. The only repulse he felt came from his aunt. It was a more than welcome change after feeling the constant suck of the revenant's shadow.

The string of ancient words grew ragged, her voice and face straining with each refrain, until she leapt from her seat. The bowl tipped on its side as she slammed her hands down on the table. Shaking her head, she stared out the window at the waning summer sun as it passed behind the rooftops.

A smirk crossed Cecil's lips. "Perhaps you wore him out. I told you it was too soon to put him in another body."

"He isn't gone!" she cried, her voice rough and foreign. "If I tore him apart, I would know!"

"Maybe he left you again. He was good at that, wasn't he?"

Lady Rose's eyes clouded, darkening until they were nearly black. The chandelier danced overhead, its lights blinking erratically as a weight fell against Cecil's chest. He planted his feet to counteract the futile urge to run, knowing she would never let him get that far. Glass bulbs shattered overhead as Cecil ducked behind the table. Wires sparked in the empty chandelier and the filaments buzzed with excess power. She crossed the rug, energy spiraling around her as she approached him.

"If you don't stop, I'm going to leave." As the porcelain scrying bowl cracked and exploded in a hail of shards, he cried, "Claudia, get a hold of yourself before you kill us both!"

Lady Rose locked eyes with him as she stood over him, the blackness surging deeper, but in an instant, they turned to green as if nothing had been amiss. The pressure receded like the tide, taking with it the room's heat. Cecil exhaled, watching his breath roll out in a puff of condensation. For a moment, he wondered if there had been a reason she spent time in the madhouse after all.

"Did you see anything?" he asked hesitantly as he rose, brushing the glass from his trousers.

"No, but I can feel him somewhere," she finally said. "He's too far. He's beyond my control again."

"Well, what did you do with him? I thought you sent him after the vivalabe again. He couldn't have gone far in that flea-bitten body."

"I don't know. He was following the boy. He was supposed to break in and steal it, but the boy warded the whole house with protection sigils."

"Alastair couldn't just batter through?"

"The boy used blood," she spat as she gathered up the vials and the large shards of glass and dumped them into the bin. "As long as he's alive, the house is sealed."

"He's a practioner?"

"Alastair insisted he wasn't when he previously dealt with him. Then again, he said Miss Jardine was of little consequence and look what's happened. Cecil, the boy knows what happened to him, and I think your little friend has been keeping a secret from us, too. She is more than she lets on." Lady Rose stared at her hand as a bead of blood ran from a cut in her palm. "We shouldn't have brought her in. We should have taken the book by force and been rid of her. We still can."

The hair rose on Cecil's neck at the thought. From across the room, he gave her a look he hoped would strike her dead. "Emmeline is to be my wife, and if you have any love left for me, you will leave her alone."

A cackle escaped Lady Rose's lips. "Of course she is. Never could separate yourself from business, could you? I never should have brought you into this. You're as useless as your uncle."

"I wish you hadn't."

"Well, your little friend would be dead if you didn't. Always remember, you wanted it."

No. No, she lured him. She made him. *She* did it. Grabbing her arm, he growled, "You played on a child's need for protection."

She met his gaze, unflinching. "I played on a man's need for power."

With a twitch of her hand, the air squeezed from his throat. Cecil groped for his neck but found his hands forced to his sides. Her lips twisted into a sharp grin as she drew closer until they stood eye-to-eye. Cecil's body jerked with each failed breath, his eyes widening in alarm. His vision tunneled nearly to pinpricks as his head was forced back by unseen hands. The pressure grew greater until he feared his neck would snap, and in an instant the whole world would go black. A small part of him wished it would.

In a rush, the sensations ripped away and he tumbled forward. Staggering into the table, Cecil gripped the edge and drew in a ragged breath. His neck and chest ached and the world spun around him. Before he could orient himself, Lady Rose grabbed him by the lapels and shoved him against the wall. She brought his face within a breath of hers, her green eyes glowing.

"Get me the boy tomorrow or you and Miss Jardine will pay dearly. Do you understand me? Bring him to me."

"You would have me disrupt our plans for some petty revenge? Have one of your street roughs do it if you want him so badly," he wheezed, his throat raw. "Besides, you should be happy Lord Rose is finally gone. He treated you like dirt. He was dead weight—"

The slap came hard and fast, insulting in its simplicity and pain.

"You will do as I say, do you understand? We need him more than I need you."

"Fine!" He shoved her away, brushing the touch of her hard fingers from his clothes. When he looked down, he found his coat covered in streaks of bright red blood. "I will do it, but you have to leave Emmeline out of this."

"You and I both know that isn't possible. She's as deep in this as you are. Maybe more so, since she is doubly involved."

"What do you mean?"

Lady Rose turned from him, walking into her bedroom without looking back. "Ask her who she shares a blood-bond with."

As the door shut, Cecil's eyes ran over the carnage of blood, glass, and broken wood at his feet. When had his life become this?

Chapter Twenty-Nine
Blood and Lace

Adam grimaced at the ripping, hiccupped sound of Immanuel retching behind the bathroom door. "Are you all right in there?"

"Uh huh," came the faint reply.

Pushing open the door, Adam found his companion kneeling beside the toilet with his arms on the seat holding his head. Adam wetted a washcloth and squatted beside him. With gentle strokes, he wiped away the sweat from Immanuel's cheeks and the tang of bile from his lips, but his companion didn't move. He kept his eyes locked on the floor.

It took everything in Immanuel's power to not think for a few seconds, to not set his mind and heart racing until he could no longer stomach the pace. It was only for Adam that he stopped. If he vomited on Adam's best set of tails or his favorite shoes, he would never forgive himself.

"You don't have to go, you know. We could stay home. They won't be able to get to you or the vivalabe with the wards, right?" Adam asked, shooing Percy away from the open toilet.

Immanuel shut his eyes and rubbed his hand across his pulsing sinuses. "I don't know. Either way, I can't stay here. I only think they need the vivalabe, but if they don't, something horrible could still happen. There are only a few of us who know, and— and— I can't let your sister and the Earl go there without any idea of the danger they might be in. I *have* to go."

"That and you're afraid Sir William will sack you."

"That's the last thing on my mind right now."

He inhaled slowly, fighting the urge to belch and vomit again. All those people would be at the museum. There had been pages and pages of names in Sir William's desk, and they would all be at the mercy of a few. What could he do? When the mere thought of getting dressed in tails and showing up to mingle made him ill, how could he stop a cabal of practioners? Grabbing the edge of the bowl, he released a mouthful of vomit. His stomach cramped against the unnatural purging as he coughed against an already raw throat.

"Immanuel, I would like you to think of yourself for once," Adam said softly as he rubbed his back. "What good will you be to anyone in this state?"

Ignoring his question, Immanuel flushed the toilet, wiped his mouth, and staggered to his feet. Percy nuzzled at the backs of his legs as he crossed the hall with a heavy, swimming head. Adam stood somewhere in the haze of his vision, but he kept him from sight as he buttoned his stiff shirt and slipped on the trousers Adam had carefully tailored the day before. Raising his eyes, Immanuel stared at his reflection in the mirror, but before he could see himself, Adam slipped in front of the glass and held his gaze.

"What are you doing?"

"If you insist on going to the party, I want you to go with confidence. It seems like you will need it."

Adam carefully combed Immanuel's golden curls aside to reveal his damaged eye and the long scar running across it. Grabbing the jar of pomade, he lightly rubbed it into his lover's hair. Once he was satisfied, he straightened Immanuel's waistcoat and jacket before carefully knotting his ascot. Finally, Adam stepped back and planted a reverent kiss on his lips. Immanuel closed his eyes and rested his forehead against Adam's. There was no one he loved more than Adam, but that love tore at him like a knife in his ribs. He wanted him at his side in battle, but he wanted him home out of danger. More than anything, he wanted to ensure Adam would be safe. Immanuel coughed, fighting the tears knocking at the backs of his eyes.

"Why am I always caught in the middle of something, Adam?" Immanuel croaked.

"I don't know, darling, but it will be over tonight," he replied, his hand gently stroking Immanuel's cheek. His face hardened for a moment. "One way or another."

"I'm afraid."

"I am, too."

Adam's arms closed around him, pulling him so close he could scarcely breathe. Resting his head against Adam's shoulder, Immanuel shut his eyes against the fear squeezing his ribs and threatening to send a wet cry from his throat. When Adam pulled back, he carefully brushed a loose curl from his face. His bright blue eyes passed over him, lingering on Immanuel's narrow hips and blotted eye.

"Here, take a look."

As Adam stepped away, Immanuel's eyes lit up. For a brief moment, he saw himself as he used to be. He saw the untainted boy in Germany who floated through life with a naivety he envied. A smile spread across his face as Adam joined him at the mirror. Their fingers interlaced, their hearts pulsing as one. He looked like the man he wanted to be. With a gentle tug, Adam pulled the chain and vial out from under Immanuel's shirt and let them fall across the front of his waistcoat.

"Now, it's perfect," Adam said softly with a tired grin. "Is there anything I can do to make you feel better? Anything at all."

Immanuel opened his mouth to speak, but the words hung in his throat. "There is one thing. Unbutton your shirt."

Raising a henna brow, Adam unbuttoned his waistcoat and the shirt beneath it. "Do you really think we have time?"

"Not that." Immanuel swallowed against the knot in his throat. "I don't know if I can protect you tonight, but I want you to have a chance no matter what happens."

Removing the boutonniere from his lapel, Immanuel jammed the needle into the tip of his finger. In one continuous stroke, he drew the sigil of protection over Adam's heart. He pictured warm arms wrapping around him, police rushing in, bars and chains surrounding treasure, a dragon guarding its hoard. Instead of sealing it with a final tap of his finger, Immanuel kissed the spot directly over his heart. A shiver ran from Immanuel's form through Adam's. His companion stared up at him, his breath heavy and his pupil's wide.

"Is that what magic feels like?"

Immanuel nodded as he lightly blew on the thin traces of blood in hopes they would dry.

"Then, we must do magic most nights."

Immanuel laughed despite himself as he touched the sigil, satisfied when it didn't smudge.

The moment Adam finished buttoning his jacket a steamer horn sounded outside their window. Percy trotted toward the windowsill, but Immanuel snatched him up and deposited him on the bed out of sight.

"That must be Hadley and Eilian. Are you ready?"

Immanuel nodded as he grabbed the vivalabe from the top of the dresser and slipped it deep into his trouser pocket. Reaching into the inner lining of his jacket, he confirmed that the stiletto Peregrine had lent him was still inside. He hoped to god he wouldn't have to use it. More than anything, he hoped he was wrong and that the gala would be as awkward and dull as he first imagined.

At the bottom of the steps, Immanuel stopped in the parlor doorway. As Adam reached for the front door, Immanuel cried, "Wait, there's something I want to show you."

Tucked behind his books on evolution, Immanuel pulled out a

journal and a photograph. Immanuel gave the boy a wistful smile. It was time Adam got to know him.

⚬⚭ ⚭⚬

Emmeline Jardine lingered in the Natural History Museum's vestibule, her owl-like eyes sweeping over the steady stream of guests passing through the double doors, but Lord Hale was nowhere to be found. She swallowed hard at the thought that she had been stood up only days after their engagement. If he didn't show or he had changed his mind about their relationship, she wouldn't have the nerve to go back into the gala and face her aunt and uncle. Of course Aunt Eliza would have something to say. She ground her teeth at the thought. As Emmeline stepped out of sight to calm her nerves, the hairs on the back of her neck prickled. Looking around the massive stone column, her eyes landed upon two familiar faces. Her breath hitched upon seeing Claudia sweep past the threshold.

Her dress was crafted from a deep emerald silk overlaid with swathes of black lace. Within their knots and woven threads were the silhouettes of creatures. Beetles and bees, tarantulas and butterflies creeped across lace leaves. As Claudia and Cecil grew closer, Emmeline realized the creatures were raised, and for a moment, she wished she could run her hands over the noblewoman's form like she would have if her mother had worn such a beautiful dress. Upon seeing the strange light in Claudia's unnaturally green eyes, all thoughts were dashed aside. She couldn't put her finger on what it was. It wasn't anger or sadness or even hatred; it was something wild. Within her gaze was something ever shifting, changing before it could come to fruition. At her side stood Lord Hale. Emmeline's lips curled into a grin upon seeing him, but when his gaze fell upon her, the joy fell short of reaching his eyes. Beneath them were deep bags and the faint outline of what looked like a bruise on his cheek. When they passed, he stuck out his elbow for Emmeline to take. Cecil gave her a faint smile and gently squeezed her hand as she joined them.

Together they entered the great hall. Emmeline's head fell back as she took in the massive steel tree trunks that held up the museum's cathedral vaults and the wide, golden chandeliers that now hung from the glass ceiling. The room had been decorated with tall palm trees and lush planters brimming with exotic flowers the likes of which she had never seen. Lords and ladies huddled alongside curators who described the strange specimens while waiters passed through the vast room with plates of hors d'oeuvres and flutes of champagne. When Cassandra had asked if she was going, Emmeline had never expected such finery.

Across the room, she spotted her friend standing beside Miss Elliott's stoically beautiful form, talking animatedly with Adam Fenice and Immanuel Winter. *Cassandra.* Emmeline's heart sank. Since she had gotten engaged, she couldn't get Cassandra out of her mind. Cass was the first person she wanted to tell, and each time she wanted to write her a note or dash to the Spiritualist Society, she had to remind herself that it was impossible. Guilt rang through her. What had she done?

"I need to speak to you privately," Cecil whispered the moment his aunt stepped away from them to greet an older gentleman in a fine set of tails.

"Oh?" Emmeline asked, a cheeky smile sneaking across her features, but when she saw Cecil's somber expression, her mirth faltered. "Is something the matter?"

Lord Hale looked over his shoulder to make certain his aunt's attention was elsewhere before steering Emmeline into a dead-end hall. Hiding between two misshapen yew trunks, Cecil stood so close that she could feel a faint puff of air on her cheeks with each breath. He rested his hand on her arm, and with the other, he gently stroked her neck and the curve of her cheek. His gaze traveled over her hair and eyes, drinking her in until he reached her pouted lips. For a moment, she thought he would kiss her, but he didn't move. Instead, he cast his eyes to the floor or the wall behind her but refused to meet her gaze.

"Cecil, what's wrong? Please tell me."

When he finally locked eyes with her, her heart sank at the fear tinging every fiber beneath the surface. His grip tightened on her as he asked, "Do you love me?"

"Of course I do. You know I do."

"Do you trust me?"

"Yes?" Emmeline's mouth dried at his pulse pounding against her skin. It wasn't a beat of desire but one of unbridled terror. "Cecil, what is this about? You're scaring me."

Leveling his gaze with her, he replied with his voice tight, "Emmeline, things may happen tonight, things that I should never have agreed to, but it's too late for me. I'm bound to my promise. It was foolish." Cecil drew in a rattling breath. "I fear you won't feel the same way about me after it has happened— that I won't be the same. If you leave before Claudia returns, you may have a chance. *We* may have a chance."

"I don't understand. A chance of what? What are you talking about?"

Cecil glanced behind him, his eyes widening in alarm as his aunt drew closer. "Just know I didn't understand what she intended to do until it was too late."

Before she could reply, he drew back, pretending to study an information card. With a cough and a hardening of his jaw, he regained some semblance of composure. Claudia sauntered over to their hiding place with a flute of champagne gracefully wrapped beneath her slender fingers. Under the bowers of dead yews, her bronze curls took on a metallic sheen and her skin an alabaster shine that made Emmeline wonder if she was truly of their world. A sharp smile spread across her lips as her gaze slid between them as if unaware of the barely smothered looks of fear on their faces.

"Ah, my lovebirds, now is not the time to hide. You must come back to the party. One must be social even while in love."

Slipping between them, she eyed Cecil, who wouldn't meet her gaze, before turning to Emmeline. She lightly lifted her chin, her nails pressing into her cheek. With her other hand she swept the hair from Emmeline's forehead, but when the glass grazed her cheek, Emmeline felt a vibration ring through her. It was barely more than a low hum, but it spread through her body, working its way down until it reached her heart where it spread with each beat. Claudia threaded her arm through Emmeline's, compelling her feet forward even as her head swiveled back to Cecil who lingered in the hall.

"Dear Cecil told me of your engagement, and I couldn't be happier," Claudia crooned as she led her back to the throngs of guests and the bright nave where a pink, sun-kissed sky still shown. "Come, come. The fun will begin any minute now, and we mustn't keep them waiting."

◦◦◦

Immanuel's heart pounded in his throat as he stepped into the vestibule. He would have run from there in an instant if it weren't for Adam and the Dorsets at his side. Hadley gazed at him tenderly from her husband's arm and gave his wrist a gentle squeeze.

"Are you nervous?" she asked soft enough that only Immanuel could hear. "Parties aren't Eilian's forte either, except on the rare occasion when they involve artifacts and exhibits."

"She's right, you know," Eilian chimed in with a lopsided grin. "Have you seen the exhibit for the silphium? We haven't heard heads or tails of it since we sent in the seedling."

"I have. It's the centerpiece of the exhibit. Mr. Nichols has been hard at work perfecting it since I arrived. The director hopes it will bring in more interest in the botanical wing and of course, more donations."

"He will regret that soon enough."

Immanuel turned to find Peregrine Nichols at his elbow as they entered the great hall. "Lord and Lady Dorset, this is Mr. Nichols, the junior botany curator."

The moment Eilian proffered his hand, Peregrine grasped it, giving it a hardy shake without even noting that it was made of metal. Raising Hadley's hand to his lips, he gave her a graceful bow. "It's a pleasure to make your acquaintance. I have wanted to personally thank

268

you for your generous donation, Lord and Lady Dorset. I hope you don't mind me asking, but I would like your permission to send off a few specimens to New York and Paris. They have expressed an interest in it and well, it would be a great opportunity for research which is *far* beyond my expertise, as Winter here will tell you."

"Of course you may. I donated it so it could be studied. Feel free to send it to whomever you see fit, but if I may, would you be willing to send me any findings they uncover? The silphium has been in my family for years, and I would like to learn its history," Lord Dorset replied with a genial grin.

"I certainly will. Now, if you will excuse us, Winter and I need to take care of some museum business," Peregrine replied, giving Immanuel a pointed look.

Immanuel excused himself, watching as Eilian and Hadley drifted over to the Hawthornes who stood near a mammoth skeleton. At his elbow, Adam followed a step behind. He scanned the crowd, giving each person who caught his eye a graceful nod and a manicured smile. Immanuel's gut churned as Peregrine threaded them through the throngs of patrons, taking them out of the way to go around cases of fossils and petrified plants where Sir William held court with donors whose names appeared proudly emblazoned on brass plaques. Immanuel stooped as they passed a short case, in hopes the director wouldn't catch a glimpse of his unfortunately remarkable features.

"Despite my feelings on the matter, Elliott would like me to bring you both to her," he stated curtly as they climbed the stone steps to the bridge that overlooked the length of the hall.

At the center of the rail, Judith Elliott and Cassandra Ashwood stood together, watching couples walk arm-in-arm below and the heads of the museum hobnob with aristocrats. Upon hearing their steps ringing on the stone, the women turned. Immanuel was relieved to find them somber but not afraid.

"Mr. Winter, Mr. Fenice, it's good to see you. Has there been any sign of Lady Rose or Lord Hale?" Judith asked.

Peregrine shook his head. "They aren't here yet, as best as I can tell."

With a wave of Judith's hand, they moved to the other side of the catwalk where the vestibule stood in full view. Immanuel stared over the rail, watching a familiar black head circle a column as the trickle of guests flowing into the museum slowed. When Emmeline raised her gaze, he leaned back out of sight.

"Emmeline is here. Do you— do you think she is part of all this?"

Cassandra pursed her lips, pushing a strand of wavy brown hair behind her ear without taking her eyes off the girl below. "She is, but I don't know if she knows it."

"Wait, she's spotted someone."

They watched as Emmeline linked arms with an auburn-haired man, a smile brightening her features. Immanuel's throat tightened at the sight of the woman at their side. She looked nothing like Lord Rose, yet there was something about the predatory roll of her hips and the polished control of her features that sent the icy thrill of fear through him. For a second, the filthy mortar walls rose around him, engulfing his senses in offal and paralyzing pain.

"Let's rejoin the party. We can watch them better below."

Immanuel jerked back to reality. He turned to follow Judith but found Adam watching him with an all too familiar look of concern. Had he seen him slip? Casting his eyes to the ground, he pushed it from his mind. The best thing he could do was pretend he could forget. At the bottom of the steps, they skirted the crowd, taking up position at the edge of the main aisle where they could see to the far side of the room through the glass-paneled cases that littered the hall. Judith snatched a passing glass of champagne and watched Lady Rose from under her lashes.

"Nichols, what's down that hall?" she asked as Lord Hale led Emmeline out of sight.

"Nothing important. It's a dead end."

"Keep an eye on them."

"Should we get her away from him?" Immanuel said, keeping his back to the alcove.

Ignoring Cassandra's nervous glance, Judith threw back the fizzing drink in one gulp. "Not yet."

Reaching into his pocket, Immanuel ran his thumb along the letters and symbols inscribed into the vivalabe's brass face. How easy it would be to spy on them if he didn't have to worry about it being stolen. His nerves reeled at the thought of someone taking it from him. It gave him a second sight that allowed him to track the beings that haunted him, and he wouldn't give it up easily. Hazarding a glance behind him, he watched Lady Rose speak to the assistant director, her teeth flashing with every word. Immanuel quieted his mind and searched the crowd for anyone who radiated the vibration Peregrine had mentioned, but no one seemed out of place apart from Lady Rose.

"Are there others here? Other Interceptors?" he asked, keeping his voice low.

Judith's eyes followed someone in the crowd. "Only us."

"Just three?"

Adam's hand gently squeezed his arm in a fleeting but intimate embrace as he passed into the blurred side of his vision.

"Mr. Winter, you must understand, it *is* the solstice. There are only so many of us in the London office to cover a large area. The next office of our size is in Edinburgh."

"How many people get involved in—?" Adam stammered. *Why was the word so bloody hard to say?* "In witchcraft."

"You would be surprised. The thing is, we have little proof as to what they plan to do, and we were lucky my superiors gave us three tonight. Then there's the problem of having too many Interceptors in one place. Lady Rose would certainly feel it and run or at least be much less amicable. Rather than give ourselves away, we will simply watch and act when the need arises."

"What are we waiting for them to do?" Immanuel whispered, casting a glance to where Emmeline and Lord Hale stood.

Judith cocked her head, her hazel eyes running between Immanuel and Peregrine. "You didn't tell him?"

The impish man shrugged and barred his arms tightly across his chest. "I have been very busy. Besides, I didn't see the need."

Shooting him a reproachful look, she opened her mouth to speak but quickly closed it. Judith locked eyes with Peregrine for a long moment before turning to Immanuel with softer features. "Yesterday we received word from our contacts in Germany about the grimoire. When it left their possession months ago, they had been attempting to send it to one of the book's previous owners without knowing she had died in a fire by the time they sent it. According to our sources, the grimoire is a guide to unlocking the secrets of death: communication, revival, peering into the spaces between life and death, namely a realm called Eidolon. The reason the book was originally hidden away was due to an association with an otherworldly being."

"Like— like a demon?" Immanuel asked, his eyes as wide as Adam's.

"In a sense. Many magical items are tied to the power of something outside our world. Some creatures are merely curious about humanity, others treat us like pampered pets, and many want to exploit our world. We believe the creature tied to the grimoire is malevolent. Our German contact said it hasn't been summoned for centuries, but from their records, it appears to have not ended well, especially once it grew accustomed to its new body."

"Its new body? Immanuel, we should leave," Adam whispered, his eyes bulging as he reached for Immanuel's arm but let his hand drop.

Judith fell silent, her eyes traveling with Lady Rose's path. "Don't worry, Mr. Fenice. We won't let it get that far. It isn't as if they could perform the ritual here with all these people around."

"Then what are they doing here?"

"That's what we're here to find out. Hopefully enjoying the gala."

Swallowing hard, Immanuel asked, "And Miss Jardine's role in all of this, do you think she is to be their sacrifice?"

"I don't know. If she is bound to the book, then she will be worth more alive, but…"

Immanuel turned in time to find Emmeline hooked onto Lady Rose's lace-clad arm. The air squeezed from his lungs at the woman's sharp smile, so at odds with the way she gently patted Emmeline's arm. How could Emmeline follow the wife of the man who ruined their lives, who killed her mother? *How?* As she passed, her face contorted into a grimace before falling into a well-mannered grin. Perhaps it wasn't so willing after all.

"Did you see that? Surely, we have to do something to get Emmeline away from them."

"As I said to Cassie, we will do nothing of the sort until we have to. We aren't to interfere until then, do you understand? Don't make me regret involving you, Mr. Winter."

A gong rang through the great hall. Sir William stood at the entrance to the new exhibit flanked by the museum's numerous grey-haired chairs and senior curators. For once the director wasn't scowling or staring down his patrician nose, but as his eyes swept over the crowd to find Immanuel and Peregrine standing together, his usual rigor remained beneath his welcoming façade.

"Would my junior curators join me, so we can begin?"

Pushing past them without a word, Peregrine knocked into Immanuel's arm as he headed toward the front of the crowd. Immanuel locked eyes with Adam, every unsaid reassurance passing between them. In his mind's eye, he traced the familiar sigil hidden beneath his lover's shirt and sealed it with a final tap, hoping to fortify them against the hollow fear bubbling in his gut, but as he took a step forward, a firm hand closed around his sleeve. Cassandra Ashwood stared back at him, her eyes pleading a warning she dared not say.

Chapter Thirty
Bees and Wasps

The gong sounded in the direction Emmeline had just come, but even as the rest of the guests turned to see what was happening, Claudia compelled her toward the far side of the room, away from the crowd. Her hand had closed around Emmeline's arm like a steel band, yet what kept her moving forward wasn't her firm grip but the feeling that someone else steered her legs and that once again her soul hadn't settled in her body correctly. When they finally reached the void at the end of the sea of guests, Cecil appeared at her side. His brows furrowed and he stood unusually straight.

Without casting a glance in his direction, Claudia patted Emmeline's hand and said, "My apologies, Emmeline, but I must leave you now."

"You aren't going to see the exhibit? Are you unwell?" Emmeline asked, searching the woman's features for any sign of pallor or weakness. Even if she had only shown up to be seen, it was much too early to depart.

"Don't fret about me." Holding Emmeline's hands in hers, she stared up at the glass ceiling where night chased the remaining colors of day. "I have something I must attend to. Besides, I am certain you would appreciate my dear nephew's company over mine. He has been brushing up on his botany lately and will give you a tour I'm certain you won't soon forget." Leaning close, she kissed Emmeline's cheek, sending a wave of cold through her that set her hair on end. "Don't worry, we will see each other very soon."

Motioning for Cecil to follow her, Claudia sauntered toward the vestibule. Emmeline stood rooted in place, watching their lips move in a silent exchange. Cecil shook his head and his aunt rebuked him with a pointed finger, casting a quick glance toward Emmeline. With a final rough command, Cecil turned on heel as Claudia slipped out the door and into a waiting steamer. At Emmeline's side, he stared ahead, the muscles of his jaw flexing and grinding as they trailed behind the guests flowing into the exhibit hall. Emmeline opened her mouth to speak but found she didn't know what to say. Twirling the ring on her finger with her thumb, she bit back the urge to pry when her betrothed could scarcely look at her. She had never seen Cecil truly angry before, not at her, and she wanted to keep it that way.

"I'm sorry," he said suddenly. "My aunt knows how to get under my skin."

"It's all right. So does mine."

Cecil gave her a tired smile and brought her hand to his lips. Rubbing her palm between his, he said softly, "You remember what I said before about leaving? There's still time. You can still get out."

"I told you, I want to be with you."

He nodded, cursing himself for letting it get so far. His aunt had been right, he had let his feelings get in the way and had dragged the one person he cared about so deep into the mire that she would surely drown with him. As they drew nearer to the entrance with only twenty people before them, Cecil closed his eyes. A wave of energy swept down his body and across the stone floor. One by one half a dozen columns of energy reverberated back, dissonant notes ringing in the darkness. Drawing in a deep breath, he let another wave flow, but this time, he listened closely for a familiar tone. Two bodies resounded at nearly the same pitch, one note longer than the other, but it was close enough that he could confirm that what Lady Rose said had been true. Cecil opened his eyes, searching for the source of the energy. In the crush of jostling bodies, it was too hard to tell.

"Emmeline, I have been meaning to ask you a question," he began slowly. When she looked at him expectantly with wide owlish eyes, he continued, "Have you ever heard of a blood bond?"

She shook her head, the curls hanging on either cheek swinging in agreement. "What is it?"

"It's when someone uses their blood to fortify magic done on another person. Blood is our life force, so infusing magic with that life force ties it directly to their soul. It binds the practioner and the subject together for life. Have you ever experienced that?"

Emmeline looked up to find him staring at her expectantly. Behind the nonchalance, she found a strange mixture of wariness and weariness, the prelude to jealousy she knew so well. "I believe I have."

His gaze sharpened with surprise.

"Last summer I fell into the Thames and drowned. By the time a young man pulled me out, I was dead, but he used a potion of some sort that brought me back. He told me later he didn't know how it worked or what it would do, but it worked. I guess we are tethered to each other whether we like it or not. Is there a way to dissolve it?"

"Death."

She laughed. "I don't think so. In case you're wondering, there was and is nothing between us. He was merely a Good Samaritan. We run into each other occasionally, but trust me, the bond is all that holds us together."

"Good." Cecil forced a chuckle and cleared his throat. "I don't want to say I was worried, but blood bonds are often intimate."

"I can see that. Perhaps you can explain this, but after the accident, he gained some abilities from me."

"Really?"

Emmeline ran her fingers along the fine fabric of her fiancé's Saville Row suit. "He told me that if he touches the dead, he can see their final moments like a medium. Is that normal? Being able to pass something like that?"

Cecil's tongue felt too large in his mouth as he swallowed against the knot in his throat. "It is quite unusual. Have you," he paused, trying to figure out how to put it into words that wouldn't sound absurd, "ever reanimated anything?"

Cocking a dark brow, Emmeline's lip curled.

"I don't necessarily mean on purpose."

"Don't be vulgar, Lord Hale. I'm a medium, not a resurrectionist. Why would you even ask?"

"Professional curiosity." Cecil's heart thundered in his ears as he scanned the crowd once more. "The man you're bonded to, he's here, isn't he?"

Emmeline released a derisive sigh and shook her head. "I never would have taken you for the jealous type, but yes, he's by the entrance, the one with the scar."

Beside the stone arch that led to the exhibit, Immanuel Winter stood with his curly blonde hair and mismatched eyes, wringing his hands as he watched the other patrons file in. Releasing a quick pulse, their identical frequencies rang in Cecil's ears and before his eyes appeared two columns of vacillating light that danced and arced until the tip of the flames nearly touched. Cecil blinked away the vision, replacing the shadowed room with stone and lustrous leaves. Life and death stood so near, never to unite. Cecil stared at Immanuel, committing the young man's face to memory. If this was to work, he would have to forget he ever saw him.

❧❧ ❧❧

Looking over the crowd, Immanuel's throat tightened. The sea of guests seemed endless, even if he knew there were less than four hundred including the museum staff. Sir William's keen gaze swept between the crowd and the curators.

"Quinn, gather up the dignitaries and donors. We will lead them in as the premiere group. Everyone else take two dozen guests each, except you, Winter. You will be with Nichols at the end of the line. You need to watch how a proper tour is given."

"Yes, sir," Immanuel replied as Quinn's stately form disappeared into the crowd toward the Sorrells who stood chatting with a Middle Eastern man in a paisley turban and purple suit.

Immanuel eyed Peregrine. His mouth was set in a tense line, the only sign of his usual vigor in the flicker of his petulant stare. The crowd flowed forward, but three figures fought against the tide. Through glimpses between tuxedos and satin bodices, Immanuel could make out Emmeline's inky ringlets and Lady Rose's green and black lace. His body lurched to chase after them, but the press of the crowd and Peregrine's pointed glances kept him in place. Craning his neck, he found they hadn't left but merely stood at the edge of the crowd. Panic and relief washed over him. They would likely be part of his tour group, which meant he could keep an eye on them but then Adam would be trapped with them.

As Peregrine led the remaining guests into the darkened hall lined with potted palms, Immanuel averted his gaze in time for Emmeline and Lord Hale to pass, resisting the urge to shift under the nobleman's scrutiny. When he finally looked up, he found that Lady Rose wasn't among the stragglers in the great hall.

A flash of red appeared in the blurry part of Immanuel's vision as fingertips grazed his hand. "Everything all right?"

"Yes, but Lady Rose is gone."

"Isn't that a good thing?" Adam whispered as they trailed after the rest of the group.

"I don't know."

Within a few steps, the cloistered hall rose into a soaring palace of greenery. Strange plants overflowed from pots, streaming across the floor in dendritic vines. Jurassic ferns hung across their path while poisonous plants stood behind iron fences or trapped in glass reliquaries to deter curious fingers. Each specimen was a chance for Peregrine to delineate their virtues and histories in his best sideshow bark. While the rest stood rapt, Immanuel watched Emmeline and Lord Hale. As the nobleman inspected the specimens or listened offhandedly to Peregrine's tour, Emmeline watched him. In the fifteen minutes it took to get through the recreated monastery garden in the main thoroughfare of the wing, she had only looked away once to study the brass tiles of plants and animals that lined the ceiling.

When they finally reached the bend where the silphium stood as the pinnacle of the collection, Immanuel released a silent sigh.

"Perhaps we were mistaken," Adam said as if reading his mind.

"Even so, I still need to speak to her before dinner."

"But you heard what Miss Elliott said."

"I know, but I can't let her go on with them without knowing what could happen."

"Maybe she already knows."

Immanuel bit his lip as Peregrine's voice rose dramatically during his recitation of Rome's use of the mysterious silphium. "Maybe, but I couldn't live with myself if any harm came to her."

Nodding, Adam whispered, "Just be careful."

Inside the gallery, the silphium plant sprung from a massive Grecian urn decorated with red and black figures embroiled in a static battle. As tall as a sunflower, its daisy heads clumped together to form one massive sun atop thick green stalks of tiered leaves. Protruding from the sides were drooped heads laden with heart-shaped seeds. On the opposite wall stood its nearest relatives, fennel and prairie flowers from the Americas. Sounds of surprise and whispers of its mundanity came from the guests' lips. Leaving Emmeline at the perimeter, Cecil Hale stepped closer until he stood beneath a pod of seeds, his forehead nearly brushing it. Unlike the others who circled it and disappeared into the great hall where the aroma of roasts and puddings wafted, he stared up at it with the reverence of one who understood the value of what lay beneath its weed exterior. With Lord Hale's attention elsewhere, Immanuel inched nearer to Emmeline until he stood at her shoulder.

"Emmeline, I need to speak with you."

The girl jumped, whirling around to face him. Her surprise quickly faded to annoyance when she realized who had spoken. "What do you want?"

Ignoring her attitude, he kept his voice low and asked, "Do you know the name of the woman you spoke to earlier? The one in green."

"Of course I do. It's Claudia…" Emmeline strained, surely she had heard her surname before. "Claudia Hale. Why?"

"That may be what she calls herself now, but her real name is Claudia Leopold Rose, *Lady Rose.*"

Emmeline's body tensed at the name and all the memories tied to it that she had buried in the back of her mind. Silencing the fear, she straightened her back and picked a ball of imaginary lint from her gown. Her voice edged with anger as she replied, "This again? You're obsessed with that man. He's dead. Move on with your life."

"I know, but anyone who would marry him—"

Glaring at him, she took a step toward Lord Hale but stopped when Immanuel's hand closed on her wrist.

"Please listen to me," he pleaded, following her as she shook off his hand.

"You say her surname is Rose. That is a common name, and even if she were married to him, they were obviously estranged. He could be charming when he wanted to be, and we both know the reason she might want to be away from him," she replied, keeping her voice low while casting a glance at her companion who remained rooted before the silphium. "Now leave me be. I neither need nor want your advice about the company I keep."

With one long stride, Immanuel cut her off before she could reach Lord Hale, blocking her from his sight. She glared up at him, her hands balled at her sides and her chestnut eyes aflame.

"Do you plan on accosting me all night or should I scream for help now and be done with you?"

"Just think about it, Emmeline. Why would she suddenly make your acquaintance? Another Rose tied to us can't be a coincidence.

She's planning something. I don't know what it is, but it has to do with the grimoire. You may be in grave danger."

"You're insane." But was he? Her mind flickered to Cecil's strange behavior, his pleadings for her to believe he didn't want to do something, and Claudia's early departure. Claudia… Banishing the thought, Emmeline stuck her finger in his face and growled, "Mind your own business and leave me alone. I have moved on with my life, and I suggest you do the same."

Shoving past him, Emmeline hooked onto Lord Hale's arm and urged him into the great hall. Immanuel deflated. *You're insane.* It had felt that way for months, but he had been right before and was sure he was now. Adam stood beside him, laying a hand on his back when everyone was out of sight. His companion met his gaze with an apologetic smile and a half shrug. *You tried*, he could hear Adam say. If only that were enough.

Chapter Thirty-One
The Path to Hell

Stepping into the main gallery, Adam and Immanuel were surprised to find the hired servants lighting the candelabras lining the walls. Music reverberated off the museum's soaring vaults as night swept in, reducing the ceiling's glass panels to inky mirrors. Guests mingled between the cabinets of curiosities until the gong rang once again for dinner. Sir William's urbane chuckle set Immanuel's nerves on edge as he motioned for Adam to follow him down the hall Emmeline and Lord Hale had hidden in earlier. Adam's gaze swept over Immanuel's shifting eyes before coming to rest on his hands as they fumbled to open the vivalabe.

"You're going to use it now?" Adam asked, standing in front of Immanuel to block him from sight.

"I need to know if Lady Rose is still in the museum."

Clicking the latch, the minute stones scattered across the brass plane, fanning out from the white ball, which stood as still as north. Cassandra's blue stone stood beside an amber stone that moved slightly as if pacing while the green one he knew to belong to Peregrine had taken up position at the other end of the room near Sir William and the museum staff. Emmeline's black stone froze beside a cat's eye near the exhibit. A bit of garnet gleamed so far from the rest of them that it nearly fell off the edge of the plate.

"She's gone," Immanuel said, snapping the vivalabe shut. "I hope to god I'm wrong about this. Emmeline thinks I've gone mad."

"She isn't your responsibility."

"Isn't she? We share a soul, Adam. You wouldn't understand what someone like Lord Rose is capable of, and if Lady Rose is even a fraction—"

The words died in Immanuel's throat. Something coiled and rolled in the shadows of the entrance behind his companion.

"Adam— Adam, what is that?" His companion turned, but before Adam could move, Immanuel darted ahead of him. "Stay here."

Immanuel walked to the end of the hall and disappeared around the bend with Adam at his heels. Between the wisps of candle smoke and the smell of dinner, a biting sensation sent tears to his eyes. In his blurred vision, he caught a flash of purple crepe and black linen while the exhibit hall stood empty. As Immanuel followed the strange smell deeper into the exhibit, it grew stronger. With a gasp, he ran past the monk's garden and into the room that housed the silphium.

"Adam, get help!"

Sprinting into the smoke-filled room, Immanuel's eyes widened at the tapestried walls alight with the prairie plants before them charring to columns of ash. He coughed, staggering back from the crackling blaze and raging heat. His back collided with the urn of silphium, knocking it onto its side with a crack. He paused, his eyes locked onto an empty stalk where the daisy heads had once been. As he struggled to right the shattered vase through coughs and wheezed breaths, Adam grabbed him by the arm and dragged him into the great hall.

"It's been cut! This wasn't an accident," he said breathlessly as they entered the great hall.

"Fire! Someone get the fire brigade! Fire!" Adam cried at the top of his voice.

In an instant, the entire party was in motion. Chairs overturned and glass shattered as the guests scattered and condensed into a stampede of silk at the entrance. Over the cries and clatter, Sir William called for someone to fetch buckets of water from the basement. As Adam and Immanuel reached the murky night air, Judith and Cassandra appeared through the crowd.

"Are you all right?" Cassandra asked, watching Immanuel draw in a constrained breath. "Did you see what happened? We were too far to get a good look."

"Someone set the tapestries on fire in the exhibit. They stole some silphium, too. The crown of flowers at the top was broken off."

"Arson? I should have anticipated a distraction," Judith added, eying Peregrine as he arrived a moment later.

"Lady Rose is gone. I have been through the whole crowd and can't find any of them." Peregrine craned his neck, catching the distant boom of Sir William's voice over the whirring siren of the fire steamers. "I need to get back in. My apologies that I won't be able to help you tonight, Elliott, but I would like to keep my job. Come on, Winter, I'm sure he will want you, too."

"Wait," Immanuel said, "Lady Rose left before the fire. I checked the vivalabe not long before, and she wasn't in the museum."

"They must have gone back to the Eidolon Club to perform the ritual. Let's go, Cassie. We still might be able to catch them in time."

Cassandra gave Immanuel and Adam a sympathetic look before following Judith to the waiting row of cabs. When Immanuel turned back, he found Peregrine glaring at him from under furrowed brows.

"Don't even consider it. We need you here, Winter. Besides, you have no business getting involved."

Immanuel's mind sputtered with half a dozen reasons why it was his business, but instead, he forced an agreeable smile and replied, "Let me just make sure the earl and countess are all right, and I promise I'll meet you in the hall. It should only take a moment."

Peregrine eyed him suspiciously but at the grating call of the director, he grimaced and headed back to the door where the firemen rushed from their red steamer cabs.

"What was that all about? Lord Dorset and Hadley are right there." Adam said, casting a glance over his shoulder toward the museum. "You aren't seriously thinking of going after them, are you?"

Immanuel pulled the vivalabe from his pocket, holding it under the sparse light of the street lamp as he clicked it open. Looking up, he found Adam staring at him, silently pleading with him to stay. "Adam, I have to do something. They could kill Emmeline and summon something— something horrid."

"Would she really die? You said you both have come back to life before."

"Do you really want to take that chance, Adam?" Immanuel cried, his voice tight. "As rotten as Emmeline can be, she saved my life once, and I'm not going to let someone hurt her because she's too stubborn to admit she was wrong!"

In his palm, the stones within the vivalabe scattered. Lady Rose's garnet piece stood in the distance as the black and cat's eye stones slowly rolled toward it. His eyes widened as he watched Judith and Cassandra drive away from the others.

"*Mein Gott*, they're going the wrong way! They aren't heading for the Eidolon Club." Immanuel raised his gaze to the thick line of trees at the end of the road. Their leaves rustled in the breeze, carrying with it the damp must of the earth and the tang of something much older. "Hyde Park. They're heading for Hyde Park. Miss Elliott said the ritual requires space, and—"

Locking eyes with Adam, Immanuel stepped closer. If only he could touch his face or hold his hands, anything that would help him understand. Out on the street surrounded by the jostling crowd, they could be anonymous if they were merely two men talking, but they drew eyes with a nearness that was too intimate. There would be no proper good-bye for them.

"Adam, I'm sorry, but I have been afraid far too long. I need to do something."

"Then let me come with you."

"No! I can't risk it. I don't know what I am, but I know you can get hurt. Take Lord and Lady Dorset back to the house, lock all the doors, and wait for me. You'll be safe there."

Immanuel put his hand on Adam's shoulder, wishing he could gently stroke his cheek and press his lips to his. Instead, all he had were unspoken phrases where heart and eyes met in silent grief.

"Please… If you love me, stay safe for me," Immanuel whispered, squeezing Adam's shoulder before he ripped himself away and trotted down the pavement toward the darkness of the park.

Adam stood frozen, blinking as if the whole night had been a mirage. Smoke drifted from the grand entrance of the Natural History Museum as rows of steamers came and went, carting off guests only to be replaced with police and reporters. Near the street, Eilian and Hadley waited outside their idling steamer. Their butler watched the chaos with a wary eye while Eilian wrapped his arm around Hadley who nervously scanned every face that passed. Upon seeing Adam approach, her face lit up with a relieved grin. Breaking from Eilian's arm, she hugged her brother to her.

"Thank heavens you're safe. I was beginning to worry about you. Where's Immanuel? Did he go back inside?" She searched her twin's face, the grin falling from her lips. "What's wrong? What happen?"

"I need to borrow your gun," he said flatly, his eyes flickering from his sister to the earl who now stared up at the stars.

"My gun?"

"Please, Had, I need it. I know you have it on you." When she stared at him with a raised henna brow, he added, "I don't know what's going on, but I think Immanuel may be in trouble."

Hadley dug through her beaded clutch, keeping her eyes on the police as she shoved the snub-nosed gun into Adam's hand.

"I promise I will return it to you tomorrow."

As he turned to leave, his sister grabbed the edge of his coat. She stared up at him, her freckles bright against her sudden pallor. Swallowing hard, she took a step closer, her bones casting deep shadows in the street lamp's harsh light. Slipping her arms around him again, she held him tight.

"Be careful, Adam. If anything is going on with Immanuel…"

"I will. Please go home and stay far away from here."

With that, Adam slipped the miniature derringer into his pocket and disappeared into the shadows of the museum's façade. If Immanuel was to risk his life, he wasn't about to let him go it alone. Not this time.

ｏ๑૭ ๑ઠ੦

Emmeline staggered, her silk slippers heavy with moisture and mud as Lord Hale urged her forward. A rock cut through her sole, eliciting a pained groan, but she bit it back for fear of what might happen if they stop. He had done *something*. She hadn't seen what in the chaos of running and doubling back through the museum's stone and wood passages. She had expected to hop into a cab and ride off, but instead he dragged her into the park. Trees and vast swathes of manicured lawns rose before them. In the day, the park bustled with life, but at night, the sound of horses and people were mere ghosts. Something was wrong about it. The air felt too thick, too hard to push through, and what repelled her further was the sickening pulses that rang through her body as the misty Serpentine came into view. Grabbing her head, Emmeline stumbled. Her head swam as pins slipped from her hair and the world around her turned on its side. Lord Hale turned, reaching to urge her forward with wild eyes when she swatted his hand away.

"Cecil, stop!" she cried, eyes burning.

He stared at her, his hazel eyes blank and unfeeling until the spell broke with a blink. "Emmeline, we have to keep moving. We have to reach my aunt before—"

His lips tugged into a tight line as he clenched his jaw and looked over his shoulder where a faint glow flickered between the trees. Standing on tiptoe, Emmeline gently turned his gaze back to her.

287

Stubble pricked her gloved hand as she stroked his jaw. He swallowed hard, his chest heaving as he averted his gaze.

"What is going on, Cecil? You've been cryptic all night, and now, you dragged me off without a word. I'm to be your wife for god sakes! Tell me what's going on."

He locked eyes with her, holding her gaze against the press of whatever lurked beyond the trees. "Do you trust me?"

"I told you, yes."

"My aunt wants to summon something, a creature from another realm, the one you saw."

Emmeline gasped, shaking her head. "No. No, she can't do that. It— it's was horrid. I felt it. Why would she want that?"

"Whatever happened to her has turned her mind. She thinks the creature will help her with some glorious revolution if it has a host."

"A host!" Grabbing him by the lapels, she cried, "Cecil, you still have a choice. We can turn around right now and leave. I have money enough for us to get far away from here. We can start over. You'll never have to see her again."

"You don't understand. I have to put an end to this. She thinks she has everything she needs, but," he cast a glance toward the museum and dropped his voice, "I'm going to stop her. You have to trust me, Emmeline. No matter what happens."

"I do."

"Then, we had better get to my aunt before she comes looking for us."

As he turned, she caught his arm. "Cecil, why did you never tell me she was Lady Rose?"

His brows furrowed in confusion. "She told me not to. Why?"

"I knew Lord Rose in Oxford. He killed my mother and kidnapped me."

Cecil's lip curled in disgust, his face darkening with anger as he helped her over a low fence. "But why?"

"It doesn't matter now. I'll tell you later."

As they cleared the low brush and followed the dirt path to the edge of the Serpentine, Lady Rose appeared through the rolling mist. A small fire crackled beside her, casting strange shadows over her dress that made it appear to crawl with tarantulas and beetles. Emmeline swallowed hard at the sensation threatening to smother her. Where were the policemen who walked the parks at night? Where were the vagabonds or the savage men who lurked in the shadows? Had they too been driven away by the undulant waves of energy radiating from her camp or had they felt the sudden ring of fear that women learned to trust so well?

Concentric circles had been incised into the earth, littered with strange symbols that seemed to faintly glow in the moonlight. Lady Rose knelt beside the circle, her lips moving in time with the words written in the *Corpus Grimoire.* Emmeline winced at the book lying on the damp earth, so close yet beyond her reach. When it had been hers, the interlocking rings and obscure drawings had seemed so beautiful, but in Lady Rose's hand, they had been perverted. As Lady Rose carved another symbol in the circle, Emmeline's heart skipped a beat. What was she doing to her? Upon seeing them, Lady Rose climbed to her feet, a satisfied smile snaking across her lips.

"Emmeline, you have decided to join us on this momentous occasion. I had hoped you would. Your talents as a medium will be most helpful tonight."

Biting back her fear, Emmeline mustered a smile and a nod.

"I got what you asked for," Lord Hale replied as he reached into his jacket and dropped a wad of crunched daisy heads into her hand.

"*Some* of what I asked for. This will do for now."

Reaching into the Gladstone bag near the fire, she retrieved a glass bottle filled with a viscous brown liquid. She tore the silphium petals apart before rolling them between her palms and dumping them into the potion. Fine smoke rose from the mixture, fading it to purple. After a brief inspection, Lady Rose held the bottle out for Emmeline to take.

"Now, my dear, it is your turn to fulfill your part. Drink up. If it worked for the oracles, surely it will work for you."

Emmeline held the potion at arm's length and hoped the

noblewoman wouldn't see the tremor in her hand. "And what am I to do?"

"You will tell him we are ready for his ascension to our world."

Swallowing hard, Emmeline eyed the tendrils of purple lingering around the bits of ancient petals suspended within the bottle. Her gaze flickered to Cecil who watched wearily but made no move to stop her. *Trust me.* Every nerve in her body screamed for her to throw it away and run. Run as far and fast from Lady Rose even it means death. But she didn't want to die. She wanted to do the right thing. Closing her eyes, she drank the acrid liquid. It scalded her from throat to stomach. Coughing and gagging, she tossed the bottle aside. Before she could wipe her lips, a wave of pain ripped through her stomach. She staggered forward, Lord Hale's arms wrapping around her as the ground grew closer. The darkness closed in, and just as suddenly, the world brightened with otherworldly hues that turned the Serpentine into a river of lava. With a cough, her body fell back and her soul launched forward into the veil. A towering gate rose before her, its metal red as rust and hot as a forge, but beneath her hands, it swung open. The palace blocked the park as far as she could see, and as she stepped inside the opulent hall of contorted and cracked beings, she felt the stag's eyes upon her. Fear coiled around her heart, squeezing the organ thundering in her body while the spirit realm fell as cold as Dante's ninth ring.

She followed the tiles to the dais at the creature's feet. It stared down at her expectantly, its skull-like head twitching in irritation. As it rose, towering over her with an unbridled power that scattered her soul with each breath, she hoped Lord Hale knew what he was doing.

Chapter Thirty-Two
Sacrifices

Immanuel held the vivalabe before him, watching the stones within orient themselves with each movement until once again they fell still. On the bank of the Serpentine he could make out three figures in the rough light of the fire. At their feet, the ground shimmered and smoked. For a moment, Immanuel thought it might be fog, but as he darted closer, he could see that the strange light emanated from the runes and circles carved into the earth. At its center, Lady Rose's voice cut through the air in a low chant. Immanuel's heart pounded in his throat at the sight of Emmeline lying on the ground. Her hair had fallen from its coiffure and lay spread across her face in ragged curls. He eyed Lord Hale who sat beside her, holding Emmeline's petite form close. Immanuel stepped out of the line of trees and into the thick air. He didn't know what he could do, but there had to be something. Even if it was only a distraction until Judith and Cassandra realized their mistake… *if* they realized their mistake. Swallowing hard, he drew Peregrine's dagger from his pocket.

"Let her go!" Immanuel yelled as he stepped into the firelight, brandishing the knife at Lord Hale.

The nobleman glared up at him, a mixture of shock and anger twisting his features, but it wasn't the anger he expected of an enemy.

"Well, isn't this a pleasant surprise, the boy with the vivalabe? And I thought you hadn't found him, Cecil," Lady Rose said as she stepped closer until she stood at the end of Immanuel's blade. "But you're a little late as we have already begun. Now, give me the vivalabe."

"Give me Emmeline first."

Immanuel gasped, the air squeezing from his throat as the copper-haired woman stared him down. Her green eyes glowed as he tried to draw in breath. Staggering back, Immanuel dropped the knife and grabbed for his throat. The world tunneled in until it was only a point of light until it suddenly fell away. Immanuel lurched forward, his palms and knees hitting the dirt hard as his lungs seized and his pulse pounded in his temples. Spots danced before his eyes, but through them, he could make out Lady Rose's green gown and the shadows dancing over it.

"Now will you cooperate?" she asked as she grabbed the vivalabe from his pocket.

Immanuel tried to grab her gown, but before he could get a hold, her heeled boot collided with his cheek. The blow rang through him like a shot, in an instant bringing him back to all the hopelessness of his filthy prison. Yelping, he fell to the dirt beside Emmeline, clutching his face as Lady Rose return to the fire. When he looked up, Immanuel found Lord Hale glaring at him as Emmeline's lips moved in silent speech.

You're a fool. Cecil mouthed as he nodded toward Lady Rose, *She needs you to do it.*

Staring at the nobleman in disbelief, Immanuel scrambled to his knees. With two mechanical clicks, the vivalabe sprung into a globe. Colored stones rushed around the axis while the peridot ball hung in midair like a sickly sun. Holding it ahead, Claudia readjusted the symbols in the centermost ring and carefully added a bowl filled with something dark to the left arm of the cardinal rose before placing a plate of raw meat and fruit on the right arm. Lady Rose stared down at her handiwork, double checking the vivalabe's directions before clipping it to the gold chain hanging from her neck. Reaching into her Gladstone bag, an obsidian knife flashed at her side. Immanuel's blood froze at the sight of the jagged blade and the look in her eyes when they fell upon him.

"Cecil, maybe we won't need you after all."

"Wait!" Lord Hale cried. "She's coming to."

Emmeline's head lolled back before falling forward as Cecil helped her into a sitting position. "Two…," she said, her voice barely audible. Her eyes opened a crack, a faint smile crossing her lips upon seeing Lord Hale at her side. "Two of us. It needs both of us. Otherwise it won't work. Cecil, we did it."

The nobleman bit back the angry tears that burned his lids. "He came to save you," he whispered as he wiped the clammy sweat from Emmeline's brow.

"What are you—?" Her drowsy eyes widened as she followed Cecil's gaze to where Immanuel knelt with Lady Rose hovering over him with a knife. "Oh god. You! You ruin everything."

Lady Rose's eyes flashed between the three of them, her open mouth betraying her surprise, but before she could speak, her gaze trailed to the line of trees just beyond the summoning circle. The click of a hammer being cocked rang through the night air. Between the oaks, Adam appeared in his tails with Hadley's derringer pointed ahead and his site locked on Lady Rose. His blue eyes blazed as he aimed the gun at her heart, matching her step for step as she backed toward the fire.

"Drop the knife, Lady Rose," he commanded, hazarding a glance toward Immanuel who gaped up at him in wide-eyed panic.

A knowing smile crossed her lips as she led him deeper into the circle. The wicked knife flashed in the fire light, but her eyes never left Adam's hardened gaze. "Your timing is impeccable. I was just thinking how I was in need of a handsome corpse."

Immanuel's eyes flickered to the dagger lying out of reach. As Lady Rose darted forward, Lord Hale leapt from Emmeline's side and collided with his aunt, dragging her to the ground with a shrill cry. Immanuel scrambled to his feet, grabbed the stiletto as he ran to Adam's side. Staring down at the two nobles, Adam trained his gun on Lady Rose ready to pull the trigger, but each time she came into view, Cecil fell over her as he struggled to take the knife from her iron grasp. The circle of symbols beneath them pulsed, the air thickening with smoke and the smell of moist earth.

"Do it!" Lord Hale cried, leaning back before being dragged close to her by a clawed hand.

Adam pointed the gun again, holding his breath as he waited for the right moment that wouldn't come. "I can't unless I hit you."

Lady Rose bared her teeth at him as the cords on Cecil's neck strained against invisible binds. In a strangled voice, he yelled, "Just do it! I can't hold her much longer."

From the edge of Adam's vision, a figure rose. Emmeline stumbled forward, her steps unsteady but purposeful as she moved toward the fray, a rock clutched in her hand. She stared down at Claudia Rose. When the sorcerous looked up at her, her lime eyes brimming with furious betrayal, Emmeline saw only Lord Rose's unforgiving smile as her world burned. Channeling every ounce of anger and spite, she hurled the rock down at her. It crashed against the edge of her forehead, leaving a bloody gash. Lady Rose stared up at her in disbelief. Then, her eyes slid shut and her body relaxed beneath Lord Hale's form. As soon as Emmeline stepped back, Immanuel's hands were on her, guiding her out of the inner circle. She couldn't believe she had done it. She didn't even remember grabbing the stone.

Leaning back, Lord Hale watched his aunt's chest rise and fall. A part of him was relieved. "She's still alive. One of you, bind her hands with your belt. I—"

Cecil hissed, grabbing his stomach as he stood. Staggering forward, he fell to his knees on the carved earth. Emmeline pushed Immanuel away and ran to Cecil's side. As she grabbed his arm to help him up, her head swam at the blood dripping onto the glowing patches of dirt beside him. He raised his gaze to meet hers, fear and horror crossing their features at the realization. Pulling her to him, Lord Hale kissed her as he wished he had done all season. Long and deep, burdened with every night he longed for her and every time he envisioned a life beyond all hope. The backs of his eyes burned as the symbols beneath them danced with renewed energy. His heart lurched, but he kept his lips to hers and his arms locked around her trembling form. This was what he wanted to remember last.

Strange voices filled his ears along with the sounds of a chattering, grinding world beyond his own. Shoving Emmeline back, he stared down at the runes beneath his feet, which had gone from a faint green to a violent red.

"Take her out of here! Get her far away!" he cried, pushing her into Immanuel's arms as he and the redhead stared at him in disbelief.

"It's coming?" Immanuel asked, watching the nobleman lurch forward as if tugged by a string.

When Lord Hale looked up at them, his eyes were not his own. They were black save for the sliver of a pupil which had turned a deep crimson. Lord Hale was gone and in his place stood the creature. A cry tore from his throat as he grabbed his head, his nails digging into his scalp.

"Get it out! Get it out!"

"No..." Tears filled Emmeline's eyes. "No! Cecil!"

Emmeline dove forward, but Immanuel and Adam caught her, dragging her back to the tree line as Lord Hale's body twitched and whipped against his will. His muscles bulged under the strain of the beast's power until the seams of his suit ripped. Falling to his knees, Cecil stared ahead.

"Cecil?" Emmeline peeped, her fingers digging into Immanuel's arm which barred her chest.

"You can't go near him, Emmeline. We don't know what it's capable of."

"But he's my fiancé. Cecil wouldn't— Cecil, please come back!"

Rising, Cecil stepped over his aunt's body and through the flames flickering from the sigil at his feet. The cords of his neck strained as he stood at the edge. His body tensed and jerked, but when he looked up at them, there was only him. His face glistened with perspiration as he staggered closer and locked eyes with Emmeline. Adam trained the gun on him with trembling hands.

"I'm so sorry, Emmeline, but this is the only way," Lord Hale said, his eyes brimming with regret.

He swallowed down the monster threatening to usurp his mind and body, and in one swift motion, he shoved Adam back and yanked the gun from his hand. Immanuel threw himself in front of Emmeline, steeling his arms around her as a retort echoed through the park.

The fire flared behind them, its heat all-consuming until suddenly it shrank into silence. For the first time since entering the park, Immanuel could breathe again. He slowly raised his gaze, hoping that what he heard hadn't been real. Lord Hale lay in the center of the circle, his chest ringed with blood and his fingers loosely curled around the derringer. Looking between them, Adam stared at his empty hand where the gun had been. As Adam stepped back, Immanuel pushed Emmeline into his arms. She latched onto him, burying her face in Adam's chest.

"Adam, don't—," he paused as Emmeline released a sob, "don't let her see."

With the edge of his foot, Immanuel kicked dirt over the symbols until he reached Lady Rose. Keeping his eyes locked on hers, he carefully pulled the lethal blade from her hand and threw it into the Serpentine. Immanuel knelt beside Lord Hale's body. Even in death, his brows were furrowed in concentration, his neck taut. Drawing in a steadying breath, Immanuel pushed the tip of Peregrine's dagger into his finger until a bead of blood appeared. He unbuttoned Lord Hale's waistcoat and shirt, trying to ignore the burned skin that ringed the hole over his heart. Closing his eyes, Immanuel thought of life. He pictured the sea and the creatures teeming with life just below the surface, children playing, flowers springing through an unseasonable snow,

Adam's smile upon waking. Tapping his finger in the center of the twisting sigil, he leaned back and waited for a breath.

Immanuel shook his head and closed his eyes again, tracing the sigil from memory. Once again, he sealed the symbol, but nothing happened. He leaned closer until his head rested over the bullet wound, but the only heartbeat he heard was in his own ears. Behind him, Emmeline wept openly into Adam's chest as guilt-ridden tears surfaced in his eyes. Meeting Adam's red-eyed gaze, Immanuel shook his head. Adam hugged Emmeline closer as Immanuel buttoned Lord Hale's clothes and folded his hands over his chest. Immanuel sat back on the muddied ground, covering his mouth to stifle a cry at the image of Lord Hale right before—

Immanuel hung his head as voices called over the hill. He had failed Emmeline, but worst of all, they had failed Cecil Hale.

Chapter Thirty-Three
Open Doors

All activity at Interceptor headquarters ground to a halt as they arrived. Immanuel and Adam flanked Emmeline as Judith led them through the halls and up to her office, but at every turn, eyes probed them, searching for any hint of what had transpired in Hyde Park as Emmeline kept her scalded gaze on the carpet. As he had done with Immanuel at the museum, Adam glared at anyone who dared to eye them with suspicion. When they reached her office, Judith ushered them in and locked the door. Before Immanuel could offer her the seat, Emmeline sank into it and sat with her head in her hands. Her torn gloves cradled her face as she stared at her feet. It had been that way the entire time they were in the steamer. She never spoke. She just stared.

Squatting beside her, Immanuel croaked, "Emmeline, I'm sorry. I didn't think this would happen. I only meant to... I thought you were in danger."

Emmeline glared up at him, her lips white with anger. "Leave me alone.”

“I just—”

“Immanuel, let her be,” Adam replied, squeezing Immanuel’s shoulder as he rose to his feet. “We all had a hand in this.”

Standing behind Emmeline, Adam slipped his hand into Immanuel’s. More than anything he wished he could wrap his arms around him and tell him everything would be all right, but it felt wrong knowing Emmeline would be without her companion. That they had caused a tragedy that would live with her forever. Adam opened his mouth to give Emmeline his condolences when the door flew open and Judith walked in with a huff. She lingered behind her desk, looming over it rather than sitting down.

“The three of you were incredibly reckless. This whole mess could have been avoided if you or Lord Hale had come to us. We could have put a stop to this earlier, Miss Jardine.”

Emmeline stared defiantly at her from under her bangs.

“Lady Rose has been taken into custody, the grimoire confiscated, and,” Judith stopped to fish into her pocket, “I can return these to you.”

Placing the vivalabe on the table, she reached over Emmeline and stuffed the derringer into Adam’s hesitant grip. “As you probably know, Lord Hale is dead.”

Immanuel winced. “I— I tried to resurrect him, but it didn’t—”

“Magic can’t supersede free will.”

“Can we get on with this?” Emmeline said through clenched teeth. “I told you everything. Now, can I leave? Unless you plan to arrest me, too.”

“You’re lucky, Miss Jardine, because my superiors wanted to do just that, but I convinced them to release you to your aunt and uncle under the provision you don’t get involved in any more magic or become part of *any* club. That includes the spiritualists.”

Emmeline’s lip trembled. Hardening her jaw, she raised her gaze to Judith’s. Her brown eyes steeled with rage, but her voice stayed level as she replied, “That’s fine. I don’t plan on being a medium anymore or staying in England a moment longer than I have to. I'm taking my inheritance and going somewhere I don't know anyone."

"Very well. You may go, Miss Jardine. Your aunt and uncle are waiting downstairs for you."

Without a glance back at Adam or Immanuel, Emmeline leapt from the chair and stormed out of the room. The door slammed behind her, reverberating through the empty hall. Her legs trembled with each step, and by the time she reached the iron staircase, her entire body shook with sobs. Gripping the railing, Emmeline rested her head against the cold metal as her legs buckled beneath her. First Mama, now Cecil. Why did she never get to say good-bye?

Footsteps sounded down the hall, sending Emmeline scrambling to her feet. She wiped at her nose and eyes as a familiar face appeared at the end of the hall. Cassandra's cocoa eyes softened with worry and then relief upon seeing Emmeline, but before she could embrace her friend, she stopped short at the sight of Emmeline's cutting glare.

"I just heard what happened. Are you all right?"

"No," she replied, sniffing against her will as anger overtook her sadness. "Cecil's dead."

Cassandra gasped. "Oh, Em, I'm so sorry."

"Sorry? You're sorry? You lied to me and kept me in the dark, and now, you're sorry. Are you happy now? The man I loved is dead, and you and Aunt Eliza have me all to yourselves again," Emmeline venomously spat.

"You know that was never my intention. I thought I was helping you. We can still fix things. I know you're in trouble now, but I could help. We could start a new medium business or maybe you could work here with us."

Emmeline released a bitter laugh, the void within her gnawing away what little love she had left. "You can't fix this. No one can. Besides, look what all of this has brought me! My mother's dead, my fiancé's dead, and now, I'm not allowed to be a spiritualist anymore. See what good *this* has done."

"But, Em—"

Cassandra reached for Emmeline's arm, but the raven-haired girl kept her at bay with trembling rage.

"Don't. You. Dare. Your help has done enough damage."

Pushing past her, Emmeline stormed down the steps. Interceptors eyed her as she passed, lingering on her reddened face before trailing to the ring on her finger. As she burst into the street and the night air drew her anger into emptiness, the blood-red gem on her finger flashed. At the curb a steamer idled to take her back to Wimpole Street, but instead, she kept her head down and walked toward the Victoria Landing Fields, her gown sweeping behind her. She was done with people, but most of all, she was done with love. No, that wasn't it. She could never pretend her feelings for her mother and Cecil weren't worth the pain. She was done with death and loving things that would leave her behind.

෧෬ ෨෨

Immanuel eyed the empty seat, resisting the urge to run after Emmeline. Adam would tell him she needed her space, but how could he make it right for her? He had tried… he had tried so hard to bring him back. He never thought he wouldn't be able.

"Is she always like that?" Judith asked.

"How could you say that? She just lost her fiancé," Adam cried. "I think she has the right to be cross with everyone after tonight."

"Even after all that, she still has feelings for him?"

"Of course she does."

Judith sighed and sank into her chair. Leaning forward on her elbows, she looked from Adam to Immanuel. The latter stared miserably at the floor while Adam watched her warily, his body inching closer to Immanuel's.

"My apologies for my momentary insensitivity. This job is rarely easy, but today has been worse than usual. As I said, you were incredibly reckless going after Lady Rose and Lord Hale alone, but I must commend you on how you stopped her."

301

Immanuel gnawed on his lip, his fingers working at his cufflink. "We didn't stop her. Emmeline and Lord Hale did. They're the heroes in all of this. If it weren't— if it weren't for me, he might still be alive."

"There's no telling what could have happened. You could be right, but you did a good enough job that my superiors would like to ask you if you and Mr. Fenice would consider joining the Interceptors."

His mouth ran dry. "Join the Interceptors?"

"You would still keep your job at the museum. We can work out the rest of the details in the coming weeks."

Adam released a nervous laugh. "You said *we*, but I don't have magic like Immanuel has."

"Neither does my partner, Cassandra, but these pairings seem to work quite well." Her hazel gaze lingered on Immanuel, who wringed his hands. "Just think it over. Maybe after a vacation, the answer will be clearer. It looks as if you could use one." Judith rose, opening her door for them. "I have a cab waiting for you downstairs. We look forward to hearing from you, Mr. Winter. A man of your skillset would be greatly valued here."

Immanuel forced a weak smile and led Adam down the wood-lined halls and out into the hot night air. Climbing into the cab, Immanuel let his head fall back against the seat as he rubbed the bridge of his nose and shut his eyes. What had he gotten himself into? More importantly, what had he gotten Adam into? When he opened his eyes, they were outside 126 Baker Street. Shutting the front door behind them, Immanuel leaned against it, relishing the stillness. Tinkling footsteps drummed on the floor as Percy appeared in the doorway to the parlor, his tail flicking as he stared at his masters. Adam hesitantly squatted beside him and scratched his head.

"What are you going to tell Miss Elliott?" Adam finally asked as Immanuel scooped up the cat and held him close to his chest.

"You aren't seriously considering that I should—?"

Adam shrugged. "It's up to you, but I don't know if I would want to go back to pretending magic doesn't exist. She thinks you could be a great help, and I do, too."

Leaning close, Adam pressed his lips to Immanuel's until he felt his face bloom into a reluctant smile. Immanuel closed his eyes. He never would have thought that a failure could open up a new realm of possibilities. As a younger man, the man who mocked him from photographs and dreams, he would leapt at the chance to fight for good and discover the secrets that lay just beyond their reality. But if the gala was any indication, he would be putting his life and Adam's at risk.

"What if I make a mistake again? What if someone else dies because of me?" Immanuel said, his voice cracking as he buried his face in Percy's smooth bones. *What if you die because of me?*

"But what if that never happens? What if you're as fantastic at your job as you are with everything else? You would do more good there than you ever would at the museum."

Adam's arms wrapped around Immanuel's shoulders, leading him up the stairs to their bedroom. As they passed each window, Immanuel spotted the shimmer of blood and oil. With the dangers of being an Interceptor came a new found freedom he and Adam had never dreamed of. They could be together, they could be known, and they could forge a life sheltered under Her Majesty's protection. At the bedroom door, Immanuel let Percy jump down as Adam's hands traveled over the buttons of Immanuel's waistcoat. Clothes fell away in the midnight stillness. Bodies lay vulnerable and bear beneath skimming fingertips that hummed with magic and eyes filled with longing for immortality. Drawing Adam close, Immanuel traced the symbol for protection over Adam's heart. He focused on the smoothness of his skin and the dusting of henna hair as he banished the vision of Lord Hale's splintered heart peeking through his skin.

Immanuel closed his eyes and rested his lips against Adam's neck. The words hung in his throat, coming in spurts. "The only way I'll do it is if you'll promise me something."

"Anything."

"To be my partner. In life and death and everything in between."

Adam locked gazes with him, tracing the lines of copper in Immanuel's eye. Once more tragedy would lead to something better.

Giving himself wholly to Immanuel, he whispered, his voice hoarse, "Always."

About the Author

Kara Jorgensen is an author and professional student from New Jersey who will probably die slumped over a Victorian novel. An anachronistic oddball from birth, she has always had an obsession with the Victorian era, especially the 1890s. Midway through a dissection in a college anatomy class, Kara realized her true passion was writing and decided to marry her love of literature and science through science fiction or, more specifically, steampunk. When she is not writing, she is watching period dramas, going to museums, or babying her beloved dogs.

For more info, please visit KaraJorgensen.com or subscribe to her newsletter**, Her Ladyship's Missive**, to receive a *free short story*, news about releases and sales as well as future projects.

Join her Facebook group, **Lady Jorgensen's Interceptors**, to chat with other fans, indulge in Victorian goodies, and get news before anyone else.

Also by the Author
The Ingenious Mechanical Devices

The Earl of Brass (IMD#1)

The Gentleman Devil (IMD#2)

"An Oxford Holiday: An Ingenious Mechanical Devices Companion Short
Story"

The Earl and the Artificer (IMD#3)

"The Errant Earl: An Ingenious Mechanical Devices Companion Short
Story"

Dead Magic (IMD#4)